# WE SHALL NOT SLEEP

## Anne Perry

headline
review

First published in Great Britain in 2007 by
HEADLINE REVIEW
An imprint of HEADLINE PUBLISHING GROUP

First published in paperback in Great Britain in 2008 by
HEADLINE REVIEW
An imprint of HEADLINE PUBLISHING GROUP

1

Cataloguing in Publication Data is available from the British Library

ISBN 978 0 7553 4411 6 (B format)
ISBN 978 0 7553 0293 2 (A format)

Typeset in Galliard by Palimpsest Book Production Limited,
Grangemouth, Stirlingshire

Printed and bound in the UK by
CPI Mackays, Chatham ME5 8TD

HEADLINE PUBLISHING GROUP
An Hachette Livre UK Company
338 Euston Road
London NW1 3BH

www.headline.co.uk

*New York Times* bestselling author Anne Perry lives in Portmahomack, Scotland, and her well-loved series featuring Thomas and Charlotte Pitt has been adapted for television. THE CATER STREET HANGMAN was watched by millions of viewers when it was broadcast by ITV. Also available from Headline is Anne Perry's critically acclaimed William and Hester Monk series.

Praise for Anne Perry's novels:

'Perry writes passionately and with deep humanity about the horrors of trench warfare, revealing its terrible consequences through the eyes of her characters' *Yorkshire Evening Post*

'An incisive study of the ethics of politics and morality in war-time, with a thrilling narrative pace – intriguing, with great moral scope. It is a terrific piece of writing' *Lady*

'A complex plot supported by superb storytelling' *Scotland on Sunday*

'Perry stirs your conscience as well as your soul' *Northern Echo*

'A beauty, brilliantly presented, ingeniously developed and packed with political implications that reverberate on every level of British society' *New York Times Book Review*

'Perry's characters are richly drawn and the plot satisfyingly serpentine' *Booklist*

*Also by Anne Perry and available from Headline*

To all the women who kept the home fires burning

Take up our quarrel with the foe:
To you from failing hands we throw
The torch; be yours to hold it high.
If ye break faith with us who die
We shall not sleep, though poppies grow
In Flanders fields.

John McCrae

# Chapter One

'Home for Christmas this year, Chaplain?' Barshey Gee said with a wry smile. He turned his back to the wind and lit a Woodbine, then flicked the match into the mud at his feet. A couple of miles away in the gathering dusk the German guns fired desultorily. In a little while the bombardment would probably get heavier. Nights were the worst.

'Maybe.' Joseph would not commit himself. In October 1914 they had all imagined the war would be over in months. Now, four years later, half the men he had known were dead; the German Army was in retreat from the ground they had taken and his Cambridgeshire regiment had advanced nearly as far as Ypres again. They might even make it tonight, so every man was needed.

They were waiting now, all around him in the gathering darkness, fidgeting a little, adjusting the weight of rifles and packs on their shoulders. They knew this land well. Before the Germans had driven them back they had lived in these trenches and dugouts. Friends and brothers were buried in the thick Flanders clay around them.

Barshey shifted his weight, his feet squelching in the mud. His brother Charlie had been mutilated and bled to death here, shortly after the first gas attacks in the spring of 1915. Tucky Nunn was buried here somewhere, and Plugger Arnold, and dozens more from the small villages around Selborne St Giles.

There was movement to Barshey's left, and to his right. They were waiting for the order to go over the top. Joseph would stay behind, as he always did, ready to tend the wounded, carry them back to the casualty clearing station, sit with those whose pain was unbearable, and watch with the dying. His days were too often spent writing the letters home that told women they were widows. Lately the soldiers were younger, some no more than fifteen or sixteen, and he was telling their mothers how they had died, trying to offer some kind of comfort – that they had been brave, liked, and not alone, that it had been quick.

In his pocket Joseph's hand tightened over the letter he had received this morning from his sister Hannah at home in Cambridgeshire. He had refused to open it yet. Memories could confuse him, and take him miles from the present and scatter the concentration he needed to stay alive. He could not think of evening wind in the poplar leaves beyond the orchard, or, across the fields, the elms motionless against a sunset sky, starlings wheeling up and out, black fragments against the light. He could not allow himself to breathe in the silence and the smell of earth, or watch the slow tread of the plough horses returning along the lanes after the day's work.

There were weeks to go yet, perhaps months, before it was over

Teversham came to the open flap, his face frightened and smeared with blood in the lantern light.

'Captain Reavley, you'd better come. There's two o' the men beating a prisoner pretty bad. If you don't stop them they're loike to kill 'im.'

Joseph shouted for one of the orderlies to take over from him, and followed Whoopy outside, almost treading on his heels. It took his eyes a moment to adjust to the dark, then he started running towards the back of the operating tent. The ground was rough, gouged into ruts and shallow craters by gun-carriage wheels and earlier shelling.

They were ahead of him, a group of half a dozen or so crowded together: the lightly wounded on guard duty. Their voices were sharp and high-pitched. Joseph saw them jostle closer, an arm swing in a punch and someone stagger. A star shell went up and momentarily lit the sky, outlining them luridly for several seconds before it faded and fell. It gave him long enough to see the figure on the ground, half curled over with his face in the mud, as if he had tried to protect himself.

Joseph reached them and spoke to the only man he had recognized in the brief light. 'Corporal Clarke, what's going on here?'

The others froze, caught by surprise.

Clarke coughed, then straightened up. 'German prisoner, sir. Seems to be hurt.' His voice was uncertain and Joseph could not see his face in the dark.

'Seems to be?' Joseph said scathingly. 'Then what are you doing standing around shouting at each other and throwing punches? Does he need a stretcher?'

'He's a Jerry prisoner!' someone said angrily. 'Best put him out of his misery. Bastards spent four years killing our boys, then think they can just put their hands up in the air, and suddenly we'll bust our guts bandaging 'em up and looking after 'em. Oi say the war's still on. Their brothers are over there,' he jerked an arm towards the gunfire, 'still troying to kill us. Let's shoot back.'

There was a measure of agreement in murmured angry voices.

'Very brave,' Joseph said sarcastically. 'Ten of you kick an unarmed prisoner to death, while your comrades go into no-man's-land and face the Germans with guns.'

'We found him loike that!' The sense of injustice was hot and instant. Others agreed vehemently. They turned, looking at each other.

'He was escaping!' someone explained. 'Going off back to 'is own to tell 'em where we are, an' how many. We had to stop 'im!'

'Name?' Joseph demanded.

'Turner.'

'Turner, sir!' Joseph snapped.

'Turner, sir,' the man obeyed sullenly. 'He was still escaping.' The resentment in his voice was clear. Joseph was a chaplain, a non-combatant, and this soldier considered him inferior. Joseph had compounded that now by interfering with a holy-Joe attitude and interrupting natural justice.

'And it takes ten of you to stop him?' Joseph enquired, allowing his voice to rise with disbelief.

'Two of us,' Turner replied. 'Me an' Culshaw.'

'Go and join your unit,' Joseph ordered. 'Teversham and I will get him to the dressing station.'

Turner did not move. 'He's German, sir . . .'

'So you said. We don't kill unarmed prisoners. If it's worth bothering, we question them; if not, we leave them alone.'

'Morning, Chaplain?' Harrison said questioningly, as Joseph crouched beside him. 'What are you doing this far forward?' He searched Joseph's face, knowing there must be some kind of trouble to bring him this close to the firing. 'We lost Henderson. I'd like to write to his family and tell them myself,' he added, a note of apology in his voice.

Joseph had known he would. It was the sort of thing Harrison would not leave to others. Such news should always be broken by someone who had at least known the dead man. However good the regimental chaplain was, a letter from him was still, in a sense, impersonal.

'It's about Culshaw and Turner,' Joseph told him.

Harrison frowned but he waited for Joseph to continue.

'Caught a German prisoner trying to escape,' Joseph said, making it as brief as possible. 'Boy of around sixteen, thin as a scarecrow. Beat him almost to death. Whoopy Teversham caught them and stopped it.'

Harrison stared at the ruined tree stump ahead of them, and the carcass of a horse beneath it. Joseph knew Harrison loved horses. He even liked the stubborn, awkward regimental mules.

'Hard to stop it,' he said after a while. 'It just goes on and on, one death after another. Men get angry because they feel so helpless. There's nothing to hit out at. Culshaw's father was in the navy, and his elder brother.'

'Was?' Joseph asked, although he knew what Harrison was going to say.

'Both went down last year,' Harrison answered. 'His sister lost her husband too. No idea what he's going home to . . . if he makes it.'

'Nobody does,' Joseph said quietly. He thought of his own

9

home, instinctively moving his hand towards his pocket, and then away again. He knew the letter was there.

Hannah's husband, Archie, commanded a destroyer. Would he survive the last few weeks or months of war? Would any of them? Joseph was still alive, unhurt except for the dull ache in his bones that cold brought, and which reminded him of his smashed arm and the deep shrapnel wound in his leg, which had invalided him home in the summer of 1916. He had been tempted to stay in Britain. At his age he could have. Not that he would have been happy. However, it would have been a betrayal of his men still out here, and of the women at home who loved them, and trusted him to sit with the injured, not to leave them to die alone.

'It can't ever be the same,' he agreed aloud. 'The England we fought for is gone anyway. We all know that.'

'You used to teach theology in Cambridge, didn't you?' Harrison asked. 'Will you go back to that?' His face was curious, surprisingly gentle.

Joseph smiled at the innocence of the question. He had gone to teach at the university as a form of escape. Eleanor had died in childbirth, and their son with her. His bereavement had been insupportable, his faith too shallow to sustain him. The thought of ministering to the human needs of a congregation overwhelmed him, and he ran and hid in the purely intellectual teaching of Biblical languages.

'No,' he said in answer to Harrison's question. 'It's a little divorced from the reality of living.' What a weight of dismissal that carried. When you cradled a man in your arms as he bled to death in the freezing mud, theory was nothing, however beautiful to the brain. Only being there counted, staying with him, no matter what else happened, no matter if you were freezing and terrified also, and just as alone as he. The promise – 'I will not leave you' – was the only one worth keeping.

Harrison looked sideways at him. The light was broader now, cold and white, and they could see each other's face. He lit a cigarette, cupping the brief flame in his hands. 'Everything's changed at home. Women do half the jobs we used to have now. Couldn't help it – the men were away or dead. Or, of course, crippled! But it's still different.' He stared at the dregs of his tea. 'God, that tastes foul! But how long will clean water and no more guns be enough, Chaplain? We'll be strangers, most of us. We're heroes at the moment, because we're still fighting, but what about in six months, or a year? There's always something to talk about: people we know, the news, what's on at the cinema. Ask each other if we've read any good books? But that can't go on for ever. One day we'll have to deal with the ordinary things. We'll get used to each other, stop being polite and careful. Then what will we talk about? When I'm home on leave now people can't do enough for me. I'm given the best in the house.'

Joseph said nothing. He knew exactly what Harrison meant, the intended kindness, the meaningless conversations, the silences they couldn't fill.

'I still have nightmares on leave,' Harrison said softly, blowing out smoke. 'I can hear the guns even when they aren't there. I think of the men who won't come back, and I see that terrible stare in the faces of too many who look as if they're whole, until you see their eyes. We're frightened we'll be killed in the last few weeks, and we're frightened of going home and being strangers and alone, because we don't fit in any more.'

But to Joseph that was better than the desert of emptiness

that awaited him afterwards, the banality, and the agonizing loneliness. He would never be able to lose himself in academic studies again. They were such a small part of the enormity of life. He needed the touch of mind and heart, the passion of friendship.

Joseph waited several minutes before he answered. Everything Harrison said was true. He was afraid of the emptiness of going back himself. He was needed here, desperately needed, so much that the burden of it was sometimes crushing.

'I know,' he said at last. 'We're all afraid of the future, because we don't know what it will be. But we can't let men kick a German prisoner to death, whatever they feel. If we are no better than that, in God's name, what have ten million men died for?'

'I'll talk to them,' Harrison promised. He pinched out his cigarette, then threw the dregs of his tea away. 'It won't happen again.'

The following day, 12 October, Joseph was back in the casualty clearing station with more prisoners. They were coming through the lines every day. Most of them were marched back into camps where they would be held as the army moved eastwards over the old battlefields towards the borders of Germany. The few who were seriously wounded were kept in the clearing stations until they could be taken on without risking their lives.

Sometimes there was information to be gained from them, but it was of little use now. The terrain had been fought over back and forth and was known intimately, every dugout, every trench. Only the craters were different as the guns fired ceaselessly, churning up old clay, old corpses, the wreckage of armour. The movement of regiments changed too often for yesterday's prisoners to tell what tomorrow's deployment would be.

Joseph was occupied mostly with speaking to prisoners of

medical issues, translating their needs to the doctors, and then translating back the treatment they would receive. His German had been fluent even before the war. He had spent time there studying, and he cared for both the land and its people. Like any other Englishman, the idea of fighting Germany had been troubling and unnatural. He knew the soldiers on the other side of the lines were too much like the men from his own village that he talked with every day. It was the governments, the tide of history, that were different from one country to the other.

He had been behind the lines last year and seen the suffering of the ordinary people, the hunger and the fear. He remembered the German soldiers who had helped him wheel the broken gun carriage with the man he and Edgar Morel had gone to look for. They had shared schnapps and sung songs together. Hunger, fear and wounds were the same in any language – and weariness, and the love of home.

Now he was standing in the resuscitation tent, talking to a prisoner with an amputated leg. Rain beat intermittently on the canvas. The man was not much more than twenty, his eyes sunken with pain and the shock of being suddenly mutilated, his country beaten and himself among strangers. Nationality seemed an irrelevance.

Joseph had tried all the assurance he could give with anything like honesty: that the soldier would receive medical treatment such as there was, food, transport when he was well enough, and that he would not be further injured.

Joseph knew that he should attend to the wounded of his own regiment, even though they were none of them seriously ill, but the terror in the man's eyes haunted him. He looked like Hannah's elder son, the colour of his eyes and the way his hair grew off his brow. Joseph did small jobs – fetching and carrying, running errands – always returning to the man lying motionless in the sheets, the stump of his leg still oozing blood.

'When will your armies be in Germany?' the man asked him shortly after midnight.

'I don't know,' Joseph said frankly. 'There's still a lot of hard fighting. The war may be over before we actually cross the border.'

'But you will get there, tens of thousands of you . . .' He left the sentence hanging as if he did not know how to finish it. There was sweat on his face, in spite of the cold, and his teeth were clamped together so the muscles of his jaw were tight, bulging under the grey-white skin.

Suddenly, with a sense of shame, Joseph knew that the man's fear was not for himself. The desperation of his fighting had not been out of hate or the hunger for a German victory, simply the driving fear of what would happen to his family when enemy soldiers poured into the homeland of those who had killed their comrades, their friends and brothers, and revenge for it all lay open before them. Perhaps he knew what had happened to Belgium in 1914, and had been repeated over and over in every town and village. It might have appalled him as much as it did British soldiers to see the beaten and bereaved people, the burned-out farms and the eyes of the women who had been raped.

If the tide had gone the other way – and there had been years when it had seemed inevitable that it would – then German troops would be marching through the little villages of Cambridgeshire: Selborne St Giles, Haslingfield, Cherry Hinton, and all the others. The enemy would have the cobbles of the familiar streets where Joseph had grown up. German soldiers would be sleeping under the thatched roofs, tearing up the gardens, perhaps killing the beasts to provide food, shooting those people who resisted. Women he had known all his life would be confused and humiliated, ashamed to smile or be seen to offer a kindness.

He saw the fear in the German's eyes, and the bitter knowledge that he had failed to protect his women, perhaps his children. He would rather have died in battle. And yet what use was he to them dead? What use was he to anyone, a prisoner, and with only one leg?

Could Joseph tell him with any honesty that his women would not be violated, nor his house burned? After four years of horror, inconceivable to those who had not endured it, and slaughter that numbed the mind, could he say the victors would not take payment for it in blood and pain? Some men retained their humanity even in the face of hell. He had seen it. He could name hundreds of them – living and dead. But they were not all men, by a long way not all.

Should he comfort this man, lying ashen and broken-bodied in front of him, by telling him lies? Or did he deserve the truth? A dubious honour.

What would he want himself? Would he want to think Hannah was safe, even if it was not true? And her children – the boys and Jenny? What about Lizzie Blaine, who had been such a friend to him when he was home wounded in 1916? The thought of her frightened and shamed by a German soldier was so hideous his stomach churned and for a moment he was nearly sick.

He had not heard from her lately. He had tried not to count how long it was, but he knew exactly. It was six weeks and two days. He would not have expected it to hurt so much, but every mail call without a letter from her was like a blow to a place already aching.

The German was still watching him, uncertain now if he was going to answer at all.

'Where is your family?' Joseph asked him.

'Dortmund,' the man answered.

Joseph smiled. 'It'll be a long time before they get that far.' He tried to sound confident. 'The worst will have worn off by then. There'll be some discipline. They'll be regular troops. Most of the volunteers will have gone home. We're all tired of war. Vengeance has little flavour once the blood has cooled a bit.'

The man blinked hard, the tears running down his cheeks. He was too weak to raise his hands to check them. 'Thank you for not lying to me,' he said quietly. 'If you had said British soldiers don't do such things, I would not have believed you.'

'Most of us don't,' Joseph told him.

'I know. Most of *us* don't either.' There was defiance in his voice and his eyes were hot with anger.

'We've all changed,' Joseph said sadly. 'Not much is as it used to be.'

The German closed his eyes and retreated into some grief or pain too deep within himself for anyone else to guess at.

Joseph waited a moment longer, in case there was anything further the man wanted to say, then he turned and walked away. It was raining harder and the canvas rumbled with it. He kept in the shelter of the walkway between the tents. The ground was wet, the light shining on pools of water.

His thoughts returned to Lizzie again. He could not think of going home without her filling his thoughts. He remembered how she had been his driver all the time he was there two years ago, too badly injured to handle a car himself. In spite of her husband's murder, she had found the strength and the courage to help him look for the man who had so fearfully betrayed them all, and to confront him when at last they could no longer avoid the truth.

Joseph had begun by liking her, finding her company easy because she understood loss and never evaded it with trite words. She knew when to talk, and when to stay silent and allow the pain to take hold, and then slowly absorb it and pass through.

And she could be fun. Her humour was quick and dry. She had an easy laugh; the light of it reached her eyes, which were very blue in spite of her dark hair. If ever she felt sorry for herself she fought it alone, without blaming others. And yet she was imperfect enough to be vulnerable, to make mistakes. She needed help now and then.

Why had she not written?

Did she sense the growing affection in him and know that she could not love again – at least not love a man who had seen four years in the trenches and was so immersed in the horror of it he was changed for ever? Weren't all men changed? Could any of them be whole enough again to make a woman happy? No woman wanted to grieve for ever. Women created life, affirmed it, loved no matter what else happened. They needed to nurture, and begin again.

Perhaps only women like his sister Judith, who was here at the Front, could understand and speak to soldiers as equals, could endure the nightmares and the ridiculous jokes, the miseries that seared the heart and would not be let go. To forget the dead would be to betray them, and was unforgivable. It would be to deny honour, to deny friendship, to make all the injury and the loss not real any more.

Judith understood. She had been here since the beginning of

the war, driving her ambulance with the wounded and the dead, facing the hunger and cold, the disease, the horrific injuries, the despair and the hope, just like the rest of them. It was ironic that he could talk to Judith, yet at the same time he didn't need to because she knew it all, just as he did.

The rain was soft and cold in his face as Joseph crossed the mud back to the admissions tent to see if there was anyone just in who needed help.

Would he be able to offer anything of tenderness or honesty to any woman who had no experience of war? Or would the gulf between them be made uncrossable by the ghosts of too many friends lying dead in his arms, too many journeys across no-man's-land with terror and grief tearing him apart, too many long nights being deafened by the guns?

Lizzie, why don't you write? Don't you know what to say any more? What horror could there be in the future as terrible as that which we have already endured in the murder of Theo and the betrayal by Corcoran?

He stopped still, his feet covered in mud. He was not ready to go into the tent yet. He needed a short break before finding the next man to talk to, to try to comfort, or if not that, then at least to help him to a drink of water, or to turn him on to his other side for a little ease.

He had not acknowledged to himself until this moment that Lizzie meant so much to him – far more than friendship, more than laughter or comfort or someone to trust. The thought that she might not write again brought a loneliness he was not equipped to endure. It was pointless to evade it, even if it were possible – he loved her.

\* \* \*

18

In London Joseph's brother, Matthew Reavley, was sitting in the bare impersonal office opposite Calder Shearing, his superior in the Secret Intelligence Service.

'A month,' Shearing said, pulling his mouth into a tight line. 'Possibly a week or two longer, if the Germans hold out around Ypres, but not much more. There's still hard fighting in Menin, Courtrai – and Verdun, of course. Casualty figures are bad, on both sides.' He did not need to look at the names on the map, he knew them all, better than the furniture of his own house, or the neglected garden behind it.

'Talks by early November?' Matthew asked. 'Ceasefire?'

'Probably,' Shearing replied. 'But we're not ready. We're still arguing with Wilson, and the French.'

His voice was raw with emotion. There was a wealth of anger in it, although suppressed because it had to be. This had been the most devastating war in history. It had spread to almost every corner of the world. Thirty-five million people were missing, dead or injured; a continent spread with ruin. The balance of power was altered for ever. The old rule was swept away. The Kaiser was toppled, the Austro-Hungarian Empire crumbling. In Russia a revolution had occurred that was even more terrible than that which had swept the Bourbon monarchy from France. America had emerged as a new world power.

'Wilson's fourteen points,' Matthew said grimly.

It was a vexed subject. President Woodrow Wilson of the United States was in effect the chief arbiter between the opposing forces, and as far back as January he had laid out his principles upon which peace should be negotiated.

Shearing's neat, strong hand clenched on top of his desk. 'Don't argue it, Reavley. Not now.'

'He has no grasp of history,' Matthew said, not for the first time. 'If we force his terms on Germany, it will lay the foundation for another war just as bloody as this!'

'I know!' Shearing snapped, the muscles of his face tightening. 'We all know it, but the man doesn't listen to us. He has the mind of a country schoolmaster, and the soul of an army mule. But what matters is that he has the power of a nation that didn't join the war until close to the end, when the rest of us were already on our knees. He rescued us, and, very politely, he doesn't intend to let us forget it.'

'If he were a European country schoolmaster it wouldn't matter,' Matthew said drily, leaning back in his chair. He had grown comfortable in Shearing's room only lately, now that he understood why there was nothing personal in it. 'He would at least grasp the reasons for our ancient quarrels, and know that we can't be forced to get over them by common sense, especially an outsider's idea of what is sensible.'

'I know!' Shearing repeated sharply. 'Dermot Sandwell has tried pointing out that if we destroy Germany's heavy industry with punitive restrictions we will cripple the economy of the whole continent. Germany in violent recession could create a vacuum, which would suck in all of us, in time. Five or six years from now we could have an economic depression unlike anything we've seen before.'

'Is Sandwell right?' Matthew asked with sudden chill.

'God knows,' Shearing replied. 'Probably. And yet if we don't prevent them from rearming we'll be back where we started, and deserve to be.' He smiled. It was very brief, but there was warmth in it, even a momentary revelation of something very close to friendship. 'I suppose you still don't know who your "Peacemaker" is?'

Matthew took a deep breath, startled by the sense of defeat in himself. 'No,' he admitted.

'I'm sorry,' Shearing said quietly. 'I suppose if I could help, you would have said so?'

There was irony in that Shearing was a dark, intense man who never spoke of himself. Matthew had learned from someone else of the tragic and heroic history of Shearing's family. It was only after that he had finally trusted Shearing and understood his fierce loyalty to his adopted country. Not a trace of his original accent remained. His English was not only correct, it was completely colloquial. Nothing except the darkness of his eyes and an occasional sadness in his smile gave him away. Many times before that, Matthew had feared Shearing himself was the Peacemaker.

There was a gleam of humour now in Shearing's eyes as he looked back at Matthew. Perhaps he knew it too, or guessed it.

'Yes. And if I think of anything, I still will,' Matthew said.

Shearing tidied the handwritten notes in front of him and locked them in his desk. It was an unnecessary measure since the room would be locked also, but it was his habit to be careful, even though the notes would not be decipherable to anyone else, even if they were found.

'Bring me more, as soon as you have it,' he instructed Matthew.

'Yes, sir.' Matthew stood up. 'Good night, sir.'

'Good night, Reavley.'

Matthew returned to his office, locked away his papers and collected his mackintosh. Outside in the dark street, he turned left along the pavement and began to walk briskly. It would take him about half an hour to get home to his flat, by which time, in the fine, cold drizzle, he would be pretty wet. Still, it was better than looking for any kind of transport. Buses were crowded and irregular. Taxis were rare. Everyone was competing for the little petrol there was, and he could easily walk the distance. In fact, after sitting most of the day at a desk, sifting information, he was glad of the strange sense of freedom the dark streets brought to him. They were crowded with other people also hurrying, their heads down, their collars high. The occasional gleam of car headlights shone on the wet surfaces: smooth tarmac or rough cobbles, the sharp edge of a kerb.

He would have known the way blindfold. He passed the tobacconist on the corner. The man's son had been killed at Gallipoli, and a younger son had lost an arm at Verdun. His daughter's husband had been blinded at Messines. The greengrocer's son was in the Royal Flying Corps. He was still fine, but his mother had been killed in a Zeppelin raid here at home. And so it went on. Everyone had lost someone, even if it were a lifelong friend rather than a relative.

He crossed the street, facing into the wind. The rain was heavier. The 'Peacemaker' that Shearing had referred to was the codename Matthew and Joseph had given to the man who had conceived a wild plan to prevent the war entirely, back in the summer of 1914.

Matthew could remember walking across the sunlit cricket pitch that afternoon in Cambridge as if it had been yesterday, and yet in a way it seemed like another lifetime. It was not an important match, mostly just for pleasure. He could still see the cloudless sky and the white gleam of flannels and shirts. The women wore long, pale muslin dresses. Wide hats shaded their faces, and their hair was elaborately dressed. It had been a golden afternoon, which seemed as if it would go on for ever.

He had gone to shatter it, at least for his own family. He had to tell Joseph that their parents, John and Alys Reavley, had been killed in a car crash on the Hauxton Road. That evening, as they sat in the silent, strangely empty family home, the village constable had come to express his sympathy, and mention quite casually the news that in Sarajevo the Archduke and Duchess of Austria had been assassinated by some Serbian madman.

John and Alys Reavley's deaths had proved to be murder also. John Reavley had found one of the two drafts of a proposed treaty between Kaiser Wilhelm and King Edward. It would allow Germany to invade England, France and Belgium and absorb them into an expanding German Empire, and then in time take the rest of Europe as well. Their price was German help to regain the old British colonies of the United States, and of course to keep all the rest of the British Empire – India, Burma, Africa, Australasia and the various islands around the earth. The result would in effect be an Anglo-German empire greater than any the world had seen before. It would bring global peace, but at the cost of national honour, and individual freedom.

John Reavley had been coming to London to show the treaty to Matthew, who, because of his job, could bring it to the attention of the right people, making it impossible to carry through. John had died because of it. But before he had left Cambridge, he had hidden the treaty, and no matter how the Peacemaker's men had hunted for it, they had not found it. Matthew and Joseph had discovered it on the eve of war. It was still in its hiding place in the barrel of the unused punt gun in their home in Selborne St Giles. Without both copies, the Peacemaker had not been able to present it to be signed by the King, and there had been no time left to get the Kaiser's signature on another.

Once war had begun the Peacemaker had turned his efforts

– and those of his followers – towards making peace again as soon as possible. In the early years his intent had been to sabotage by propaganda the British recruitment, which was all still voluntary then. Later he had sabotaged the scientific inventions that might have saved thousands of lives at sea, both in the Merchant and Royal Navy, and tens of thousands of tons of vital supplies of both food and munitions.

Still later he had used propaganda again. The reports of failing morale, escalating casualties, the pointlessness of so many deaths for an ideal that had been flawed from the beginning, were designed to undermine British resolve and productivity.

Matthew had wondered if the fearful explosion in Halifax, Nova Scotia, had somehow been the Peacemaker's doing. It had happened on 6 December the previous year. The *Mont-Blanc*, carrying over two and a half thousand tons of high explosives destined for the war effort, had struck a Norwegian ship in the narrows at the harbour entrance. Abandoned by its crew, the *Mont-Blanc*, rather than blowing up immediately, as they had expected, drifted into the harbour itself until it rested against one of the piers. Then it exploded so violently that every shred of it, in shattered and burning debris, fell on churches, houses, schools, factories, docks and other ships. Over twelve thousand houses were damaged. Far more importantly, well over four thousand people were killed or injured. It was the biggest man-made explosion that had ever occurred.

The devastation was bitter and its effects lasting.

But it was the personal murders that hurt Matthew the most sharply – his parents, the man who had stolen the treaty and brought it to England, Gustavus Tempany, Owen Cullingford, Theo Blaine. He knew that was foolish. No man or woman had more than one life to give, or to lose, but the death of someone whose face you know, whose voice is familiar, whose laughter and pain you have shared, wounds a different part of you, and reason doesn't help its healing. He remembered Shanley Corcoran, with a unique stab of pain, because his end had been worse than merely death.

And, of course, he remembered Detta Hannassey, beautiful Detta who moved with such grace, and would now never walk with ease and grace again. That was different, and perhaps the Peacemaker was not so much to blame, but that did not lessen the hurt.

Now, in October 1918, Matthew still did not know who the Peacemaker was, and could only guess at what else he might have done that was outside SIS knowledge. There could be a hundred other schemes, a thousand.

Matthew crossed the dark street. A taxi swept by, lights gleaming on black puddles, wheels spraying dirty water high. He leaped backwards, hand up as if to ward it off, memory drenching him with sweat for the other times when the Peacemaker's men had twice so nearly killed him. Once had been in the street in what would have looked like an accident. He straightened his coat and went on, feeling foolish.

Of course he had spent more hours than he could count trying to find the Peacemaker's identity, and stop him. He had suspected several people, and one by one ruled them out, only to find that his facts were turned on their heads by another piece of contradicting information. Most painful, as well as most compromising, was that it could have been Calder Shearing. The evidence had piled up. It was only last year that Matthew finally knew his innocence.

He had suspected John Reavley's one-time friend Ivor Chetwin. When the sinking of the *Lusitania* in 1915 had kept Matthew at home, Joseph had gone in his place to the beaches of Gallipoli in search of the final proof, and found their suspicions were wrong.

They had both believed it could be Aidan Thyer, Master of St John's at Cambridge. They still had Thyer under suspicion, as well as senior cabinet minister Dermot Sandwell, close to the heart of government.

Now it looked as if the war were going to end and they would never know. That would mean victory, peace, and a very personal failure. He had let his father down. John Reavley had never wanted his son to enter the intelligence services. That is what he and Ivor Chetwin had quarrelled about. His father had never liked the deviousness, the secrecy and lies it involved, the manipulation and betrayal inherent in its methods of gathering information.

Soldiers who fight face to face have a certain honour. They also endure a kind of physical horror that comes as close to hell as a human being can conceive. The suffering, not only of body but perhaps even more of mind, belonged in a realm outside the imagination of sane men. Matthew had heard it discussed, but even the words of poets – and there had been some of the most powerful in the English language – could barely evoke it.

Men who returned on leave did not speak of it, not even his own brother, Joseph. John Reavley would have been proud of Joseph, silently, joyously proud of him. Joseph had kept his word to his men throughout, swallowing his own pain and going forward again and again.

What would John Reavley have said of Matthew? Would he have

understood now what vital work the intelligence services did? How many lives they saved, silently, unknown and unrecognized?

He was only a couple of hundred yards from home now. Soon he would be able to take off his wet clothes and make himself a hot cup of tea. He would have had whisky, but it was becoming harder to get, and he would save it for later. There were shortages of just about everything: food, petrol, coal, clothes, paper, soap and candles.

Inside, the flat was cold. He put on the kettle and cut himself a couple of cheese sandwiches, piling on Hannah's home-made chutney brought back with him from his last visit to Cambridgeshire. She had wanted to give him more, offering him all sorts of things he knew she could not really spare.

She was lonely, with Archie at sea almost all the time. They had grown much closer since the summer of 1916 when she had seen so much loss, and forced him to tell her far more of the truth of his life as a destroyer commander in the North Atlantic. Before that she had been happy not even to imagine it in any realistic detail.

Matthew understood why, and he admired her for at last taking that great step forward. But she had hated most of the changes the war had brought. She had never wanted the rights, and the responsibilities that went with them, which so many women now were forced to accept, willingly or not. She was nothing like Judith, who had gone without hesitation to France to drive an ambulance. Hannah was happy with her children and the village. She had stepped into her mother's shoes, taking on the organization of village affairs, the knowledge of families' loyalties and needs, the constant small kindnesses that bind a community together and make it possible for them to survive shattering loss.

The end of the war would be a blessing for Hannah. At last she would be able to sleep without nightmares about Archie, or about her elder son joining up, as he was so keen to do before it was too late to fight for his country.

Matthew ate the sandwiches slowly. The cheese was a little stale, but the chutney masked it. He thought again about having a whisky, and knew tea would be better. Despite the shortage, it was too easy to let one whisky become a second, and a third.

For Judith the end of the war would be quite different. Suddenly she would be purposeless again, a single woman nearly thirty, in a marriage market almost bereft of young men. Those there were would want someone more comfortable to be with than she was: less passionate, less demanding, possibly, even, less brave or clever. The nation was tired. Beauty was good to look at, but disturbing and exhausting to keep. What would she do with all that fire that burned inside her?

He was jerked out of his thoughts by the sound of the door-bell. It startled him, and it rang again before he stood up and walked into the hallway to answer it. Even then he hesitated. He spent very little time in his flat. He worked long and irregular hours, and when he had a day or two off he went home to Cambridgeshire. It was most unusual to receive a visitor here.

He opened the door slowly, keeping his weight at least half behind it so he could force it closed hard, if necessary.

'Major Reavley.' It was a statement, not a question. The bland face of the man in front of him held no doubt at all. He was of average height, his hair dark but thinning, his brows colourless, his features unremarkable, except possibly for his eyes. They were steady and penetrating. He wore the drab suit and white dog collar of a man of the Church.

'Yes?' Matthew answered without moving to allow him in.

The man smiled very slightly, more with his eyes than his mouth. 'I have a message for you which might have very little meaning for anyone else, but if it fell into the wrong hands could cost me my life,' he said quietly. 'Very much more important, if it did not reach you, it could alter the peace which faces us. The outcome of the war is now inevitable, but what follows it is not. There is still much to play for.' This time the smile reached his lips as well. 'I dare say it is just as cold inside, but it will be more discreet.'

For Matthew there was only one decision possible. 'Come in,' he offered, stepping back and allowing the man to pass him before closing the door again and making sure the lock was fast. 'If you are cold, perhaps you would like tea, or whisky? How about a sandwich? It's only cheese and chutney, but the chutney is good.'

'Thank you, I have little time. I do not dare wait here too long, but a sandwich would be welcome.' The man had a very slight accent, as if German were his native tongue.

Matthew boiled the kettle again while he made a sandwich, and then took the plate and tea through together.

'What is your message?' he asked, sitting down opposite the man. In the light from the lamp it was clear that he was well into his forties, and there were lines of strain and weariness in his face, especially around his eyes and mouth. 'Is there any point in asking your name?'

'Not really. I am only a messenger,' the man replied, swallowing hungrily.

'Army chaplain, by your clothes,' Matthew remarked. 'Does that mean anything?'

'No. It's just a convenient way to travel. But like you, I have a brother who is, or was. He was killed on the Somme last year.'

'I'm sorry.' Matthew meant it. He could imagine losing a brother very easily. He read casualty lists. He had nightmares about it.

The man finished the whole sandwich and drank the last of the tea before speaking again. 'Thank you. I imagine you are still interested in knowing the identity of the Peacemaker, as I believe you call him?'

Matthew felt the sweat stand out on his skin, and yet inside he was suddenly cold. No outsider could know the name they had given him. Who was this man? The silence in the room was so intense he could hear the faint sounds of footsteps outside in the street.

'For the death of your parents,' the man went on, watching Matthew's face, 'but also because he will have a very great effect on Britain's demands at the peace negotiations that cannot be more than weeks away now. I would estimate about the second week in November. If we make the wrong decision we will pay for it in pain all over Europe, perhaps in a world way bloodier and more terrible than this one. Not only this generation will be lost, but our children's generation as well, with weapons we have not dreamed of yet.'

'I know!' Matthew said harshly. His chest was hurting. It was hard to breathe. The weight of grief seemed almost crushing. He remembered his father so vividly he could hear his voice and smell the faint, familiar aroma of pipe tobacco and Harris tweed. Fragments of a dozen rambling jokes filled his mind. He was conscious of the man in the other chair watching him, seeing his intolerable hurt, and he resented it.

'We must not let that happen,' the man said softly. 'And if you do not stop the Peacemaker, he will rebuild his plans to create an Anglo-German empire out of the ashes of this war, and then there will be another war, because Europe will never let that happen. Britain at least will not. We know that now. Perhaps if we had been wiser, we would always have known it.'

'The Peacemaker – who is he?' Matthew demanded.

'His name is no use to you without proof.'

'Then what are you here for?' Matthew knew he was being unfair, but he had waited four long, bitter years for this and seen too many good friends die by the Peacemaker's hand. To be offered knowledge at last, only to grasp it and find it a mirage, was like being openly taunted.

'To tell you that his counterpart in Germany is willing to come through the lines and travel to England to expose him, at the cost of his own life, if necessary, rather than see this holocaust descend on Europe again.'

Matthew's mind raced. Could it be true? Or was it one more chimera, another trick to obtain a final chance of destruction?

'You have nothing to lose by bringing him through and listening to him,' the man said with infinite weariness in his eyes. 'We are beaten. Germany has lost over a million and a half men on the battlefield alone. The people are starved and broken, the land devastated, the government in ruins. No one who loves Germany, and is sane, wants to see that again. Manfred will come through the lines, if you tell him where and when. But it must be soon. We have no time to debate, or to weigh and consider. If you meet him, give him safe conduct. He will come back to London and tell your Prime Minister personally of the entire plot from the beginning. You already know much of it yourself. I imagine you still have the original of the treaty, or at least you know where it is.' Again it was not a question. He probably did not expect Matthew to answer.

'This man – what is his name?' Matthew asked. Should he hesitate? Was there anything else to ask, any answer he could check? He was used to double-cross, triple-cross; it was the nature of his business. If the man were setting up some trap, he would carry with him at least one fact that could be checked. Its honesty meant little. Even an amateur used one truth to verify the other lies.

The man hesitated also.

Matthew smiled. There was an irony in their situation, and an absurdity, at this last stage with seas of blood already spilled.

'Manfred von Schenckendorff,' the man answered. 'Where should he come through the lines?'

There was only one possible answer. Joseph was in Ypres, as he had been since the beginning. He had friends there, people he could trust. 'Ypres,' Matthew answered. 'Wherever the Cambridgeshires are. It changes from day to day now.'

'Of course. Your brother.'

'You knew he was there?' Matthew was surprised, and slightly disconcerted. This man had too much knowledge to be simply a messenger. Was this a last chance at vengeance by the Peacemaker, because Matthew and Joseph had been responsible for too many of his failures? No, that was absurd! He must have had far more plans than they could ever imagine. Countless people must have helped, or hindered. It was absurd to think Matthew and his family were high in the Peacemaker's mind, now of all times.

And yet it was John Reavley who had seen the original treaty and taken it, foiling the plot that would have betrayed France and prevented the war in the first place. Perhaps the Peacemaker would never forgive that.

The man was waiting for him, watching his face. 'We planned carefully,' he said at last. 'We assumed it would be the Cambridgeshire lines at Ypres. But if you had preferred somewhere else, we would have made it so. It will be as soon as he can come. It is not easy. Two days, perhaps three. We cannot afford more.' He rose to his feet and stood still for a moment, then offered his hand.

Matthew rose also and grasped it, holding it hard for a moment. He was tempted to ask who he was, and how he knew so much, but he was already certain he would receive no answer but the same tired, enigmatic smile. Then he let it go, and took the man to the door.

Afterwards, alone again, he stood in his silent flat, looking at the familiar, rather worn furniture, his favourite painting of cows on the wall, his shelves of books. In a few days he would know the identity of the Peacemaker at last. This time he would not know it through deduction, with its potential for error; he would have certain knowledge. How fitting that in the end the Peacemaker should be betrayed by his own, a man choosing compromise rather than dominion, honour rather than power, a hard peace that might last.

Tomorrow morning Matthew would go to Shearing and tell him the news, then leave immediately for the Western Front, and Ypres. He must be there when Schenckendorff came through. This really was the beginning of the end.

He thought of his mother and father driving along the Hauxton

Road to bring him the treaty, nearly four and a half years ago, in that last golden summer when the world had seemed so unbreakably innocent. In spite of himself, his eyes filled with tears.

# Chapter Two

Across London, in Marchmont Street, the man Matthew thought of as the Peacemaker was standing in his upstairs sitting room with the lights out and the curtains wide open, staring down at the street. There was very little he could see, even though his eyes had grown accustomed to the dark, really no more than the occasional gleam of hooded headlamps on the glistening wet road as now and then a car passed by.

It was nearly the end of the struggle. There was just one more big hand to play, and then it was over. Peace was inevitable now – of a kind – but nothing like the peace the world could have had if his plans had succeeded in 1914. He had seen the horror of the Boer War at the turn of the century. The slaughter, the waste, and the shame of it had never left him. He had sworn that such things would never happen again if there were anything, at any price at all, that he could do to prevent it.

He had tried. God knew, he had done everything in his power, and sacrificed the time and substance of his life in the cause. And yet war had still broken out, and continued for four long, ruinous years. He and his cousin Manfred von Schenckendorff had almost prevented it four and a half years ago. They had been days away from success when John Reavley, a retired Member of Parliament and sometime inventor from a Cambridgeshire village, had stumbled on the treaty and understood what it meant. In his narrow-minded patriotism, he had stolen it. The Peacemaker had learned what had happened and had had him killed before he could show it to anyone, but in spite of all his efforts he had failed to retrieve the treaty, and the one copy he had was insufficient to take to the King.

Then there had been the idiotic assassination in Sarajevo, and Europe had hurtled towards war. Some people had estimated that the dead and lost – those crippled, maimed or damaged in heart and mind – amounted to over thirty-five million. The futile, blind idiocy of it boiled inside him with a rage so intense it caused him physical pain.

He had done everything he could, and failed. Now, if he did not succeed in forcing the Allied powers to create a just peace, it would all happen again. A handful of years, and a new war would foment like a disease incubating in the body, and a new generation would be slaughtered just as this one had been.

He had tried persuasion, but was not listened to. President Wilson had no conception of European politics, and no understanding of history. He wanted to dismantle Germany's heavy industry, destroy her army and navy, shatter the heart of her people and weigh them down with debt that could never be repaid. He could not see the damage that would do to all of Europe, perhaps to the whole world.

The torrent of his despair was interrupted by the sound of footsteps on the stairs. He knew Mason would have come on foot, but how had he not seen him in the street? He had been waiting for him all evening.

'Come in!' he said sharply in answer to the knock.

The door opened and the manservant announced Richard Mason.

The Peacemaker nodded and the manservant stepped back to allow Mason in. They had conducted this ritual often enough over the last five years that it needed no words.

The Peacemaker went back to the window, closed the curtains, and then turned on the lamps near the two large chairs. The yellow light shone vividly on Mason's face. It was gold across his high cheekbones and broad mouth, making his nose look even stronger and his eyes darker, the lines around them accentuating his weariness. His hair was thick and black, so that he barely looked English, although in fact he was born and bred in Yorkshire, and he loved its wild moors and dales and the storms along the coast as a man can love only the land where his roots are deep into the earth.

The Peacemaker had no need to ask the question that was in his mind. He and Mason had known each other since Boer War days. They had seen the same horrors and made the same covenants with the future, and both had failed.

'Three or four weeks at most.' Mason was just back from the Western Front where the troops were now moving forward so rapidly that it was hard to keep up with the numbers of prisoners or the land gained. The fighting line was always advancing and the casualties were still high. Each report looked much like the last, except that the names of the towns were different.

The balance of hope and tragedy was especially poignant. As a journalist, he found it difficult to write without his own anger pouring through, and he did not want it to. The whole continent had suffered enough, and there would be far more pain and loss still to come than most people realized. The aftermath of war would very rapidly overtake the first wild joy of the cease-fire. Unlike the Peacemaker sitting opposite him in this safe, elegant room, he had spent the last four years reporting from every battlefront in the world. He had lived in the violence and the fear, the cold, the hunger and the stench of death. The war was not simply an idea and a set of emotions to him; it was a terrible, physical reality.

He looked at the Peacemaker's face in the lamplight, one-sided in shadow, as his own must be, and to him now the imbalance in it was disturbingly visible. In the lit side were the dreams and the compassion of the early years, the vision of healing; in the shadowed side towards the open room were the arrogance and the disregard for the curbs of morality, the refusal to see the dreams of others. The Peacemaker had argued over and over that the greater end justified the smaller ugliness of the means.

Joseph Reavley had said that the means were inextricably bound into, and part of, the end. Being a chaplain, he had put it in religious terms. He had said that if you picked up and used the devil's tools, you had already served his purpose, because using them had changed you, and that was all he wanted.

Mason had thought it fanciful, an easy sermon. Now, sitting in this quiet room, he knew it was true. The Peacemaker was no longer the man with whom Mason had planned such noble things five years ago. They had used means he despised, and still they had not achieved their ends of peace. They had fought a war inconceivable even a decade ago, and brought ruin that seemed endless and irredeemable. Art, society and faith had changed for ever. A kind of innocence had been lost.

He remembered how the Peacemaker had envisioned the revolution in Russia as the birth of a new social order sweeping away the old tyranny and putting in its place justice for the ordinary man. Mason had been to Russia and seen the blood and the violence, and the same old weapons of oppression, secrecy and deceit, no more skilled and certainly no more merciful.

Above all, he could see in the Peacemaker an imbalance of judgement, a hunger for glory that disturbed him. His visions were of an order that ignored the passions and the vulnerabilities of men.

The Peacemaker broke the silence between them, leaning forward a little. 'We have to affect the terms of the armistice now!' he said urgently. 'Before Wilson can force a punitive settlement on Germany and start an economic ruin which will draw into it the whole of Europe. Germany is the key, Mason. Never forget that! They'll rise again. Let it be as our friends – not as our enemies. Think of the future. Whatever you believe of the morality of any of it, the simple truth is that we cannot afford revenge. The ordinary German soldier is no different from the ordinary British soldier. How often have you told me that? The mothers and the widows in a German town are the same as those in London or Cambridge or anywhere. Think, Mason! Use your intelligence, not your sentimentality.'

Mason's resolve had been firm, yet in one short speech the Peacemaker had moved the ground under it, and it wavered. Revenge was the last thing Mason wanted. There was nothing left to take, no one left to hurt any more terribly than they already had been. How could he have been so certain only a few moments ago?

'There is nothing I can do,' he said. It was an evasion, an escape from responsibility, and he knew it before the words were finished.

'For God's sake, man, you can try!' the Peacemaker snarled, fury suddenly twisting his features. Then with an effort so profound the strain of it was visible, he forced himself to lean back and lower his voice. 'If we don't make a just peace – one on which we can build a new and united Europe – then economic chaos will ruin every chance we have of building up what is left of our civilization. We must repair the spirit of our people so they have a will to work, and a faith that it is to some purpose. Can't you see that?' His face was pale, his eyes glittering. 'Do I have to explain to you what happens to a nation if we rob it of its identity, its means of regeneration, its faith in its own worth and destiny?' He flexed his long, thin hands. 'If Germany accepts that the terms are just, we can be allies in the future. If they can't, then they will hate us. Secretly, violently, they will plan revenge, and it won't matter how long it takes, they will have it. Nothing good is built upon hatred.'

Mason knew that was true, but the use of the word 'allies' shivered through him with all the warnings he had not seen or understood the first time, before John and Alys Reavley were murdered, or Sebastian Allard, or Owen Cullingford, Gustavus Tempany, Theo Blaine, and every village in Britain bereaved of its youth.

He rose to his feet, surprised at how stiff he was.

The Peacemaker stared up at him. 'What?' he demanded.

'I'll consider what there is to say that will cut across emotion and make them look at reason and reality in the future,' Mason answered.

The Peacemaker stood also, an inch or two taller than Mason. 'There's no time to weigh and measure,' he said grimly. 'It sounds like the evasion of a moral coward who won't say "no" to a man's face.'

At another time, even months ago, Mason's temper would have risen to such a charge. Now he was too weary, too clenched inside in his gut with the reality of death to be stung by the wound of words. He smiled. 'And that sounds like the attempt at manipulation of an armchair warrior who is used to shedding other people's blood,' he answered. 'I told you, I would consider what I think, and then act accordingly. I am just as aware as you of how little time there is.'

And without looking back to see if the Peacemaker's face were twisted with rage or pain, or simply blank with surprise, he walked to the door, down the steps, and finally into the dark, windy street.

By late afternoon the following day, Mason was back in Yorkshire, in the land he loved. He had booked a room at a pub in a village in the North Riding and, after a supper of home-made sausages – he did not ask what went into them in these times of hardship – he put on good walking shoes and set out in the evening light. He was high up, and the whole panorama of the dales spread out in front of him, valleys already shadowed, high slopes gold in the sun. The purple was fading from the heather and the dark bronze bracken gave the colour a sudden depth. The sky was ragged with clouds towards the west, and there was a chill in the air with the sweetness of great distances and clean winds.

The South had a gentleness with its great trees and richly harvested fields, its winding lanes and meal-drift autumn skies, but it never healed him as this land did. It was too soft, too comfortable. It forgave too much.

The North was different. The bones of the earth were naked here, and there was a beauty in it that spared nothing. You could stand on a narrow road like this and stare across the hills, fold after fold, wind-scoured, to the horizon. In a month's time, when at last there was peace in the world, there would be the first snows on the shaws, pale-gleaming. The air would smell of it. The wild birds would be flying in for the winter, long skeins of them across the sky, wings creaking. The reeds would spear upwards in the rippled water of the tarns. Strangers would disappear, and only the men who loved them would walk these ways.

There was wood smoke rising below him. Over the hills he could see, perhaps five miles away, the roofs of the next village, and the church spire high above them.

He turned and continued climbing. He would be tired by the time he got back to the pub, and bitterly cold, but he would not lose himself up here. There was only one road, and he was long familiar with it. He needed to be alone in the night with the wind and the stars.

He thought of Judith Reavley. The painful memory was something he should let go of. Their last parting a year ago had seemed final and yet he kept turning it over and over. He could not change to please her. Her dreams, like Joseph's, had no foothold in reality. She fought battles she could not win, for ideals that were rooted in religion rather than the nature of men or of nations.

And yet her face haunted his mind. He found himself watching women who walked as she did, with the same ease, the stride that was a little too long for femininity, and yet filled with its own grace. He would hear someone laugh, and turn to find her, then disappointment would cut deep when he realized it was a woman he had never seen before, but who, for a moment, had sounded like her.

He wanted her ridiculous hopes to be attainable, and he was angry because they were not, and she would always be hurt. He was angry with Joseph Reavley for not having taught her better, protected her. And yet how could he? He was just as naïve himself. Perhaps Matthew, the second brother, was more of a realist. At least he was not a preacher, trying to create a belief in God in the trenches. That was a dreamer's errand if ever there were one.

He turned and walked back down the hill with the cold night wind in his face. A blaze of stars swept above him from horizon to horizon, so low in the clear sky he felt as if he should have been able to gather them with his hands.

The following morning he took the bus into Harrogate and had lunch in the Rat and Parrot with Robert Oldroyd, who had retired from schoolteaching the year Mason had started there. Oldroyd was nearly ninety now, white-haired and bent, but still interested in everything, and as inquisitive and irascible in his opinions as always.

'Read your pieces,' Oldroyd said, nodding slowly and staring at Mason. They were sitting opposite each other at a small table near the window. 'You did well, boy. Don't want to get your head too big for your shoulders, but you have a nice turn of phrase. Say what you mean, no nonsense, no silly pretensions of making yourself immortal. Make us feel as if we are there with you.' He reached his gnarled hand for his glass of cider and drank deeply before continuing. 'Would like to have been with you, once or twice.'

'Would you, sir?' Mason said doubtfully. He was grateful for the praise. He had admired Oldroyd intensely in his boyhood. A word of praise from him then had been as precious as an accolade from anyone else. If Oldroyd acknowledged you were alive it made everything worthwhile. You became important, and the wildest dreams were possible. It was half a lifetime ago, but the memory lingered with an innocence he thought he despised, and yet for some reason he clung to. 'It was pretty grim most of the time.'

'Course it was,' Oldroyd agreed, ignoring his lunch of bread and cheese. 'Do you think I don't know that?' There was a challenge in his voice.

That was exactly what Mason had thought, and anger at the old men who stayed at home burned hot inside him. The delusions of glory and the ignorance of what real death was like in the mud and terror of the trenches were what made war like this possible. 'Where exactly would you like to have been?' he asked, and then wished he had not. The cruelty would serve nothing. Oldroyd belonged to the past. It was pointless to try to drag him into the harsher light of the present. He would die of old age soon, still understanding nothing.

'One place?' Oldroyd asked, thinking about it, his face pursed up, eyes almost lost in the folds of his skin. 'I would like to have walked into Jerusalem last year, with Allenby. I could just about imagine it from what you wrote, but you saw it, you were there. December the eleventh. You didn't say much about his big cavalry victory at Megiddo last month. Damascus has fallen and Aleppo won't be long. But Jerusalem is different; it'll always be different.

Went in as a man should, to the Holy City.' He looked at Mason. 'Jaffa Gate, wasn't it; with that big, square tower above it, and the crenellated walls. Crowded with people, you said. All looking down at one Englishman, alone and on foot.'

'Did I say that?' Mason thought it sounded overemotional, sentimental, and he despised himself for it.

Oldroyd was watching him intently now, judging. 'Yes, you did. Did you lie?'

Mason was too tired to be offended. He picked up his bread to eat it. 'No. That's how it was. It just sounds . . . predictable.'

'Shouldn't it?' Oldroyd asked. 'Did you expect differently?'

'I don't think I expected it to happen at all.' Mason was quite honest. 'After so much dust and blood it all seemed ridiculously pedestrian – weary and aching men doing things we have become desperately used to. No trumpets, no drum-rolls, just a bald, middle-aged Englishman in an army uniform. Apart from his badges of rank, he looked just like anyone else.' He bit into his bread and continued with his mouth full, 'I was actually thinking about the future of the Middle East after the Turkish Empire is gone. Who will rule what, and how? Will the ordinary people be any better off, any freer from hunger or oppression?'

'Heroes are ordinary people, Mason,' Oldroyd told him. 'They're not ten feet tall. It's the inside that's different, not the outside. You could walk past Christ in the street, if you weren't looking for him.' He sighed. 'Come to think of it, most of us do.'

'Maybe that's why we usually put Him on a cross.' Mason said grimly. 'At least that's different. Although I think it's peculiarly appropriate as a symbol of humiliation and pointless suffering. No wonder Europe worships him. We see ourselves, our whole race, in one image of the ultimate defeat.'

Oldroyd leaned forward, his bony hands clenched, his face so grave his skin was tight across the sharp bones of his cheeks beneath his sunken eyes. 'It's what a man fights for that defines who he is, boy! And a man who doesn't love anything enough to pay what it costs doesn't deserve to have it. Sometimes it costs pain and blood and terror. Sometimes it's years of quiet weeping. Sometimes it's waiting in the dark, without giving up.' He blinked, as if seeing other times and people for an instant. 'My grandfather fought Napoleon at Waterloo in eighteen fifteen. My father fought in the Crimea, Battle of the Alma, eighteen fifty-four. I was twenty-three. Heard Campbell tell us, "There's no retreat from here, men. You must die where you stand." He died in my arms. My son lost his legs in the Zulu Wars, eighteen seventy-nine, at Rorke's Drift – hundred and thirty-nine of us against four thousand Zulus. My grandson fell at Passchendaele. Fifty thousand we lost in the first day.'

Mason said nothing. In spite of himself, the ache in his throat was too tight and hard for him to swallow.

Oldroyd blinked. 'Of course we lose sometimes. What has that to do with anything? It's not winning or losing that says who you are, it's the courage that makes you stand fast, with your eyes forward, and fight for what you love. Never let go of hope. Real victories happen one by one, and they're over the enemy inside. If I didn't teach you that, boy, then I didn't teach you anything.'

Mason put his hand up and pushed the heavy hair off his forehead. 'You sound like the chaplain in the Cambridgeshires at Ypres, and an ambulance driver I know.'

'Woman driver?' Oldroyd asked him quietly.

'Yes.' Mason was surprised. Judith's face was as clear in his mind as if they had parted only days ago rather than after the court martial last year.

'Thought so.' Oldroyd nodded. 'Women are as brave as any man. They die to save their own, without a second thought. But then that's love, isn't it? Loyalty. Women never give up, not when it's someone they love. Many a child wouldn't be here if they did.' Oldroyd sipped his cider. 'But a good woman'll fight for anyone that's hurt. It's someone's need that draws them, anything vulnerable.'

That was just what Joseph Reavley would have said. Mason knew it as he sat there in the crowded tavern with the voices and the laughter around him, the smell of ale, the sawdust, the light gleaming on pewter tankards hanging above the bar, and horse brasses on the wall. That passion was what Judith looked for in a man because she had seen it and understood it in her brother. She had felt it herself and had carried its burden for years.

Then quite suddenly he realized that for all its weight, that passion was far less crushing than the doubt and the sorrow he carried himself. He was looking at what he had lost, not at what he had won. It was not only she he had lost; it was something of the best in himself. No matter how difficult it was, or what comfort of surrender it cost him – and sometimes it was easier not to fight any more – he must change himself. He must become who he wanted to be, a man he could look at in the mirror with some sense of respect, at least for his aspirations, if not his accomplishments.

'Yes, you're right,' he said.

Oldroyd blinked again. 'Of course I'm right, boy,' he said gently. 'Except I was a bit over myself when I thought I could teach you, or anyone. You can tell people, that's all. Life teaches, or it doesn't. Be damn grateful you got the chance to try a bit harder. Where are you off to now?'

'Back to Ypres,' Mason replied without hesitation. 'I have things to do there, before the end. Would you like another cider?'

Oldroyd pushed his glass across. 'Seems like a good idea. Don't mind if I do.'

Matthew Reavley crossed the English Channel on the night of 13 October. He had told Shearing only that he was pursuing information about a British collaborator with the Germans, which was part of his job anyway. It would be time enough to speak of the Peacemaker if Schenckendorff really did provide proof of his identity.

The weather was overcast with a sharp wind and a choppy sea, but the physical discomfort was small compared with the constant danger of torpedo attack. Even at this late stage, when surrender was only weeks away, the war at sea continued. Ships still went down with loss of all hands.

It made him think of his brief time aboard the *Cormorant*, Archie's destroyer, before it was sunk in the Battle of Jutland in 1916. He still woke at night with the smell of burning corticene in his nose and the screams of men trapped in the gun turrets on fire, above the crash of metal and hiss of steam. Mostly he remembered Patrick Hannassey at the railing and the impact as Matthew struck him. There was an incredulous moment as they stared at each other, and Hannassey knew he was going over to be crushed by the bow of the German destroyer as it was sucked back in its own wash, then lurched forward again. It smashed into the hull of the *Cormorant* with Hannassey between them.

Only afterwards had Matthew learned that Hannassey was a murderer and a spy, but not the Peacemaker himself.

Now he stood on the deck staring towards the dark coast of Belgium ahead and willed himself not to think of it, not to think of Detta. They could never have been happy together. She was an Irish patriot more than she was anything else. She lived to crusade – if not for Irish independence, then for something else. If the battle were ever won, she would only look for a new torch to carry high.

They disembarked at Dunkirk towards dawn and Matthew waited around a cold railway station for the first train eastwards to Ypres. It stopped several miles short, where bombing had destroyed the tracks. He was tired and cold and very hungry, but rations were short and he was grateful for a tin mug of hot tea given him by an army cook at the railhead. It was probably better not to enquire.

He was in uniform but he had removed his insignia of the rank of lieutenant-colonel, a recent promotion, and substituted that of major. It was less conspicuous. He dared not tell anyone the truth. They had learned in the past that the Peacemaker had allies in the least expected places. Any rank was sufficient to ask for a lift towards the lines. 'Intelligence service,' he said with a smile, to explain his absence of kit or weapons. 'Trying to run down a traitor.'

'Before it's too late, eh?' the young driver said with understanding. 'Know where you want to be, sir? If I can help, I'll be happy to. Nothing filthier than a man who turns against his own.'

'Gathering information. The man I need to see will be just behind the front lines.'

Matthew cranked the engine for him, then climbed into the

front seat. They pulled away on to the early morning road, which was crowded, mostly with wounded coming back towards the hospitals.

'Looking for anyone in particular?' The driver swerved expertly to avoid a loose dog running after small groups of wounded men on foot.

'I'll start with the chaplain of the Cambridgeshires.' There was no point in being secretive about seeing Joseph. He would have to ask people for directions in order to find him. Evasion had become a habit with him. He did not like it because he found he was being evasive even when there was no need.

'Oh, Captain Reavley? You said your name was Reavley. He related to you, then?'

'My brother.' He was proud to say that, especially here, so close to the fighting.

The young man nodded and concentrated on the road ahead. It was muddy, and potholed at best; at worst gouged out by mortar fire and littered with debris. In the ditch there were broken wheels and shafts from wagons, old boxes half rotted away, and sometimes even the carcasses of animals, mostly horses. That was something that sickened Matthew more than he had expected it to. They looked so vulnerable, having loyally gone to the slaughter by men's rage and futility.

He could smell the front line long before they reached it. It was like nothing else he had ever known, thick and cloying. He gagged at the mixture of raw sewage and the sweet, stale odour of rotting flesh.

The driver glanced at him, then ahead again. 'You'll get used to it,' he said cheerfully. 'I expect you'll be sick the first few times you step on a corpse thrust up by the mud, especially if it's been there for a year or two and you realize it's one of our own. But you'll get on with it.' He sniffed. 'And if they're right, it won't be for much longer anyway. If you're around in no-man's-land, watch for craters. Some of them are pretty deep, and God knows what else is floating in them. Not much gas left now, but it's heavy, sticks to the low bits, so stay higher an' you'll be all right. Don't need to tell you about the barbed wire; you can work that out for yourself.'

Matthew studied him in the now broad daylight. He was a lieutenant, and he looked by his build and the fine texture of his skin to be about eighteen or nineteen. But from the weariness in his eyes and the dry, painful humour of his voice he was an old man, long past his prime.

'Thank you,' Matthew replied. 'I'll probably just be speaking to people, prisoners coming through the lines. But I'll remember your advice.'

'You'll have to find the prisoners before you speak to them,' the driver pointed out. 'Chaplain's back at the casualty clearing station now and then, but mostly he's forward. I'll take you as far as I can.'

Again Matthew thanked him.

They continued on in silence past columns of men walking slowly in the opposite direction. They moved as if half asleep and their eyes seemed to see nothing. They put one foot before the other, shambling unevenly on the ruined road, and their faces were vacant. Had they been lying rather than standing, Matthew would have assumed them dead.

Suddenly he saw the human cost not in numbers of millions but individually, each an irretrievable loss. He was no longer aware of the stench, or the far-distant noise of guns beyond the flat horizon as the armies moved inexorably forward, closing on the old battlegrounds, and then at last moving towards Germany itself.

He had no wish to speak now, nor did he care if the young driver thought it was a squeamish stomach that held him silent. When they reached the field hospital, he thanked him and left.

Inside, he asked an orderly if he had any idea where Captain Reavley was. When he could not help, he went to the next person, and the next. Finally it was a mild, good-natured American first-aid volunteer called Wil Sloan who told him and offered, if he would work his passage by helping carry stretchers, to take him further forward to a casualty clearing station where Joseph was most likely to be.

'Known the chaplain since the Christmas of 'fourteen,' Wil said with a smile as they started out. 'I drive with his sister most of the time. I guess she must be your sister too, eh?'

Matthew swallowed hard. He could not think of Judith in this mud and rain, working day after day trying to do the impossible, seeing men die all around her. She had never spoken of it in the few times he had seen her at home on leave. Had she worked to forget? Or did she simply believe he would never understand the reality, and to allow anyone to believe less was a betrayal of the courage and the pain? If she had thought that, it would only have been the truth.

But then he never spoke of his work either, because he was not allowed to. It was founded on lies and delusions: who could deceive the more efficiently, his own kind of betrayal.

Three times they got stuck in waterlogged craters, and Matthew had to climb out and help dig while Wil struggled with the steering wheel and the reluctant engine to get it started again.

Matthew was scratched, bruised and splattered with mud by the time they finally reached the casualty clearing station where Joseph was. It was only a series of tents with some wooden duckboards to make walkways between. Even before locating Joseph, however, he needed first to fulfil his obligation to Wil, and help load the stretchers into the ambulance.

He worked hard, slipping and staggering between the evacuation tent and the parking area, trying desperately not to drop anyone. The stretchers were not as heavy as he expected. Many of the wounded were only boys, light-boned, no muscle on them yet. Their faces were hollow with shock and there seemed to be blood on everything.

Matthew saw Joseph, recognizing his outline by the angle of his shoulders and the way he stood, unconsciously favouring his right leg. The left still ached when he was tired; it probably always would do. Joseph gave no sign of having recognized him, but then he was not expecting to see Matthew here. He was absorbed in his work, seeming to know exactly where to be, what to say, and when he could help.

Matthew was awed by it. It was his brother whom he had known all his life, and yet it was a stranger whose moral courage dwarfed his own. How could any man keep his sanity in this? There were broken bodies everywhere, ashen-faced, wounds hastily bound, the blood seeping through. He saw one soldier, of not more than eighteen or nineteen, with a scarlet stump where his leg should have been.

Finally the ambulance door closed and it jerked, stopped, then plunged forward, sending up sprays of mud. At last it picked up speed and disappeared into the rain. Matthew walked over to where Joseph was standing with the last of the walking wounded.

'Good afternoon, Chaplain,' he said quietly.

Joseph stood motionless, then slowly turned. He stared at him with momentary disbelief, then, as Matthew smiled at him, with dawning joy.

'Matthew!' He clasped his hand and wrung it so hard he crushed his fingers and it was all Matthew could do not to cry out. At home he would have hugged him, but here in the midst of so much absurd mixture of chaos and discipline, it seemed the wrong thing to do.

'Hello, Joe,' he replied instead, grinning back.

'What are you doing here?' Joseph demanded. 'The war's not over, surely?' He looked momentarily bewildered. 'They're still fighting like hell ahead.' He gestured slightly eastwards towards the old battlefield of the Ypres Salient, and beyond it Passchendaele, which was on the verge of being retaken. The German border was still miles away.

'Not yet,' Matthew answered. 'Another three or four weeks at the most. That's not why I came.' The excitement was sharp in his voice, and he could not control it.

Joseph looked at him, searching his eyes and finding no grief in them, no holding of darkness he needed to share. 'The Peacemaker? You've found him?' His hand tightened again on Matthew's.

'Almost,' Matthew answered. 'In a day or two we'll know. Get these men back to help of some kind, and I'll tell you.'

Joseph was puzzled. 'Why have you come, instead of writing? He can't be out here!'

'I'll tell you,' Matthew repeated. 'Get your wounded to wherever they need to be.' He was standing still in the mud, and the rain was getting harder.

Reluctantly Joseph obeyed, knowing which had the greater urgency. It was gathering dusk before they sat together in Joseph's bunker, shivering over a dixie can of hot, muddy tea.

'Well?' Joseph demanded.

The rattle of guns was muted, far in the distance forward, but every now and then one of the big howitzers sent over a shell the weight of three grown men, which exploded closer to them, shaking the ground and sending up massive gouts of earth.

'A messenger came to see me.' Matthew swallowed and tried to conceal his distaste at the oily residue in the tea. At least the warmth of it eased the clenched muscles inside him. 'A priest, or that was how he was dressed. He said the Peacemaker's counterpart in Germany, Manfred von Schenckendorff, is going to come through the lines at whatever point I would suggest. I said here, of course. He'll give himself up, so we can take him to London to expose the Peacemaker to the government. To Lloyd George personally.'

'What?' Joseph stared at him, his face almost comical with disbelief in the yellow light of the lamp. 'And you believed him? Matthew . . .'

Suddenly Matthew's elation vanished. Was he so hungry for justice, before it was too late, that all sense of reality had left him? 'Think about it!' he said huskily, feeling the heat burn up his face. 'Half Europe is ruined. America has lost over three hundred thousand men, killed, wounded, or missing, but we've lost over three million! Germany's lost twice as many, and Austro-Hungary even more. The estimates we have altogether are beyond thirty-five million. God Almighty, Joe, what man with even a shred of sanity left could ever bear to imagine that happening again?'

Joseph closed his eyes, overwhelmed by the vision.

'The Peacemaker is planning to urge a settlement that will allow Germany to rise and begin it all over again,' Matthew went on. 'He hasn't forgotten his dream of dominion that would force peace on us all, a servitude of spirit and the slow strangulation of individuality under the heel of law made by people to whom we are strangers.'

'And does this Schenckendorff believe that?' Joseph asked. 'Why now? Why not years ago, or always?'

Matthew searched his mind and answered reluctantly. 'Perhaps it was a dream with some nobility in the beginning. If I had ever seen war, real war like this, I might have done almost anything to prevent it happening again.'

'Sold your countrymen, without asking them if it was what they wanted?' Joseph's voice was quiet, his face bleak. 'Or if they understood the price?'

'Nobody understands,' Matthew replied. 'You can't imagine . . . this!' He swung his arm around vaguely to indicate the battlefield beyond the clay walls of the dugout. 'It's a human abattoir. I don't know if you believe in heaven any more, but you must believe in hell!'

Joseph smiled faintly. 'I believe in summer nights with the sky pale with stars, and in the poplars at sunset, and in spring the beech woods carpeted with bluebells so dense you can't put your foot down between them. I believe in clean water and a quiet bed, in laughter and gentleness. I believe that some men have the courage and the honour to face anything at all, and die without self-pity or complaint. I believe in the possibility of friendship, the love that never betrays. That's as close to heaven as I can grasp at the moment.'

Matthew sighed. 'Schenckendorff is coming through the lines here. He knows your name, naturally. It seems like the obvious place. You should hear what he has to say. I expect your German is better than mine – colloquial, anyway. Mine's a little rusty. Don't get enough practice. And I might need your help with the mechanics of getting to him, and making certain I can get him out of here and back to London.' He looked at Joseph gravely. 'We're so close to it, it would be easy to forget the Peacemaker might still think he has it all to play for, and take the chance to kill him – and us.'

Joseph winced. 'I suppose he could. Why should anyone think themselves safe here?'

Matthew started to laugh, then stopped almost immediately.

'Nothing we can do except wait.' Joseph finished his tea as if it had been fit to drink.

Joseph had one of the better dugouts, and he made room for Matthew in it. At least it was dry. But he slept badly that night, as always excited to have seen Matthew, wondering if he was sleeping or only pretending to. He was concerned for his welfare in the filth and danger he was unaccustomed to. Joseph lay in the dark of the familiar space, knowing where everything was: the rickety table, the one chair, the shelf with his books and the picture of Dante Alighieri who had written so brilliantly about a different hell.

Joseph was the eldest of the four siblings. He was quite aware that worrying had become a habit with him, and had increased since his father's death. He was not ready for the responsibility of caring for the other three, foreseeing dangers, comforting loss, finding a reason and an answer for pain. There was no answer, but you did not tell that to people you loved, and who had learned to rely on you. He was the wrong man to have chosen the Church as a calling, but there was no way out now.

What if this Schenckendorff was one more trick of the Peacemaker's? Matthew had looked so excited, so hopeful, all because some man had turned up on his doorstep in London and said he was a priest! Anyone could say that. Heaven help him, Joseph had said exactly that himself when he and Morel had been behind the German lines looking for Geddes before the court martial last year. He had been believed too.

They wanted to find the Peacemaker so desperately, and time was running out. After the war was over, what chance would they have? But, if he were honest, what chance had they ever had? Maybe their hunger for revenge was the Peacemaker's final act of destruction of the Reavley family?

He drifted into half-sleep, and confused dreams. Then, without any warning, it was daylight. Cold and stiff, moving as quietly as he could, he got up, shaved and began the long routine of paperwork, letters of condolence, and helping the wounded. He tried to comfort, advise, assist with practical things like eating or drinking with bandaged hands – or none at all – dressing with a shattered arm or leg, simple tasks that had suddenly become monumental.

Matthew woke late, and excused himself to find something to eat.

There was no word of any German prisoner asking to see either Joseph or Matthew, and there were so many coming through the lines in the general area of Ypres that it was impossible to check all the names. Joseph continued with his usual duties. More often than not he was far forward of the casualty clearing station, beyond even the old trench line, as the armies advanced. That day British troops took Messines and were advancing on Menin.

Matthew spent the day restlessly, trying to look as if he were collecting some kind of information that would justify his presence in the junior intelligence work he had told Colonel Hook, the regiment commander, he was engaged in. He spoke to German prisoners, but there was nothing of use they could tell him, and the pretence would wear thin soon.

It was the middle of the afternoon of the sixteenth when Snowy Nunn came to tell Joseph that Colonel Hook wanted to see him. 'Roight now, Chaplain,' he added, his fair face puckering up with apprehension. 'It's another German prisoner. Oi don't know what anybody done to this one. Officer an' all, by his uniform, and the way he stands. He's got a foot all mangled up, so looks loike someone ran over it, or something.'

'Right.' Joseph's heart sank. Another piece of random brutality, pointless but so very understandable. 'I'll be there.'

Snowy nodded, his eyes grave. 'Whole lot more for the hospital, Oi reckon. Some o' the poor sods are knocked about pretty bad. Look loike hell, they do. Oi thought winning weren't much fun after all, an' we waited long enough for it. But Oi reckon losing's got to be a whole lot worse. Roight away, Chaplain, he said.'

'I'm going,' Joseph said impatiently. He resented Hook sending for him over some breach of discipline. There were going to be lots of instances of loss of self-control. He had known people nurse loved ones over years to a painful death, never complaining. Then when it was all over and there was some ease at last, they were suddenly overwhelmed, letting slip the courage and the selfless endurance that had governed their lives throughout the sacrifice. He could sense the same longing for peace, and fear of change now. They wanted to go home to what they had originally left, what this whole bloody war had been about saving, but it wasn't there any more. The past never is. The England they had paid for with such a price no longer existed.

He walked quickly through the mud, used to keeping his balance in it, not avoiding the rain because he was already wet and there was no point.

He found Colonel Hook in the command bunker nearly a mile further east. He looked tired and he was even thinner than he had been a year ago at the court martial.

'Ah, Reavley.' He looked up from his maps spread out on top of a packing case. 'Odd thing's come up.' He looked puzzled rather than angry, and it was unusual that he had addressed Joseph by name rather than rank or calling.

Joseph stood to attention. 'Yes, sir?'

'Got a German officer, says he's a colonel, but I think he might be more senior than that, although my German's not good enough to be certain. Know everyday language well enough, but not the differences of education and class. But he's asked to speak to you.'

'Is he badly injured?' Joseph was surprised. Snowy Nunn had mentioned only a crushed foot.

'Not at all. Painful, no doubt, but he didn't even refer to it,' Hook replied. 'He didn't ask for a chaplain, he spoke of you by name – Reavley. Seemed to expect you to be here.' The demand for an explanation was clear in Hook's eyes.

Was this the Peacemaker's ally in Germany at last? 'No idea, sir,' Joseph said, his voice husky. He cleared his throat. 'I'll go and talk to him. Where is he?'

'Casualty clearing station,' Hook replied. 'His foot's a mess.

Looks like someone pinned him to the ground with a bayonet.'
His face was pinched with disgust. 'Damn stupid thing to do. If
I thought I had a cat in hell's chance of catching the man who
did it, I'd have him up on a charge.'

'What's his name, sir?' Joseph's heart was pounding. Could
they really be this close to the Peacemaker at last?

'No idea!' Hook said impatiently. 'They've only got one
colonel. Go back and bloody well ask!'

'Yes, sir.' Joseph stood to attention, and then hesitated. He
knew Hook wanted to say something more. Their eyes met for
a moment. Joseph smiled.

Hook shrugged. 'Get out,' he said quietly. 'Go and find out
what the poor sod wants. No favours.'

'Yes, sir.'

'You mean "no, sir",' Hook corrected him.

It was Joseph's turn to shrug. He went out without replying.

It was raining harder again, just like last year, and the year
before. The wet khaki had rubbed his skin raw at his neck, and
his feet were getting new blisters by the time he caught up with
the ambulances. There were very few men around. Most of the
troops had moved forward, beyond Ypres now. Joseph remembered the town well, the places where in 1914 and 1915 they
had eaten quite decent food, drunk wine, even sung around the
piano in one or two of the better *estaminets*. He wondered how
many of the people were still alive after occupation. Or had most
of them fled ahead of the German Army, back somewhere into
France? How many of the buildings were still standing after the
incessant bombardment? He had heard that Passchendaele was
in ruins; nothing left but scattered stone and burned wood.

He walked back the way he had come through the mud to

the cratered road. Thirty minutes later, he was back in the casualty clearing station, standing by the cot of a German officer whose foot was swathed in bloody bandages, his face white and masklike with the effort of controlling his pain.

'Captain Reavley,' Joseph introduced himself. 'I believe you wanted to see me, Colonel?'

The man stared at Joseph's uniform as if trying to understand his insignia, and the Military Cross and Distinguished Service Medal. These were both front-line awards, and yet he was still a captain. 'You have been demoted?' he said in German. He spoke very quietly, the subject being a delicate one, and there was sympathy in his eyes.

It was Schenckendorff, Joseph was sure of it. He thought he was speaking to Matthew, and had therefore expected a major. And certainly the chaplain's collar confused him. Only the name was what he had been told.

But he must be careful. 'What is your name and rank?' Joseph asked. 'Why did you send for me?'

The man was exhausted, and to surrender must be almost intolerable for him. His accent was discreet, highly educated. He probably spoke English, even if he chose not to now. But if he really was the German ally of the Peacemaker then he would be the man who had obtained the Kaiser's signature to the original treaty, and he would unquestionably be of the old aristocracy.

'Why did you ask for me?' Joseph repeated.

'I asked for Major Reavley,' the man replied, drawing his breath in sharply as another wave of pain overtook him. 'I did not know you were a man of the Church. It does not seem to make sense.'

'It makes excellent sense,' Joseph told him, moving a little closer but remaining standing. One did not sit on the narrow cot of a wounded man; the sheer alteration of weight could hurt intensely. 'I am chaplain of the Cambridgeshire regiment, the remnants of which are still here at Ypres. I refused promotion because I want to stay with the men, not move back to Regimental Headquarters.'

Schenckendorff nodded fractionally, both understanding and respect in his eyes.

'I think it is my brother, Major Matthew Reavley, that you want, Colonel Schenckendorff,' Joseph went on.

The man's face tightened. It would have been impossible for him to have grown any paler. Joseph realized with a sudden, searing pity for him, what this decision must have cost. He was a man who loved his country and had once believed passionately that it could dominate and govern with a lasting peace. Now he was coming through the lines to betray in turn the trust that had deceived him. The courage and the grief of it were over-whelming. For the first time Joseph saw with wrenching power the meaning of defeat, not just of a nation but of individual men and the dreams they had lived and died for. Perhaps heroism could only be truly measured in those who had lost, and faced the ultimate truth without flinching.

'Yes,' Schenckendorff agreed at last. 'I would be obliged if I could speak with him. It is . . . necessary.'

'He is here,' Joseph told him. 'I'll bring him as soon as I can. But as you will be aware, we dare not tell anyone else who you are, or why you are so important.'

Schenckendorff did not answer.

'You must tell no one,' Joseph said urgently, lowering his voice even further. 'Be as invisible as you can be, just like any other prisoner. We have no idea where the Peacemaker . . .'

he hesitated, '. . . where your counterpart may have allies,' he amended. It was brutal, but he could not afford to be unclear. 'He may have guessed that you have come to us, and he will see it as a betrayal, one he cannot afford.'

'I know,' Schenckendorff said in no more than a whisper. 'He will kill me. Perhaps he will do that eventually anyway. With him the cause was always first.' He spoke with difficulty. 'Perhaps that is the germ of his moral decay, that he cannot see some weapons destroy the men who wield them in a subtler and deeper way than the enemy they kill with their use. I will be extremely careful, Captain Reavley.' The shadow of a smile touched his lips. 'I have to survive in order to tell your Prime Minister what my . . . counterpart . . . has done. He will not believe it from anyone else. Even I may have some difficulty. It will be necessary for you to be there, and to swear to the existence of the original treaty your father took. Do you still have it?'

Joseph smiled very slightly. 'Who is the Peacemaker?' he asked.

Schenckendorff smiled back. It was a thin, painful gesture but not without both humour and comprehension. 'The treaty would help,' he said, evading the question. His voice was growing weaker, as if the pain of his broken foot, the shock to the bones and the extensive loss of blood, and no doubt several days of bitter deliberation before the struggle to get through the lines, had exhausted his physical and mental strength. He had risked being shot as a deserter.

Joseph debated within himself whether to tell the doctor in charge here that Schenckendorff was of special importance and to take care that he did not die of neglect to his wound. That was possible in the vast crowd of German prisoners pouring through the lines now in their tens of thousands. Not all of them would be fed, treated and cared for. And Allied soldiers must come first, always. But he could give no reason. The doctors were harried to exhaustion. Burdening them with secrets was foolish, especially one that they would not understand. The risk was higher than any advantage. He decided against it.

'I'll have my brother here by this evening,' he said instead. 'Get as much rest as you can. Sleep if possible.'

There was a flash of appreciation in Schenckendorff's eyes that he had not indulged in platitudes. 'Good night, Chaplain.'

Joseph managed to find Matthew and get the message through to him. He arrived back at the casualty clearing station by sundown. He saw Schenckendorff briefly, but now he was feverish and in intense pain. The wound in his foot was messy. He had lost a great deal of blood, and there was a fear of septicaemia.

'You'd better start praying,' Matthew said grimly when he found Joseph in the storage tent. He was sorting through supplies and trying to tidy them up after the night's casualties. 'That foot looks pretty bad. Hope to hell they don't have to amputate it. It would make him hard to move. We won't convince anyone if we can't get him to London.'

'Did he tell you who the Peacemaker is?' Joseph asked, turning from the table where bandages, lint, disinfectant and suture thread were laid out.

Matthew looked back at him steadily. 'No. Did he ask you if you still had the treaty Father took from the Peacemaker?'

'Yes. But I didn't answer him.'

Matthew chewed his lip. 'Joe, do you think that's what he really wants? Is he still on the Peacemaker's side and they need to get that treaty back before the armistice, just in case we expose it then?'

The thought had crossed Joseph's mind and he could not dismiss it. 'Maybe,' he said unhappily. 'Perhaps we'd better not tell Judith anything until we know more. Damn it.' He swallowed hard. 'Damn it! I'd begun to hope we had him.'

Matthew gripped Joseph's shoulder hard. 'Maybe we have.'

Joseph looked at him. 'Have you thought what it would cost a man in Schenckendorff's position to turn against his own like that? I can hardly imagine the courage and the moral strength to face the fact that you had dedicated your life to a cause that was fatally flawed, and you would give yourself to the enemy to undo your own efforts, then accept whatever they choose to do to you.'

'Nor can I,' Matthew agreed. 'Which is part of why I dare not believe it yet. He's either a true hero, or a very clever double-trickster. Either way, he's a brave man.' He sighed. 'And he could die of that damn foot. What did it, Joseph?'

'Bayonets, by the look of it.'

'God in heaven! For what? What's the point of that now?'

Joseph did not answer. For a man who had seen half the men he knew killed, the rage to commit such an act was easy to understand, and impossible to explain.

# Chapter Three

It was another long night of casualties. More German prisoners coming through the lines voluntarily, or taken in desperate, failed battles. Joseph worked between the first-aid post and the casualty clearing station. He finally got a break at almost half-past one in the morning when he lay down in his dugout. He was exhausted and filthy, but here it was at least dry. Matthew was curled up, apparently asleep, and Joseph took care not to disturb him.

He woke with a jolt to find Tiddly Wop Andrews bending over him. There was a thread of daylight coming down the steps. He could see Tiddly Wop's handsome face was gaunt with weariness and what Joseph recognized as pain, and was now also creased with new anxiety.

'Chaplain!' Tiddly Wop said urgently. 'Wake up! The colonel wants you roight away.'

Joseph struggled to the surface of comprehension, his head

pounding. 'Why? What is it now?' His first fear was that Schenckendorff had died. Then he realized that Hook had no idea how much that would matter. He struggled to sit up. Every bone and muscle in his body hurt. 'What's happened, Tiddly? Have you been injured?'

Before the war Tiddly Wop's hair had been long, and when he was worried he pushed it back off his brow as if it still were. He did it now, unaware of the movement. 'Just a gash in the side, Chaplain. Nothing serious. And Oi don't know, Chaplain, but it's bad. Looks loike hell, he does. Something at the clearing station, that's all Oi know. You'd better go now. That's whoi Oi didn't even get you a mug of tea. No toime.'

Joseph was suddenly ice cold. 'Have you seen Miss Reavley?' he demanded, his mouth dry. That was always his first thought.

'Yes, an' she's foine, sir. But you'd better go,' Tiddly Wop urged.

Warmth flooded back into Joseph as if the blood had started pumping again. That was absurd. Judith had been here for four years, and usually he managed not to imagine what she faced, or he would cease to function at all. It was the only way to survive.

He struggled to his feet and followed Tiddly Wop out into the pale, misty daylight. The rain had stopped and there was a watery sun gleaming on the mud. Here and there it shone on a flat surface of a crater, making it look like polished steel.

It was a fifteen-minute hard walk to the colonel's command bunker. Joseph went down the concrete steps and parted the sacking over the entrance. He asked for permission to enter. When it was given he went in and stood to attention. This was further forward than the casualty clearing station. It was an old

German bunker, and deeper than the British. The floor was dry and the walls lined with pretty decent wood.

'Sit down,' Hook ordered, gesturing to an ammunition box turned on end. The Germans must have taken the chairs when they retreated. Tiddly Wop was right, Hook looked dreadful.

'I'm afraid there's been a death at the clearing station,' he said grimly. 'I've no choice but to call in the military police, but I want you to be there. You know how to keep your head and deal with these things.'

Joseph was confused. There were deaths every day – in the trenches, in no-man's-land, in the ambulances, first-aid posts, clearing stations, in the fields and on the sides of the roads, violent, desperate death, all the time. Hospital was the best place to die, not the worst.

'One of the nurses,' Hook added. 'Sarah Price.'

'I'm sorry,' Joseph said automatically. 'I'll write to her family. What happened?'

'For God's sake, Reavley!' Hook snapped, his voice near the edge of control. 'I wouldn't have woken you up to tell you if it were an accident! The poor girl was hacked to death with a damn bayonet!'

For the second time since waking up, Joseph was stunned into complete immobility. He struggled to grasp what Hook had said, and yet the words were clear enough. A nurse had been pretty brutally murdered. Of course the police had been sent for; there was no other possible action. 'Yes, sir,' he said slowly.

'Be there, please,' Hook asked. 'The men are going to take it very badly. I don't want . . .' he looked for the right word, '. . . I don't want revenge. I suppose it was one of the German prisoners, but we can't have them all massacred. Do what you can, Reavley.'

'Yes, sir.' Joseph stood up sharply. His mind was racing now to Schenckendorff. How would they get him out? He could not tell Hook that he needed to leave. Perhaps they would find out what had happened quickly and it would all be settled in a day or two, then Schenckendorff's fever would have broken and he could travel. He would be in pain, but so were tens of thousands of men. War was about pain, of one sort or another.

Hook drew in his breath as if to add something further, then let it go again in silence.

Joseph excused himself and went to find Matthew, before going to the casualty clearing station.

Matthew was standing with a group of other men around a small fire with a dixie can of boiling water. He was about to make tea. Joseph spoke to him. He turned round, regarding Joseph with some concern. He did not ask what was the matter, but it was clear that Schenckendorff was on his mind too.

'You'd better come,' Joseph said simply.

Matthew thanked the men for the tea, leaving it behind him, and fell in step with Joseph as they walked away in single file between the old craters. Only when they could move side by side did Joseph tell him what Hook had said.

'I suppose he's sure?' Matthew asked, hunching his coat collar up. 'That's going to make it harder to get Schenckendorff out, isn't it? They'll be pretty unhappy about German prisoners, even injured ones. And I was worrying about him dying!' He pulled his mouth down in a hard line. 'I suppose the only good thing is that he was too ill to be suspected. Filthy irony of it.'

'He wasn't too ill to stand,' Joseph replied. 'Not early in the evening, anyway. You'd be amazed what a man can do, injured almost to death.'

'Murdering a nurse?' Matthew's voice rose in disbelief. 'What the devil for? He's on his way to London to give up his ally, and pretty certainly to be hanged!'

'No one in the casualty clearing station knows that,' Joseph pointed out. 'At least, please God, no one does. Let's hope this priest of yours was careful.'

Matthew increased his stride towards the clearing station. All men were moving forward in file towards the ever-shifting front line: the wagons of ammunition boxes, two tanks mired in mud and making heavy weather of churning it up on their huge tracks, and mule teams pulling guns forward on carriages.

Judith Reavley pulled her ambulance into the mud as close to the casualty clearing station as she could and climbed out. She was tired and stiff from driving most of the night, and more than anything else she wanted a hot drink to ease the chill from inside her, then to find Matthew. Wil had told her he was here – that he'd given him a lift – but in the two days since then she'd been too busy during daylight hours to look for him, the influx of German wounded adding to the chaos at the casualty clearing station. First she must help unload the wounded, and then, when they were safe, check her engine, which was misfiring. She had thought when she was here at about three o'clock with Wil Sloan that she would lose it altogether. It was early daylight now and she was alone. Wil had stopped to help another ambulance overturned by shellfire. Mist hung over the craters, softening the harsh lines of the old supply trenches and for the moment making them look more like cart tracks than the gashes in the land that they were.

Judith stood, turning slowly, looking for someone to help.

It was a two-man job to carry a stretcher. Someone must have seen her coming. A doctor hurried by fifty yards away, increasing his step to a run, but he took no notice of her. She started towards the admissions tent. She was halfway there when another doctor came out and she recognized him immediately. It was Cavan, one of the best surgeons in the army, a man with whom she had worked on some of the worst nights during the battles of Ypres and Passchendaele, and in the long, desperate days since. His courage had merited him a VC, and his rash loyalty had lost him it.

He saw her, went back to the tent opening and shouted something inside. Two more men appeared and ran towards the ambulance. Cavan came to her – his face was grave, his eyes smudged around with shadows of exhaustion. She assumed he had lost many wounded through the night. There was no point in saying anything comforting to him. They had both had this happen so many times the understanding needed no words, and nothing helped anyway. Even if the task had been hopeless and the men too mutilated ever to survive, it was still death.

'Judith!' he said the moment they were out of the hearing of the wounded. 'Something pretty awful has happened. Sarah Price has been killed.' He took her arm and held it, closing his hand to grip hers, almost as if he were afraid she might sway and overbalance.

'I'm sorry,' she said sincerely. She did not particularly like Sarah, but it was somehow harder to make it this far, and then be killed in what had to be the final weeks of the war. By this time next month it could all be over. 'What happened? There's not much falling this far back now.'

'Not shelling,' he said. 'She was murdered.' He was frowning, his face puckered with distress. 'It was brutal. She was cut about with a bayonet, in the pit of the stomach, and left out where the waste is put.'

'You mean . . . ?' she stopped. She tried to picture Sarah Price lying in the mud behind the operating tent where they disposed of blood-soaked bandages, old swabs, litter that would not possibly be reused in any way at all, and the sodden clothes and mangled, amputated limbs of the worst injured. 'Who did it?' She felt her stomach churn with horror, then a hot wave of fury. Sarah was trivial, made fun of things that were important, laughed too loudly, flirted in a silly way, showing off. But she was also kind, and generous, always willing to share even a simple biscuit, or pretend she had not heard a joke before, and find it funny all over again. 'Who did it?' Her voice rose sharply, too loud, and she pulled her arm away from his.

'We don't know,' Cavan replied. 'One of the German prisoners, I expect.'

'I suppose it has to be,' she agreed. 'Why aren't they keeping them guarded properly?' But even as she said it, she remembered odd moments of rage breaking through what looked like banter taken a little too far, ugly comments that stayed in the mind, petty cruelties that betrayed an underlying contempt. Please heaven it was a German, but she was not certain. 'What are they doing about it?' she went on.

'Sending for the police, I suppose' he said with a slight shrug. 'No one really knows. It must have happened some time during the night. I hope no one gets it in the neck for not having guarded the prisoners. I reckon there are just too many of them for anyone to watch. And they came through the lines themselves, most of them. Poor devils are glad the war's over, at least for them.' He gave a rueful gesture. 'They might have thought we have more food than they do.'

It was impossible to think of the prisoners as enemies any longer. She had found her sense of pity disturbing; they looked so desperately like their own men. More than once her mind had turned to the Peacemaker, and she had wondered what he was like. She had even thought that had she known him as a man rather than a power behind the murder of too many people she had loved, she might have liked him. At the very least she would have understood his dreams. Was that a disloyalty to her dead parents, and to Owen Cullingford, whom she had also loved? Every one of the dead was precious to someone. It was contemptibly arrogant to imagine that those dear to you, woven into your life so the loss of them tore it apart, were really more valuable than all the uncountable others.

What had happened to Sarah Price? It could as easily have happened to Judith herself, or any of the other women here. Now a hot drink was trivial, almost forgotten. Her wet skirt flapping about her legs, cold and heavy, was no more than a discomfort. She gave Cavan a smile and a little mock salute, then walked over towards the admissions tent and the extended tents put up to shelter the wounded Germans, as well as their own.

She was barely inside when she saw Joseph. He turned at the sound of her footsteps on the boards. She felt a sudden pinch of anxiety at how tired he looked. He would have to deal with the men's grief of this new loss, and the fear and blame that followed.

'Judith!' He excused himself from the orderly he was talking to and came over to her quickly, almost pushing her into a corner away from earshot, so that she was pressed against a pile of boxes and stretchers stacked upright. 'Sarah Price has been killed—' he began.

'I know,' she cut him off. 'Cavan told me. Murdered with a bayonet.' She swallowed hard, her throat tight. 'It's horrible, but I suppose we shouldn't be surprised. Victory and defeat are too close to each other here, and both of them have their bitterness. War is probably the most hideous thing we do to each other, but we've become used to it. I don't know about you, but I'm scared sick of going home.' She looked at him, searching his eyes and seeing understanding leap to them, and laughter, and pain. They knew each other now in a way they could not have in a lifetime at home.

'That's not all, Judith,' he said in little more than a whisper. 'Matthew's here. I didn't have the privacy to tell you before. I left him asleep. The Peacemaker's German counterpart has come through the lines to give him up before he can affect the terms of the armistice so the war starts up again within a few years.'

'Wil Sloan told me Matthew's here. I haven't had a chance to look for him. But you know who the Peacemaker is?' She was amazed, excitement surging up inside her now, her heart beating faster, blood suddenly pounding.

'Not yet.' His hand tightened on her arm. 'The German's here, but he doesn't trust us enough to give us the Peacemaker's name. He'll travel to London to tell Lloyd George. We've got to keep him safe until we can leave. He's got a badly wounded foot and was feverish last night when I met him, but the orderly says he's better now.'

'Are we going?' Without giving it even a thought she automatically included herself. 'He'll need an ambulance. Can we explain it to Colonel Hook?'

Joseph hesitated only a moment. Before the war he would have evaded an answer, protecting her; now he knew her strength. 'No. I think Schenckendorff's genuine, but we can't be sure,' he said. 'And even if he is, it's possible the Peacemaker knows he's crossed through the lines, and there could only be one reason why. He wouldn't take the risk.'

'Murder him too? His own—' She stopped, realizing what she was about to say, and bit her lip. 'Schenckendorff?'

'Yes. Looks like someone already put a bayonet through his foot, more than once.'

She drew in her breath to swear, then remembered his sensibilities and checked herself. 'So Matthew's here on this secret mission?'

'Five days ago Schenckendorff sent a message to him in London, asking where he should come through, and if Matthew would be here.'

A chill touched Judith more than the wet skirts around her legs. Now she understood why Joseph was afraid it was a trap, a last attempt at revenge on the Reavleys who had thwarted him from the start.

He must have seen the fear in her. 'We'll get him out,' he assured her. 'It'll be over soon. It's wretched about Sarah Price's death, but that may be solved pretty quickly. We can't wait for it, anyway. I'll explain it to Colonel Hook, if I have to. Matthew's rank should make it pretty simple. He's recently been promoted to lieutenant-colonel but at the moment he's pretending to be a major, not to draw attention. He'll just have to take the chance and explain who he is.'

Judith nodded. 'I've got to see if I can fix my engine before I need it again. I'll be lucky if it lasts the war out. I really need some new parts.'

'Good luck!' he said drily.

'Luck won't do it!' she retorted. 'I need a light-fingered friend willing to "liberate" a few spark plugs and one or two other necessities of life.'

He had stopped bothering to warn her to be careful. He gave a very slight smile, and walked away.

Judith spent the next hour taking apart various pieces of her engine, cleaning them and attempting to make them work again. Finally she resigned herself to the fact that without new spark plugs it was pointless. She abandoned the task and went to find a mug of hot tea and something to eat, even if it was only a heel of bread and some tinned Maconochie stew.

The clearing station was unusually tense. She passed medical orderlies moving briskly over the duckboard paths from the tent for the walking wounded to that for the lying wounded, their heads averted as if they dare not look at her. They were embarrassed, because she was an ambulance driver, not so very different from a nurse. It was as if she were somehow related to the victim. She opened her mouth to speak to one she knew well, but he had passed her without meeting her eyes, and it was too late.

She found nurses Allie Robinson and Moira Jessop in a supply tent. They were busy boiling a pot of water on a portable stove. The place was full of boxes stacked up and a half-open bale of sheets.

'Just came in?' Moira asked Judith. She was a Scots girl with red-brown hair and wide eyes.

Judith shook her head. 'Spark plugs are burned out,' she said resignedly. 'Got enough for tea?' She looked at the pot.

'Of course. I suppose you've heard about poor Sarah?' Moira asked.

Allie Robinson gave a little grunt. 'What I want to know is what she was doing there at all! Everyone's been warned, as if we needed it. Did she think German prisoners were going to respect her and treat her like a lady?' She looked defensively at Judith, seeing her surprise. 'Of course I'm sorry for her!' she snapped, the colour rising in her fair skin. 'Everyone is. But she flirted like mad with the Germans, led them on like a—' She stopped short of using the word that was obviously in her mind. 'You have to take some sort of responsibility,' she finished. 'Now everybody's scared stiff and all the men are going to be suspected, until we can prove who it was.'

'Why men?' Judith asked.

Allie and Moira glanced at each other, then away again.

'Because of how it was done,' Moira answered. 'Like rape, but with a bayonet.'

Judith imagined it, and felt sick.

'Sorry,' Moira apologized. 'But she was pretty . . . loose. The last time anybody saw her she was with somebody, we just don't know who.'

'Are you sure?' Judith was trying to deny it to herself, refusing to believe.

'Of course we're sure!' Allie snapped. 'Stop being so naïve!'

Judith saw the fear and anger in her face, and knew with chilling familiarity that it was her own fear speaking. She despised Allie for her facile criticism, as if any of it altered the tragedy, but she also understood it. If it were somehow Sarah's fault – if she had behaved differently, it would not have happened – then the rest of them could find a way to be safe.

'No matter how silly she was, she didn't deserve that! She was used and thrown away, like so much rubbish, Allie!' Moira said with disgust.

Allie looked away from her. 'We're all used and thrown away,' she said bitterly. 'Just this time it's against the law, that's all. They're getting police in. Not that they'll find anything, but I suppose they have to try. Where do they even begin? Men are coming and going all the time, our own wounded, German prisoners, VADs, doctors, people bringing supplies, even burial parties. Could have been anybody at all. Like Piccadilly Circus here.'

'Well, obviously it was one of the German prisoners,' Moira said impatiently. 'It's just a matter of finding out which one. She flirted with all of them, stupid creature!' The pot boiled and she made three tin mugs of tea. She passed one to Judith. 'Sorry there's no sort of milk, but it's tea, more or less.'

'Thank you,' Judith took it and sipped tentatively. She had forgotten what real tea tasted like, and this was at least hot. 'I don't suppose you know anyone who has decent spark plugs?'

'Good luck!' Moira said ruefully.

'You could try Toby Simmons,' Allie suggested. 'He has some imaginative ways of getting hold of things. At least that's one way you could phrase it.' Her face pinched with distaste. 'Gwen Williams says she thinks he's behind this. He was always making vulgar remarks, and Sarah wasn't above flirting with him. Too openly, if you ask me.'

'Nobody did ask you,' Moira told her.

'You didn't, because you like him!' Allie retorted. 'You never thought there was anything wrong with what he did, even when he was caught in the empty theatre with Erica Barton-Jones.'

'Really?' Judith was surprised. Toby was handsome, and sometimes amusing, but Erica Barton-Jones was from a very good family, and fully expected to marry into a title of some sort – at the very least into money.

'That's rubbish,' Moira said quickly, her face flushed. 'That was just spread around by Sarah, as a piece of spite.'

'Why would she do that?' Allie asked.

'How do I know? Boredom, fear, loneliness, sheer stupidity,' Moira snapped. 'Why do we do any of the things we do? She was lonely, and she had nothing much to go home to. Not that many of us have.'

Allie was silent, her face filled with a sudden, overwhelming grief.

Moira looked at Judith. 'It's as if something has sort of . . . broken,' she said quietly. 'Yesterday we were all stiff upper lip, and today nobody knows what to say or do. I don't know how many of us actually liked Sarah, but she was one of us, and nobody at all should be used that way, and left . . . exposed like that.' She put her arms around herself, holding them folded tight, protectively. 'I feel . . . naked too, as if every man's looking at her, and seeing me as well. I know that's idiotic, but I can't help it.'

'It'll be better once they find out who did it,' Judith tried to reassure her, although she feared it was a lie. Suspicions might be proved wrong, but did one ever forget them? Trust broken is not easy to mend; sometimes it is not even possible. 'Thanks for the tea. I've got to see if I can find some spark plugs.' She put the mug down and, with a small wave of her hand, went outside into the cold mid-morning light.

In the empty resuscitation tent Joseph reported to Cavan to ask what he could do to help. He knew Cavan well and had an immense respect for him. After Major Northrup had been killed, it had been Joseph who had saved Cavan's life at the court martial, although he could not save the VC for which he had been recommended for his extraordinary courage under fire. Naturally they did not speak of it now; a gentleman did not mention such obligation.

'Glad you came,' Cavan said sincerely. He was sitting on an upturned box emptying stew out of a dixie can, and there was a mug of tea on the makeshift table. He was wearing regular uniform, but his blood-splashed white coat was slung over the back of a hard chair. 'Need all the help we can get to keep control of this.' He looked up at Joseph. He was in his middle thirties, an angular man with fair hair and tired, heavy-lidded eyes over broad cheekbones. With long rest and regular food he would have been handsome.

He did not bother with explanations; he knew Joseph understood. 'Police are here already. Damn nuisance, because nobody can leave until they get this sorted out. Means we're piled up with German prisoners, and this fellow Jacobson won't even let our regular ambulance crews in and out, except the women, in case it's one of them.' He looked exhausted and thoroughly fed up. He shook his head. 'God, what a bloody stupid mess. Sorry, Reavley. See what you can do to help. Jacobson's in the first tent at the end.'

'Yes, sir.' Joseph was outside on the wooden slats that formed the connecting pathways between the tents before he fully realized what Cavan had said – no one could leave. He, Matthew and Schenckendorff were imprisoned here until this crime was solved. It would probably be only a couple of days, but it was already 17 October. What if it took longer?

The air was cold with a raw wind coming in from the east. He walked quickly, his boots clanking on the wooden slats, but they were firm under his weight, not like the constantly rocking duckboards in the trenches, the best of them covered with chicken wire to help men avoid slipping when they were wet.

He reached the tent and knocked on the doorframe. He heard the command to enter, and pushed it open. Inside it had been cleared of most of its medical supplies, no doubt because they were needed, as much as for the convenience of the police. The man sitting behind the bare, wooden table was plain-faced with dark hair brushed straight back and a short bristly moustache. He appeared to be of average height. Only his hands holding a pencil above a clean sheet of paper were in any way remarkable. They were slender, fine-boned, with particularly well-shaped nails. His insignia said that he was a captain.

The other man in the tent was fairer, his nose a little crooked as if at some time it had been broken, possibly on the rugby field in youth. He stood a little distance from Jacobson's chair and he stared at Joseph with undisguised curiosity.

'Yes?' Jacobson enquired. He looked very pale and his voice was sharp. It was apparent that he was nervous, and Joseph guessed that he was probably a civilian policeman fairly recently drafted to the Front. The stench of it would turn his stomach, and the scale of death everywhere must be something he had read of, but could never truly have imagined until now.

'Captain Reavley, sir,' Joseph replied. 'Chaplain. Captain Cavan thought I might be able to help.'

Jacobson's face relaxed; even the tightness of his shoulders eased a little. 'Oh. Good. Yes, Captain. I'm obliged. This is a very ugly business, and there are only Hampton and myself to deal with it.' He indicated the other man briefly. 'We need to question everyone: doctors, orderlies, nurses, and of course the patients . . . men . . . injured men.' He did not seem certain what term to use. 'I'd be grateful if you could help. You might know better how to deal with it, what to say. Colonel Hook says you're . . . experienced.' He was obviously at a loss to understand what that might mean.

'Yes, of course. You'll have to give me some of the facts, or my questions won't be of much use,' Joseph agreed. He had no intention of telling Jacobson about the other crimes he had solved, or the decisions and the grief of the past.

Hampton shifted his weight from one foot to the other, but he did not interrupt, and Jacobson ignored him.

'Sarah Price,' Jacobson said grimly. 'Twenty-five-year-old nurse. Been here just over a year, according to my information – pleasant enough, and good at her job. Turner, slightly wounded man on guard duty, found her at the back of the operating tent, on the ground near where the . . . the waste is left for removal.' He looked embarrassed because he could not think of any words that were decent to describe what he knew were amputated limbs from injured soldiers, parts of their bodies that could not be saved. He was shivering as he tried to control his feelings. 'What . . .' he swallowed, '. . . what do you do with it . . . the waste?'

'Bury it,' Joseph replied. 'As deep as possible.'

'Never be found,' Jacobson said with relief. 'Maybe whoever killed her was hoping the same would happen to her. Could be why she was left there.'

'Possibly,' Joseph agreed, trying to save Jacobson's emotions. Then he realized how false that was. They could not afford to cater to squeamishness, even as a mercy. 'Bodies come back to the surface here, sir, quite often,' he continued. 'New shell holes, craters, even new graves dug. He couldn't hope to conceal her. More likely he just left her there because that's where it happened.'

Out of the corner of his vision Joseph saw Hampton nod. He looked as if he had been here at the Front longer than Jacobson. Possibly he was not in the regular Criminal Investigation Department, merely seconded for this crime.

'What time was she found?' Joseph asked.

'Just after half-past six this morning.' Jacobson rose to his feet. 'You'd better come and see the body, and where she was found.' He motioned Joseph to follow him. 'Hampton will get on with investigating the physical facts.' He did not bother to glance at Hampton, but led the way out.

Joseph had seen more dead men than he could think to count: whole ones, white and motionless. They did not look as if they were sleeping; it was profoundly obvious that the spirit that made them unique and alive was not there any more. And he had seen men who had died in agony and terror, blown apart, half their bodies gone, soaked in blood, mutilated beyond recognition. Some of them had been men he had known in life, friends he had cared for and with whom he had shared deep and unforgettable emotions. Some he had held in his arms as their lives bled away. Still he had not seen a body that shocked him as this one did.

No one had tried to make her decent, on purpose, so the sight of her would stir rage and pity, and leave whoever saw her so wrenched and violated of all decency that they would never forget or forgive what had happened to her. The most private parts of her womanhood were lacerated and exposed as if whoever had done it had hated not only her, but also all that was female. It was grotesque, and Joseph stared at it as if every woman he had known and loved were torn apart on that wooden table, and everything to do with the act of sex debased. She had in effect been raped with the blade of a bayonet, almost certainly still affixed to the rifle.

No wonder Jacobson looked sick. It wasn't just the stench of the latrines, or a hundred miles of corpses half rotted in the mud over the last four years; it was this desecration of the source of human life.

'Cover her up,' Joseph said hoarsely. 'God in heaven, she didn't have to be left like that!'

'Yes, she did, Chaplain,' Jacobson said at his elbow. 'I need your help. I don't want any feelings of mercy for your man, any loyalties to anyone and pity for the living, or ideas of peace and forgiveness to make you let this man go. You've seen fighting and I haven't, but a man who would do this to a woman has to be stopped. If we say this is all right and it doesn't matter, then I don't want to live in the England we just spent four years of hell to defend.'

Joseph took off his jacket and laid it over the lower half of Sarah Price's body. He was shuddering with cold without it, but he did not even think twice. Anything was better than leaving her. He wondered who Jacobson had lost: brothers, perhaps even a son. Many boy soldiers were as young as fourteen or fifteen. They hungered and died just like anyone else. Perhaps that was why the trenches shocked Jacobson so profoundly. He was thinking of someone in particular.

'What do you want me to do?' Joseph asked.

Jacobson sighed. 'Captain Cavan said you'd solved other murders out here. Didn't elaborate, he just said you had a way of finding the truth. Originally I was thinking of your helping to keep control of things. Everyone's pretty upset. They've enough to deal with in ordinary war; they don't need this on top of it. But any other help would be good. We need this closed as soon as possible; get back to some kind of sanity – as much as there's any kind of sanity out here.'

'What are you going to look for?' Joseph asked. 'There's a bayonet on the end of every rifle on the Western Front! And blood on all of them. And on most of us in a casualty station.' He swallowed hard as if there were something stuck in his throat. 'There's nothing to say this was personal to her. It looks like hatred of all women. A madman.' He thought as he said it that it was a shallow remark. Who could stay sane out here where all men's life expectancy could be counted in weeks? Life had a different meaning.

Jacobson did not pick him up in it. Perhaps he saw the regret in Joseph's face as soon as the words were out.

'Opportunity, to begin with,' he replied. 'See who we can weed out with that. Get rid of any man who was accounted for all night. Won't be so many, but perhaps more than in civilian life. For a start, I expect all the doctors were busy, and can prove it, and maybe some of the ambulance drivers too? Orderlies? Understand you speak German pretty well?'

'Yes. It was fair before the war, and I've had plenty of chance to practise it since then. Do you want me to start with the German prisoners?'

Jacobson debated with himself for a minute before replying. 'Let's narrow it down a bit first. Can hardly expect them to tell us the truth anyway, can you? They'll try to blame us, and we'll try to blame them. It's natural.'

'It'll be difficult,' Joseph warned. 'People come and go all night long in a casualty clearing station. Usually it's mostly wounded and drivers, but right now it's prisoners as well. It's not guarded, except the German prisoners, and that's by men not wounded badly enough to go home, but not fit for the front line. Sometimes men bring in a friend or someone they have found or rescued, or come to visit someone too ill to be moved, but I'll see what I can learn.'

Jacobson put his hand on Joseph's arm. 'First speak to some of the nurses, Chaplain. They'll be pretty badly upset. They know you. They're used to seeing you around. Maybe they'll tell you things they won't tell me. See if you can find where people were. Find out what you can about this girl.' He gestured towards Sarah Price on the table. 'And take your coat, man. You'll freeze, and we need you. I'll see she's decently covered.'

Joseph left the hut with his jacket back on again, cold from the dead body rather than warm from his own. His shirt was stained with dark blood from where the cloth of it had touched her.

The wind outside was knife-edged. There was no ice on it, but it was hard and flat from the east and it stung the skin. Who had such a fury of hate in them that they had done this to a woman? Had life and death become so cheap?

He walked slowly along the wooden boards, passing nurses, who smiled at him nervously. One or two even stepped off into the mud to avoid being too close to him. He was a chaplain and a man they knew; what must they be feeling about others?

What lay behind the savagery that had swept over some man until he had lost everything within himself that made him decent, all gentleness, all respect for life or dignity or hope? Had war changed him, or had it merely stripped from him the veneer that concealed the barbarism, which had always been there, just hidden from view?

Did he know the man, and had failed to see it? What manner of priest does not recognize hell when it is in front of him, face to face? A man so blunted by the sight and sound and smell of suffering that he has shut himself off from the pain of it, a man who refuses to see, because seeing hurts? Seeing forces you to acknowledge that you must also act. The excuse of ignorance is stripped away, leaving you naked before the truth.

He stopped outside the pre-operation tent. He was not ready to go around it to the treatment tents yet, even though he was so cold his muscles were tight and his teeth clenched.

Who had done this? One man must answer for it. But was one man alone responsible, or were they all, because they had taken young men and taught them that fighting and killing was necessary for the nation to survive? And it *was* necessary! Surrender was not just a matter of ceasing to fight, it was to forfeit all the freedoms that gave you the chance to make any choice about good and evil, for you and your children, and maybe even their children as well. Imprisonment of the mind passes down the generations.

Perhaps it was how you fought that made the difference. Or maybe some of the soldiers that lived on and went home were just as much casualties as the dead. What had war done to the man who had torn Sarah Price open that way? Could they ever heal him and make him something like whole again? Or must they simply execute him, for the sake of society? Whose was the guilt?

He would speak to the nurses one by one. He must get some sense of order into his mind; learn all he could about that night.

First eliminate the impossible. Where had Sarah been working, and with whom? Could other people establish that beyond doubt? It was a busy place – men coming and going all the time, but with their attention on the injured, and on their own jobs and the terrible urgency of them.

But if he could find the time when she must have been killed, then it would be possible to eliminate most people, and events might begin to make sense. Of course he would learn as much as he could about Sarah herself, just in case there were any personal element to her death, but her tragedy could so easily have been no more than being alone in the dark at the wrong time.

First he walked around the admissions tent into the wind and across the open space to where he found Judith in the lee of the supply tent, very carefully fitting new spark plugs into the engine of her ambulance.

'Don't ask me where I got them!' she warned him. 'Believe me, you would prefer not to know.'

He had had no intention of asking. He was a lot wiser now than he had been two years ago. Odd how your family was the last to realize that you had grown up, or learned from your mistakes.

'Were you here last night?' he asked her.

She smiled at him. Her face was smeared with engine oil and more than a little mud, but she still had the same steady eyes, the high cheekbones and the passionate and so very vulnerable mouth. What on earth was she going to do in St Giles after the war? Marry some local worthy who would never begin to understand her . . . ?

He repeated the question.

'Driving back from the front line, most of it,' she answered. 'I dropped wounded off here at about three, helped with them, had a cup of tea and something to eat. I cleaned the ambulance. I suppose I left again about half-past four. I got lost somewhere about Polygon Wood, I think, but it could have been any other hill with tree stumps on it. I got back here about daylight.'

'Are you sure of the times?'

She frowned. 'I think so. Why? Was that when she was . . . killed?' She said it with difficulty, and he could hear the pain in her voice.

'I don't know yet,' he answered. 'How many wounded did you have?'

'Six, same as usual.'

'Badly hurt?'

'Yes. Does all this matter?'

'I don't know yet. The culprit was probably one of the German prisoners, but we have to be sure. Was Wil Sloan with you?'

'Wil?' She was startled. 'Yes, of course he was. You can't suspect him, for heaven's sake!'

'I need to place everyone, Judith, or I can't begin to make sense of it. Someone did a terrible thing to Sarah Price.'

She turned away. 'I know! It *must* have been one of the German prisoners. I dare say they hate us all. Or at least some of them do. They look just like us, don't they, especially when they're hurt and covered with mud and blood. I hate this!'

He touched her arm gently. 'It'll be over soon. Or this part of it will. But we've got to find out who did that to Sarah. Apart from justice, and stopping him doing it again, Matthew and I need to get Schenckendorff back to London. They're not going to hold up the armistice negotiations because of this mess here.'

'Can't you explain it to Colonel Hook and get away anyhow?' she asked.

'I don't think so. We don't know who the Peacemaker is, or what allies he might have here. He may know Schenckendorff has crossed over. It won't take a genius to guess it could be here. He'll know Matthew's left London, and probably where he's come to.'

Her eyes widened, fear sudden and gripping. 'Joseph, be careful!'

'I am. Tell me about Sarah Price, honestly. We haven't time for blurring the edges with kindness.'

She pursed her lips. 'I didn't know her well – I don't think anybody really did. She was a bit flighty, enjoyed a laugh and a joke, even if it was pretty silly. Didn't seem to take anything very seriously and that annoyed some people. She seemed awfully shallow.' She looked away for a moment, towards the edge of the light from the lamps, then back at him with painful honesty. 'I think she stopped allowing herself to feel when her brothers were killed. She wasn't going to let herself feel that kind of loss again. She made light of pretty well everything, and she drank rather more than was good for her. She flirted and led a few people on, but most of us knew it was just the way she was. We all deal with loss and fear in different ways. That was hers.'

One of the orderlies crossed over at the edge of their vision and she waited until he was beyond earshot before she continued. 'She didn't gossip and she didn't tell tales. And she was generous with things. I think she had stopped valuing anything, so it was easier for her to give it away. Almost as if she knew she might not make it home.' Her lips tightened. 'I'm not sure she had any home now. I remember her saying once that there was only her grandmother left. I don't know what happened to the others. Her mother died in the winter of nineteen sixteen, and she lost both her brothers at the Somme.'

She took in a shaky breath and let it out with a shiver. 'Hell, Joseph, I think I might drink and flirt and behave like a fool if that were me. Catch the creature who did this to her!'

'I'll try. But we have to get Schenckendorff back to London.'

'I know. At least we've got Matthew here to help.'

He stayed with her a few minutes longer, and then spoke to some of the nurses. They all said more or less the same as Judith had, although they were less frank with him than she had been, and some were less kind.

He walked into the last tent at the end of the row without hope of learning anything new, or even remotely helpful. There was just one nurse there, standing with her back to him, cleaning surgical instruments on a wooden table. Her dark hair was tied up and back, but the natural curl in it made it impossible to keep tidy. Her neck was slender and there was a grace uniquely beautiful in the line of her shoulders. It reminded him of something gentle and happy that he could not immediately place.

She must have heard his boots on the floorboards because she turned. Her blue eyes opened wide and the scalpel slid out of her fingers on to the floor with a clatter.

Joseph also stopped abruptly, his heart pounding. It was Lizzie Blaine. It was absurd. He was shaking and his hands were stiff and clammy, even in the cold.

'Hello . . . Chaplain . . .' she said awkwardly.

'Lizzie . . . Nurse . . . Blaine.' He found his tongue clumsy, words idiotic, banal. Of course she had said she might join up, after her husband had been murdered in 1916. He had thought she was just searching for something to do, ideas not reality. 'I . . .' he swallowed, 'I thought you were going to be a driver.' He remembered the miles she had driven him during that nightmare time when they were looking for a traitor. She had been the only good part of that summer.

She bent and picked up the scalpel, holding it in her hand to keep it separate from the clean ones. 'I started that way, but they needed nurses.' She smiled. 'I'm quite good on ordinary roads, but out here it's a different thing altogether, and I'm not so clever at the maintenance. I'm not inventive enough.'

'Have you been in this section long?' How had he not seen her before, or at least known she was here?

'A few weeks. People are being moved around all the time, to fill in the gaps. Are you here because of Sarah Price and what happened to her?'

'Colonel Hook asked me to help, if I can. Did you see Sarah last night?'

'Yes, of course. We were both working in the admissions tent and then the operating tent. She was in resuscitation for a while. She has . . .' she stopped and took a breath, 'had more experience than I do.'

'Do you remember what time you last saw her?'

She flinched, understanding exactly why he asked. 'Not really. I saw her coming and going up until we had a new lot of wounded in at about half-past two, or three o'clock. I went to admissions.' She looked down, avoiding his eyes. 'I hate that. I feel so helpless and I'm never sure if I'm making the right decisions. Some of them die before any doctor even gets to them.' She stopped abruptly, violent emotions naked in her face.

'I know,' he said gently. This time he did touch her, just fingers on her arm, but tender with the ache to comfort her that burned through him.

She looked up. 'Yes, of course you do. You must spend hours there, doing what you can. I'm sorry. It's . . .' She stopped, knowing there was no way to finish.

'Did you know Sarah?' Joseph asked. 'Can you tell me anything about her?' He would value her common sense. She was older than many of the other nurses, and he already knew her wisdom from two summers ago, the steadiness she had shown in the midst of her own grief. She herself had been suspected of having killed her husband in a terrible way, knowing that his brilliance could have saved thousands of lives. He might even have turned the tide of the war. She had been afraid, but she had never sunk to anger or bitterness. How sweet that memory was now. It was like sudden sunlight on a winter landscape.

'Not very much,' she answered. 'She seemed a nice enough girl, a bit flighty.' Her face was blank for a moment. 'But then she was alone, with nothing in particular to go home to.' She said the words with only the slightest tremor. 'Her parents are dead, and her brothers, she had only a grandmother. I heard her say that, and for a moment I saw something more than the rather trivial person she seemed to be.'

She looked away for a moment, and he saw that she was struggling with emotions. He wanted to say something wise and gentle that would comfort her. He wanted overwhelmingly to reach out and touch her, but it would be completely inappropriate. It would startle her and she would be embarrassed; worse than that, it would be an abuse of the trust she needed to keep in him as chaplain. He put his hands behind his back, clasping them hard enough to hurt.

94

'Did she flirt, to lead anyone to suppose . . .' He did not know how to finish the sentence.

Lizzie gave a tight, little smile, meeting his eyes. Then, seeing him colour faintly, her smile widened. 'Probably,' she agreed. 'But that's no excuse.'

Of course she had not seen the body. The bestial intimacy of it flooded his mind with a revulsion so violent it made him feel physically sick.

Lizzie saw it in him, and without hesitation moved forward, putting her hand very lightly on his sleeve. 'I'm sorry. Was it terrible?'

'Yes.' She had seen her husband's body. She was a nurse. He should be able to trust her strength. 'Yes, it was bad. Please be very careful.' That was a ridiculously inadequate thing to say. The thought of anything happening to her was worse than if it had happened to himself. How had he not realized that she was so much more than a friend, even the best kind of friend to whom one could talk of the innermost things, or keep silence and still feel the warmth of trust? He had crossed a boundary within himself and there was no way to retrace his steps, even if he might want to. Part of him did want to; he was afraid to care again so much. In fact, he was more afraid, because new places had been carved out inside him to a depth he had never touched before, an emotion that was not part of him, but all of him.

'We are all being careful,' she said wryly. 'None of us goes anywhere alone. It's all ridiculous and ugly. I find myself talking to someone quite naturally, a doctor or an orderly or driver, or a man wounded but not disabled by it. Then suddenly I remember, and I can see that he does too, and neither of us knows what to say. I'm frightened of him, embarrassed, and he knows it and is sorry for me, or angry because I'm being unjust. It's all horrible.'

Joseph nodded. It was a situation he had never faced before, and he tried to imagine it. 'It won't be long,' he said. 'We'll be able to prove pretty soon that there were only a few people it could have been, then all the others will be cleared.' Please God that was true. Apart from the other ugly and dangerous things, they had to solve the murder and be free to get Schenckendorff back to London. But he dare not tell Lizzie that, for her own safety.

'Is that what you are doing?' she asked. 'Helping the police?'

'Yes. Can you account for any of the men last night, from three o'clock onwards, or when you last saw Sarah?'

She thought hard before answering. 'I was working with two of the orderlies most of the couple of hours when the new cases came in. I don't think they were out of the admissions tent for more than a few minutes at a time, and then it was to take them into the pre-operations tent.'

'Names?' he asked.

'Carter and Appleby. I think the surgeons were operating all the time, or with people in resuscitation.' She looked at him anxiously, searching his eyes. 'I saw people after that, of course, but about five or six in the morning. You don't look at watches when you're trying to stop people from dying. And everyone was covered with blood. We always are.'

He nodded. There was nothing to say. He took brief notes of all she told him, then reluctantly left her and started to speak to the injured British men who had been here last night.

The first he saw was Major Morel. They had known each other since Morel had first come to Cambridge as Joseph's student in 1912, to learn Biblical languages. He had been there when Sebastian Allard had died. That had been his first experience of the shock and emotional confusion of murder. They had served four years of war, seeing most of the same horror, enduring the grief for loss of men they both knew. Morel had been the leader of those who had come so close to mutiny last year, and together he and Joseph had gone east and through the lines into Germany to bring back the one man guilty of murder. Morel had been promoted afterwards.

He had been injured in the shoulder last night, and was now among the wounded. Joseph found him propped up in a bed in one of the treatment tents. He was very pale, his cheeks sunken, but that was not so much the new injury as the weariness and hunger of four years in the trenches. His dark eyes were red-rimmed and looked enormous.

'Hello, Reverend,' he said with a twisted smile. 'Have you come to do your holy duty, or to find out if I killed that poor woman? I hope to God it wasn't one of us. What a bloody miserable way to end the war.'

'Do you think it might have been one of us?' Joseph asked him.

'Of course not!' Morel said in assumed horror. As always, he was struggling between intellect and dreams. He desperately did not want it to be one of his own men. For all his pretence at an armour of cynicism and his biting, irreverent wit, his care for his own men was deeper than any loyalty duty could impose. They had journeyed through a kind of hell together, seen the deaths of half of those they loved, and it was not over yet. Those who survived were weighed down by the ghosts of lost lives – joy and pain to carry for those who had forfeited their own chance to feel it all.

Joseph looked at him. His skin where his uniform usually

protected it was clear and fine, apart from the scratches and louse bites they all had. The bones of his shoulders were fragile, and yet his eyes were those of an old man. Everyone was like that, but Joseph knew Morel, and that made it different.

'Do you mean not British, or not the Cambridgeshires?' he asked.

Morel grimaced. 'I'm a realist, Reverend. Not the Cambridgeshires. I know a lot of people are saying it had to be one of the Germans and, since they're not locked up because we've nowhere to put them, it's a nice thought. But it could have been pretty well anybody. I don't envy you your job of finding out who, and I suppose you have to. You would, anyway.' He winced. 'You never could leave well enough alone, even when nobody else knew there was even a problem.'

'I've learned,' Joseph said rather tartly.

Suddenly Morel's face softened and a sweet affection shone through. 'I know.' Then it vanished again. 'But I hear there are a couple of policemen this time, so you won't be able to hide anything. Don't even try!'

'I have no intention of trying!' Joseph snapped. 'There's nothing ambiguous about the morality of this.' Even as he said it he knew that that might not be true. When was it ever utterly one-sided? Had the man who had done this been born violent – bestial? Or had the army taught him how to hate, and that killing was the answer to rage? Had the war created what he was now?

Morel rolled his eyes, and did not bother to answer. Instead he recounted what he knew of men's comings and goings through the night, from the time he had arrived, in pain but very definitely conscious and observant.

Joseph thanked him, asked what he could do to help, then moved on to the next man, who as it turned out, could tell him nothing.

That evening Joseph joined Matthew in the dugout. There was no spare accommodation in the clearing station now that only the most seriously wounded could be moved on. Anyone able to stand remained, imprisoned by Jacobson's command. The Germans were herded together, but they had only the barest shelter, apart from those for whom exposure might mean death. Even Wil Sloan and the two other male VADS were not allowed to leave.

'It can't last,' Matthew said grimly, trying to get a candle lit in a tin in order to create a makeshift stove to boil water. 'Saw Judith at last,' he snarled. 'Looks a bit thin but just the same spirit.' He threw away another match. 'Damn this thing! How the hell do you ever manage?'

Joseph did it for him with the ease of practice.

'Thank you,' Matthew said drily. 'I hope I leave here before I do enough of that to become as good as you are.'

'I've had four years' experience,' Joseph replied. 'Although I usually manage to cadge from somebody else.'

Matthew looked at him gravely. 'You love these men, don't you, Joe.' It was an observation; there was no question in his voice.

'Of course,' Joseph answered without hesitation. 'If you can pass through this with men, and not care for them, then you aren't fit to be called human. It's a kind of friendship no number of years of safety could forge. There won't be anything like it again in our lives. We leave part of ourselves here with those who'll never come home: an obligation, a debt.'

He swallowed hard, his eyes stinging. There were so many of them, men like Sam Wetherall, the friend he'd loved the most, who was not dead, and yet who would also never come home. War robbed men of many different kinds of things. For Sam it was his identity, and everything it meant. Eldon Prentice, in 1915, had seen to that – another victim of the Peacemaker.

'We've got to get this solved, and get Schenckendorff back to London,' he said. 'His foot is a bit better today. His fever seems to be breaking.'

'That's the least of our worries,' Matthew answered grimly. 'Somebody butchered that girl, which would be bad enough at any time, but out here nurses are viewed pretty well like angels. They're the one link with the women they love who represent home and decency, and everything they're fighting for. For one or two I spoke to, it was as if something inside them had been violated too.'

Joseph stared at him, realizing suddenly that that was what he had seen in Morel, and in others he had spoken to. They assumed it was rape, although it had not been said in words. That kind of violation was a deep internal injury to any decent man also. The vulnerability was different, but it was there, too often un-acknowledged, and unhealed.

Matthew gave a little shrug. 'If we don't solve it soon, Joe, there's going to be a whole lot more violence, possibly towards the German prisoners. Our men want it to be one of them, not one of our own. I've heard some ugly things said. The veneer is thin; it won't take much to break it.'

It was another hard night, but most of the casualties were taken to a clearing station five miles away, and closer to the actual fighting as it moved eastwards. Joseph arrived back to find Matthew waiting for him outside the tent for the walking wounded. His face was haggard and his uniform sodden wet in the rain. As soon as he saw Joseph he strode towards him, splashing through the mud with complete disregard.

'Joe, it's getting worse,' he said abruptly. 'There's been more violence. Three or four British soldiers lit into half a dozen German prisoners and beat the hell out of them. The worst thing is that the officer in charge didn't do anything to stop it. He didn't even punish them for it after. What in God's name is this . . . this whole bloody slaughter for . . .' he swung his arm around violently to encompass the entire battlefield, 'if we end up acting like barbarians ourselves? We might just as well have surrendered in the first place. We had nothing worth saving.' He was so shaken that his hands were trembling and he could barely keep still. 'We've got to get Schenckendorff out of here,' he went on, deliberately lowering his voice. 'If he still thinks we're worth saving.'

Joseph understood his anger. The sight and the stench of so much suffering, and so unaccountably many dead, had temporarily torn away his normal reserve. He was used to the intellectual tensions of waiting, of cat-and-mouse games of the mind, but the sheer physicality of the line was new to him.

'Who were they, do you know?' Joseph asked.

'Two of them were Black and Youngman. I don't know the other two.'

'Bill Harrison's men. I'll go and speak to him.'

'The officer already knows!' Matthew said impatiently. 'I told you, he didn't give a damn, and he just let it go.'

'I'll deal with it,' Joseph promised, and turned and walked away.

He found Harrison surprisingly easily. He was already in the casualty clearing station. Stan Tidyman, one of his men, had lost a leg, and he had come to see if he was still alive, and give him all the support he could.

Joseph looked at Stan's grey face and sunken eyes, and waited until Harrison was ready to leave. Not that one was ever ready, but there came a time when it was necessary.

He waited outside and spoke to Harrison as he stepped on to the boards and into the wind. His face was tight and vulnerable with pity and he looked relieved to see Joseph.

'There's not much you can do right now, Chaplain,' he said grimly. 'But he'll be pleased to see you.'

Joseph felt a stab of guilt. 'Actually it was you I was looking for,' he answered. 'Four men beat more injured German prisoners last night. Two of them at least were from your unit, Black and Youngman. It's got to stop, Bill. Apparently the lieutenant on duty didn't do anything. It isn't good enough.'

'I didn't know,' Harrison said unhappily. 'They're on guard duty, and they resent it. They're only slightly injured and they want to be pressing forward with the rest of the regiment.' He gave a tiny, rueful smile. 'We've been telling them to go and kill Germans for the last four years, Chaplain. Some of them hated doing it so much they were almost paralysed at the thought of deliberately blowing another man's body to pieces, even if he was German. They look just like us, walk and talk, have homes, parents, pet dogs, things they like to do.'

He was obviously distressed and there was disgust deep inside him, but he refused to evade the issue. 'I've had to punish men because they couldn't pull the trigger, and I hated doing it.' He did not shiver, even in the rain. 'I've seen hundreds of men aim high, on purpose. And I've seen those who didn't, and the nightmares they've had afterwards.'

He shook his head. 'We gave medals to the ones who can do it without flinching. They were ordinary men when they came here, bakers and blacksmiths, bank clerks, farm boys, bus drivers. A lot of them have lost brothers, friends, even parents at home from the bombings.' His voice dropped. 'Wives have been unfaithful over the long years alone, sweethearts have found someone else. It hurts. It doesn't seem fair to punish them now for being what we've made them into.' His grey eyes looked steadily into Joseph's with an honesty that would not flinch or accommodate. 'I'll speak to them, but I'm not going to punish them, sir.'

Joseph admired his loyalty, stubborn though it was, and perhaps technically wrong. He could understand it, and he knew that from Bill Harrison he should even have expected it.

'What if it takes us a while to find this man?' he asked. 'Closed up here like this, these incidents could get worse, especially since they got away with it this time. I know that what someone did to Sarah Price was bestial, but that isn't the reason for this, it's the excuse. Next time someone may be critically injured, or even killed. Then we will have to charge whoever did it with murder, because beating to death an injured and unarmed prisoner is murder, Bill. You know it, and so do they. So do the Germans, incidentally.'

Harrison stood very stiffly, shoulders square. 'I'll talk to the men, Chaplain. I won't let that happen.'

'Good.' Should he trust him? What if the violence did break out again, and this time Schenckendorff were killed? He dare not say anything. The Peacemaker had eyes and ears in all sorts of places, followers who were often good men, idealists whose dreams were more passionate than their understanding of human nature or the strength of human individuality, and the bloody-minded courage of ordinary men. But they killed for another man's vision, and Joseph could not afford that. They were so close. This was the last hand to play against the Peacemaker, win or lose.

It was not Harrison's honour he could not trust, it was his wisdom, his ability to see evil where he had a right to expect it would not be.

# Chapter Four

It was Judith's turn to be questioned by Jacobson. She had known it would come, and tried to prepare herself for it. He was speaking to all the women, asking them where they had been at the time of Sarah's death and which of the men they could account for. Had anyone looked troubled recently, or had they noticed anyone behaving peculiarly? It was the obvious thing to do, but Judith was still uncomfortable when she was commanded to enter the tent that had been hastily put up for the detective. Someone had found a table, two chairs and a box for him to keep his papers in. There was a duckboard floor, but it was bitterly cold.

Judith went in and closed the flap behind her. She stood to attention, not out of any particular respect, but because it marked her as part of the army, and was a tacit statement of unity with the others. He was civilian, even if he was employed by the military police for this specific crime.

'Thank you for coming, Miss Reavley,' Jacobson said without expression. He pointed to the wooden chair opposite the desk. 'You may sit down.'

She considered it for a moment. It would be more comfortable, but it would also instantly put her on a physical level with him and take away any resemblance she had to a soldier.

'Thank you, but I prefer to stand,' she replied. She was also not going to call him "sir". 'I sit a great deal,' she added. 'I drive an ambulance.'

'Yes, I know.' He indicated a piece of paper in front of him on the table. 'You've been here a long time.'

'Since the beginning.'

'Then you will know the other people here as well as anyone can. You will have known Sarah Price.'

'Not much. I'm a driver, not a nurse,' she pointed out.

'Don't you bring wounded men here to be treated?' he asked.

She thought he was a plain man, but in other circumstances he would not have been unpleasant. There was intelligence in his face. 'Yes,' she answered. 'The orderlies help me unload them off the ambulance, then I turn around to go back for more.'

He blinked. 'Don't you tend them at all on the way?'

'I can't drive an ambulance through the mud and shellfire and tend the wounded at the same time!' she said tartly.

'Don't you have anyone to help you?' He looked at her with intent.

'Yes, most of the time.'

'People trained to give medical help?'

'Of course, otherwise they wouldn't be of any use.' She was keeping her temper with difficulty. It was unfair to resent him – none of this was his fault – but he was still an outsider probing with a civilian's lack of understanding for the terror, the grief and the loyalties of soldiers.

'Nurses?' he questioned. 'Orderlies?'

'VADs,' she answered.

'What happens if your ambulance breaks down?'

'I mend it!' she said with her eyebrows raised.

'Yourself?'

'Of course. There's no one else.'

'You must be extremely competent. Where do you do the regular maintenance work?'

At last she saw his point. 'Usually here. But I don't often see many nurses. None of us has a lot of time to stand around.'

'But you see a lot of orderlies, other drivers, doctors, soldiers?'

'Of course. But I have no idea who attacked Sarah Price. If I had, I would tell you.'

'Would you, Miss Reavley?'

'Of course I would!' The anger burned through now. It was a stupid question, and offensive. 'No decent person would defend a man who killed one of the nurses! Or any woman, for that matter.' She stood even more stiffly. 'We work together, Mr Jacobson. We have done in more hideous circumstances than you could imagine. You know nothing about it. I can see that in your face, even if I didn't know. We have a kind of loyalty to each other that peacetime couldn't create.'

The ghost of a smile crossed his face, full of regret.

'I believe that, Miss Reavley, which is why I think that one of you could well be defending a man with whom you have shared danger and pain, perhaps who has even saved your life, because you cannot believe he would do what he has. You will have different judgements of right and wrong from mine, and debts of honour I couldn't understand.'

With amazement like a slow-burning fire inside her, she realized what he was saying. 'You think I would defend the man who did this?' she said incredulously. She could feel her temper slipping out of control. 'I want him found and arrested even more than you do! The worst that can happen to you is that you fail!' Her voice was shaking now, and she was gulping for air. 'I could be assaulted or murdered, or both. So could my friends! Of course I want him caught . . . and . . . and got rid of . . . like . . . sewage!'

'Even if he were, for example, your friend Wil Sloan?' Jacobson asked. 'A man who would never hurt you, surely?'

She felt the heat burn up her face. 'That's disgusting. Wil would never even think of doing something like that!'

'What kind of a man would, Miss Reavley? Do you know who would, and who wouldn't?'

He had caught her, this ordinary civilian who knew nothing about the reality of war. She had walked straight into his verbal trap without seeing anything of it. She hesitated, unable to frame an answer. He was right: she was trying to protect those she cared for most, because they could not be guilty, not because she feared they were. But any answer like that would sound ridiculous.

'Of course I don't,' she said at last. 'All I know is who couldn't have because they were somewhere else.' How lame that sounded.

'And was Wil Sloan somewhere else?' he asked, almost casually.

Her mind raced. How could she say anything that was of value without making him suspicious? She did not even know when the murder had happened, or if he had already spoken to Wil. The only time she and Wil had been at the casualty clearing station was roughly between three o'clock and half-past four. If it were not then, would Jacobson even be asking?

'Miss Reavley?' he prompted.

She tried to look innocent. She must not seem too clever, or that in itself would make him distrustful of her. 'We were both in the ambulance most of the night,' she answered. 'Miles away from here.'

'But not all of it,' he pointed out. 'You brought the wounded back. Surely that was your entire purpose?'

'Yes, of course. We were here a couple of times, a little before midnight, and again at about three.'

'And when did you leave each time?' His face was almost expressionless.

'The first time about quarter to one, the second at half-past four, roughly.'

'So there were over two hours that you were both here,' he pointed out.

She wanted to say something sarcastic, referring back to their whole purpose, but swallowed her temper. 'Yes. We have to get the wounded off and into the admissions tent, then clean the ambulance and refill with fuel.' She nearly added that it needed maintenance too, but since she did that without Wil, it would be walking into another trap. Where had Wil been the second time? She did not know. But he could not have killed Sarah. No one who knew Wil would have had such an idea even enter their minds. He was hot-tempered on very rare occasions, but never towards women. He was generous to a fault, and idealistic, otherwise he would not even have been here. He was American, and had come voluntarily in 1915, when his own country had had nothing to do with the war. Like many others, he had simply believed it was the right thing to do, and so he had done it. He was patient, funny, too honest, a little unsophisticated, and one of the kindest people she knew.

Again Jacobson prompted her, more abruptly this time. 'Miss Reavley?'

She took a gamble. 'I don't know where he was at midnight,' she answered. 'I was trying to think, but as far as I can remember, he went to the tent with the walking wounded. You'll have to ask him.'

She saw the lack of interest in his face. So Sarah had been killed between three and half-past four. The cold bit inside her like ice. She took the risk, certain beyond any doubt at all that Wil would have done the same for her. 'The second time I had to clean the spark plugs in the ambulance. They get dirty quite often and then they don't work. It took us a while to get the wounded in, and after that he got me some tea and a piece of bread and jam. Jam's rationed now, so that's not easy. Then he held the lamp for me. The engine was in a bit of a mess, and I needed two hands.'

'I see.' He was looking at her more closely, almost narrowly, as if he were trying to discern something about her. It made her feel uncomfortable. Did he know she was lying? Had Wil said something different?

'Ever had any trouble, Miss Reavley? Any unwanted attentions?' he asked.

'No!' she said, and knew she had answered too quickly.

His eyes widened. It was obvious that he did not believe her. She felt her face colour. 'Nobody has behaved badly!' she said curtly. 'I deal with wounded men on the battlefield, Mr Jacobson. We all have one aim in common – to stop them dying, and get them to the nearest medical help. Nobody has time or thought for much else.' It was not his fault that he knew nothing about the Front, and it was unfair that she was angry with him for it, but she was. And she felt frightened, and guilty for lying, even though it was necessary. Her friends were in trouble, and he was an outsider who did not understand.

'That is clearly not true, Miss Reavley,' he said steadily, 'or I would not need to be here. And while I haven't fought on the line, I've seen plenty of men under pressure. Emotions are close to the surface. It results in violence sometimes, and people close to death want to touch life and all the pleasures it offers, sometimes even the source of life.' His voice dropped a little. 'At those times it does not have to be someone you love, anybody will do. Please don't tell me you are unaware of that, or that it shocks you. You have seen four years of war. You cannot be blind to the realities of men's fears or needs, or the extremities of death.'

Her face was burning hot and she knew it. He had touched a nerve in her, and without knowing why, she felt a passionate need to defend the desperate vulnerability she had seen so often. 'Of course I'm not!' She was shouting at him, although she had not meant to. She heard herself and could not stop. 'We are all . . .' Now she did not know what to say, and he was still staring at her.

'You do not want to betray anyone whose weakness you have seen and understood,' he finished for her. 'You protect each other. As well as loyalty, and honour to men on whose courage your life may depend, you cannot afford to antagonize them.' There was gentleness in his face, even pity. 'You will have to work with them in the future, and with the other women who may love them, or hate them. But I remind you, Miss Reavley, that you will also work with the other women who may become their victims in the future. I can see that you have a very terrible conflict as to where your duty lies.'

'No I don't!' she said hotly. 'I don't know anything!'

He did not believe her. She could see it in his eyes, and in the slight smile touching his mouth. She must control herself, or he would be even more certain that she was lying. She stood rigidly upright, her hands by her sides, touching the seam in her skirt, as a soldier would stand to attention. 'If I should learn anything that would help you, Mr Jacobson, I shall inform you of it immediately. Is that all? Because if it is, I would like to get back to my duties.'

'For the moment, Miss Reavley. But please remain here. I will wish to speak to you again.'

'Unless I am needed,' she told him. And before he could protest, she turned and marched out. There were duties to do. Nurses were always short-handed and the men wanted more care than they could give. A lot of it did not require any skill other than she had. At the very least there would be errands to run.

It was mid-morning when she found Lizzie Blaine unpacking medical supplies. She did not know her well. Lizzie had moved into Selborne St Giles with her husband after Judith had already left for France. She had heard of her from Joseph, who evidently regarded her highly, and with affection beyond what one might have for a kind neighbour, and in the one or two times they had met here she had liked her instinctively. Lizzie had a penetrating honesty that Judith found comfortable, because it was not only when she was with others, but within herself. She made no excuses and never shifted blame, and neither her friendship nor her courage was ostentatious.

'Can I help?' Judith offered.

'Please.' Lizzie pointed to an unopened box. 'You'll have to check that everything is what it says. They get put in the wrong places sometimes.' She glanced at Judith again, frowning a little. 'You all right? You look a bit upset.'

'Furious,' Judith said ruefully as she bent to the box. 'I've just been talking to Jacobson, the policeman. He misunderstood everything I said, and I wound up talking too much, and now he thinks I know more than I do.'

'That's stupid,' Lizzie turned back to the unpacking. 'You'd hardly defend anyone you knew was guilty!'

'That's not what he thinks,' Judith explained. 'I suppose I could lie about a small incident that looked bad, but I hadn't believed it really was. The man just doesn't understand what friendship is out here, and it made me angry.'

Lizzie smiled. 'And then you felt guilty for that? I know what you mean.'

'I suppose we all do.' Judith started to unpack the box, looking at each item carefully. 'But things like that don't happen out of the blue. Whoever it is must have bothered other people from time to time, even if it was only stupid remarks, or being too free with his hands. Although we don't know whether he raped her or not. We're just thinking he had because rumour says it was that sort of killing.'

'I suppose so,' Lizzie kept her face averted and now there was no emotion in her voice.

'Everybody's stupid sometimes,' Judith went on. 'You just realize why, and if it isn't bad, you forget about it.'

'Yes.' Lizzie's fingers were tight on a box lid. It slipped from her grasp and scattered tablets on the bench top, half a dozen on the floor. She drew in her breath sharply, as if to swear, then bit it back.

Judith bent and picked them up. She regarded them for a moment, uncertain.

Lizzie held out her hand. 'The amount of dirt and mud we eat, it's too precious, even off the floor, than to waste it and have someone perhaps die without it.' She examined the tablets, then put them separately in a small screw of paper and wrote on it what they were.

Judith looked at her more carefully. There was something remote about her, closed off and hurt, as if she were afraid. 'Do you know somebody who's been bothered?' she asked as gently as she could.

'No,' Lizzie said quickly, without looking up from what she was doing. 'I don't know that I would recognize it if I did. Sarah used to flirt like mad, and I've no idea how far it went, but I'm not telling Jacobson that. There are enough people saying she deserved it.' Her face was flushed and her knuckles white where she gripped the small box she was holding. Her voice was thick with anger when she spoke again. 'It's a vicious and idiotic thing to say! What happened to her was not flirting gone too far, it was violent and brutal, a crime committed by a man who has no decency left in him. He has descended into something less than human. Please, let's talk about something else. I liked Sarah, silly as she was sometimes. She was only trying to survive.'

'I'm sorry,' Judith said immediately. She had forgotten for a moment that Lizzie had probably known Sarah quite well. Friendships could grow quickly out here – bad experiences shared, an act of kindness, and bonds were forged. 'I'm talking too much because he made me angry and I behaved like a fool. And I'm afraid too.'

Lizzie looked at her with a sudden smile. 'We all are,' she admitted.

However, that evening Judith was back in her vehicle with another VAD who had not been at the casualty clearing station when Sarah was killed. They were driving towards the fighting, which was moving steadily further ahead with each new assault, stretching the supply lines.

Judith thought back to her exchange with Lizzie. Lizzie was afraid, and Judith had an increasing feeling that it was something more personal that troubled her, and she guarded it not only from Jacobson but even from other women. Was she afraid for someone in particular – a man she was fond of, or worse, who had threatened her? It was a hideous thought that there was someone here who either was guilty, or looked it, and somebody else was carrying the burden of that knowledge. If so, then surely her life could be in danger too? They were all used to death; the place was saturated with it. It did not startle or horrify any more.

The gunfire was growing heavier in the distance, over towards Courtrai. The roads were worse here. She could see huge craters in the intermittent light of the star shells.

Perhaps they were all pretending not to know anything for precisely that reason. How could Jacobson, or anyone else, protect a witness? There was no such thing here as safety of any sort. She wished Lizzie could have trusted her. She felt an acute awareness of failure. She should have tried harder, said different, gentler things, and been far less occupied with herself.

She was one of the fortunate ones in that she could leave the field hospital, though Jacobson had told her not to, and he had refused to let Wil come with her. But the fighting was still going on, and there were more casualties to be brought back. The war plunged on inexorably towards its last days. Individual lives had never mattered in these circumstances.

She drove eastward through the darkness towards the glare and the roar of guns.

German prisoners came through that night as well, some captured, several badly injured. More came willingly, with an air of desperate bewilderment. Most were passed on immediately without coming anywhere near the casualty clearing station. They had been hastily bandaged, often lame or half blind, and then made to trudge on foot through the mud towards the railhead and the journey back into France. Only the wounded who could not be taken without jeopardizing their lives were kept here.

It could not continue like this for many more days. Tension was mounting, not only with overcrowding of men critically injured, and the growing expectation of peace, but above all the endless questions by Jacobson stirring up suspicion and anger over all kinds of old loves and betrayals, fears of violation too deep to name or face. Beyond the question of who could have been guilty, the speculation of rape was more divisive than anyone had imagined.

Judith found that people she had known since the earliest years of the war, and beside whom she had fought illness, disaster and grief, held views she could not accept. Even Cavan surprised her. She admired him intensely for his courage, both physical and moral. After the stand in the trenches for which he had been put up for the VC, and then the murder of Major Northrup, she had risked the firing squad herself last year to help him escape. The other men had gone, and Cavan had chosen to remain and face trial. That decision had infuriated her, but he had refused to be swayed. She had known it was born of supreme honour to duty, and she never forgot it in him.

Now he stood at the operating table, having just amputated a man's shattered foot. He was exhausted and there was blood on his white coat and up both his sleeves. It was even splattered on the pale skin of his face, hollowed about the eyes by exhaustion.

'Thank you,' he told Bream, the orderly. He looked at Gwen Williams, the nurse who had assisted him. 'Call me if he gets feverish, but I think that should be all right.'

Judith had remained to help after bringing the man in. Cavan had already complimented her for getting him there alive.

'I'll fetch you some water,' she said, turning to go outside.

'Yer can't go alone!' Bream waved sharply as Judith reached the tent flap. 'I'll get it, after I've taken 'im to resuscitation.' He gestured at the unconscious patient.

'It's only fifty yards away,' Judith protested. 'I'll be perfectly safe.'

Bream opened his mouth to protest. He was about twenty. A London clerk before the war, he was too flat-footed to make the infantry.

'For goodness' sake!' Gwen cut across him. 'Nothing's going to happen to her.'

'It can 'appen to anyone!' Bream replied, his eyes wide. 'Well, any woman. We've got a madman round 'ere, and no one knows 'oo 'e is.'

'No it won't,' Gwen contradicted him, shaking her head irritably. 'Some women invite disaster, of one sort or another. If you behave with sense, don't lead people on and act like a – I'm sorry – like a tart, then people won't get the wrong idea.'

'The right idea being what?' Judith asked with brittle civility. She had thought she liked Gwen. Suddenly she didn't. They were strangers in culture and belief, allies only by force of extraordinary circumstance.

Gwen stared at her as if she too had seen her clearly for the first time. 'I'm surprised that the chaplain's sister should need anyone to tell her the right way to behave,' she said coldly.

'We weren't talking about my behaviour, or Sarah's,' Judith pointed out. 'We were talking about whoever it was who killed her – which as you put it so pithily, was "the wrong idea".'

'Judith, let it be,' Cavan said wearily. 'It's over. It's a tragedy that we can't undo, like pretty well every other bloody useless death here. Some wretched man forgot that you are only allowed to kill the enemy, who's wearing a different uniform from you and carrying a gun at the time. An enemy who's wearing a dress and whose weapon is her tongue has to be treated differently. Someone forgot that, or simply stopped caring.'

Judith stared at him. She had thought she knew him as well as it was possible to know almost anyone. She had seen his superb courage under fire, his tireless, selfless work, never giving up on anyone, no matter how mutilated or how ill. She had seen him share his food, sit up all night to watch and comfort men, seen him encourage those learning to nurse, young doctors afraid to try tasks that seemed impossible, or offer solace and refrain from blame when they failed. And yet he was speaking of this horror as if it were simply one more foreseeable tragedy. He even had some pity for the man.

He looked back at her very directly. His blue eyes did not waver in the slightest, but there was regret in them now, and a very faint colour in his cheeks. 'We can't teach a man to tear another man apart with a bayonet, and then expect him to control his temper when he feels someone made a fool of him,' he said grimly. 'When fear has reduced you to nothing in your own eyes, the contempt for yourself doesn't heal just because someone says the war is over. Some of our men have a sanity so deep nothing can break it, but that's not true for all.' He shook his head, his lips tight. 'People can lose their belief in anything. When they see the good die hideously, some of them find they have nothing left to cling on to. Let Bream get the water. Don't go out alone. It's arrogant to think your virtue will protect you.' He turned to Gwen Williams. 'Or you,' he added coldly.

'You didn't know Sarah,' Gwen retaliated, her cheeks pink. 'She led men on. She flirted and she teased.' Her voice grew sharper. 'I'm not saying she deserved it – of course she didn't, no one does. But she did behave badly – stupidly. Nothing like this has ever happened before, or to anyone else, and that should tell you something.'

Bream shuddered. 'It tells me we didn't never 'ave German prisoners before,' he said firmly. 'Leastways, not so many we couldn't keep 'em locked up. Yer wrong, Doctor, it weren't any of our boys who did it to poor Miss Price. They may be a bit loud at times, even a bit free with their 'ands now an' then, but nothing more'n that. They're gettin' ready to go 'ome, an' no one knows who'll make it even now. This close, it's kind o' scary to think yer could still end up staying 'ere in the mud for ever.'

'Nobody stays in the mud for ever, Bream,' Judith told him gently. 'At least . . .' she gave a sudden wide smile, 'at least in a sense we all do and, when it comes to it, I don't see that Flanders mud is any better or worse than London mud, or Cambridgeshire mud, for that matter. The point is, the part of you that matters goes on to eternity anyway.'

Bream was staring at her as if she had suddenly changed into a totally different animal in front of him.

Cavan smiled also, lighting his face with sudden warmth. 'Chaplain's sister, Bream. You'll have to excuse her. She's probably been preached at since she was born. Prayers over the porridge, no doubt.'

'Actually maths,' she corrected him.

'Prayers over the maths?' Cavan asked in disbelief.

'Maths over the porridge!' she explained. 'My father was a mathematician. Don't ask me where Joseph got religion from; I have no idea.'

Gwen looked from one to the other of them with a sense of somehow having been made light of, but she knew there was no use pursuing it. She turned sombrely to Judith. 'You can mock all you like, but there is a very wicked man around here, who was stirred to violence by something that Sarah Price was foolish enough to do, and she paid a fearful, terrible price for it. Whether he was German or British, he's still out there. But if you behave decently, you will be perfectly safe. I'll prove it. I'll go and fetch the water for Dr Cavan.' And without waiting for anyone to argue with her, she marched out of the tent and into the darkness beyond.

Judith did not hesitate. She went straight after her, catching up within half a dozen yards.

'You don't need to!' Gwen said loudly.

'I prefer to.' Judith kept pace with her along the boards with difficulty, her feet slipping on the wet wood and clattering loudly. 'Do you really think Sarah brought this on herself? Did you see anyone bother her before? I mean, was she having a romance with anyone?'

Gwen glanced sideways at her once, then kept on walking. 'I have no idea. I know how she was generally rather loose in her manner, which is foolish as well as vulgar. I suppose I should have told her about it, but I thought she'd just ignore me, and get angry. I was wrong, wasn't I?' There was a sharp acknowledgement of guilt in her voice.

Without warning Judith's anger evaporated and was replaced by pity. Gwen was not an easy person; very few people actually liked her. Most people treated her with tolerance and included her in the general sharing because that was what everyone did; it was a habit for survival. 'No,' Judith said gently, falling into step beside her. 'She might easily have been worse, just to spite you. Maybe we all should have said something.'

'I could see it,' Gwen argued. Her voice was so low Judith could only just hear her above the squelch of the mud as they stepped beyond the boards on to the earth. They were now far enough from the fighting that the sound of guns was only a rumble in the distance. Curiously, as the battle moved ahead of them, she did not feel relief, but a sense of being left behind, no longer of the most use she could be.

'Maybe everyone could,' she replied. 'It wasn't your responsibility.'

Gwen shot her a quick glance, then they reached the water supply and she began to fill the pail she had brought. 'Not your brother's keeper? Your brother wouldn't agree with that,' she said wryly. 'Do me the kindness to be honest, Judith. Apart from the cruelty of it, lying won't work because I know what you really think. You don't often hide it.'

Judith was chastened. She had not realized that her dislike of Gwen was so apparent, or that she was quite so free with her own opinions. A little tact, a little kindness would have been better. 'I'm sorry,' she said sincerely, and the moment after, wondered if that sounded dishonest too. Then Gwen smiled at her, and she knew it was accepted, at least for now.

It was three days since the murder of Sarah Price and Jacobson did not appear to be any closer to knowing who had killed her. Suspicion grew, often absurdly. There were brief outbreaks of anger and violence, but no more German prisoners had been seriously hurt.

News of the fighting came every day. The British were advancing on Lille and the Belgians had occupied Zeebrugge and stormed Bruges. Someone said that the British forces in Syria had entered Homs. Everything was closing for a German surrender, but it hadn't happened yet. The hope itself was a kind of strange, exciting and disturbing thought, so very close, and yet men were still dying every day, sometimes hundreds of them.

Judith heard many other arguments over Sarah Price, some like those in the operating theatre, others quite different. Some young men, knowing their own innocence, were hurt when nurses were afraid of them.

On the third night after Sarah's death, the fighting was so heavy all ambulance crews were needed. Judith and Wil Sloan drove beyond Menin to pick up some badly wounded. It was cloudy, but there was no rain, and after a while the sky cleared, moonlight showing the devastated landscape and shattered buildings. Tree stumps were gaunt, motionless, but looking as if they writhed, pointing half-amputated limbs upward, reaching towards some help that never came. The lights showed rutted tracks swimming with water, glistening pale on the craters, punctuated by the black silhouettes of broken guns, wheels, even an occasional foundered tank, its giant caterpillar tracks high in the air. Judith knew there were also bodies drifting to the surface, but one could not tell their mud-caked outlines apart from the banks and paths.

'I guess even the Badlands are going to look good after this,' Wil said with a half-smile. 'Main Street will be pretty wholesome.'

'I'm sure it will,' Judith agreed. 'Specially on a sunny day.'

He was silent for some time. She looked at him and in the light of the star shells saw a sombreness in his face. When he had first come late in 1914 he had been very young, barely twenty. It was some time before he told her that he was actually running away from his home town, even from America altogether, after an ugly incident in which he had lost his temper and beaten a man.

Now the world was different, and Wil himself looked so much older. He had not put on weight – no one did on army rations – but his leanness had turned to muscle and there was a grave maturity in his face. He had not lost his Midwestern accent, but he had picked up a great many very English expressions, which he had begun using with humour, but now they were part of his nature and he no longer noticed them himself.

'I'll miss you,' he said suddenly.

'For a little while,' she conceded, not certain what else to say.

'Home won't be the same as when I left,' he went on. He bit his lip. 'Some of that's good. Maybe they'll have other things to think about than what a fool I was.'

'You still worried about it?' she asked with surprise. 'Come on, Wil! That was years ago. The whole world's grown sadder and wiser since then.'

'You don't know small-town people,' he retorted. 'They can hold a grudge for generations.'

'Of course I know small-town people,' she said with a laugh. 'How big do you think Selborne St Giles is? Everybody's related to everybody else, and has been for a thousand years! If you go into the shop in the morning they can probably tell you what you had for breakfast. They can certainly tell you who's quarrelling with whom, and what about.'

He smiled; it was a wide and unusually charming expression. 'Perhaps I'll stay in England. Do you think I can?'

'Certainly, and welcome. But don't you want to go home?' She looked away from the road for a moment, then hit a violent rut and concentrated again. 'Are you really that scared of it, Wil?'

'No!' He hesitated. 'Well, maybe. I never got to go back and say anything, and now they've got real heroes, men who fought, even some who died. Possibly not from our town, but not far away.'

'Every town has someone who died,' she answered.

'I guess you Brits have some for every street, eh? I'm sorry.' His voice dropped. 'I'm just not sure where I belong any more.'

'Nobody is.' She realized how intensely she meant that. She had been something of a misfit in the local society before the war, not content to marry suitably and become absorbed in home affairs as everyone else was. But that world no longer existed anyway. But what sort of world was it now? Women, old men, children, a million men gone, and near enough two million more injured or maimed who would need care. The jobs women had held over the last four years would, for the most part, have to be given back to the returning men. She would have to earn money. She couldn't possibly expect Joseph to keep her. Anyway, it would bore her to weeping not to do anything. Wil Sloan was certainly not the only one who had no idea what to expect.

'There's something vaguely comfortable about the place you are used to,' she added aloud. 'Even if it's plunging around in the mud being shot at.'

'Only a Brit could say something like that.' He stared straight ahead, his eyes very bright in the momentary headlights of an ambulance coming the other way. 'And I will miss you,' he repeated.

She could think of nothing that sounded right to say in return, or that would tell him the affection she felt for him. There were friendships to miss that nothing could replace. There would never be anything else like this again, thank God, but those who survived it would share dreams and nightmares that no one else could know.

Joseph was standing outside the resuscitation tent when he heard a movement behind him and turned to see Lizzie in the entrance. In spite of the anxiety in her face he felt a quickening of pleasure. He drew in breath to ask if she were looking for him, and then realized that she was almost certainly seeking a doctor. One of the patients must be in trouble for her to have left him.

'Can I get someone for you?' he asked instead. 'I know where Cavan is.'

She looked disconcerted. 'It's not really . . .' she started, and then as if annoyed with herself, straightened her shoulders and met his eyes more coolly. 'It's not really necessary,' she replied. 'He'll certainly be busy.' She turned away, ready to go back into the tent again.

'Can I help?' he said quickly – not because he thought he could, but because he could not let her go without some response.

She hesitated, as though the decision were difficult for her. 'Have you no one in greater need?' She seemed annoyed with herself, as if her question was foolish but amending it would only make the situation worse. 'Private Fields is coming round. He isn't going to be able to feel his leg. It's still there, but he's going to be frightened . . .'

'I'll come,' he said, moving forward immediately and catching up with her so he was on her heels as she went back in. It must have been he she was looking for in the first place, or perhaps it was someone else, someone who knew Fields. Joseph could not place him.

There were several beds occupied, but Lizzie went straight to the furthest over by the canvas wall at the other end. The boy on it was fair-skinned, sixteen at the most, and his left leg was heavily swathed in bandages. There were also cuts on both his arms, blood already seeping through the gauze. Joseph met Lizzie's eyes questioningly. He had to know the truth, whatever he decided to say.

The gulf between them was no longer there. She understood as if he had spoken aloud everything he meant.

'Shrapnel through the flesh,' she said quietly. 'It will heal. But he was in a lot of pain. They had to give him morphine. I'm not sure he would believe me that his leg's still there.' She did not add that he would believe Joseph, but it was there in her certainty. He felt self-conscious, his face flushing at the compliment, even if it was not meant as such. She was thinking of the boy, not of him.

Lizzie looked down as the boy stirred, breathing more heavily, and his eyelids fluttered open. A wave of fear came over him as he registered the pain, and her presence. He wanted to speak, and did not know what to say.

'Hurts like hell, doesn't it?' Joseph said very quietly, moving a step closer to the bed. 'I got shrapnel in my leg in nineteen sixteen. But it healed. Hardly ever aches now – only if the weather's really cold and wet for a long time, and I get tired. I expect yours will be the same. Only you're a lot younger than I am, so you might do better.'

'Chaplain?' Fields gasped, turning his head a little and trying to focus his eyes. 'It's . . . it's still there? I thought . . .' He stopped, embarrassed. He desperately wanted to be brave.

Joseph nodded. 'Our surgeons are pretty good. The bone's not damaged. Don't think that'll make it hurt any less.'

Fields gave a weak smile. 'As long as it's there . . .'

'It is . . . I give you my word.'

'. . . then I don't care.'

'You will,' Joseph said cheerfully. 'I remember how mine hurt. I thought it would never stop. Actually it was only a few weeks, but I think I was a pretty good nuisance most of the time.'

'I'll bet you weren't.' Fields closed his eyes as another wave of agony passed through him. His skin was ashen white.

Joseph reached down and touched his hand lightly. 'Don't bet anything you can't afford to lose. I'm not saying it to make you feel better. It's the truth.'

Fields tried to smile, and nearly succeeded.

Lizzie pushed the damp hair off his forehead with her fingers. She had nothing more she could give him to ease the pain. All she could do was come to him as often as she had time. Now she glanced at Joseph, her eyes bright and soft, and then moved to the next man.

Joseph stayed with Fields, a silent presence, simply being there, until he drifted off into either sleep or unconsciousness. Afraid it was the latter, he touched the pulse in the boy's wrist. It was not strong, but it was steady.

He should go back to the admissions tent, but he must speak to Lizzie first. He wished to ask her why she had not answered his last letters, but if she had been training for this, in a hospital somewhere away from St Giles, perhaps she had not received them. And then here in Flanders she certainly would not have. She might even have thought he had stopped writing, and she would not have pursued him. She would have thought it indelicate, afraid he read into her answers a warmth he did not welcome. How absolutely far that was from the truth!

Now he felt awkward, in case it was he who had presumed to go too quickly beyond simple friendship.

She heard him approach and turned around from the medicine table quickly, fear in her eyes.

'He's asleep,' he assured her. 'His pulse is not strong, but it's regular, not fading or skipping. At least he's got a little while away from the worst of it. I must go back to the admissions tent.'

'I know. Thank you for coming. Not to be afraid helps – a bit.'

He smiled. 'Some of the time.'

She looked away, a slight colour in her face. 'You weren't a nuisance, you know.'

'Ask Hannah. I don't think she'd agree with you, if she were honest.'

'She'd never give you away!'

'Lizzie, why did you stop writing?' Then instantly he wished he had not said it, but it would only make it worse to try taking it back, somehow explain it away. He did not want to know the answer anyway; it might be what he was afraid to hear.

'Because I was out here at last,' she said very quietly. 'To begin to realize what it was really like. I'd wanted to be a driver, like Judith, but they needed nurses. I started training in Cambridge, actually quite a long time ago. I didn't tell you because it seemed so . . . mundane at the time. Safe at home. Then out here they kept moving me. I didn't know whether you were still writing to me, or not. There was no one to forward anything.'

'I was.' Then in case it sounded like blame, he added quickly. 'But it doesn't matter now.' He wanted to add something else, something that would capture the old lightness, the ease they had had with each other in St Giles, driving through the lanes, seeking a terrible truth, his leg aching like an abscessed tooth.

'Thank you for coming,' she said in the moment's silence, fitting it in as if she were afraid what he might say if she allowed him. 'It was what I hoped you would do. I know you have to go back to the admissions tent. You'll be needed there too.' She looked at him an instant longer, then turned back to the medicines.

It was final, and there was nothing for him to do but go back as he had said he should, his heart bumping in his chest, a mixture of hope and confusion in his mind.

\* \* \*

Richard Mason was sitting in a casualty clearing station to the east of Messines with a colleague about to return to file his stories in London. It was raining outside the admissions tent and even inside it was chilly.

'Bit unreal, isn't it?' Harper said thoughtfully. 'Used to think at one time that it would never end, and now we're nearly there. There's only one way it can go, and everybody knows it. But we go on shooting at everything in sight as if there were still something to fight about and it could all make a difference. It's as if we got so insanely into the habit of it that we can't stop.'

'That's probably close to the truth,' Mason remarked. 'Have you ever thought how we are suddenly going to start enforcing the law and saying you can't shoot people any more, or stick a bayonet into them, if you think they thoroughly deserve it?'

'You talking about that bloody horrible business up with the Cambridgeshires near Ypres?' Harper asked, pulling a sour face, although it might have been the last of his tea that caused it. Mason had avoided the sludge at the bottom by leaving the final couple of mouthfuls, but then he had been here many times before.

'What are you talking about?' he asked absently.

'Haven't heard?' Harper winced again. 'Some damn lunatic hacked a nurse to death in the clearing station nearest to Ypres. No idea who, or why. All pretty violent and disgusting. Killing any woman is bad, but one of our own VADs is beyond the pale.'

Mason's head swam. His mouth was dry and there was suddenly a senseless roar in his ears, as if he were in the middle of a river. 'VAD?' His mouth could hardly form the letters.

'Yes. Nurse or ambulance driver or something,' Harper answered. 'As I said, pretty vile. I dare say they'll shoot the bastard when they find him. You were talking about the general difficulty of settling back into civvy life . . .'

Mason swallowed, feeling as if he had a stone in his chest. 'What was her name, the VAD?' He felt bruised and sick.

'Don't know,' Harper replied. 'Don't think they said. Got to tell the poor girl's family first anyway. Pretty rotten way to be killed.' He frowned. 'You have family up there? I'm bloody sorry. I didn't know.'

'No,' Mason said with a feeling of being bereaved. Judith was not family. She should have been.

'Still pretty rotten,' Harper responded. 'Don't think you can make a decent story out of it, one that should be told right now. But of course I can't stop you going up there if you want to. Last throes of battle, and all that.'

Mason was barely listening. He made a pointless remark, wished Harper well, and went outside to enquire for any sort of transport that would take him towards Ypres. He was prepared to set out and walk if necessary.

He was impatient. He asked two or three people for a lift, and was refused because ambulances were full, or staff cars were going in the wrong direction. As dusk was mantling the ruin of the fields and woods, he set out on foot, leaving the broken town, bombed out and abandoned, fire-blackened skeletons against a lowering sky.

He passed columns of walking wounded. This time their numbers were swelled by thousands of German prisoners as well, just as gaunt and shell-shocked as the British. He had seen them before, tens of thousands of them, and it still moved him to an intense pity, but he had no time for it to scorch his emotions. He must find Judith.

He moved from one first-aid post to another, using his press credentials. His name alone had earned a kind of respect so people were willing to help him. They wanted to talk, to ask what news he had, and when he expected the war to end. Troop movements were no longer secret; they were reported in the newspapers because it was one victory after another, as relentless as a tide coming in. He tried to answer with the honesty these men deserved, remembering that some had been here for long, desperate years and lost entire platoons of friends. Some were the last survivors of regiments raised from factories, neighbourhoods, villages. They would go home to quiet streets and drawn blinds.

He did not tell them that he knew there was a strong German counter-attack on the River Selle, or that Dunkirk was finally shelled by long-range guns. He did tell them that he had heard a rumour that there were peace demonstrations in Berlin.

Every place he asked if the ambulance crews included Judith Reavley. Many knew her, but events were moving too rapidly for certainty of anything any more. A regiment that had been here a day or two ago was further forward now, and ambulances went wherever they were needed.

'Could be in the casualty clearing station that's closed off,' one lance-corporal told him grimly. 'Been a murder there, so I heard. Don't know why the hell there's such a fuss. Been thirty million murders, last reckoning.'

Mason was shivering. 'Who was killed?'

'Half Europe,' the lance-corporal replied.

'In the casualty clearing station?' Mason had no heart to banter. His chest was so tight it was difficult to breathe. He thought of all the times he had seen Judith since their first encounter at the

132

Savoy Hotel in London in 1915. The occasion had been about getting some coordination among the women wanting to help the war effort, sort the chaos into something useful. She was there because she was a VAD on the Western Front and knew what they actually wanted. She had been wearing a blue satin dress, which elegantly hugged the curves of her body. He could still see in his head the way she had walked with the easy grace of one whose mind is so absorbed in her purpose that she cared not a jot what other people thought of her. She had barely glanced at him. Even then the passion in her face had captured him.

Later it was the vulnerability. Once he had found her slumped over the wheel of her ambulance, pulled in at the side of the road, only just behind the front line. He had been terrified that she was wounded, even dead. He was overwhelmed with relief to find her breathing. Then he saw her face, her eyes empty of the fire and the will that had always been there before. He had hauled her out of the driving seat and forced her to walk with him along the road, talking to her, angry, fighting with her, anything to make her care again. When at last she did, he had held her in his arms and whirled her around for the sheer joy of having her back.

And then last year they had quarrelled. It had not been violent, in a way that might be healed, but quietly and with certainty. She still cared passionately for the same hopeless, naïve ideals she had started out with, and he knew them for the delusions they were.

Except that perhaps they were not. Perhaps Oldroyd was right, and that faith, whether founded in dreams or in reality, was the only thing that was worth fighting or dying for. Or, more importantly, worth living for.

But he knew that if it were she who had been murdered in the casualty clearing station, it would be for him as if the light had gone out everywhere. There would be nothing left to win, or to lose.

The lance-corporal did not know who had been killed; he could only say that it was a nurse.

Mason moved on, mostly on foot. Always there was the smell of death and the knowledge of cold and pain, the sound of guns in the distance and squelching, struggling feet beside him.

He found her in the ambulance bay at the casualty clearing station miles from the lines now, somewhere behind Ypres. She was bent over the engine, muttering to herself, an oily rag in her hands and her hair wet and falling forward over her face.

The relief was overwhelming. He wanted to laugh and shout and run over to her across the earth and stones, clasp hold of her, swing her around and then kiss her so hard and so long she would fight for breath. Of course he could not do so. They had parted as enemies, at least ideologically. He had denied everything she had believed in, and her loyalty to her dreams was greater than to him. Perhaps that was the way to survive. Maybe she was one of the few who would come out of this something like whole?

He walked towards her and stopped. She did not look up.

'Broken?' he asked. 'Or are you just cleaning it?'

She froze, then very slowly turned round and looked at him. Her eyes widened, then suddenly the disappointment and the hurt were there. His heart pinched. That was what he loved in her: the passion and the courage to care enough to be hurt and not grow bitter or run away.

She straightened up and took a deep breath. 'Hello, Mason.

Come to report on our murder? Or are you just passing through to the Front? I think we're well beyond Menin now.' She sounded nervous, even defensive.

He made himself smile, trying to look as if he were at ease. Would she believe such a pretence? Perhaps. She had no real idea how he felt. There was no certainty in her eyes, none of the confidence of a woman who knows she is loved.

'So I hear,' he agreed. 'I came about the murder. Actually . . .' Should he tell her the truth? It might not be wise, but there was no time to retreat from a lie. A couple of weeks and the war could be over. Would he find her after that?

She was waiting.

'Actually I heard about it near Messines, but they didn't know who the victim was, just that she was a VAD. I was afraid it could be you.'

Her face barely changed. In the reflected light from the lamps he could not see if she was blushing or not. 'I'm all right,' she said, looking away. 'It's just rather rotten for everybody because we have no idea who did it, so we are all looking sideways at each other, and misunderstanding half of what's said. You don't want to think it's anyone you know, but you can't help wondering.' She stopped again, still keeping her face averted as if she were concentrating on the engine. 'The worst thing is that you realize that some people have very different ideas from the ones you thought they had. I am happier not knowing some of the beliefs they have about . . . assault.' She straightened up and faced him, eyes hot and angry. 'And if you write any of that down I'll not ever forgive you.'

It was on the edge of his tongue to say that she had not forgiven him from last time, but he bit it back. He needed to begin again with no memories of failure. He was stunned by how overwhelmingly important it was to win her, and how hard it would be. He refused to face the possibility that he might not succeed.

Matthew was surprised to be called to see Jacobson, who was still questioning people, not yet to any appreciable effect. Matthew had not told anyone except Joseph of his true rank or position in the Secret Intelligence Service. With the Peacemaker's connections and his network of informants, he could not afford to trust even those of the most seeming innocence. People betrayed innocently, made a casual remark, gave a confidence to someone they thought they knew well, and it was too late to regret. Far better Jacobson take him for the more junior officer he pretended to be.

'Major Reavley,' Jacobson began. 'Sit down.' He waved to the chair. Sergeant Hampton was standing behind him, his face almost expressionless. 'You are not with the Cambridgeshires, in fact you are not regular army at all. What are you doing here, sir?'

It was a blunter opening than Matthew had expected, and certainly more immediate. It left him no choice but to tell some version of the truth. 'I'm with the Secret Intelligence Service, Inspector. I can't discuss my reason for being here.'

'Really?' Jacobson looked sceptical. 'Can you prove that, Major?'

'I could, of course, but you would have to get in touch with Colonel Shearing in London, and you would have to send your message in some secure way. Otherwise you could ask the chaplain. He would vouch for me.'

'Isn't he your brother? Hardly an unbiased witness,' Jacobson pointed out. 'And you didn't say what you were here for. The fact that you are an intelligence officer of some sort doesn't automatically mean you couldn't have committed a crime. Whoever did is in His Majesty's service in some way or other.'

Matthew was startled. Being suspected was a possibility he had not even considered. And yet what Jacobson said was true. Whoever was guilty had very probably had a good record, possibly even a fine one, up to this point.

Jacobson was waiting. Behind him Hampton shifted from one foot to the other.

'I cannot tell you what I am here for,' Matthew repeated. 'It would jeopardize my mission, to the point of failure.'

'Are you saying you distrust the inspector?' Hampton asked a little sharply.

'We make no exceptions,' Matthew told him. 'For anyone. I'm surprised you don't know that. I had never met or heard of Sarah Price before her death. I have no idea who killed her. If I had, I would already have told you. Also I am unaware of the movements of anyone here that night. I was asleep in a dugout a mile or two away, so I cannot offer any information of use.'

'Were you alone?' Jacobson asked.

'No. My brother was there.' Even as Matthew said it he realized that Joseph had come in very late and, being used to the conditions, had slept for several hours without waking. He would not honestly be able to swear that Matthew had been there as well.

'Asleep or awake?' Hampton questioned.

He would be caught in a lie, especially if Joseph were asked without knowing the reason. He would answer honestly. 'Asleep.'

'All night?' Jacobson asked.

Matthew hesitated. He had got up twice and walked outside and lit a cigarette. He knew the smoke would disturb Joseph, and even more than that, he found the underground bunker claustrophobic. The second time he had gone some considerable distance along the old trench.

'All night, Major?' Jacobson repeated.

Someone might have seen him. 'No,' Matthew replied. 'I got up a couple of times and went along the line a bit to smoke a cigarette. But I was the best part of a mile from the admissions tent, and I walked in the opposite direction. I wasn't gone longer than fifteen minutes.'

'Did anyone see you?'

Matthew tried to recall exactly what had happened. His mind had been on Schenckendorff and the possibility that this was one more trick of the Peacemaker's. Alternatively, if Schenckendorff were exactly what he said, how could Matthew make sure they got him back to London alive?

'Major Reavley!' Jacobson said impatiently. 'Either you saw someone, or you did not! Which is it?'

Matthew remembered one picture vividly, perhaps because he did not understand it. He had been tired, sickened by the stench, shivering with cold, but in the flare of star shells in the distance he had seen a man and a boy struggling. There had been a quick lunge, as if with a bayonet, then the boy had fallen, and the man had picked him up and carried him. He had seen the man's face for an instant, in profile. He had a large nose. It had made Matthew think, idiotically, of the cartoons of Mr Punch.

'Yes,' he said abruptly to Jacobson. 'I saw a man with a profile like Mr Punch, and a boy.'

'Soldiers?' Jacobson said sceptically.

'Of course. Who else would be out there?'

'What were they doing? Did you speak to them?' Hampton put in.

'No. The boy was hurt. The man was carrying him,' Matthew answered, still trying to make sense of it in his mind.

'Did you offer to help?' Hampton pressed.

'No. I don't have any medical training. He was going towards the casualty clearing station anyway.'

'What about helping to carry him?' Hampton would not give up.

'He was only a boy!' Matthew protested. 'It would have been more awkward for two of us than for one.'

Hampton shrugged.

'I see.' Jacobson nodded. 'And you made a point of telling us that you did not know, nor had you ever heard of Miss Price, until the news of her death, is that right?'

'Yes.'

'Are you certain of that, Major Reavley?' This time it was Hampton who spoke.

'Yes, of course I am,' Matthew said somewhat tensely. 'How would I? I haven't been to the front line before. Most of my work is in London.' It seemed a stupid question.

'Indeed?' Jacobson raised his eyebrows. 'But Miss Price has not been here so long, in fact less than a year. And she has been home on leave even during that time.'

'Which she took in London,' Hampton added.

'There are four or five million people in London.' Matthew told him with a touch of sarcasm. 'Curiously, so far as I know, my path and Miss Price's did not cross.'

Hampton took a step forward. 'That is not true, Major Reavley.

In going through her effects I found not only a photograph of you and her together – to judge by the clothes and the general surroundings, from some time before the war – but also a note from you, undated. From the tone of them, it is quite clear that you had a relationship of some warmth, even intimacy. It must have been nice to find an old friend out here in this waste of mud and death. But she wasn't so friendly any more. How did it happen, sir?'

Matthew was stunned. This was becoming grotesque. 'It may look like me, but I'd never even heard of her until after she was killed!' he protested.

Hampton moved a piece of paper on the table beside Jacobson and picked up a photograph, laying it where Matthew could see it. It showed a young woman, very pretty, with fair hair and a wide smile. She was facing the camera, and beside her was a handsome young man, posing a little self-consciously. He too was fair, with level, light eyes and a strong-featured face, not very unlike Joseph's, and profoundly recognizably Matthew, in his university days. He had on a cricketing pullover with a Cambridge badge. His arm was around the girl. Sarah Gladwyn. He remembered her well. She had been courting a friend of his, but had found she preferred Matthew, and the courtship had ended. It had all been embarrassing, and he knew he himself had not behaved well.

'Sarah Gladwyn,' he said aloud, his voice hoarse. He felt the heat burn up his face. 'Her name wasn't Price. I . . . I never connected them. It was years ago!'

'Yes, Major, we can see that,' Hampton agreed. 'But you said you didn't know her at all.'

'I didn't! Not by the name you told me!' Matthew protested.

'So you say.' Disbelief was heavy in Hampton's voice. 'But she was killed shortly after you arrived, and no one can account for your movements. The only person who can vouch for you at all is your own brother, the chaplain. If I may say so, he is a rather unworldly man, and obliged by his calling to think the best of people, not to mention by his relationship to you.' Hampton took a couple of steps around the table. 'I advise you not to make a fuss, Major. I am arresting you for the murder of Sarah Gladwyn Price. We will inform the chaplain, so he can make any arrangements you wish for your defence.'

Matthew drew in his breath, then let it out again without saying anything. The whole thing was a nightmare. He felt the canvas walls of the tent sway around him and blur in a hideous unreality. And yet Hampton's hold on his arms was hard and very real indeed.

# *Chapter Five*

Joseph was writing letters at the table in his bunker, catching up with condolences. There was a terrible grief to the senselessness of the slaughter, this close to the end. Dusk was falling rapidly and he found himself straining his eyes in the lamplight as the ink on the page blurred in front of him. He put the pen down for a moment, blinking. He was even more tired than usual. These last few weeks seemed to be the hardest. It was foolish. They should have been easier, now that the ceasefire was in sight.

They would even know who the Peacemaker was. He had given up hope of that until Matthew had come, and then Schenckendorff had actually crossed through the lines. Fortunately his foot seemed to be healing. The swelling was reduced and the infection they feared had not materialized. As soon as Jacobson found out who had killed poor Sarah Price, Joseph and Matthew, and perhaps Judith, could leave and take Schenckendorff with them. It was still only 21 October. They would have probably a couple of weeks left.

He was startled by the sound of boots on the step and someone banged loudly on the lintel. Even before he could reply, Barshey Gee pulled the sacking aside. His face was smeared with mud and he was clearly very upset.

'What's happened?' Joseph rose to his feet in alarm.

Barshey came in, letting the sacking fall. 'Chaplain, that daft policeman has gone and arrested Major Reavley for killing the nurse. He's got him locked up back in the hut next to where they have the German prisoners.'

'That's absurd!' Joseph refused to believe it. Barshey must have it wrong. 'Matthew's an intelligence officer. He isn't even stationed here. What the . . . ?' He started to push past, but Barshey clasped his arm, holding him tightly.

'No, Chaplain. From what Oi hear, that other policeman, Hampton, was looking through Miss Proice's things, and he found a picture of Major Reavley and her, going back to before the war, and it looked loike they knew each other pretty well.' Barshey looked acutely embarrassed. 'But he says the Major denoied it. And of course he can't say where he was when she was killed . . . at least he can, but there's only you would know it, and you were asleep. And seeing as you're his brother anyway, he doesn't put a lot of weight on your say-so, if you'll pardon me.'

There was no point at all in being offended, and no time to waste. He had to prove to Jacobson that Matthew was innocent. He had no idea even where to begin, let alone to reach any conclusion. The idea was preposterous but then Jacobson obviously didn't know Matthew.

His mind raced. Could he get in touch with Shearing in

143

London and have him use some authority to persuade Jacobson? But Matthew had said Shearing did not know what he was here for. And did men in charge of intelligence units ever emerge from their secrecy to do such things? Would the police take notice of him anyway?

Joseph knew almost nothing about Matthew's work. No one did. By its very nature that was obligatory. There was no one to support the intelligence officers. They fought in secret, and there was no praise for them, except from their own.

If the police could not blame a German then Matthew was the obvious scapegoat: a man in uniform who stayed safely at home in London, sleeping in his own bed every night. He had never even got mud on his shoes, never mind shrapnel or a bayonet in his body.

'What are you going to do, sir?' Barshey asked, pulling himself to attention carefully to avoid cracking his head on the ceiling. He said it as if he were waiting for orders to help.

Joseph's mind was suddenly clear. 'About the only way I can prove he didn't do it is to find who did.'

'Haven't you been troying?' Barshey asked with a frown.

'Not hard enough,' Joseph answered grimly. 'I left it to the police, and they've made a complete mess of it.'

'What'd you loike me to do, sir?' Barshey offered.

Joseph was not even sure what he was going to do himself, let alone how anyone else could help, but he was loath to refuse even the slightest assistance. There was no one else he could turn to, apart from Judith. Even Barshey's trust was a kind of strength. 'I have a pretty good idea about who couldn't have done it because they were accounted for during the hour or so when it must have happened . . .' he started.

144

Barshey's eyes widened. 'You know when it happened?'

'Only roughly. She was seen alive at three, and the state of her body when she was found at about seven means it has to have been no later than around four.' He did not need to explain how a dead person changes in the first few hours; they were all far too familiar with it, in strangers, friends, even brothers.

'But not *all* accounted for,' Barshey observed. 'Want me to work on that, sir?'

Joseph hesitated, torn by indecision. Barshey was loyal and willing. He knew she was dead; did he know how brutally and intimately she had been destroyed as well? That kind of assault on a woman was a thing that tore gut-deep with all of them, violating emotions they were not even aware of. But there were other loyalties that weighed just as heavily: debts on the battlefield, secrets trusted in the long hours of watch in no-man's-land, between life and death.

'I need to know more about Sarah Price,' Joseph said thoughtfully. 'Maybe she was chosen at random, but maybe not. She might have had some liaison that was at least the start of this. I thought I knew most of the men, but it seems I don't. I half expected the violence towards the German prisoners, but nothing like this.'

'Nobody wants to think that sort o' thing about anyone they know, Chaplain,' Barshey said grimly. 'And with respect, sir, most of us want to show a man loike you the best soide of ourselves. Men that'd swear a blue streak usually koind of keep a close lip when you're there.'

'You're saying I don't see the real man?' Joseph shrugged. 'I know that, Barshey. I make allowances.'

Barshey did not look convinced, but he was too gentle to say so.

Joseph saw it in his eyes and understood. 'All right, I'll tell you what you can do to help. Give me a more honest picture of the men you think I've judged too softly. Help me to see them as they are. Somebody killed that girl pretty obscenely. I saw her body. It was worse than you think.'

Barshey was startled, then overwhelmingly disgusted.

'I'm not as other-worldly as you think,' Joseph told him quietly. 'I've heard some confessions that would surprise you, especially from men who knew they were dying. I just can't think of anyone I know doing something like this. There was a hatred in it I hadn't imagined.'

'Oi hope it's not someone from St Giles.' Barshey's face pinched as if he expected a blow. 'Oi'll think about it, an' Oi'll ask.'

'Don't think long, Barshey. It's going to be too late pretty quickly.' It hurt even to say it aloud.

'Oi know that.' Barshey did not offer any words of comfort. The belief in everything working out for good had long ago been swept away. One believed in honour, courage and friendship, but not in any certainty of justice.

Joseph found Judith helping with nursing shifts in the tent for the walking wounded. It had been a quieter evening than usual so far, perhaps because the front line was now moving further east, and the injured men taken to a casualty clearing station closer to. There were half a dozen patients, two standing, and four sitting in various degrees of discomfort. Some had obviously received no more than first aid – a bandage to stop the worst of the bleeding, a sling for a broken bone. Others were already treated and waiting to be told where to go next, their uniform sleeves cut away, bandages clean and white. There were two nurses in attendance, an orderly and a young surgeon.

Judith looked at Joseph's face and excused herself from the man she was helping, leaving the job for the orderly to finish. She crossed the space between them in a few strides. 'What is it?' she asked anxiously. 'What's happened?'

Using as few words as possible he told her, and saw her eyes widen with horror. 'I'm sorry,' he finished. 'We have no more time to be gentle. Quite apart from getting Schenckendorff to London, we've got to find out who the murderer is to save Matthew.'

'They can't believe it was him!' she said desperately, struggling to find it so absurd as not to be serious. 'Why on earth would he? He only arrived here a couple of days before she was killed! It doesn't make any sense. Anyway, where would he get a bayonet?'

'Judith, there are weapons all over the place, rusted ones, broken ones, ones people have dropped or lost. And what does sense have to do with any of it?' he demanded, feeling panic rush up inside him. 'Why would anyone want to do that to her? The authorities need to blame somebody and open up the station and get on with ending the war. They want to get the men out of here, and start operating it as normal again, probably even move it forward. It's too far behind the lines now. Above all, they want to say the matter is closed, and forget all about it.'

'Even if it isn't the right man? That's monstrous!' She waved her hands, refusing to believe it. She ignored the curious glances of the orderly and two of the wounded men.

'Look around you!' Joseph said impatiently, keeping his voice low. 'How many men are dead? What's one more, if they can close this over and say it's ended? They don't know Matthew; he isn't one of them.'

'But somebody really did it! Somebody—'

'I know.' He lowered his voice with an effort, breathing in and out deeply, trying to regain control of himself. 'We have to find him, British or German, and we have to do it in the next two or three days, at the most. We need to begin by getting to know everything we can about Sarah Price. She didn't deserve it – nobody could – but she may have done something to provoke it . . .'

Judith's face tightened with anger. 'And what does one do, exactly, to "provoke" being hacked to death, Joseph?' she said savagely. 'Funny how one never thinks one's brother could be just like the rest of men!'

'That's the point, Judith,' he said with barely a flicker of change in his expression. 'It's probably someone that nobody thinks of as having violent or uncontrollable passions, or having been so wounded in mind that at times he no longer behaves like ordinary sane people. But somebody knows him, has worked beside him, fought beside him, shared rations, letters from home, all the things we do and the ways we get to know people.'

'Was that why you said it?' she demanded, her eyes wide and angry. 'To make me think of that?'

'Not altogether,' he admitted reluctantly. 'I do think that she might have said or done something that infuriated someone. If it is entirely random, we don't have much chance of finding him, do we?'

Judith's face crumpled with regret. 'I'm sorry. I suppose we don't. I'd rather think she was stupid than that Matthew could . . . could be . . .' She did not finish the sentence. She took a deep breath and looked a little away from him. 'I feel guilty because I didn't even take much notice of her. I thought she was trivial and empty-headed. Father always used to say I was too quick to judge. I thought I'd learned.'

She bit her lip hard. 'We've got to get Matthew to London with that German officer, whatever his name is, because we've got to expose the Peacemaker. My war won't finish until we have done! I'll start finding out. At least I've plenty of time, compared with usually, and I have an excuse to be here. I suppose I even have an excuse to ask questions now. At least nobody can tell me it's not my business.'

'We have to succeed—' Joseph started.

'I know!' she cut him off, not wanting to hear him say it, even though she had accepted that it was true.

She began next day with the other medical staff, knowing she had a better chance with them than Joseph did with the soldiers. None of them had been here very long because it was the nature of a casualty clearing station for the wounded to move through it as quickly as possible.

'No more time for being charitable about it,' she said briskly to Erica Barton-Jones as they were in the storeroom, taking delivery of some clean blankets, having sent away those too torn or saturated in blood to use any more.

'I thought they'd arrested someone,' Erica replied, heaving the grey blankets up. She was not pretty but there was a grace and strength of character in her face that was in some ways more attractive. She was a highly practical woman and she held whatever grief she had experienced deep inside her.

'They have,' Judith replied. 'My brother.'

Erica was incredulous. 'The chaplain? That's idiotic!'

'No, Matthew. He's an intelligence officer.' She had no

compunction at all about shading the truth. 'He's out here on some mission or other, which of course he can't tell us, and they don't believe him. He can't prove it because it's secret. That's what intelligence is about.'

'So what are you going to do?' Erica's face was tense and anxious. 'You could ask questions, of course, but what makes you think anyone will tell you something they haven't told the police? Not that I'm saying you shouldn't try.' There was an uncharacteristic flash of sympathy in her eyes, perhaps because she thought Judith would not succeed.

A flare of temper burned up in Judith. The pity made it worse because it twisted her emotions even more.

'Because I know what questions to ask,' she snapped back. 'For example, before anything happened, who was Sarah nursing? Did she flirt with any of the doctors or orderlies?' She saw Erica's distaste. 'And don't screw your face up and pretend it couldn't happen. We're all frightened and tired, and sick with seeing people suffer, and we can't do much to help them. We don't get close to anyone for long because people are moved around all the time, lots of them die, but we still can't help the need to touch someone, emotionally or physically. Life can be too hard, too unbearably lonely without it. Friendship is almost the only life-line to sanity and the things that are worth surviving for.'

Erica stared at her, her eyes shadowed, her lips pulled tight. She looked as if her mind was racing and she wanted to speak, but the words eluded her.

'Well, who was she nursing?' Judith repeated. 'Don't tell me you don't know, because you do! You are in charge and you never miss anything. You're the most efficient nurse on the whole Ypres Salient. Did she go anywhere near the German prisoners?

I haven't seen the rosters, but we both know they don't mean anything. People go where they're needed. An emergency happens and everything changes.'

'It's not on the roster,' Erica said reluctantly. 'But I'm pretty sure she did. We had a bit of a panic about one of the Germans who had lost an arm – thought he was going to bleed to death – and another one with a mangled foot, but he's recovering quite well. We lost a couple, but we never had much of a chance of saving them anyway. They were bad when they got here.'

'Who? Did she quarrel with anyone – flirt too much? Was she careless?' Judith rattled off the questions, hearing her own voice demanding and knowing it made little sense. The answers would prove nothing. 'Did she go back again afterwards?'

'I wish I could say she did, but she stayed pretty much with our own,' Erica replied. She stood stiffly; her grey dress was soiled and very crumpled but she carried herself with such high head and ramrod back that on her it had a kind of style. 'Mary Castalet did most of the nursing for the Germans,' she continued. 'There are only a few here, you know. About eight. Anyone fit to move got sent on. We need the beds. Some of them are on the floor anyway, poor creatures.'

Her elegant face puckered in distress. 'Imagine having fought for four years out here, losing the war, terrified that your wife and children will be treated pretty much the way you treated the Belgians, and then being wounded and lying on the floor of the enemy's field hospital! I wouldn't wish that on a dog.'

Judith refused to let her mind picture it.

'How well are they guarded, really?' she asked.

Erica thought for a moment. 'Not closely,' she said, meeting Judith's eyes levelly. 'Most of them came here voluntarily. They're wounded and they need treatment. Why would they escape and where would they go, assuming they were fit enough to go anywhere?'

Judith forced herself to ask the next question. 'What about our men going in and hurting them? If that happened, couldn't they as easily get out?'

Erica's face hardened, although her anger was not directed at Judith, but at the whole tragic ridiculous turn of events. 'Don't be stupid! You know the answer to that already – we can't spare men to guard Germans from our own soldiers.'

'Then possibly a German prisoner, not wounded too badly to walk, could actually have got out and gone looking for someone vulnerable, like one of the nurses?' Judith pointed out. 'Maybe one that was childish enough to taunt them, or try flirting?'

'I suppose so. But the other prisoners would have seen it. They're in there like sardines in a tin.'

Judith thought about it for several moments. Ideas raced through her mind. It would be easier for all of them if the murderer was one of the Germans. It was going to be bitterly painful to have to acknowledge that a British soldier could have done such a thing. It had to be someone they knew, because there wasn't anyone they didn't know, or had not fought beside, shared rations with, jokes, loneliness. They all wanted it to be a German.

But that might also be more difficult to prove. And might they want it enough to be tempted into making it look that way, whether they were sure of it or not? Nothing was clear enough. That was a sickening thought but once it was in her mind she could not get rid of it.

'Describe Sarah to me,' she said instead, picking up the blankets again and resuming folding them. They were rough to the touch and smelled stale. 'What was she really like? I saw her only a few times when we were helping the wounded inside, and she came over to give a hand, or when she gave us tea, or food.'

Erica hesitated.

'Come on!' Judith said urgently, her patience slipping. 'How was she in a crisis? What did she talk about if you had a really sick man and you had to sit up all night with him? What did she think was funny? What did she cry over? Was she saving money for anything? Did she write to anyone? Who did she like, or not? Who didn't like her?'

'What on earth can that have to do with who killed her?' Erica was making a clearly visible effort to keep her own patience. 'Judith, for God's sake! Nobody's saying it, but everybody's thinking it! Some man went crazy and raped her!' She shuddered violently. 'It wasn't just a quarrel and somebody slapped her too hard. You're talking as if it were all reasonable. It isn't!' Now her voice was growing uncontrollably louder. 'Reasonable people fight sometimes. If they're men they might even hurt each other badly. But this wasn't human. There was blood everywhere. It was like a wild animal!'

'Foxes do that to chickens sometimes,' Judith replied. 'But animals don't kill for hate, and they don't indulge in years of organized slaughter of their own kind, and leave nothing standing but mud and ruins. This was very definitely human.'

Erica put down the blankets she was holding. The lamplight flickered in the draught through the tent flap. It danced on her face, accentuating the lines of strain. 'I'm only answering your questions because they've arrested your brother,' she said, her voice shaking a little. 'Sarah was all right in a crisis, pretty stupid the rest of the time. I never sat up all night with her. I took care to avoid it. According to Allie and Moira, she talked about men. And as to what she thought was funny, it was pretty juvenile: flirting, teasing, making people look silly. There was a cruel streak in her. I think it was partly because she wasn't respected very much, and she knew it.' Erica turned away and her shoulders under the grey dress were stiff, as if she disliked herself for what she had said.

'Underneath the laughing and the flirting, she was pretty desperate,' she went on quietly. 'She didn't have a lot to go home to. She wasn't a bad nurse, but she didn't do it because she loved it. It was a job. What did she cry over? Nothing. I never saw her cry.' Her face tightened and she avoided Judith's eyes even further. 'Now that I think it over a bit harder, I think possibly she didn't dare to, in case she couldn't stop. Who did she like? Men, any men who would flirt with her. Who didn't like her? I didn't. She thought I was a stuck-up bitch, and said so, several times. Ask anyone, she wasn't discreet about it. Or about much else either.'

'In fact she was rather common?' Judith included with a slight lift of her voice to make it a question. Then she remembered hearing that Erica's younger brother was an RFC Squadron Leader who had been burned to death when his plane crashed over Vimy Ridge, and wished she had been gentler. Matthew and Joseph were still alive, at least for now.

'If that's your conclusion, don't attribute it to me,' Erica said sharply. 'And don't say I said that she deserved what she got, because I didn't.'

'I'm not trying to make trouble!' Judith exclaimed. 'I've got more than enough already. I'm trying to find out who killed her!'

'You're trying to save your brother from being hanged,' Erica corrected her, turning to face her squarely, eyes hot and full of pain.

Judith felt as if she had been slapped. It was perfectly true. Before Matthew had been accused she had cared very little who had killed Sarah Price. Her mind had been on Mason returning and stirring up feelings in her she had been determined to leave buried, and also the amazement of finding someone who would identify the Peacemaker at last, and the need to get him home to England in time. Sarah's death was horrible, but not personally wounding.

'At least you don't lie about that,' Erica said with a bleak smile. 'Good luck. You'll need it. Everyone has their own ideas about who did it, and whether they really want to know for certain, or not. Some of us don't.'

Judith finished the job with the blankets, then went to find out who had been on duty guarding the German prisoners the night Sarah had been killed.

It had stopped raining outside, but the air was cold and it flapped her wet skirts around her ankles, making her legs and feet almost numb. The boards creaked when she stood on them and the wind rattled in the canvas and whined through cracks where it could not be tied down.

It took her some time and argument before she learned the names of both men who had been on guard duty. One was Lance-Corporal Benbow, the other Private Eames. Both had recently been wounded themselves, and they were still insufficiently healed to be back on front-line duty. She found Eames first. He was in a dugout brewing up a cup of tea in a dixie can over a flame, waiting patiently for it to come anywhere near boiling. He had fair hair and long, bony wrists that poked out of his uniform blouse. He moved stiffly, the wound in his shoulder still aching.

'We were there all night, miss,' he said in answer to her question. 'I'd an 'ole lot rather think it was one o' them Jerries 'oo done that to 'er, specially seein' as 'ow she were over that way towards the shed w'ere they're kept. But Benbow were with me all the time, and no one came out o' the 'ut that I saw till about three in the morning, an' that were just ter stick 'is 'ead out, and straight back in again.'

'But you saw Sarah Price?' Judith said quickly. 'Where? Who with? What was she doing?'

He shook his head, still watching and nursing the flame under his dixie can. 'She were alone, miss. Just walking along the boards wi' something in 'er 'and. Couldn't see what.'

'What time?' She refused to let the faint glimmer of hope slip out of her grasp. 'You were on guard duty, you must have an idea.'

'About 'alf-past two, near as I can remember. Or maybe three.'

'Was there anyone else near her? Think! It could matter a lot.'

It was clear that Eames was thinking, his brow furrowed and he was deeply withdrawn into himself.

Judith waited.

'I don't know,' he said at last. 'I was thinking about the Germans.'

'What about before that?' she asked. 'Earlier in the evening?'

'She went to the Germans' shed,' he replied. 'But she came out and she were fine. I told 'er . . .' He stopped.

'What?' Judith demanded. 'What did you tell her?'

He chewed his lip, eyes still concentrating on the candle flame. 'I told 'er to give the poor sods a chance,' he mumbled. 'They aren't all bad, any more'n we're all good.'

Judith breathed in and out slowly. 'Why did you say that, Private Eames?' She did her best to sound patient.

He was silent for several moments.

'She was murdered, Private,' she prompted him.

He looked away from the candle at last, his eyes grave.

'I know that, miss, an' I wouldn't 'ave that 'appen to anyone. Wot they did to 'er was 'orrible. But she did tempt them something rotten. Told 'em all sorts o' things as'd 'appen to their women w'en our boys got into Germany. I know she were just ignorant, miss, an' she 'ad lost some of 'er friends and family, like all of us.' He looked across at her, the tea forgotten now. 'But that in't the way ter treat people as can't fight back at yer.' He was struggling to find the words to explain it to her. He understood his own laws of honour, but they had never been set out for him; they were simply learned by acts throughout youth, things he had seen other people do.

'It's all right, Private, I know it isn't.' Judith felt a warmth inside her, as if she had swallowed the tea and it had opened up like a fire. 'Could it have been one of the Germans who got back at her?'

'I dunno, miss. I don't think so. But there was a bit of a scuffle a while before four, an' I went to 'elp.'

She thanked him, and left him to brew his tea.

It was some time later that Judith found Benbow. He was a year or two younger, and quite clearly worried. She could draw nothing from him except an approximate agreement with what Eames had said. It surprised her. He seemed a strong man, a good soldier. He was not much more than nineteen, but he had been promoted from the ranks and he had an easy confidence about him that even a severe limp could not reduce.

The question as to when he had last seen Sarah, and who with, troubled him, but he did not hesitate in his answer. 'I wouldn't like to say, miss, and perhaps be wrong.'

She had to be content with that, as she told Joseph at dusk when they stood in line with forty others to receive their rations. It was a clear evening, banners of cloud shredded out and streaming across the north with a sharp wind carrying the sound of heavy gunfire in the distance.

Joseph looked unhappy. 'I've come across the same thing,' he said quietly. 'No one wants to tell tales that could be misread, but they all want it to be over. I can't help wondering if I would be any different if it were not Matthew they were accusing. If it were somebody from London that I didn't know, somebody who had sat out the war at home, as far as I could see, would I care?'

'Don't say that!' she told him sharply. 'Just because it—'

'I know,' he cut her off. 'But that's how some men see it. I was talking to Turner, who beat the German prisoner the other day. He's got a brother-in-law who has bad eyesight or flat feet, or something, and has spent the entire war at home sleeping in his own bed every night and making a fortune on the black market. I think Turner would see him shot in a trice.'

'We probably all would,' Judith agreed as they shuffled forward a few steps. 'But we could live with it only if he was guilty, if it was one of us and not a German. What happens to make somebody who looks just like the rest of us suddenly go barking mad and do something like this? Why?'

Joseph did not answer. Ahead of them someone laughed loudly, then suddenly bit it off and there was silence. The click of ladles against a metal can was loud.

'I'm not sure what madness is,' Joseph said at last, keeping his voice so low that those next to them and behind could not hear. 'Or maybe I mean that I don't know what sanity is, or exactly how one keeps hold of it.'

The remark frightened her, because he had always been the one person who knew what he believed. But it was unfair to expect him always to hold up the light for everyone else. He must have his dark nights of the soul too, moonless and starless like everyone else's, otherwise what use was he? Without knowledge of despair, was hope real, or only an untasted thought?

'You might lose sight of what's good,' she said firmly. 'You don't lose the memory of it or the certainty that it is what you want; that is sanity. You might have to kill, but you do it reluctantly, and without hate.'

He put his arm around her in a quick, silent hug. Even in the chill of the wind, the warmth of it touched her mind if not her flesh.

'From what everyone says she wasn't a bad nurse,' he went on exploring the ideas. 'I thought she might have made a mistake that turned out badly, or told tales, or anything else that was stupid, and might have caused somebody to get hurt, lose an arm or leg, or even die. But I haven't found anything. She seems to have been perfectly competent, and if anything, better than some others. She flirted, and occasionally, when the rations were decent, drank a bit too much and was silly, but only to laugh too loudly and be a bit of a nuisance. Some of the men even thought it was quite funny. Nobody took advantage of her. She had a few romances, but short-lived, just while a particular man was here, usually too badly wounded to do much anyway.'

They moved another step forward. 'It was just . . . just grabbing at life, while she could,' he added very quietly. 'She was frightened and lonely, like everyone else. According to one of the orderlies, all she really wanted was to marry and have children.' He stopped. 'At least that's what he thought.'

Judith could barely see his face in the uncertain lamplight, but there was a deep understanding of loss in it, and a pity that hurt. She thought of Eleanor and the baby who had died at birth. Would Lizzie Blaine ever be able to take Eleanor's place, or at least make a new place where the old hopes could begin again? At that moment she wished more than anything else in the world, more than anything for herself, that it would happen.

It was not until he turned that she saw his eyes and realized that he was thinking of Sarah Price, and perhaps of Mason, who had fallen so far below the courage and the hope Judith needed to feed her heart. Suddenly her eyes filled with tears and she turned away. It was strangely painful to be known so well. It left her wounds exposed too. And yet it meant she was not alone. As long as Joseph was alive, she never would be.

'We'll find who did it,' she said, needing to say something practical, to stop looking at the things too delicate to touch. Times, places, who was where, who saw what, were what mattered. But now they were at the head of the queue, and it was not until they had received their bread and stew that they were able to move into a quiet corner of a supply tent and resume talking.

'Practical,' Judith said firmly, taking a mouthful of stew and trying not to think what it tasted like. 'After you've dismissed all the people who couldn't have killed her because they were proved to be somewhere else, who's left?'

Joseph gave a bleak smile, but there was a flash of humour in his eyes. 'Sherlock Holmes? After you've removed all that is impossible, whatever is left, however unlikely, has to be the truth,' he quoted roughly. 'That's the trouble – very little indeed is left. Most people are accounted for because it was a pretty busy night, but in the poor light and with people coming and going, there are still quite a few I'm not certain of.' He ate another couple of mouthfuls of stew before going on. 'The trouble is, I think several people could be lying. I can understand it.' He looked at her over the top of the dixie can. 'No one wants to think it's someone they care about. Perhaps they owe a debt to some friend, a pretty big one, and so they lie to protect them, certain it doesn't matter because they would never do such a thing anyway.'

Judith looked down quickly, feeling the guilt burn in her face for her own lie to protect Wil Sloan. It had been for exactly that reason. He could never do such a thing. She knew him too well even to imagine it for an instant, but others didn't, and he might be blamed. Jacobson didn't know anyone, and didn't understand the men, any of them, let alone an American medical volunteer. Did Joseph know she had lied? She was not going to tell him, not now, anyway.

'Yes, it's difficult,' she agreed. At least her lie would not affect Matthew, and owning up to it would hurt Wil without helping anyone else. She bit into the bread and chewed it until she could swallow. Her throat was tight. 'We'll just have to work harder.'

Judith could not tell Lizzie why Matthew had come here, but naturally she knew he had been arrested. Everyone did. The sense of relief was palpable for most of them. He had not actually been charged yet; Jacobson was still gathering evidence, hoping for something more concrete, witnesses who had seen something, heard something. But it was only a matter of time.

News was coming about the front line moving east, towns falling one by one. The fighting was still bitter, with murderous losses on both sides, but the end could not be much longer in coming.

Judith was in the evacuation tent, making room for more wounded to be moved into it.

'I need to see one of the German prisoners,' she said urgently to Lizzie. 'It's important. For Matthew.' She was almost on the edge of telling Lizzie why, but she remembered with a stab of pain still fresh what it had cost Owen Cullingford when she had told him about the Peacemaker, and she kept silent, startled how sharply the sense of loss still dug into her.

Lizzie must have heard the emotion in her voice. She did not argue, or ask for further explanation. 'You'd better come with me,' she said, looking away the moment after she had agreed. 'I have a duty there as soon as we've finished this, but I expect you know that.'

Judith felt guilty. She was using Lizzie, whom she'd quickly come to regard as a friend, but she would have used anyone at all to help Matthew, and to get Schenckendorff to tell them all he knew about the Peacemaker. Her mind told her that he must not be permitted to influence the terms of the armistice; her heart demanded that he answer for the deaths of her parents, and of Owen Cullingford.

'Thank you,' she said sincerely.

A flicker of a smile warmed Lizzie's face, then she led the way. There were two guards on duty, as usual, but they took no notice of nurses coming and going, and to them Judith, in her VAD grey, was just the same. The thought flashed in her mind to wonder if nurses were always invisible to them. Had Sarah come and gone this way without being noticed, and might it make a difference?

Inside the hut eight men lay on narrow cots, close to each other. Dark blankets partially covered their bodies; white bandages were stained with blood. Lizzie stopped at the first bed. Judith went on, looking for a man whose foot was bandaged.

She found him quickly, making only one mistake first. He was not at all as she had expected. He looked leaner, more vulnerable lying in the cot, his hair untidy from the rough pillow, his face tired and unshaven, furrowed with pain. She was aware of what Joseph had said about the courage it must have cost him to abandon his life's belief and promises because his moral loyalty was to a higher principle. How many people can ever do that? The loneliness must be almost beyond the imagination. Could she have left all that she knew and loved, for any principle of right, however deep? Would not the accusation of betrayal, however false, bleed inside her for ever? Would she not weaken and eventually falter, knowing she was a stranger, not trusted, not loved?

Would he be able to go through with it, when the moment came?

The man stared straight ahead, not looking at her because he did not expect to be spoken to. She was anonymous, just another nurse, an English nurse who was here only out of duty. The young man in the bed beyond him looked no more than sixteen or seventeen. There was barely down on the fair skin of his cheeks. He looked at her with fear.

'I'm not going to hurt you,' she said in German. She wanted to add that nobody would, but she knew that might not be true.

Schenckendorff looked at her, woken from his thoughts. 'It is not himself he is afraid for,' he said in almost unaccented English. 'He is afraid for his family. He comes from a village in the path of the army on its way to Berlin. They are alone there now. His father is dead and his sisters are only children, younger than he is. I apologize for him. He has heard stories.'

'Of course he's afraid for them,' she replied. 'I understand that. My brother is in danger, and I'm afraid for him.' She smiled at the boy who stared at her, an answering smile touching his mouth and then vanishing. She looked back at Schenckendorff. 'He has been blamed for something he didn't do, and if we can't prove that, they'll shoot him.'

There was no comprehension in Schenckendorff's eyes.

'One of our nurses was murdered,' she said.

'I know,' he answered. 'It was not any of us, although I suppose it is inevitable that you should think it is. I cannot help you, miss . . . ?'

She found her eyes filling with tears, and was furious with herself. 'Reavley,' she said in little more than a whisper.

His face was grey with exhaustion and pain, but he still managed to blush. 'I'm sorry,' he said so quietly she saw his lips move more than heard the words.

She had no idea what to say. She wanted to accept whatever she thought was at least in part an apology as well as an expression of sympathy, but her father's face was so vivid in her mind that the absolution would not come. 'Who is the Peacemaker?' she said instead.

He remained silent.

'They are accusing my brother Matthew of having killed that girl,' she went on. She heard the rasping emotion in her voice and could not control it. 'If we don't manage to prove that he didn't, they'll shoot him. Everybody just wants an end to it. We'd like it to be one of you, but it seems it couldn't be.

The next best thing from them is if it were someone like him, who's only just arrived here. Anything is better than it being someone they know.'

He frowned. 'Why do they think it's him? Why would an intelligence officer from London, who's never seen her before, suddenly do such a thing?'

'Because he knew her before, and told them he didn't. It was a long time ago, and she wasn't married then. He knew her by her maiden name and he didn't associate the two.'

'Don't they understand that?' he asked.

'They don't want to.' She lifted her shoulders very slightly in dismissal of reason. 'It's an answer. They can take him and the regiment will be happy, and the police can pack up and go home, get away from the smell, the mud and the hard rations. At least most of the shelling is pretty far away now, and unless there's a hell of a breakthrough by the Germans, they're not in any danger of being hit. We're sort of left behind here.' She stared at him, seeing the weariness and a pain of disillusion far deeper than anything physical could be. 'Who is the Peacemaker, Colonel von Schenckendorff?' She almost added that he owed them that much, and then changed her mind. He knew that already, or he would not be here.

'That is dangerous knowledge, Miss Reavley.'

'You think it is going to make Matthew's life any more dangerous than it is? They'll shoot him – or hang him perhaps.' To say that was so painful she faltered.

He closed his eyes. 'Dermot Sandwell,' he whispered.

She was stunned. Was that true? Could it be? She thought they had proved it could not be, years ago. Was this the Peacemaker's last, most daring trick of all, to blame someone else? Was Schenckendorff prepared to sacrifice his life to save the real Peacemaker, and ruin Sandwell?

She realized he was looking at her, even smiling very faintly.

'You don't believe me,' he observed. 'That is why I have to come to England, whatever the cost. Knowing his name will give you nothing, Miss Reavley, except perhaps a bullet in the head. I must face him, and prove it. I know dates and telegram texts, people, places. You must free your brother from this absurd charge, however you do it, and we must go to London. We have not much more time to waste. Please . . .'

She nodded. 'Thank you. I'll do everything I can.'

His smile widened. 'You are still not certain, are you? You think it could be a double-cross, a triple-cross.'

She nearly said she did believe, then something in his eyes made her feel that lying would be cheap, a thing unworthy of either of them. 'I don't know,' she admitted. 'Can I do anything for you? I'm really an ambulance driver, but I can do basic nursing, something to make you more comfortable.' It was evasive, a moment's release from the tension that threatened to snap inside her, and yet part of her meant it. They were both trapped, and he was in a different kind of pain. She would have helped it if she could.


'Matthew Reavley?' Mason said in disbelief. 'That's impossible!'

He had followed the Cambridgeshire regiment forward to get the stories that would justify his being here. The weather was grey, with a slicing wind and occasional bursts of sun, but they were beyond the old battleground with its trenches lacing through the wasteland. Here there was nothing to shelter them except a slight rise in the ground and a few scratched-out hollows for sleeping.

'Maybe,' the other correspondent said drily, shifting his position to ease his cramped legs. The guns were too close for carelessness. Snipers could shoot a long way. 'Nevertheless it's true,' he went on. 'Been a lot more convenient if it'd been one of the Germans, but apparently it wasn't. Just as well, or we could have had a bloodbath in reprisals. Anyway, who is this Reavley? Why is it impossible? That's a word I wouldn't expect to hear you use so casually.'

'I know him.' Mason's mind was racing. Judith would be desperate. He could barely imagine what she must be feeling. He should go back to the casualty clearing station immediately and do something to help. The police must be idiots. Surely a word with whoever was in charge would unravel the mess they had made?

'And nobody you know could commit a crime?' the other correspondent said with mockery in his voice. 'Come on, Mason! Whoever it is, somebody knows him! It's not like you to be stupidly sentimental.'

Mason slithered down the hill until he was well below the ridge, then he stood up. 'I know him well, you damn fool!' he snapped. 'I know his whole family. I have done for years. He's based in London, for a start. He wouldn't even know the damn woman. You can have this,' he waved his arm to encompass the entire region of the battle line. 'I have to find out what's behind the . . . the foul-up at the clearing station.'

'You can't . . .' the other man began, but he was addressing Mason's back, and he gave up.

Mason started to walk. There was no other means of travel this far forward, and the sheer physical effort of it gave him some release from the fury of frustration inside him. Why was Matthew

Reavley here anyway? What had brought him to France or Belgium so close to the armistice? Why was he not in London doing all he could to influence events the way he would want them to go?

Mason passed a gun crew hauling a cannon up the incline until it was clear of the stream. He had no time to think of helping them.

He remembered vividly his last encounter in Marchmont Street, and how the Peacemaker had been at his wits' end to prevent a punitive settlement on Germany that would create a vacuum in the economy of Europe, which might end swallowing half the world. Could it be something to do with that? Or was he being fanciful to imagine anything that any handful of men could do would seriously affect the tide of history? Was this not going to be chaos whatever they did? Delusions of grandeur again, as if any of them mattered, taken alive!

They were firing behind him, the noise almost deafening. One blessing peace would bring would be silence. He trod on a patch of shifting ground and nearly lost his balance. There were shell craters all around and a low mist rising off the wet earth. Some of it stank of old gas, and the clinging odour of decay was everywhere. He thought of the clean wind in the grass off the high dales, the scent of bracken, the silence that stretched to eternity, the blue hills beyond the hills, and the bright sky.

How ironically senseless that this policeman, whoever he was, should arrest Matthew Reavley, of all men, for a barbaric murder. Matthew had been the Peacemaker's most implacable enemy, even more than Joseph. But this was one thing the Peacemaker could not have accomplished, another absurd twist of fate. This final injustice to the Reavleys was sheer, blind chance.

And yet they had never given up. He could imagine their

efforts now. They would be doing everything possible, at any cost, to prove that Matthew was innocent. They would be outraged, burning with the stupidity and fear of it, but not self-pitying, certainly not defeated.

He was passed by an ambulance taking wounded back to the nearest casualty clearing station, but it was not the one where Judith was. The tide of events had left that behind. It would be another two or three miles before he could hope to beg a lift on any vehicle.

His feet squelched in the mud and his legs ached with the effort of pulling himself out of it again and again.

The Peacemaker had begun with such high, clear ideals. They would broker peace, prevent the slaughter and ruin of war, at a relatively small price. Except that it was not a small price. They had not seen then that the lack of open war is not the same thing as peace. There are internal prices to pay that create a different kind of war, another sort of destruction. The Peacemaker had paid, principle by principle, until the crusader in him had become a tyrant, making choices for others that they would not have chosen for themselves.

Why had Mason joined him in the beginning? So that the atrocities he had seen in the Boer War would never happen again. He was heartsick at the suffering he had seen and would have made any sacrifice to prevent another single human being from enduring such loss again. Nationality was irrelevant.

But it wasn't nationality that was the issue. It was the passion and the belief of the individual, the right to rule himself in the manner of his choice, the chance to be different, funny, invent-ive, to learn anything and everything, to question, to make mistakes and to start again. And to be bloody-minded and brave and kind, like half the ordinary soldiers he had seen. And like the crewman who had given his life on the way back from Gallipoli, rather than betray the people who trusted him. Mason would never forget him. He could still see his white face in the bottom of the boat, then in the water. In the moment of his death he had become 'everyman', the ordinary British soldier, the one Joseph Reavley had said would never understand or accept the Peacemaker's world, at the price it cost.

Without realizing it Mason had quickened his step, sloshing through the mud in what he hoped was the general direction of the casualty clearing station. He must help Judith; that was one thing about which there was no question or doubt. Where he stood or what else he believed could wait until later.

# Chapter Six

Matthew stared at the rough wood walls of the inside of the hut in which he was locked. It had been a tool shed once, then used for supplies. Now it was the only place secure enough to keep a prisoner. He had been left a cot, two blankets and a pail, that was all. He could hardly believe that Jacobson really considered him guilty of having murdered Sarah Gladwyn – Sarah Price, as she now was. He had not lied; he had never connected the present army nurse with the girl he had known in university. 'I haven't thought of her from that day to this!' he had protested with absolute honesty. It was preposterous that Jacobson stood there convinced he was lying, not a shadow of uncertainty in his face.

'Hard to believe, Major Reavley,' he said almost without expression. 'Pretty girl. Doesn't look in that picture as if you'd forget each other.'

'Know lots of pretty girls, do you?' Hampton had asked, his lip very slightly curled, not so much out of scepticism as a faint contempt, an unworded suggestion of moral callousness on Matthew's part.

'Yes,' Matthew snapped. 'Actually university is full of them. Lots of them are pretty, and some are clever as well.' Instantly he wished he had not said that. It was an arrogant remark, and in the circumstances extraordinarily stupid. It was just the sort of indifference to feelings that justified their suspicion of him. The truth was that it had been an uncomfortable episode. Sarah had been pretty and fun, in a superficial way, and he had certainly been flattered that she chose him. It had had a lot to do with beating the competition, which was not a pleasing thought, and far too close to what Jacobson assumed of him.

Sarah had been easy to like, undemanding, ready to laugh. He remembered now how pretty her hair had been, soft and always shining. Her features were no more than pleasant, but she had danced marvellously, following as if she read his thoughts in every step. He blushed now to think how much he had enjoyed that, the easy movement in unison, the way she had never been heavy in his arms, never tried to lead. Poor Sarah.

He had wanted to forget it because he had not behaved well. The flattery had turned his head and he had not considered anyone else's feelings. It was one of the stupidities of youth he preferred not to recall, but that was a luxury he could not afford now.

'I behaved badly,' he admitted, staring at Jacobson. 'We were both young, and only flirting. It meant nothing in any lasting sense, just fun at the time. She moved on to somebody else, and so did I. Sarah is not an uncommon name. I didn't see her here, and I didn't connect the woman you spoke of with the girl I had known.'

Jacobson had said nothing. Hampton's face expressed his total disbelief.

Matthew walked four paces, turned and walked back again.

Jacobson had interviewed him again, briefly, but there was nothing to pursue. There was the soldier Matthew had said he'd seen, nicknamed Punch, but he had denied being anywhere near where Matthew had been. He had brought in a wounded soldier, a fifteen-year-old, but from the opposite direction, naturally, from where the fighting was.

Jacobson had pressed Matthew about his exact position in Intelligence, and what he was here for. Matthew had considered telling him, but he had nothing with him to prove it, and he had left London telling Shearing only that he had gone to collect vital information, nothing as to what it was. If Shearing read between the lines anything of the Peacemaker, he would not substantiate that to anyone, certainly not a policeman he did not know. The Peacemaker's power was far too wide and deep to take sides like that.

Matthew's rescue depended on Joseph, and Judith. The only answer was to find whoever had really killed Sarah. The huge and ugly thought that was always at the edge of his mind was that the whole trip here was the Peacemaker's last ploy before the defeat of Germany, and the end of at least this part of his plan.

Was Matthew in some way closer to him, more of a danger than he had supposed? Or was it no more than revenge for the trouble the Reavleys had caused him from the day John Reavley had found and taken the copy of the treaty, in 1914? If he had not found it, or not understood it, might there now be an Anglo-German empire across the northern half of the world? Would there have been peace, at least on the surface, even if there were terror, betrayal and suffocated lives underneath?

No, there would not have been peace. America would not have given in. It might have been crushed, with the combined weight of old Europe against it, but not without fearful cost. The bloodshed would have been terrible, perhaps eventually even as all-consuming as it was now, just in a different place, the same protagonists only on different sides. And the shame of England would have been irredeemable.

Now it was almost over. Matthew was locked up in a shed behind the front line in Belgium, and Jacobson thought he had murdered a woman. Or perhaps he knew perfectly well that he had not, but it suited the Peacemaker to have a final revenge?

If Joseph could not prove him innocent, Matthew would be tried and shot – or more ignominiously, hanged. Or possibly the men who had cared for Sarah, worked with her, and were sickened by the brutality of her death, might come and drag him out and 'accidentally' shoot him. Of course that was illegal, but what was the nicety of the law in the face of the carnage these men had seen in the last few years? Bodies of friends they had loved had been torn to pieces beside them, shattered to bloody pulp. Death was an everyday occurrence. If some of them could not bear that their brave, funny, kind friends were slaughtered while a bestial murderer was taken home to England without a scratch on him that was not hard to understand.

He paced back and forth, four steps, turn, and four steps. He must not panic, must not lose control. Come on, Joseph! Do something!

\* \* \*

Judith sat alone in an old bunker and felt the desperation almost suffocating her. It was impossible that Matthew could have killed Sarah Price, and yet Jacobson had arrested him and seemed to believe he was guilty. Perhaps he was so pressed by those senior to him to find a solution that he was grasping at one too easily. But whatever the reason, Matthew was locked in one of the few actual buildings still standing, and Jacobson and Hampton were busy collecting more evidence to close the case. There were days, at the very most, to prove him wrong, possibly only hours.

Nobody else wanted to disturb the conclusion to the police investigation. The fear was melting away, suspicions dying and the end of the war resumed its place as the most important subject.

Judith was close to panic. Apart from Joseph, the only person to whom she could turn for help was Lizzie Blaine. She trusted her, and, at the moment even more importantly than that, she knew she had the intelligence to weigh and measure answers and reason through the tangle of facts towards some truth. Joseph knew Lizzie's worth, and this gave Judith confidence in her own judgement.

She shivered and pulled her cape closer around her,

Thank goodness at least casualties were low for an hour or two. Joseph had gone forward into no-man's-land. He had had no choice, and even if he had been able to stay here, they had run out of ideas about who else to question or even what to ask.

It was mid-morning, and for once cold and dry. Judith was so tired her whole body ached, but there was no time to sleep. She had had two or three hours, and that would have to do.

She stood up slowly. She was stiff and her muscles ached. She had slept clenched up with fear and cold. She climbed up the steps, and the wind struck her as she emerged into what was left of the old trench. Lizzie was in another bunker about twenty yards along. It was better than sleeping in the open, and there was no room in the tents.

She hated wakening her, but she could not afford to waste any more time, and there was no one else to turn to. She reached the second bunker and went down the steps, which were wet and slippery, surfaced with a thin layer of clay from disuse. She pulled the remnants of the sacking curtain open. There was silence inside, and not even a candle burning. It was a respite she knew Lizzie needed, but desperation won. She went in, allowing the daylight to fall through the narrow opening.

Lizzie was curled over on the bunk, her dark hair spread out on the hard pillow and the blanket drawn up around her. She looked as if she had gone to sleep cold, and Judith felt a deeper, sharper stab of guilt.

'Lizzie,' she said quietly. Then when Lizzie did not stir, she touched her on the shoulder, gradually tightening her grip until Lizzie sat up, pushing her hair out of her eyes and answering in a level voice.

'Sorry,' Judith apologized, and she meant it. If there had been any other way she would have taken it. 'I can't afford to wait. Jacobson's looking for final evidence to send Matthew to trial. He doesn't seem to have any doubt. Apparently Matthew said he saw someone that, from his description, looked like Punch Fuller, fighting with somebody, but it was a couple of miles from where Punch says he was. He could be Matthew's only alibi for his whereabouts at the time of Sarah's murder. I have to get to the bottom of it, and I need help. There's no one else I can trust, or who is willing to think Matthew could be innocent. Everyone else just wants it to be over.'

Lizzie rubbed her eyes and drew the blanket around her shoulders. She was so tired that waking up fully took several moments. 'Was Punch Fuller injured?' she asked. 'I don't remember that. Badly?'

'No, he brought in a young soldier, about fifteen or sixteen, who was injured. Carried him.' She said the next words with difficulty. 'But he wouldn't pass anywhere near where Matthew was. That's at least a couple of miles away from where he'd come from the line to the clearing station.' It sounded even worse aloud.

Lizzie was properly awake now. 'Then there must be some other explanation,' she said. 'On the assumption that Matthew wouldn't lie, then either he was mistaken – and since he doesn't know the men here that has to be possible – or alternatively for some reason or other Punch Fuller is lying.'

'Why would he?' Judith said miserably. 'He brought in a wounded man, or boy, in this case. What is there to lie about?'

'I don't know.' Lizzie put the blanket aside and climbed out of the bunk, shivering. She started to put on her outer clothes again and reach for the brush to untangle her hair and pin it up. 'We can start by asking Cavan, and then see the boy. I can get to see him, even if you can't.' She gave a very brief smile, then turned her attention back to her hair again.

Judith felt a sense of gratitude that was almost like a physical warmth. All she could say was a simple 'thank you'. She would have to find some way of telling Lizzie how much it meant later on.

'Hodges,' Cavan answered. They were standing in the pre-operation tent. He had just come on duty after a brief rest.

In busy times the surgeons in casualty clearing stations worked eight hours on and four hours off. That way several of them could keep two or three operating tables working all the time. Cavan was freshly shaved and looked better than Judith had seen him for a few days. 'He'll be all right. It was actually not nearly as bad as it looked. I think he was shocked more than anything.'

'Punch Fuller brought him in?' Judith asked.

'Yes. He was in a pretty bad state of shock.' Cavan's face twisted with pity. 'Poor little devil's only fifteen. Had his birthday a week ago. His best friend was just ripped to pieces by a shell. Couldn't find enough of him to bury.' He said the words clearly, but his shoulders were tight and the muscles of his neck stood out like cords. 'Hodges was barely hurt, only a cut on his thigh,' he went on. 'Flesh wound, painful, but it'll heal.'

Judith was just about to ask if she could speak to the boy, then caution stopped her. Cavan had to know Matthew was her brother, and that she would do anything she could to free him. She should be more oblique, possibly even leave it to Lizzie. 'When was that?' she asked instead.

She saw the instant flash of understanding and sorrow in Cavan's face. 'It won't help, Judith. Fuller got here just after four, and I know that time's right.'

'Are you absolutely certain?' She was aware that it was futile even as she said it, but it was fear that drove her rather than reason. 'How can you be? You were very busy. Do you watch the clock? It wasn't change of shift.'

'No, of course I don't watch the clock. It wasn't change of my shift, but it was of the guards on the German prisoners, and they're pretty regular. It was just as Benbow and Eames came off and Turner and Culshaw went on.'

'You saw all of them?'

He hesitated. 'Actually I saw Eames over by the resuscitation tent and he made some remark about it being change of duty. I went back in a moment later and Punch Fuller arrived with Hodges. I know what your brother said, but Fuller couldn't have passed that way from the lines, carrying a wounded man. I'm sorry.'

Judith wanted to argue, at least offer some other reasonable explanation, but she could not think of one. Panic welled up inside her. It was all slipping out of control. Matthew could not have killed anyone, but how could she prove it? It was as if every piece of logic or evidence she touched fell to pieces. In the end she turned away without saying anything at all.

Punch Fuller had gone back up to the Front, and she had to wait an hour before Benbow and Eames were on duty again, and every minute dragged by as she grew more and more frightened. She filled the time with petty errands, probably helping little. The wind blew up harder from the east, carrying rain with it, and the grey sky leached all colour from the earth. There was nothing in sight except mud and withered tree stumps, the ungainly angles of tents and the irregular pools in old craters, pockmarked by the wind.

Finally the hour was over and she saw Benbow and Eames coming on duty, changing places with Culshaw and Turner. As soon as the patrol was handed over, she went first to Eames. She had tried to work out some clever way of introducing the subject, but he would know why she was asking, whatever she said. Perhaps complete honesty was best. It would at least save time and the wasted energy of trying to lie.

They were standing in the lee of the treatment tents, the wind rattling in the canvas. A nurse walked past them twenty feet away, her feet slithering in the mud.

'Do you remember coming off duty the night Sarah Price was killed?' Judith asked Eames after reminding him who she was.

He looked uncomfortable, but probably that was out of pity because he could not help. 'Yes. I didn't see anything, Miss Reavley, least nothing that would be any help. That policeman, Jacobson, already asked me.'

'It's times I'm really looking for,' she replied. 'When you saw Major Cavan as you were coming off duty, was that four o'clock exactly?'

'Well, I . . . I'm not sure, not for certain.' His obvious discomfort increased.

'Don't you go off duty at four o'clock?'

'Yes, but there was a bit of a scuffle earlier, an' I waited to see what it was. There was a woman yelling an' I thought one of the nurses might be in trouble, so I went to see. Think that was when I saw Major Cavan. I don't know what time that was, closer than fifteen or twenty minutes.'

'Was it Miss Price yelling?' Judith asked immediately.

Eames shook his head. 'No, it definitely wasn't, because I saw her coming away from the hut the Germans are in as I got back. She was fine, laughing and acting happy.'

Judith was puzzled. 'Then who was it?'

'Miss Robinson. She just tripped on a broken board.'

'Was it long before you changed duty?'

'About . . . I don't know . . . a while.' Now he was so awkward she was sure he was not being honest. She was not certain why. He shifted his weight from one foot to the other, and turned his collar up against the wind. 'But Miss Price was fine,' he said earnestly. 'So it doesn't matter, does it?'

'No, I suppose not,' she conceded and, to his clear relief, she went to find Benbow.

He looked less nervous, and stood to attention in the open as she asked him the same questions.

'Yes, I heard the woman shouting out,' he agreed, looking at her gravely. 'Eames went to see what it was. It did sound like someone hurt, but it turned out to be Miss Robinson, just because she slipped.'

'You didn't go?' She was not sure why she was asking. It seemed pointless, but she wanted to sound thorough.

He shook his head slightly. 'Didn't make any difference. Sarah Price went into the Germans' hut after that to see to them.' His face was bleak, as if he were thinking of what had happened to her and the anger at it was bright in his eyes.

'But she came out all right.' That was a statement. Judith already knew the answer.

'Yes. One of the Germans came out too,' Benbow added. His expression flickered. She could not read it.

'But you watched him, of course?'

'Of course.'

She could not think of anything else to ask, and finally turned to leave.

'That was the last time I saw her,' Benbow added. 'With the German. They were still together when I went off duty. She went back inside with him.' He tried hard to keep the contempt out of his eyes and his voice, but it was too deep within him, and she could not help recognizing it.

'At about quarter-past four?' she asked.

He blinked, knowing what she had read in him, defying her to make an issue of it. 'Yes.'

She swallowed hard. She understood and part of her agreed. Pity for any wounded man, British or German, was one thing; to flirt, as if nothing stood between you, no years of slaughter, was different. Respect, yes, even honour – but not laughter and trivial flirting, as if the dead did not matter.

She thanked Lance-Corporal Benbow and left, without meeting his eyes again.

She found Lizzie coming out of one of the treatment tents. Her face was pale and there was an urgency about her that made it plain she had learned something.

'What is it?' Judith demanded. Then she saw that Lizzie was suffering some acute distress, struggling within herself to make a decision. 'What is it?' Judith said more gently. 'At least tell me!'

Lizzie took her arm and steered her away from the half-open flap and out into the wind. She walked some distance until they were clearly alone before she spoke.

'I know what happened, but I don't know what to do about it,' she said almost under her breath, even though there was no one within fifty feet of them.

'Does it clear Matthew?' That was the only thing Judith cared about.

'Yes . . .'

'Then we'll tell Jacobson, and—'

'No,' Lizzie cut across her. 'And Punch Fuller isn't likely ever to change his story.'

'Yes, he will! Joseph—'

'Be quiet and listen,' Lizzie said firmly. There was a charge of emotion in her voice so intense Judith stopped.

'Hodges' friend was blown to bits beside him,' Lizzie went on. 'He was only fourteen, Hodges is just fifteen. He was sort of an older brother to him. It must have been a howitzer.' She gulped and swallowed. 'Or something like that. Hodges lost control and ran in blind horror and panic. He went all the way from where they were behind the front line, to where Matthew saw Punch Fuller catch up with him. Punch knifed him himself, to make him a genuine injury, and then carried him into the casualty clearing station as if he'd come from the front line.'

Judith nodded. She understood profoundly.

'He'll stick to that story to save the boy's life,' Lizzie went on quietly. 'If the truth gets out he'll be shot as a coward. He's only a child, for heaven's sake. The other boy was his best friend, and he feels responsible, and guilty as hell for surviving, and now for running too. He knows Punch saved his life, and he'll die rather than betray him as well. And he does look on himself as a traitor. He's terrified and so ashamed he's not sure if he even wants to survive.'

Judith was numb. 'How do you know all this?' she said hoarsely. 'If Punch wouldn't tell you, and Hodges wouldn't betray him . . . ?'

'Some I guessed,' Lizzie answered with a sigh. Her face was very white. 'His wound is superficial. And it's obviously a bayonet. A German soldier would have stabbed him in the chest or the stomach, not the leg where it really does little harm. It's not self-inflicted, but it's not battle-inflicted either. I could work it out, and then I asked him. I didn't let him lie, and I think in a way he didn't want to. His mother's probably not much older than I am. He shouldn't even be here!' There was a sudden fury in her voice so violent her body was trembling. 'If you tell that

183

story they'll shoot him. And if you don't, they'll hang Matthew, I know that!'

Judith drew in her breath, and then let it out again. 'We have to do something. Perhaps Joseph can—'

'They won't believe him,' Lizzie said reasonably. 'He's Matthew's brother. They won't believe you either. But if I go to Jacobson, he might believe me. I can't make Punch Fuller say anything, but if Jacobson wants to catch whoever really did it, he'll let Matthew go. This could prove it wasn't him.'

Judith nodded. It was a risk, appalling, cruel, inescapable, and to do nothing was worse.

Jacobson agreed. Lizzie's story corresponded exactly to what Matthew described, and he understood enough of the terror and the grief to see how it could have happened. Such things must have occurred many times before. He did not explain, he simply let Matthew go. He questioned Eames, Benbow, Cavan and several others again. Then he arrested Schenckendorff.

Joseph, Judith and Matthew sat huddled together in Joseph's bunker. Outside the rain fell steadily, dripping down the steps. The star shells were too far away to light the sky, and the flash of muzzles was invisible beyond the slight rise in the land.

'There's no point in going to London without Schenckendorff,' Judith said quietly.

'There's no point in going at all until we can tell the Prime Minister who the Peacemaker is!' Matthew answered bitterly.

'I could tell him,' Judith said.

Joseph stared at her, his face incredulous in the yellow candle-light. 'How do you know? And without Schenckendorff, why on earth would he believe you?'

'I would go to him with Father's copy of the treaty, which has the Kaiser's signature on it, and put it in front of him,' she answered. 'Then I would tell him that the Englishman who had planned it, with his German cousin, was Dermot Sandwell. Colonel von Schenckendorff couldn't come himself because he died after being injured coming through the lines.'

Matthew stared at her, his face blank with surprise for an instant, then anger and disbelief, the struggle to understand.

'Schenckendorff's alive, and getting better,' Joseph pointed out. 'Except that they'll hang him for murder. Or more likely shoot him.'

'Lloyd George won't know that.' Judith was practical.

'It can't be Sandwell,' Matthew said at last, his voice rough. 'We ruled him out. And Lloyd George certainly wouldn't believe you. I understand your frustration, Judith, but you can't fling accusations around like that.'

'It's not an accusation!' she said vehemently. 'Schenckendorff told me it was Sandwell. When we ruled him out we were wrong. He fooled us.'

'You asked Schenckendorff, and he told you?' Joseph's voice rose sharply in amazement.

'It wasn't exactly as bare as that,' she explained. 'I told him Matthew had been arrested for the murder. I think he felt guilty because Matthew wouldn't even have been here if he hadn't come to meet Schenckendorff, at his request.'

'For God's sake, Judith!' Matthew's fists were clenched, his back rigid. 'The man was prepared to tyrannize half Europe! He's not going to feel guilty that I've been wrongly accused of a crime because I came over to get him back to London.'

'Guilt is about shabbiness of behaviour, hypocrisy, not the enormity of the sin,' she answered him. 'Isn't it, Joseph?'

Joseph put his hand up in dismissal. 'I've no idea, and it doesn't matter. We don't know whether Schenckendorff is telling the truth or not. For that matter, we don't even know for certain if he is who he says he is. It's not beyond the Peacemaker's ability to get him a false identity, as much as any identity is needed by prisoners coming through the lines.'

Judith frowned. 'Do you think, this close to the armistice, that he really has time to bother with us, even to get revenge?'

'Maybe it isn't so much trouble.' Matthew looked at her, his face pinched with a fear he was struggling to hide. 'Just a single act by one German who may be desperate, and have little to lose. It was our father who ruined the Peacemaker's plans in the beginning. He won't have forgotten that, and I don't think he's a man to forgive. If you're losing, revenge may be the only sweet taste left.'

Joseph stared at the broken duckboards on the floor, and the single piece of old matting over them. 'Or perhaps Schenckendorff is completely genuine, and his realization of what the Peacemaker has become, the slow corrosion that power has worked on the morality he started with, perhaps when they were younger, and knew each other well—'

'That wouldn't account for his killing poor Sarah,' Matthew interrupted him. 'If he did that, he deserves to hang for it.' His voice was rough with emotion.

Judith knew it was for his own treatment of Sarah, and also for the whole helpless destructive path of violence and blindness that had ended alone in the dark beside the amputated limbs and human refuse of a battlefield hospital. It was no one's fault, and everyone's. The world had changed, and much of the brutality of that had altered for ever the role of women, not only for themselves but in others' eyes as well. Nothing was safe and reliable any more. Nothing could be trusted to be as it was before.

'What I was going to say is that he may be exactly what he says he is,' Joseph explained. 'But it won't have happened suddenly. The Peacemaker could have sensed it a while ago, and struck first.'

Matthew stared at him. 'You mean instead of just having him shot he set up this elaborate plan and had him blamed for Sarah's murder?' His face tightened. 'Then there's someone else here who's the Peacemaker's man! He did it, and is making it look like Schenckendorff. God Almighty! What a revenge. A German officer and aristocrat, to be hanged for murder, when really he came through the lines at hideous cost to himself, to commit the final act of honour to his principles rather than his leader.' He pushed his hand through his hair. He sighed and caught in his breath. 'That's our Peacemaker! What are we going to do?'

Joseph looked from Matthew to Judith, and back again. 'What we set out to do: find out for certain, beyond any doubt, reasonable or otherwise, who killed Sarah Price. All we're working with now is people's stories of where they were, what they were doing, who else they saw or didn't see, and what kind of a person Sarah was.' He leaned forward a little, the candlelight gold on his cheek. 'But all the time we're thinking of what he did to her.'

Matthew turned towards him. 'What do you know that we don't, Joe? There's a lot of talk about rape or mutilation, but if anyone knows, they aren't saying.'

Judith winced. She had been refusing to think further. No one had imagined the motive was anything other than sexual, but that was not the same as giving words to the act.

187

Joseph's eyes moved from one to the other of them gravely. 'It's the violation of the inner person which is unbearable,' he answered. 'The complete loss of control of your own body and its passions and needs, the core of the way in which it belongs to you. In a woman it is if she is violated by someone else; in a man it is if his own body betrays him by degrading every decency he ought to hold and turning him into a creature outside the acceptance of his fellows. We're all afraid of it. We don't know how to stop it touching the core of identity, of life. We run away from truth, we build lies that we can live with.'

Judith stared at him. What was he trying to say was bigger than she had even considered, a more painful idea. There was something in it that touched her own knowledge of passion and change, the freedom she had won here in the slaughter, and was not sure how to deal with once her carefully outlined job was over. Without an ambulance . . . uniform, who was she then?

'We need the truth,' Joseph finished, his voice half an apology. 'Whoever it hurts. It was somebody here. In finding who, we may also find a whole lot of other things we would very much rather not know. Do you believe Schenckendorff's guilty?'

'I don't know,' Matthew said.

'No,' Judith had no hesitation. 'I think, somehow or other, it's the Peacemaker.'

Judith was not called out that night, and slept on the floor of one of the outer rooms of the hospital until four in the morning when the first casualties came in. They were some considerable distance from the fighting now as it moved eastwards towards the borders of Germany itself, and there were other casualty clearing stations far closer. These men were just the excess they could not treat.

She worked helping the orderlies, carrying stretchers, assisting those able to walk a little the few steps from the ambulance to the waiting area, or from there into a theatre.

By six o'clock the worst was over. She drank a mug of hot tea and ate a heel of bread; then she went to help the nurses. She had not their skill, but she could at least fetch and carry for them and do the simpler jobs. She was prepared to sit, with a calm face and a quiet voice, with those who were beyond all practical aid. She knew Joseph did it often enough. It was a small service, but no young man should face the final darkness alone, unnoticed and with no one to say they cared.

By eight o' clock she was sharing rations with Lizzie and trying to think of what questions she could ask to strip bare the lies that were painting Schenckendorff as a murderer. She refused to accept that there were no loose ends anywhere, no one who knew something that would eventually unravel it all.

Moira Jessop joined them, sitting on an upturned empty box, with her mug in both hands. 'In a month's time we could all be home,' she said cheerfully. 'Eating proper food. Having a bath and sleeping in sheets. I'd love to be clean.' She pulled an expression of complete disgust.

Lizzie gave a slight, bleak smile.

'What's the matter with you?' Moira asked cheerfully. 'At least now we know it was a bloody Jerry who killed poor Sarah, and not one of us. We don't need to look sideways at each other any more. Or walk around in fear, for that matter. And don't pretend half of us weren't!'

Lizzie swallowed hard, but with the dryness of the bread that was not surprising. 'Half of us were afraid it would turn out to be someone we knew well, or really liked,' she said, not looking at either of them.

'Were you?' Moira's eyes opened wider. 'Who do you like, then?'

Lizzie shook her head. 'I am speaking generally.'

Judith looked at her, not just at her face but also the angle of her shoulders and body, the slightly awkward way she sat on the ammunition box, as if maintaining her balance with an effort. She didn't know that Schenckendorff was important; she probably hadn't even known his name before the evidence that implicated him. Why was she not as relieved as everyone else? Surely she had not thought she knew something, or suspected something about one of their own men? How could she have allowed Matthew to be blamed, and said nothing? To whom could she possibly owe a loyalty like that?

Moira was still talking, rattling on about going home once all the wounded had been evacuated, what it would be like in peacetime again, which hospital she would find work in in England. Lizzie was obviously not listening to her.

Judith finished her tea and stood up. 'Let's go and clean up the theatre while there's a chance,' she said to Lizzie. 'I'll help you.'

Lizzie rose a little stiffly. 'Thanks, but don't you have to do maintenance or servicing on your ambulance?'

'Not yet,' Judith said firmly. 'The theatre'll probably be needed first anyway.' She led the way and Lizzie caught up with her. It was a bright day with a hint of chill in the air. At home, late October was one of Judith's favourite times of the year, with its rich, heartaching beauty of wind-riven skies, woodsmoke, blazing colour in the leaves, bright berries. Here it was like a harvest aborted, the barren earth too full of blood to bear the fruits of autumn.

The operating tent was deserted, the surgeons and orderlies either with critical patients, or taking a brief respite, snatched sleep or some kind of food.

As soon as the flap was closed, Judith turned to Lizzie. She had no time to afford subtlety. She liked Lizzie more and more each time she saw her, and she was perfectly sure that Joseph loved her, which mattered far more. Now she was also intensely grateful to her for her courage and decisiveness in going to Jacobson and getting Matthew released.

'What is it?' she asked bluntly. 'Everyone else is thrilled that Jacobson has arrested a German, but you're not. Is there someone else you're afraid of – maybe you thought it was them?'

Lizzie lifted her chin and stared back in surprise and complete denial. 'No! If I knew anything like that don't you think I'd have told you when they were blaming Matthew? I'd have grasped at any other answer rather than tell him about Hodges.'

'Yes, of course. I'm sorry,' Judith apologized immediately. 'But something is wrong. Everybody else is relieved, and you look as if it's worse. What is it?' She was aware the instant she had said it that she was being intrusive. Nothing gave her the right or the excuse to demand answers to what might be a very private grief.

Lizzie turned away and began to tidy up the theatre, moving soiled dishes and swabs, picking up bandages and pieces of bloody cloth cut away from a wound. That would have to be done before they would even consider cleaning the blood off the floor. 'Perhaps you'd fetch some water,' she asked, head still averted, watching what she was doing, 'if you can find anything fit to use. I'll have this ready by the time you get back.'

It was dismissal. She was not going to discuss the subject. She kept on picking up, tidying, folding. She did not meet Judith's eyes at all.

Judith obeyed because she recognized that she was not going to receive an answer, and pressing it any further would make an enemy where she wanted a friend. She went looking for water. It did not have to be especially clean because it was only to swill among the worst of the blood and mud on the floor. Nothing dropped could possibly be used again without sterilizing anyway.

She walked along the boards deep in thought. Why would Lizzie not confide in her? They had spoken openly before. Even if briefly, it had been honestly. The only answer that came to her was the one she least wanted to believe. Had Lizzie realized how deep Joseph's feelings were for her, but she could not return them? Perhaps she was still grieving for her husband murdered in the summer of 1916, and she could not yet love anyone else. Theo Blaine had been brilliant, one of the finest scientists of his generation. How could Joseph equal him in her estimation?

That was a crushing thought that Judith would not tolerate. Joseph had endured enough pain with the loss of Eleanor. Lizzie knew that, and it would hurt her to have to reject him, but you could not accept someone out of pity; that would be the worst decision of all. She could not imagine anything that would be a deeper pain, because it robbed you of belief in yourself as well as the love you longed for.

She filled the pail with cold water that was too stale to drink but good enough for a floor, then carried it back to the operating tent. She opened the tent flap and banged the pail down.

Lizzie looked up at her. Her dark hair was coming out of its pins and her skin was almost drained of colour. 'Thank you,' she said quietly.

Judith was pinched by the loneliness in Lizzie's face. She looked as if she were managing not to weep only by exercising the most rigid self-control. She opened her mouth to ask again, then Lizzie took the pail and turned away, and Judith felt clumsy.

'You'll need more,' she said. 'As soon as you've used that, I'll fetch another one.'

Lizzie did not answer, as if she could not trust herself to speak.

Judith spent the rest of the day on an ambulance run, taking men who had arrived after the murder to the next hospital along the line. Wil Sloan rode with her. He too was unusually sombre. He was too busy for her to say much on the way south with the injured men, but on the way back he sat beside her as dusk mantled the fields and hid some of the scarring of the land. They moved in their own small, noisy world, their headlamps picking out only occasional ruined buildings, skeletons of walls and windows jagged and partial against the darkening sky.

'Are you still thinking about going home?' she asked him after a violent jolt on the road where she had hit an unexpected crater.

'Oh, probably. Sooner or later,' he replied. 'Longer I leave it, harder it'll be. I suppose.'

She glanced sideways but she could not see his face in the dim light. 'I didn't mean will you go, I meant, are you still worrying about it?' she corrected his misunderstanding. 'Don't. They'll be proud of you. They'll have forgotten about your quarrel. It's history. The whole world's different now.' She said it firmly, trying to think only of the positive, and convince him.

'You reckon?' He looked straight ahead.

'Of course it is! You were one of the first to come, long before the rest of America. You nailed your colours to the mast. You should remember that.'

He frowned.

'Naval term,' she explained, negotiating the next crater, but only at the last minute and throwing him off balance so he grasped at the dashboard. 'Means attaching them to the mast so you can't pull them down and surrender, no matter what.'

He smiled. She heard the amusement in his voice. 'I know that! Just because I came from the Midwest doesn't mean I know nothing about history, even if I was a thousand miles from the sea.'

'Sorry.'

He rode in silence for a while, so obviously deep in thought she did not interrupt him.

'Do you reckon someone lost his temper with Sarah 'cos she flirted with him, then wouldn't come across?' he asked as they veered round a corner and straightened up again.

Judith realized the question was deeply serious. Wil had fled his hometown originally because of a stupid quarrel in which he had lashed out, and hurt a man far more than he had intended to. He had stowed away in a railcar and gone east until he reached the coast, then taken a ship to England to join the ambulance service as a volunteer.

'Wil? Was your fight a lot worse than you're telling me? You said he was all right, just bruised and maybe a broken jaw.'

'He was.' Wil was still looking forward, as if his seeing the road would somehow make them safer. 'I was lucky. I should stop kidding myself, Judith. I could have killed him. I lost my temper – I mean really lost it. I didn't know or care what I was doing. Maybe I would do it again?'

'What made you think of that now?' she said, puzzled by the intensity of his feelings. She had never heard that before. Was she so insensitive?

'Sarah,' he replied after a moment. 'I guess I never really thought about . . . that sort of thing before. And don't tell me he just killed her, as if being British was enough. Nobody said exactly what he really did to her, but I know there was a hell of a lot of blood. I can guess. He didn't choose a woman because she was weaker . . . lots of the men are wounded and couldn't have fought back.' His face was flushed. She could see the dark colour in the occasional flashes of light. 'I can see now that all the women feel . . . embarrassed, threatened,' he went on. 'Even some of them blame her because it makes them feel that they can be safe by not doing whatever she did. Even if they are angry with all men, as if it were all our fault, when actually we've just as . . . no, I guess it's different.' He was fumbling for words, awkwardly, trying to be honest. 'We're scared of being blamed, not of it happening to us. But we're scared that it could happen to the women we like. I'm not in love with you, or anything, but I'd want to kill anyone who hurt you!' He very carefully did not look at her, even for an instant.

'Thank you,' she said gravely. She knew that he had been at least a little in love with her a year ago, but of course she did not ever want him to know that she had seen it in his eyes, his hesitation, the things he had not said. 'I would like to think you'd hate them. But nothing's going to happen to me. Not that sort of thing, anyway.'

'You reckon that German did it?'

She hated the thought of lying to him. 'I don't know. I'm not totally sure. Do you?'

'Not really,' he admitted. 'War kind of uncovers lots of things which you didn't know were there. I never knew I could get so mad at anyone that I'd want to kill them. But it was only someone else holding me back that stopped me really hurting that guy in the bar at home. Maybe whoever killed Sarah didn't have anyone to stop them, and they simply lost it . . . so bad that all the fury and the pain they'd ever felt just boiled up to the top, and by the time they got their wits back again it was too late.'

Judith could not think of an answer. She turned the idea over and over in her mind.

'I've had men tell me about fear,' Wil went on. 'Men who want to be brave and charge over the trench wall and attack, over the top, but their legs just wouldn't move. They'd soil themselves with plain physical terror. They'd have died rather than do that, but they just can't control it. Their bodies betrayed them, not their minds or their hearts.' He turned towards her. 'Could rage, or humiliation be like that too, d'you reckon? Maybe if you felt so helpless, so . . . so put down, laughed at, not as good as the rest of the guys, that you just lashed out where you could. Anything to get back to where you were in control of something, that actually you didn't see that you'd lost it for real?'

They were within a couple of miles of the trenches. The sky had cleared and a thin moon shed light on the wet road.

'Do you know who did it, Wil?' she asked quietly. 'I think you should tell the truth.'

'No I don't.' There was no hesitation or wavering in his voice.

'But I think quite a few of the men could have. The urge to have a woman can be pretty powerful, and Sarah didn't mind using how . . . how pretty she was. Put her down a bit, and she could get her own back by making you awful uncomfortable. I'm not saying that makes anything right – it doesn't,' he added quickly. 'But if you know you could die, or get so shot up so's you might as well be dead, 'cos no woman's ever going to look at you, or maybe you've been injured so you can't anyway, then you might look at things differently.'

'He didn't just rape her, Wil,' she said softly. 'He butchered her, and left her lying on the rubbish as if she were waste as well, along with the amputated limbs! That's more than even the worst frustration anyone can feel. It's hate.'

He sat very still, letting out his breath slowly. 'Jesus! I didn't know that . . .' He was breathing hard and for a moment he sounded as if he was going to be sick.

'Wil?' She turned to look at him, and drove wildly close to the edge of the road, sending the ambulance bucking and slewing across the craters. She pulled up sharply. 'Sorry.'

'I didn't do it, Judith!' he said haltingly. 'I just know that everybody's scared, not only the women.' He wiped the back of his hand across his mouth.

'Do you know if anyone is lying to protect someone else?' she asked him. 'Maybe someone they owe a really big debt, like having pulled them off the wire, or carried them back from no-man's-land? That would be something you'd pay for for the rest of your life, isn't it?'

'Yes,' he agreed. 'That's why pretty well everyone's happy to think it's one of the Jerries.'

'But what if it isn't?' she insisted. 'We can't hang somebody who didn't do it because it's convenient. Surely to God we are better than that?'

'It isn't that easy,' he replied. 'Haven't you ever owed anybody something? Something so big you can hardly breathe for the weight of it. You have to pay debts like that. You have no choice.'

'You know something, Wil!'

'I hear wounded men talk,' he admitted. 'You don't, because you're up here driving, but I spend a lot of time with some of them.'

'What do you know? I'm not moving until you tell me.'

'I can walk back from here better than you can.'

'Wil!' she protested desperately.

'I know how some of the men feel,' he answered. 'That's all. I told you, I don't know who did it. I don't. Hell, Judith, if I did I'd have said when they had your brother!'

'Yes. Yes, I know.' She eased the engine into gear again and straightened the wheels on the rutted road. They still had over a mile and a half to go.

When Judith pulled the ambulance in and parked it, Wil went to help the orderlies with the new wounded, and she began the usual maintenance of the vehicle. She was in the back tidying and cleaning the stretchers and sweeping the floor when she heard footsteps outside in the mud, and a moment later a shadow blocked the light at the door.

She looked up and saw a familiar silhouette that made her heart jolt and her stomach tighten far more than she wished. She wanted to be in control of her emotions, but as Wil had said, her body let her down. She was hot and cold at once, and her hands were clammy.

'Can I help you?' Mason asked.

'Not really, thank you. I'm just about finished,' she said a trifle more coolly than she had intended. Although perhaps it was for the best. She did not want to hope, or imagine that she could see in him a tenderness or a belief that was not there. 'What's the news from the Front? Where are we now?'

'About two miles from Tournai, the last I heard,' he replied. 'The fighting's still pretty heavy.'

'Yes, I know. We're still getting quite a few of the casualties.'

'I heard you found the man who murdered the nurse. It was one of the Germans.'

She kept on looking at the ambulance stretchers, even though there was nothing more to do to them. 'They've arrested him, but they haven't collected all the evidence to charge him yet. He's under guard more to protect him, I think.'

Mason was silent for a moment or two. She stepped out of the ambulance, taking his hand because he offered it, and it would have been pointed had she refused it. She found herself absurdly self-conscious. His physical nearness intruded on her concentration and she was angry with herself for allowing it.

'But he did it?' he said at last as she closed the doors and they walked towards the tent where there was most likely to be hot tea. The night had closed in and the wind was harder and colder from the east.

'I don't know.' She knew the admission would leave questions he would be bound to ask, and answers that would betray more of her emotion than she wanted to share, but she refused to lie to him.

They were inside before he replied. 'You don't think he did, do you?' That was a challenge. 'Why? Because you're afraid it's what everybody wants?'

'No. I . . .' What could she say that made any sense, and yet did not betray who Schenckendorff was? That she could not do, whatever lies it cost. She was already bitterly aware of Mason's dark view of war's futility and the senseless pain of it. She had seen that bitterly and inescapably after the court martial last year. The hurt of realizing that he did not share any of her faith – blind, admittedly – in some kind of inner victory, was cut too deep into her mind ever to forget, even for a moment. There was a shadow inside him that separated them, no matter how much she liked him, or even loved him. Joseph had said he would never make her happy. She had momentarily hated Joseph for that, probably because in the depths of her belief, the passion and the light that made her who she was, she already knew it was true.

Mason was waiting. There was an urgency and a gentleness in his eyes that she had not seen before. He was waiting for her to speak, wanting to understand.

She started with the truth. 'I talked to him quite a lot. I was helping one of the nurses. Before he was accused, of course. His foot was pretty badly injured, but apparently he could stand on it. I've seen men do extraordinary things when they were so terribly wounded you wouldn't have expected them to live, let alone crawl for miles, or fight. There just . . . wasn't any anger in him. You must have to be terribly angry to rape, and then kill.'

He studied her face. She felt increasingly self-conscious but she did not look away. She had to force emotion away from herself, crush the hope inside, in case he saw it and understood. Friendship was everything – she would give him that – but love was far too dangerous, too consuming of reason, judgement, the courage or purpose to go on after it was betrayed.

'What are you going to do about it?' he asked finally.

That was not at all what she had expected him to say. She had been waiting for an argument as to why she should leave the matter to the police. She looked for mockery in him, and saw none.

'Try and find out who is lying to protect someone else, before they take Schenckendorff away,' she answered. 'Everybody's afraid, and there are . . . loyalties, debts that seem bigger than blame for a crime. We all want to end it in whatever way is least painful to us.' She thought of Wil as she said it. She was still aching with surprise at the depths of himself he had trusted her with. She had been blind to much of him beyond his easy, smiling face, his good humour, the way she could rely on him always being there. How many other people had she not bothered to understand?

'We've faced so much together we think we know each other,' she went on. 'But we don't. We know the duties, the courage, and the personal habits. We probably wouldn't even recognize each other on the street in civilian life, when you can wear what you want, choose your work – or at least some of it – make whatever friends you like. Here friendship is the one sure sanity. Do you think it'll last, afterwards?' The answer to that mattered more than almost anything else. She had not even dared ask it before. She should have asked Joseph, or Wil, not Mason. What sort of answer did she expect? Perhaps the loneliness was what all of them were afraid of, after this was all over. And for her it was even worse than for many others. She could never go back to the life she had once expected, to domestic happiness like Hannah's, or her mother's, no matter how much she loved anyone, even Mason. And would any man love the kind of woman she had become? War had released her. She was something better or worse, but forever different.

'Some friendships will always last.' Mason did not waver from her gaze when he said it. 'The good ones. Sometimes we'll want to forget this, but at other times we'll need to remember, because we've seen things other people can't even imagine. Who else would we share it with? You can't tell anyone.' She stared at him. 'We'll need somebody who understands why we laugh and cry when we do,' he went on. 'Why we look at a tree in bloom and can't take our eyes off it. Why cruelty to a horse makes us want to beat the person who did it until they can't stand. And why we sometimes feel guilty to be alive and whole, when so many of the best men we knew are here under the mud, and will never come home.'

She nodded, aching with too much memory and sorrow to speak. She put out her hand and touched his face, then self-consciously snatched it away again.

He smiled slowly, and the hope in his eyes dazzled her.

The following day Judith drove more men south and west to larger hospitals. She was only just pulling in at the casualty clearing station when Joseph came splashing across the mud towards her, his face drawn with anxiety.

She scrambled out. 'What is it?'

'They're sending Schenckendorff out the day after tomorrow,' he said desperately. 'In roughly thirty-six hours. They'll try him immediately and he'll be hanged.' He did not add all the other things that were racing through both their minds. Was he guilty or innocent? Did he really know who the Peacemaker was? Was he telling the truth, and the Peacemaker had deliberately engineered this way of having an exquisite revenge? Or was he lying, to make them all try to expose the wrong man, perhaps destroying him, and freeing the real Peacemaker? Or was it all coincidental, the ultimate farce of the whole affair?

# Chapter Seven

Judith sat on the cot in her bunker and tried to think. Nothing made any sense that was absolute and unarguable. Every possibility they had thought of depended upon so many accounts that might be lies or mistakes that it dissolved the moment they tried to prove it.

Now it seemed Sarah must have been killed later than they had thought, if Benbow really had seen her after four o'clock. Yet from the state of the body, the blood, her coldness, when she was found at half-past six, she had already been dead at least two hours. So she must have been killed between four and half-past.

Were any of the guards telling less than the exact truth, intentionally or not? Any of them could have been alone for a while, if the other had been called away by some alarm or emergency; and if both had, then it was at least possible that any of the wounded Germans who were able to walk, other than just

Schenckendorff, could have come out of the hut and killed Sarah. If she had jeered at them about what would happen to their women, that could be reason enough.

Judith shivered. Inside the bunker was sheltered from the wind, but it was small, enclosed in the earth like a tomb, and the clay always seemed to carry the damp with it. It smelled stale and cold.

How long did it take a man to rape a woman and then slash at her with a bayonet? Judith had no practical experience anywhere near such an area of behaviour, even to guess. Surely it had to be ten minutes or a quarter of an hour at least? Joseph had seen the body but he had refused to discuss it, which was ridiculous in a way. Judith was an ambulance driver; there was not any kind of death or mutilation she had not seen. Except, of course, deliberate sexual violation of a woman.

She went over it in her mind. Between four and five o'clock most people were so thoroughly accounted for that they need not be considered. Tiddly Wop Andrews had been walking wounded, with a bad slash in his side, but once it was cleaned, stitched and bound up – which had been done well before three o'clock – he had been in the resuscitation tent, and Cully Teversham had sworn to that. He had been in to see his brother, Whoopy, had been struck by shrapnel in his leg and side. Allie Robinson had accounted for Cavan for all but a few minutes here and there, certainly not long enough to have found Sarah, raped her and killed her. Not that Judith had ever imagined that Cavan could be guilty.

The guards, Culshaw and Turner, had accounted for each other, but that meant almost nothing. Snowy Nunn had been in because he had brought in Stan Tidyman, who had lost his leg.

Snowy had accounted for Barshey Gee, injured in his left shoulder and with the skin torn open on the side of his head, also walking wounded.

Except that was the heart of the problem. Barshey Gee had not been in the tent where Snowy said he was, not all the time, because Judith herself had seen him at quarter-past four outside near the entrance to one of the old connecting trenches. He was a long way from where Sarah had been killed, but it meant Snowy was lying to protect him.

And she knew this because she had been there herself, not where she said she had been when she had lied to protect Wil Sloan.

How many other people were lying to protect someone they knew and trusted, and were convinced, beyond even the remotest question, was innocent? And one of them was wrong!

She sat motionless and cold, exhausted by the hopeless tangle of it. Before Matthew and Joseph had gone, they had even talked of the possibility of Matthew racing back to London and trying to persuade Shearing to intervene, claim some sort of intelligence coup that would override even the needs of justice. But how could they persuade Shearing that Dermot Sandwell was the Peacemaker, and on the brink of sabotaging the armistice agreement? They were not even sure of it themselves.

There was a sound of light footsteps outside, and the sacking moved. 'May I come in?' It was Lizzie's voice, tight and weary.

Judith looked up. 'Of course.' Then instantly she regretted it. Just now she had no patience for anyone else. Her mind was eaten up with endless, fruitless anxiety.

'What is it?' she asked as Lizzie came down the steps and let the sacking fall closed behind her. Judith stood up. In the light of the one lamp Lizzie was white-faced, almost haggard. She sat down on the cot as if not certain her legs would support her much longer.

'They're saying that the German will be taken away in a day or so,' she said hoarsely. 'What will they do with him?'

'Try him, and then hang him,' Judith replied. The words hurt to say; there was a despair in them that she had not fully acknowledged before.

'Hanged?' Lizzie whispered. She tried to swallow and could not. Her mouth was too dry. 'But . . .'

'They believe he is guilty of a terrible crime,' Judith said harshly. 'Someone raped Sarah with a bayonet and hacked her to death. Nobody's saying that because they're trying to keep it quiet – prevent panic, or acts of revenge. But it's true. Then they left her lying like a whore, legs wide, in among the refuse. Don't you think whoever did that deserves to hang?'

'If you hang someone, and then discover you were wrong . . .' Lizzie's voice faded away and she sat down suddenly, her eyes wide and hollow, as if she were looking inward at something unbearable.

Was it possible Joseph had broken his secrecy and told her about Schenckendorff, and the Peacemaker? Judith sat on the other bunk and leaned forward. 'Lizzie . . .'

It was as if Lizzie could not hear her.

'Lizzie,' she repeated urgently, 'did Joseph tell you that . . . ?' she stopped. At mention of Joseph's name Lizzie had winced. The movement was almost too small to see, but it was as if the misery inside her had increased. Why would she feel such desperate pain if they exposed the Peacemaker, or if they failed? Did Lizzie know more of the truth than they did? Judith refused to believe that.

Lizzie was exactly what she seemed to be. Judith told herself she must not allow the Peacemaker and the suspicions he awoke to poison everything.

Lizzie sat frozen, her knuckles white. Very gently Judith put her hand over Lizzie's, without closing it. 'I think you'd better tell me. Is Schenckendorff guilty?'

Lizzie shook her head so slightly it was barely a movement at all.

'Are you sure?' Judith asked.

'Yes.' It was forced, as if her throat were raw.

'Who did?'

'I don't know.' Lizzie met Judith's eyes at last. 'I really don't. I have no idea. It just isn't Schenckendorff.'

'If you don't know who it is, how can you know it isn't him?' Judith asked. 'That doesn't make sense.'

Lizzie did not answer.

Judith waited. The bunker was silent, nothing moved. Outside boots squelched in the ruts of mud and voices came from far away.

At last Lizzie took a deep, hollow breath and let it out very slowly, then another. 'Because someone else was raped before Schenckendorff came through the lines.'

'Someone else! Are you sure?' Then like a hand of ice inside her, Judith realized what Lizzie had really said. She put her arms around Lizzie's shoulders and clung on to her, longing to be able to comfort her and knowing it was impossible. What ease of any kind could there be? She had been violated beyond imagination. How must she have felt when Sarah's body was discovered, and she knew the man who had raped her had been capable of such a thing?

Moments ticked by. They seemed frozen. Then Lizzie pushed Judith away and put her hands up over her face, the heels of her palms pushing into her eyes. 'It was dark. I honestly didn't see his face. But that isn't the worst of it,' her voice broke. She was shaking so badly her teeth chattered together. 'I'm pregnant.'

It was obscene. 'You can't know!' Judith told her. 'It's too soon! Maybe—'

'I am! It was over a month ago.'

'Over . . . then it was before Matthew came here! You knew it couldn't have been him either! Would you have let them hang him?'

'No . . . no, of course I wouldn't. If you hadn't been able to prove it wasn't him, I'd have told.' Lizzie looked up, her eyes swimming with tears. 'Do you have to tell Joseph? He . . . he'll never have me – not now . . .'

Judith felt bruised inside by the ache of pity. It was like a great swelling pain that drowned out everything else. She understood perfectly. Had it been she who had been invaded, soiled, terrified in such an unforgettable way so that her very core was no longer secret and safe, no longer even her own, she would not have wanted the man she loved ever to know it. She would have nursed it to herself, angry, confused and terribly, desperately alone.

Then she was furious. Rage scalded up inside her that any woman should be so brutalized and made to feel ashamed, as if it were her fault, so that she dared not even report the crime. It was not only the things the men said – far from it: it was what the women said every bit as much. Fear for themselves made their blame ruthless.

If it had happened to her, she could have said she ran the

ambulance off the road, or fell with a stretcher, anything to explain the cuts or bruises so no one ever knew what had happened inside her. In time they would have healed, and she might have forgotten – at least on the surface.

But what if she were pregnant? There would be no forgetting that! Unmarried, with child. Lizzie had not even any family. What was the use of winning the war here, if a woman dared not report being raped, and was left to bear the rapist's child alone?

Jacobson was not a bad man, not crude or violent, and yet when he had questioned Judith he had accused her of lying. He had assumed her a victim who would not admit it, and she had been outraged by it, even though it was not true. What would he assume of Lizzie? Would he even begin to understand why she had hidden it?

She bent down and took Lizzie's hands, only lightly, just to touch, not imprison. 'Don't tell anyone yet,' she said gently. 'We may find a better way. Don't do anything. I won't leave you alone in this, now or later.'

Even as she said the words she had no idea what she was going to do. No one else would know now, but in another two or three months it would be obvious. What would she say to Joseph then? She remembered his grief over Eleanor's death, and their unborn child. He had seemed to be numb with it, as if his heart were paralysed. After all the other losses, how could he endure this? It had seemed as if he and Lizzie were on the brink of happiness at last, and it had been snatched from them and broken into too many pieces for them even to find, let alone mend.

The grief was like watching someone you love fight for breath, struggle, and lose. She did not know what to do but kneel down and hold Lizzie close to her and let the moments pass by.

She did not even think how long it was before Lizzie finally pulled away and stood up. She said nothing. Her lips trembled and her eyes filled with tears. Then she shook herself impatiently. There was no time for weeping now.

'Thank you,' she said, her voice cracking. Then she turned and climbed up the steps past the sacking and into the cold air outside.

Judith knew that she had to tell Matthew alone. Joseph would have to know one day, but not yet, maybe not for a long time. Perhaps it would be better when they were all home, the Peacemaker was exposed and the old wounds of loss were beginning to heal. Lizzie might not bear the child. With all the fears and the violence of war, the physical deprivations, she might miscarry. Most women did not consider themselves secure in a pregnancy until after the first two or three months. She might even have the luxury of not having to tell Joseph at all. Certainly it did not have to be now.

All this turned over in her mind as she searched for the opportunity to speak to Matthew where she could be certain of being alone and uninterrupted.

She found him asleep in the bunker, when she knew Joseph had briefly gone forward towards the front line to help the stretcher-bearers. In spite of the desperate need to prove Schenckendorff innocent, that was a duty he could not abandon. They were his men from the farms and villages around Selborne St Giles. Some of them were critically wounded and might die. You could never tell; a man who appeared to have no more than a piece of shrapnel through the flesh might be so weak from exhaustion that the shock and loss of blood killed him, or the cold. Sometimes there were other wounds, masked by lesser injuries that had torn the skin and produced more obvious lacerated flesh.

Judith went down the steps, into the dark. She knew where the lamp was, and fumbled lighting it. Then she set it on the table Joseph used for writing letters of condolence, and love letters for those who found the words awkward or were clumsy with the pen, or too wounded to hold it at all.

Matthew was asleep. He did not even stir. He was curled over uncomfortably on the narrow cot, his fair hair rumpled. It was longer than a soldier's should be, but then he was used to a different kind of battle. This was not his arena. He had to outthink, outwit, and outimagine; not struggle through the mud with a rifle and bayonet, and with food, water and ammunition on his back.

She touched him gently, and when he did not stir, more firmly. He grunted, still deeply asleep. But there was no time for allowing him to rest. This would not wait on comfort, not even on need. 'Matthew!'

He opened his eyes and focused with difficulty. He searched her face for grief. When he saw neither he breathed out slowly. He had been afraid she had come to say Joseph was hurt, or even killed. It was the fear all of them lived with, all the time. It was the first thought with every startled awakening.

'Sorry,' she apologized. 'I have to speak to you while I know Joseph is away.'

'Why?' He sat up slowly, swinging his legs over the side. He was fully dressed, apart from his boots, as they all were. It was too cold to think of anything else, and all awakenings could be sudden. 'What's happened? Do you know something?'

There was no point in trying to soften it. She sat on the one chair. 'Schenckendorff couldn't be guilty,' she told him. 'There was at least one rape before he even got here. Apparently it was sufficiently like Sarah's that it pretty well had to be the same person. Less violent, of course, because she's still alive, just bruised pretty badly. Maybe Sarah fought more, which I suppose is stupid. Or perhaps he's just getting worse. The first was over a month ago.'

He blinked. 'Are you sure? It wasn't reported. Why is she speaking out now? It won't be to clear Schenckendorff; it could be to protect somebody else who might have come recently.' His mouth pulled down at the corners. 'Obviously not me. We've stirred up something of a hornet's nest by starting asking questions again. I've pushed one or two people pretty hard. So has Joe.'

'It's the truth,' she said softly. Even now, knowing the necessity, she hated having to tell him. If she could, she would have protected Lizzie against anyone at all from knowing.

His eyes widened in sudden, chilling horror. 'Judith?'

'No!' she said instantly. 'Not me! For God's sake, Matthew! Do you think I'd have let you be blamed if it were?' She sighed, swallowing hard. 'It's Lizzie Blaine. And she's pregnant.'

His shoulders hunched and he put his hand up to push his hair back, and rubbed his eyes hard, as if they hurt. He swore with deep, wrenching anger. 'Does Joseph know?' he said at last, looking back up at her.

'No. That's why I'm telling you now, while he's away,' she explained. 'She doesn't want him to, in case . . . in case it's more than he can bear. She loves him, and she's terrified it will turn him from her, or that what was love will become pity.'

He shook his head slowly from side to side. 'Judith, he's going to have to know! You can't . . . she's not going to lie about it, is she?' He tried to keep the emotion out of his voice, and failed.

'No, I don't think she'd do that, although I couldn't blame her if she did. How could she love the child, knowing how it was conceived? She's going to need a lot of help, Matthew.' She stared at him, needing to see that he understood. 'All that we can give her. I don't think she's got anyone else. First she has her husband murdered, now this! And if she loses Joseph it's going to hurt like hell. But after Eleanor and the baby, then Mother and Father, Sebastian Allard, and all the other friends since, especially Sam Wetherall, can Joseph take this as well?' She wanted him to reassure her, tell her that Joseph would be all right, that he would accept it and be strong. Perhaps if he tried hard enough he could even make Lizzie believe it.

He sat still on the edge of the cot, struggling for the answer. Finally he lifted his shoulders a tiny fraction. 'I don't know,' he admitted. 'But we can't tell him, I'm certain of that. Not yet. She doesn't need his pain to deal with as well as her own. In fact maybe she doesn't need to know you've told me. Do whatever you think right on that. Just let me know.'

She nodded, uncertain what the answer would be, and glad to have the freedom to judge for herself.

'But we know for certain now that Schenckendorff's innocent,' he went on. 'Which doesn't mean he's everything he says he is regarding the Peacemaker, but there's no way we can put that to the proof until we get to London. We have to assume he is, and get him there. I'd rather make an almighty fool of myself by trying and being proved wrong, than be a coward who could have caught the Peacemaker but hadn't the guts to put it to the test. What we'll lose as fools will be personal, and relatively little, compared with what Europe will lose if we were right, and did nothing.'

'And we need to find whoever did kill Sarah Price,' Judith added. 'He's still around.'

'The police can do that,' Matthew replied.

She looked at him, frowning. 'I don't think that's enough for Lizzie,' she answered. 'If it were me, I'd want to be sure he was put away, not for revenge, but so I was absolutely positive he wouldn't ever come after me again.'

He raised his eyes, wide with horror. 'God Almighty! I never even thought of that. Poor Lizzie.' He reached across suddenly and put his hand on Judith's. 'We will find him, I promise you.'

After Judith had gone, Matthew sat still on the edge of the cot for several minutes. The oil lamp flickered on the table, lighting the earth walls boarded up to stop them from collapsing in, the bookcase hastily knocked together out of packing cases and filled with Joseph's books, and on the wall the copy of Dante's portrait from his study at St John's. How would he bear knowing that Lizzie had been another victim of the rapist? Matthew hugged the thought of it inside him like a wound too deep to let go, in case it bled away all the strength he had.

He and Judith could work all they liked, every hour, without sleep, but he knew they would find it hard to learn anything sufficient to stop Jacobson shipping Schenckendorff out. He had promised to do it because he wanted to, and to comfort her, not because he really believed it was possible. He could not tell Joseph anything. His brother would know he was being lied to, at least partially, would work out some of the truth, and then finally worry the rest. They needed help other than his, but who else had the kind of mind that could detect and deduce, and was not bound by the loyalties or debts that crippled everyone else?'

The answer was clear even before the question was complete in his mind. It had to be Richard Mason. Judith might immeasurably prefer that they did not involve him, but circumstances had left them no choice. Matthew stood up slowly, his back stiff from the hard cot and the cold, and put on his boots. It was two o' clock in the morning, but he could not wait until dawn.

Mason was going back and forth from the front line to the casualty clearing station, writing dispatches about the work saving men critically injured in the last few weeks of the war. There was an irony to serving right to the eve of peace, and then losing sight or limbs when victory was perhaps no more than days away. And yet he had found little bitterness. Again and again he was humbled by the courage of men, and infuriated that the whole insane horror and loss of it had ever happened.

Most of the officers who had lived in these bunkers for so long were now either injured or dead, or had gone forward with the regiment over no-man's-land to the abandoned German trenches. These were better than those of the British. He had seen them himself: deeper below the ground, drier, many with electric lighting and something approaching comfort.

Of course the forward lines were beyond them too now, covering the ground rapidly, an army most often in the open, striving to keep rations and ammunitions moving along the stretched supply lines.

He had gone to sleep forcing the fighting men out of his mind and thinking instead of Judith. He woke with a start to hear a man's voice speaking his name urgently. A moment later there was a hand on his shoulder. He opened his eyes to see the oil lamp on the table burning and Matthew Reavley sitting on the upturned ammunition box that served as a chair. There was stubble on his chin and his eyes were red-rimmed, but he was very much awake.

Mason sat up slowly. 'What is it?' he asked, fear fluttering inside him. 'What's happened?' He did not bother to ask how Matthew had found him, since many people knew where he was.

'We need your help,' Matthew replied. 'I need to explain why, so please just listen. We can't trust anyone else and I wouldn't trust you if I had any choice, but I don't. I've watched you with Judith, and I can see how you feel about her. We have a very short time and we can't do this alone.'

Mason had no idea what he was talking about. 'Do what?'

'Find out beyond doubt who killed Sarah Price.'

'The German. Jacobson's almost ready to charge him,' Mason responded, knowing even as he said it that there must be something far deeper that Matthew meant. 'Is it an intelligence job?' Ironic if now that it was too late, and he had effectively left the Peacemaker's side, he might at last be trusted with information deeper than the obvious.

'I suppose it is,' Matthew answered. 'But it's also personal. Schenckendorff is innocent, at least of killing Sarah Price. I can't tell you how I know, but I do. What I need you to know now is something quite different, and which started a long time ago.'

Mason felt a chill of apprehension and dismissed it as absurd. It could not have anything to do with him. 'Yes?'

Matthew seemed still to be having difficulty finding the words, and Mason became aware of the intensity of emotion in him.

'In nineteen fourteen,' Matthew began, 'my father found a

copy of a treaty between England and Germany which could have prevented the war, but at the cost of initially betraying France and Belgium, and eventually just about everybody.'

Mason felt the semi-darkness of the bunker sway around him and blur as if he were going to faint. He knew with a hideous certainty what was coming next, but to hear it from Matthew himself, laden with his grief, gave it a reality it had never had for him before. For the first time he was face to face with what he had allowed to be done.

'It was signed by the Kaiser, but not yet by the King,' Matthew went on. 'Father understood what it would mean, and he was bringing it to me in London when he and my mother were killed in a car crash. Joseph and I discovered quite quickly that it was actually murder. A young man, a student of Joseph's, of high but blind ideals, had been persuaded to sabotage the road they were travelling on. It cost him his own life, and eventually his brother's also, and naturally his family's ruin.'

Mason's mouth was dry, his throat tight. He could not have spoken even if he could have thought of anything to say.

'The man behind it –' Matthew went on – 'we called him the Peacemaker, because we had no idea of his identity – continued to campaign against Britain and the Allies even though the war—'

Mason started to protest, and bit the words off, ending as if he had choked on his own breath.

Matthew had no idea of the turmoil inside him. He continued, lost in his own anger and grief. 'He was always trying to bring the war to an end while both sides were still strong enough to ally together in an Anglo-German empire that could dominate most of the world. It would be peace, but without any passion or individuality, any freedom to think and question, to be different, to dare new ideas, or complain against stupidity or injustice, to question or work or laugh aloud. It would be the peace of death.'

Again Mason drew breath to interrupt, but here in this bunker dug out of the Flanders earth where so many men had died hideously, all rational justification of such grandiose philosophical issues seemed not only vaguely obscene, but divorced from any kind of reality. It had once been the hope for a better, saner world, a way of avoiding all this wealth of loss. Now it looked like the arrogance of a lunatic, and as doomed as all madmen's dreams.

'The Peacemaker went on murdering,' Matthew continued quietly. 'General Cullingford; Gustavus Tempany: indirectly Theo Blaine, one of the best scientists we ever had. Perhaps even worse than murder was the corruption, and you could call that murder of the soul. Except, of course, we have to allow it ourselves before we can be corrupted. We collude in our own destruction there.'

Mason still did not answer. Everything Matthew was saying was a world from the high ideals with which he and the Peacemaker had begun, but Matthew had not seen South Africa in the Boer War: the slaughter of men; the caging of women and children in camps, starving and imprisoned. He had had no conception of what total war was like, before this.

He looked up at Matthew's face in the lamplight. 'If you had known, in nineteen fourteen, what this would have been like, the sheer, overwhelming horror of it, would you have tried to stop it?' he asked, then wished he had not. He sounded like an apologist for the Peacemaker, and he was frightened by how powerful the compulsion was within him to be honest, to cleanse himself from lies. But he had asked, and he had to wait for the answer.

Matthew looked surprised. 'Maybe,' he admitted. 'I don't know. If I had, I hope it would have been openly, without betrayal. But it would have been futile. The balance of power was fatally flawed in Europe. We could never have bought peace without coercion, and oppression. The Austro-Hungarian Empire was collapsing from within. So was Russia, in its own way. If you are asking me if I could see that at the time, no, of course not, not clearly enough to have done anything useful about it. Could you?'

'No. But I might have thought I could,' Mason had already come closer to honesty than he should have. 'What is this to do with finding out who murdered Sarah Price?'

'The Peacemaker hasn't given up yet,' Matthew said with a jerky little laugh. 'He's still in power, and there's the armistice and its terms to negotiate, and all the peace after that to fight for. If we get it wrong we could sow the seeds of another war just as terrible as this.'

'Didn't you say he wanted peace?' Mason asked, remembering everything the Peacemaker had said about crushing German industry and creating a huge vacuum in the economy of Europe, which might suck them all in and consume them.

'Peace on his terms,' Matthew amended. 'He still hasn't learned that you can't force people without at the same time destroying them. He may well be an idealist, but that does not excuse the lies, or the betrayal of trust. It is the final arrogance to blind us so he can lead us whatever way he will, and we would have no power to resist. The fact that he believes he is right is irrelevant. We all believe we are right. Some of us even are.'

Mason smiled very slightly, with only a gesture of the lips. 'You want the right to go to hell in your own fashion?'

The shadow of humour touched Matthew's face as well, uncertainly. 'If you like to put it that way, yes. The point is, one of the Peacemaker's allies in Germany has come through the lines, and is willing to come to London and identify him to Lloyd George.'

Mason now saw with hideous clarity what Matthew was doing here in the front line, and why he cared so intensely that Schenckendorff was not executed for a crime he had apparently not committed. Possibly even if he had committed it, the price was too great, at least to the Reavleys. Mason wondered what Joseph thought of it.

Matthew mistook his silence. 'I know it's not simple,' he said earnestly. 'Much that the Peacemaker wanted is right, and perhaps to begin with he was the most far-sighted, the sanest of us all, but he usurped power to which he had no right. He is a man fatally flawed by the weakness to abuse it. Right or wrong in his vision, he can't be trusted not to betray, to kill, to corrupt in order to keep that power in his own hands. And once he has it, it's too late to change if you find you have no way to control him, or to take it back from him.

'Our war was worse than anything we could have imagined,' Matthew went on, still watching Mason intently. 'But what would his empire have been? And how long might it have lasted? I don't know. We didn't make the choice, seeing all the way; no one ever does. We do it step by step, doing our best with each one, trying to see where it will lead. Sometimes we're wrong. But to decide for others, against their will, has to be an arrogance we can't allow. That kind of power is more than any man has the wisdom or the morality to handle, or to give up when he should.'

Mason was desperately tempted to ease his hammering

conscience by telling the truth of his own part in it. He longed to explain what he had seen in Africa and why he had tried so desperately to stop it happening again; why he had seen the same vision as the Peacemaker, and believed in him. It would be a relief to speak honestly, justify at least his beliefs, however they had ended. But it was a luxury he could not afford: a selfishness to ease his own burden of guilt. It was an excuse too small for the cause, and the immeasurable sacrifice of others. Mere discomfort was so trivial it would be obscene to mention it.

He looked up at last and met Matthew's eyes. 'So that's why you need to get Schenckendorff off this charge, and to London. What can I do to help?' He could have told them who the Peacemaker was, but he would have to tell them how he knew, and why should they believe him? It would appear entirely self-serving. The Peacemaker would deny it. Of course he would. Mason was stunned at his own gullibility; even now he had no proof. There was not and had never been anything in writing. The Peacemaker had always said it was for the protection of them both, above all of the cause; but perhaps primarily it was for his own safety. He trusted no one. It was oddly painful to understand now that that had always included Mason himself.

If the Reavleys knew his part in it all, they would not dare to trust him. They would not know how totally he had at last understood what he had done, and seen it in its futility, its final ugliness.

He must tell them nothing, however the guilt twisted inside him, and set him apart and alone.

'Help us find and prove who killed Sarah Price,' Matthew told him. 'Or at least demonstrate irrefutably that it wasn't Schenckendorff.'

Mason's decision was without shadow. It was a long path back, one he might never complete, but he knew how to begin. 'When do we start?'

Joseph returned from the front line with more wounded. As soon as he had seen them into the orderlies' care he went to Matthew. They stood together in the evening light as it splashed red and pink over the puddles across what had been no-man's-land. It was one of the few places where they would be uninterrupted.

'It isn't Schenckendorff,' Matthew said. 'But we're not much closer to knowing who it is.'

'I didn't think it was him,' Joseph replied unhappily, staring across the now gaudy mud. The sunset burned in the sky to the north-west. Perhaps it was foolish, but he had hoped for something more definite than that. He was weary, his body ached and he had several gashes on his arms from old barbed wire still embedded in the clay. 'Doesn't it help with proving who did it? How are you certain?' Then he asked the question to which he would rather not have had to know the answer. 'Who lied?'

Matthew's face was almost invisible in the shadows, but his voice was pinched. 'I know because one of the other women was raped violently, almost a month before Schenckendorff came through the lines.'

Joseph drew in his breath, only beginning to imagine the horror of it.

'Don't ask me who,' Matthew said quickly. 'I can't tell you. I believe it, that's all that's necessary for anyone else to know.'

'I see. Poor woman.' Joseph could understand very easily why the only chance for healing might lie in anonymity, the certainty that none of her friends or colleagues were ever aware it had happened, still less that she was the victim. 'Can you help her?' He understood also why she had chosen Matthew, a relative stranger, to tell. She might find it too difficult, too humiliating, if it were a man she knew, even the chaplain.

'I'll try.' Matthew seemed happy to dismiss the subject, at least for the present.

Joseph saw Lizzie very briefly during the long, busy night. More wounded men were brought in, none of them critical except for a junior officer of nineteen who had lost a leg. Cavan struggled all night to save his life. The shock of the amputation, and then the long journey in the ambulance, had left him in a bad state.

Joseph was so exhausted he was shuddering with cold by the time he sat on the floor in the empty Resuscitation tent. Cully Teversham brought him a mug of tea and two slices of quite reasonable bread.

'You need that more than anyone, Chaplain,' he said cheerfully. 'Wish Oi could get you some hot Maconochie's, but there's none left, not till the next lot comes.' He frowned. 'Is he going to make it?'

'Probably.' Joseph spoke more from hope than expectation.

'If Oi can foind anything else fit to eat, Oi'll bring it,' Cully said with a shrug.

'Thank you,' Joseph acknowledged the kindness. He wanted to see Lizzie again. He wanted to hear her voice, see the smile in her eyes when she recognized him and not just one more soldier. He knew she would be too tired to talk, but they understood the same emotions too well to need more than a glance. He remembered vividly driving together in the Cambridgeshire lanes two summers ago. He had not needed to explain anything to her then. She had understood his confusion and how slowly he had been forced to face the truth of betrayal, and that it had hurt him almost more than he could face.

And here they had both spent nights fighting to save young men's lives, knowing the searing physical pain they must be feeling. But just as deep as that, they could imagine the lifelong wound of being crippled, less than whole, limping when other men ran.

Was she also afraid of returning home to an emptiness after this hideous familiarity was over with: its horror and its companionship, its idiotic jokes, physical deprivation, its desperate, heart-tearing loyalties? What purpose could possibly be consuming enough to take its place?

He saw her come into the tent, and forced his aching legs to support him as he rose to his feet. He walked over to her, stopping just short of where she was, very careful not to crowd her, nor assume too much. But he wanted to be closer, even just to reach across and put his hand near hers. He saw that it was slender, bruised where she had carried a weight too heavy for her, the nails very short, one broken.

He had no idea what to say. Nothing was profound enough. She turned and smiled at him. In spite of her dark hair, her eyes were the bluest he had ever seen. What could he say that was comforting and not idiotic, so false as to be a denial of trust?

'I talked with Matthew,' he told her. 'He said that Schenckendorff couldn't be guilty. There's evidence that makes that certain. He couldn't tell me exactly what, and I couldn't repeat it if I knew.'

She turned away quickly, looking hurt, as if she had read in his face something she did not want to see.

'I'm sorry,' he said, puzzled. Who was she afraid for? Was she also terrified that someone she liked, or admired, someone she felt protective of, had killed Sarah? He could not believe it of her. He remembered so vividly her clarity of thought when Shanley Corcoran had so misled them about the project in Cambridgeshire, and it had cost Theo Blaine his life. There had been anger, bewilderment, grief, but always that honesty, above all with herself.

There was a gulf widening between them now and he did not understand it. The pain it caused him, the sense of loss almost took his breath away, as if he were hollow inside. 'Lizzie, I can't repeat things like that. How would anyone trust me if I did? I understand why Matthew has to keep silent—'

'I know,' she said quickly, but she looked at him for only an instant, then away again. 'I didn't ask you, Joseph. No one wants to talk about it, but you keep on asking. I'm . . . I'm so sorry for Sarah Price I don't think I could ever find words for how much I . . . feel for her. But I can't undo any of it. Nor have I any idea at all who did it.' Her fingers were clumsy with the bottles and dishes she was stacking. One slipped out of her hands. He lunged forward to catch it, but he was no more skilled than she, and actually knocked it further away until it crashed on the floor and broke in half.

He felt idiotic. 'I'm sorry,' he apologized.

She gasped, then blinked several times rapidly, tears in her eyes. Then she started to laugh. It was a sharp sound, growing higher and more desperate until she couldn't stop.

He kicked the broken dish out of the way with his foot so no one would tread on it, then he put both arms around her and held her as her laughter turned to weeping. Her whole body shook, her slender shoulders relaxing against him for minutes. The softness of her hair touched his cheek. He would never forget the feel of her: the stiff cotton of her grey uniform dress, the smell of antiseptic and blood and soap.

Then she pulled away and sniffed, turning aside with sudden strength so as to keep her face from him. 'I'm sorry. This is completely feeble. I won't do it again.'

'We all need . . .' he began, not knowing how he was going to finish.

'Don't make excuses for me, Joseph!' she said huskily, reaching for a handkerchief and blowing her nose fiercely. 'Pity doesn't help anyone. It's self-indulgent and a complete waste of the time in which we could be doing something useful. These men need nursing, not weeping over. There'll be plenty of time later . . . if there's any point then. I've taken twice as long cleaning this up as I should have anyway.' She yanked her apron straight and turned away to continue working.

He had no idea why the distance was widening between them, as if the friendship that was so immeasurably precious had been tarnished by some act he could not remember committing. And it mattered. It was more a part of him than all the turmoil of these last days of war playing themselves out around them: the violence and fear, comradeship, hope of peace and dread of the unknown. They all spoke of going home, and yet all but the most naïve knew that the homes they had left no longer existed as they had known them. The whole world was changed; the past lay behind a closed door.

Lizzie had been a friend in the way Sam Wetherall had been: candid and funny and gentle, and yet always keeping her own honesty a clean and separate thing, brave enough to stand apart, and generous enough to remain beside and share the darkness as well as the light.

He knew now, watching her straight back as she walked out of the tent flap, that he had loved Eleanor because he had wanted to, promised to. But he had never liked her as he did Lizzie, and the best of lovers were surely friends as well? He loved the women who stayed at home and preserved all that they treasured, whose sacrifice was in ways as great, but he could never explain to them what the front line had been like. No one could.

He must not let Lizzie go. He strode out of the tent into the darkness and saw her figure ahead of him, pale for a moment as she passed by the light of an open flap, and then dark again in the shadow. He ran to catch up with her. If she were angry or confused that he was so determined to clear Schenckendorff, he must explain to her why he had no choice.

'Lizzie!' he called, breaking into a run.

She slowed, but did not stop.

He caught up with her. Without thinking he took her arm, then felt her stiffen. Even that slight pulling away hurt him. It created a distance he did not want. 'Lizzie, it's far more than simply for justice that we have to prove Schenckendorff's innocence.' He kept his voice low so that in the darkness it would not carry even to the closest tents, or anyone standing just outside in the shadows where he could not see. He had to tell her, explain the importance, and the urgency.

'It doesn't—' she started.

'Yes, it does,' he cut across her. 'To me. My parents were murdered just before the war.'

'I know,' her voice was gentle. 'In a car crash. At least, I didn't know it was murder. But—'

'It was. My father had discovered a plot to stop the war with an Anglo-German alliance to betray Belgium, then form a new

228

empire to divide up most of the world.' There was no need, and no time, for details. He felt her stiffen with surprise. 'It was led by a man whose identity we spent all the war trying to discover, because he never gave up plotting to make the plan still work, if he could only end the war, even if it was by Britain losing. He tried all sorts of ways. We know at least some of them: destroying morale, sabotage of our scientific inventions, which was why he had Theo murdered – and other ways of corruption and mutiny as well. Many people were murdered, including General Cullingford, because he worked out this man's identity. We named him "the Peacemaker". Now he is trying to affect the terms of the armistice, and if we don't stop him, he could succeed. He has immense power.'

She was turned towards him and there was no doubt in her voice. 'How can you? You said you don't even know who he is!'

'Schenckendorff does,' he answered simply. 'He has been his ally since the beginning, but now he realizes that the Peacemaker will try to enforce terms that will enable the whole thing to start again. Germany will rise from defeat in a short time, and a new Anglo-German empire will become possible. He will never give up trying. Schenckendorff has seen the horror of this, and he will come to London with us, even if he is hanged for his part in it, rather than see his country dragged into such destruction again.'

Her voice was thick with emotion; so intense she could barely force the words. 'You have to get him there, Joseph, whatever it costs, absolutely anything. You must stop this . . . Peacemaker . . . from letting this happen again!'

'I know.' Without thinking, he put up his hand and touched the stray wisps of dark hair that crossed her brow. 'We'll do everything we can. But Jacobson is convinced that Schenckendorff killed Sarah Price, and we haven't yet worked out any way to make him doubt it enough to let us take Schenckendorff out of here. Tomorrow, or the next day, Jacobson will charge him and send him back for trial. There's nothing you can do. I just needed you to know why it matters so much.'

'I understand,' she whispered. Then she pulled away from him and walked quickly to the nearest tent flap and went in without looking back.

Judith was alone in one of the treatment tents, watching the man whose leg had been amputated. She felt helpless, inadequate to ease his pain or offer any comfort that was real. How on earth did Joseph manage to do this day after day and not make things even worse by talking rubbish, promising hope that did not exist, saying it would get better when they all knew that nothing would heal the loss? Driving an ambulance was so much simpler. She had nothing to contend with but an inanimate machine, shortages of parts and of fuel, filthy weather, cratered roads, the constant danger of being shot or blown apart. And, of course, the knowledge that she might not get the injured men to help before it was too late.

Still that was uncomplicated compared with trying to find faith and keep your own inner strength clean of lies to cover your despair, or the confusion that threatened to drown every shard of light. How did he manage to cling on to any idea of a God who loved, whose plan made sense and who had even the faintest idea of what it was like to be human?

She heard the tent flap pulled open with a surge of relief simply that there would be someone else there, a voice other than her own.

It was Lizzie. Her face was white, her dark hair pulled loose from half its pins and curling untidily. She closed the flap behind her and came over to Judith, glancing at the man in the bed moving restlessly in his pain.

'Can you help him?' Judith asked.

'No,' Lizzie answered quickly. 'He just has to get through it alone. I expect Joseph will come and sit with him again, if he has time. There are so many . . .' She bit the inside of her lip, avoiding Judith's eyes. 'And he has to get Schenckendorff back to London.'

Judith was startled, and then the moment after knew that she should not have been. Of course Joseph would trust Lizzie. He had no idea of the burden that it laid on her.

Lizzie rushed on, not allowing herself time to hesitate. 'We don't seem to be having any success finding out who killed Sarah. I'm going to go to Jacobson in the morning and tell him the truth, all of it that I know.' Her voice wavered and she swallowed. 'But I have to tell Joseph myself, first. He should hear it from me, not from someone else, gossip and half a story. I—'

'Not yet,' Judith interrupted. 'At least wait until tomorrow. We might still . . .'

Lizzie looked at her levelly, blue eyes bright with the grief burning inside her. 'So you can find something in a day? We've been trying everything we know since it happened. I'll go as soon as I can find Joseph alone again. I'm only telling you because you'll have to help him . . . I think. He . . .' she could not bring herself to say it.

'He loves you, and he'll feel like hell,' Judith finished for her. 'Wait. Just another day. Please!'

Lizzie hesitated, hope fighting against reason.

'A day,' Judith insisted. 'Jacobson won't send Schenckendorff out yet. He's still trying to find a witness who can tell a straight story. There have been so many lies; he has to find a clear thread. Please . . . then we'll tell Joseph, I promise. But don't, please don't until you have to.'

'A day,' Lizzie said wearily. 'Then I must. I know what it means. What will anything that's left be worth if I don't?'

Judith admired her passionately. It was like looking at a man about to go over the top into the gunfire, and she was keeping him balanced on the parapet. But she could not let go of hope, not for a few hours more.

# Chapter Eight

Ever since Matthew told Mason about the Peacemaker, from his family's point of view, from the murder of John and Alys Reavley right up to the struggle to get Schenckendorff back to London, Mason had been tormented by the weight of his lie to Judith, albeit by silence. He had hidden his own part in the Peacemaker's plans because he had seen confession now as a self-indulgence for which there was no time or emotional energy. They needed his practical help, not his admission to a complicity that would render him useless in their estimation.

Now he was standing on the fire-step behind one of the old parapets, staring across no-man's-land as the morning light picked out the ruts and pools in the gleaming mud, the paths between the old craters a tangled web between the wreckage. There was a faint mist over it, shining silver as the sun struck it. It hid most of the smaller mounds that were bodies of men and horses churned up by the shifting pattern of shell-holes and seeping water. At this hour it was possible to imagine that some time far in the future it could be beautiful again.

Judith was beside him. It was one of the few places they could be certain of not being overheard. She was desperate to find the truth of who had murdered Sarah Price, partly because she knew all these people in the regiment – and particularly in the casualty clearing station – and felt the pain of suspicion tearing apart the few certainties they had after years of hardship and the loss of half the people they knew. More urgent than that was her need to clear Schenckendorff from suspicion so they could take him to London and expose the Peacemaker.

That was the burden that crushed Mason now. Matthew had told him about the deaths of his parents and how the Peacemaker had killed others, and – almost worse than that – had corrupted and sabotaged, sinking lower into the abuse of both knowledge and power. Mason had listened and said nothing about his own part in it.

He looked at Judith. Her face was calm and pale in the harsh light and he saw very clearly the weariness in her, the depth of emotion, the intense vulnerability in her eyes and mouth. And yet he knew her courage also. If he wished her ever to speak to him in the time ahead, whatever it held for them, then he could not build it on such a vast lie as the silence about his alliance with the Peacemaker. He had already carried it almost too far to forgive. Once Schenckendorff was cleared and they left Ypres it would be too late.

He had thought how he would do it, which words he could use to begin, and now that he was faced with it they all sounded trite and self-serving. They had talked about Schenckendorff, and a silence had settled between them that at least for her seemed comfortable. If he said nothing now it would become a lie; one from which he might never be able to return.

'Judith . . .'

She turned to look at him, waiting for him to speak.

There was no alternative to honesty; he would make it brief and perhaps brutal, like a quick knife thrust.

'I used to believe in the same ideals as Sandwell does, or did in the beginning,' he told her.

It was a moment before she realized the meaning of what he had said. Then, very slowly, a light of astonished disbelief filled her face, and after it, pain. 'You know,' she said, her voice husky. 'When?' she swallowed. 'Always?'

'Yes. I always knew it was Sandwell. I didn't know that he had killed. I should have. I could see the power was taking him over, the desperation to stop the slaughter at any cost. What is one life here or there, taken quickly, when tens of thousands are dying slowly and hideously every day?' He waited for her answer as if it were a verdict on him – hope or despair.

He saw the flicker of uncertainty, as if, for a moment at least, she had understood.

She frowned. Her words came very slowly, with intense thought behind them. 'If that is a serious question, I think the difference may be in small acts, one by one, when you can refuse to do the violent thing, the irreparable thing. But then that might also be cowardice, mightn't it? And to say he should have asked us isn't really honest either, because we couldn't have given an answer that had any meaning. Most of us had no idea what the alternatives were. We hadn't seen war. We wouldn't have known what we were being asked to choose.'

'So what were we supposed to do?' he asked, surprised that

she had addressed the problem with pity rather than rage. 'Just let Europe stagger blindly into a holocaust rather than try everything possible to stop it?'

This time she did not hesitate. 'Yes. Rather than sell our honour, yes, he should have argued, pleaded – perhaps uselessly – but not tried to sell us without our knowledge.' She stared across the cratered land in the broadening light. Now the waste of it was easier to see. The mist no longer softened the outlines or hid the corpses. 'It wouldn't have worked anyway. Trying to make a nation of Englishmen do what they don't want to is like trying to herd cats into a barn. You can't do it. There's always some awkward cuss that's going to go the other way, or stop and demand to know why. It isn't practical, Richard; it never was. Some of us might buy peace at that price, but you'd never get us all to.'

He was watching the light on her face, not on the land. 'I know,' he admitted. 'At least I do now. There'll always be someone like John Reavley, and Joseph, and perhaps tens of thousands of others, just as willing to die for their dreams. I'm not sure how practical they are, but I'm beginning to believe that they hold the one hope we have of survival into something that is still worth keeping, worth having paid this much to have.'

She turned to meet his eyes, searching, trying to read into the depth of his mind to see if the final honesty was there inside him.

He answered impulsively, and yet he was absolutely certain that the very best of himself meant it. 'I'll come to London with you, and tell Lloyd George all I know, and that will back up everything Schenckendorff says. He will have to believe us.'

She stiffened with instant fear. 'You'd be admitting to treason,' she said in a whisper. 'Don't you know that?'

'Yes.' Said aloud like that, it brought a fear he had not fully realized before, but it did not alter his certainty that that was what he had to do. It was a payment he owed, and it was the only way she would ever look at him with the shining honesty that she did now, with the possibility of the kind of love that he could not turn away from, even if his life were the price. He would be clean; he would have given all he could to pay for his mistake.

'Are you sure?' she asked.

He was sure. He did not know if he would still have the courage when he was alone, and knew that his name would go down in history not as Britain's greatest, bravest and most articulate war correspondent, but as a man who had betrayed his own country for a flawed ideal. If he faltered later it would be because of fear crowding in; weakness, not a change in belief. 'Yes, I am sure,' he said firmly. 'I love you. More than anything else I want to be the man who can live up to your dreams, and your courage to pay what they cost.'

She gave a little nod. It was a very small, very certain gesture, and then she smiled. Then she touched his face and leaned forward and kissed him, long and tenderly. For those moments he felt an infinite happiness he thought it would be impossible ever to forget.

Later in the morning, when Judith found Joseph in his bunker, having just finished more letters, she knew that he saw the happiness in her immediately, and that he also probably recognized it as what it was. But she had no intention of telling him that Mason had always known the Peacemaker, or – at this point – that he was willing to come to London with them and tell the

Prime Minister so. They still needed Schenckendorff, otherwise they could not expect to be believed against a man as powerful as Dermot Sandwell. Alone, Mason might be written off as a lunatic, a man too shocked by his experiences at war to have retained his balance of mind.

Mason had nothing whatever on paper; it was all words, and they could be denied. There was nothing to prove any of it. Even the knowledge he had could have been obtained many other ways. Mason had realized only now that he had given Sandwell information for nearly five years, of one sort or another, but none of it was classified. It was only his own observation, put together through the wisdom and knowledge of his experience. But Sandwell had told him nothing, beyond aspirations and purposes, which of course could as easily have been his own, or a fabrication.

And Schenckendorff had not brought any papers with him. It would have been impossible to keep them after capture, even if he had dared to take the risk of removing them from Berlin.

The only written proof was the treaty John Reavley had hidden in the house in St Giles.

'We've got to think,' Judith said. 'Have you made a list of all the people it still could be, so we can concentrate on them and eliminate them? It's the first of November. We can't have much longer or they'll have ended the war and we'll be too late anyway. Jacobson must be working on it all the time. He's out there like a dog worrying a bone. And Hampton is too.'

She sat down on the cot, and Joseph turned himself round on the box to face her. He looked tired, and there was an unhappiness under the surface courage that twisted her inside to see. She knew it was because of the gulf that had opened up between Lizzie and himself, and he could not understand it.

Judith ached to be able to reach out and help, tell him that it was because Lizzie loved him intensely, not because she didn't. But would he be able to bear the knowledge of what had happened to her, and that she was now carrying the rapist's child? She did not know. He had been so desperately hurt by Eleanor's death, and the scars had taken years to heal. Might this new blow even rock his faith? Wasn't that the foundation of his strength, and would the inner sweetness in him then be gone?

Mason had told her today, as they stared over no-man's-land, that of course Joseph would have to know. Soon Lizzie's pregnancy would become obvious. Then she would either have to tell him, or walk out of his life for ever, without explanation, and that might hurt him even more.

Mason told her how Joseph had been in Gallipoli when he had first met him. He had tried to describe his compassion, his tireless work for the wounded, no matter how exhausted he was himself, his steadiness in the unspeakable horror of it. He had said the sea was red with human blood.

Then he had told her about his long argument with Joseph in the open boat in the Channel, after the U-boat had sunk their steamer and left them to find their way back to England the best they could. The others had died, leaving only Joseph, Mason and the injured crewman. Joseph had been willing to die, if that was what it cost to prevent Mason from writing his story on Gallipoli, and sabotaging morale for the recruitment needed to prevent surrender. Yes, Joseph could take disappointment, betrayal, even defeat, and survive them all.

Her eyes had prickled with tears of pride, and of happiness that Mason believed so well of Joseph. Still, she wanted to protect both Joseph and Lizzie as long as she could – and perhaps all the others here as well, except the one man who was guilty. It was the very last resort of all to tell Jacobson about the earlier rape.

Joseph was holding out a piece of paper to her with names and times and places on it. She took it and read.

'An awful lot of this doesn't make sense,' she said at last. 'For a start, I really don't believe it could possibly have been Major Morel. I know he's a bit odd, and I think he really would have led a mutiny last year.' She glanced at Joseph's wry expression. 'All right, he did. But I don't believe he would rape anybody. He's a rebel in his own way, and he'd fight any cause he believed in, but violence against women isn't a cause.'

'And Tiddly Wop Andrews?' Joseph asked. 'He said Moira Jessop saw him in the supply tent the only time he wasn't with the walking wounded, but she says she wasn't there. Why would she lie?'

'I suppose she was somewhere she shouldn't have been,' Judith answered. 'Or she's already lied to protect someone else, and she can't go back on it. But I can't believe it's Tiddly Wop. We've known him for years! He's good-looking, but he's as shy as . . . as a choir boy.'

'That's rubbish, Judith, and you know it,' Joseph said gently. 'He was shy at home. He's been on the battlefront for four years. He's not a boy any more. He's twenty-six, and a soldier.'

She was startled. 'You don't believe it could be him, do you?'

His face was tight. 'I don't want to, but we've all changed. The whole world's changed. Nobody is who they used to be.' He looked at her earnestly. 'It won't only be those of us who've been here who are changed, or on other fronts, it'll be the people at home too. Read Hannah's letters between the lines. She hates some of what is new, but she knows she can't escape.' He gave a very slight shrug. 'We don't look at anything the way we used to, socially or economically. The old rules of how to behave have been swept away. Distinctions in social class are blurred more and more all the time. We've been forced to see the courage, intelligence and moral value of men we used barely even to notice. They aren't going to go home and doff the cap any more. We know, in a way we can never forget, that we are all equal when it comes to injury and death, human need, the will to live, above all the honour and the self-sacrifice to go over the top and, if need be, to give your life for your friends.'

'I know,' she said softly. 'Do you think we'll ever forget? I'm so afraid that once we've grown used to the silence and the comfort again we'll sink back into the old bad things as well: the indifference, the malice, the inequalities, the stupid lies that we only believe because they're comfortable. Will we go back to ignorance of what real pain or real sorrow is, and complain about stupid little things again as if they mattered? Will we take offence over trivia, get greedy for more than we need, forget that we are more alike than any differences there are between us? Will we even remember to be grateful just to be alive and at home, able to see and hear and walk? Will we remember to look after those who can't see or hear? And those who are alone, and will always be alone?'

'I don't know. But I know what we'll deserve if we don't,' he said softly. 'If there is a God, a resurrection – and I have to believe there is – then when we meet those who paid, I want to be able to look in their faces and say that I honoured their gift.'

'So do I. If I can't, maybe that would be hell,' she agreed. 'And I still hope it wasn't Tiddly Wop, or Barshey Gee, or Major Morel.'

'Or Cavan,' he added. 'There's something odd about his story. I don't know what yet, and I wish I didn't have to find out, but I do.'

'Cavan would never have killed anyone!' Judith said aghast. 'Even you can't imagine that!'

'I don't,' he replied. 'But he's lying. I need to know why, unless we can solve it first.'

'I will!' she said, standing up. 'I'll go to it right now.'

'Be careful!' Joseph said with quick fear, standing as well. 'You're not safe just because you're an ambulance driver, Judith.'

She swivelled to face him, one hand on the sacking. 'I know!'

Joseph started to look for Tiddly Wop Andrews. The soldiers were all finding the enforced idleness a strain, especially since they were held here, in a sense, captive and away from the last of the fighting. Most of them were torn between relief that now they would get home uninjured, and the sense of having let down their friends by not being there at the very end. They felt useless. Hours dragged by in small jobs that were largely no more than filling in time. There was no point at all in shoring up trenches; they would never be used again. Rifles had not been fired so they did not need cleaning. It was still done, but it was a waste of time. The only thing that actually had value was helping the injured, but there was only so much that an unskilled man could do.

Tiddly Wop had been mending duckboards. There was no point – they would not need them much longer – but it was better than idleness. He put down the hammer as Joseph's shadow fell across him.

'What can I do for you, Chaplain?' he asked. 'I really don't know anything more.'

'Yes, you do,' Joseph answered, squatting down on a pile of sandbags opposite him. 'Where were you the night Sarah Price was killed, Tiddly? The truth.'

'I was in the evacuation tent,' Tiddly Wop said doggedly. 'I already told you that.'

'Yes, you did. And Cully Teversham told me so too. But Moira Jessop said you weren't, the first time I asked her. And she said the same thing to Jacobson.'

Tiddly Wop looked unhappy. 'Don't know why she'd say that.'

'No, nor do I,' Joseph agreed. 'She said later that you might have been; they were all so busy she couldn't be sure. But that's not true either. The evacuation tent was actually pretty quiet. Between half-past three and half-past four there was no one in there at all. And that's the time that counts.'

Tiddly Wop blinked. 'Is it? Is that when . . . when she was killed?'

'Yes. Didn't you know that?'

'No. I . . . I saw her earlier.' Again he looked away. 'She was pretty upset. I tried to make her feel a bit better.' He mumbled the words as if he were embarrassed by them.

'What was she upset about?' Joseph persisted.

'Lots of things,' Tiddly Wop answered, his voice thick with sadness.

'That's not an answer,' Joseph told him. 'This girl's dead, Tiddly. We need to know what happened to her, and why. Why may be the only way we catch the man who did it. I'm not going to repeat it if I don't have to. What was she upset about?'

'She was afraid of going home,' Tiddly Wop said slowly, searching for the words he needed. 'She knew things had changed. She'd only been out here a year or so, but she realized that it isn't ever going to be like it was before. So many young men are dead, and two or three times as many are injured, or crippled, or just different.' He looked sad and puzzled. 'And women aren't the way they used to be either. She felt she wouldn't fit in anywhere, nobody would marry her because she's pretty enough, but she hasn't any . . . I don't know . . . she didn't think with all the women there are who are well-bred, know how to behave, charming and modest and good at domestic skills, that anybody'd choose her. And she's got a bit of a reputation. She's nearly twenty-six. She flirted a good bit. She had a sort of a fling with Benbow, until he got too keen and she ended it. Then she . . . I don't know . . . made sure she could still attract men by flirting something rotten with the German prisoners. Safe, if you like. They can't do anything, poor sods. She just wanted to boost herself up a bit.'

He looked earnestly at Joseph, to see if he understood.

'I told her that was silly, but she knew that already. Made people angry with her. She was pretty enough, more than most. I said to her not to sell herself cheap. I didn't go too far because I didn't want her to think I was after her, but I tried to get her to think well of herself.' He searched Joseph's face anxiously.

Joseph saw the kindness in him, the sense of pity for a young woman afraid and foolish, probably like thousands of other women who saw what had once been an assured future disappearing as an army of young men melted into the earth, and all the old patterns of behaviour shifted and nothing was safe any more.

'When was that?' Joseph asked.

'About midnight,' Tiddly answered. 'Maybe one o'clock.'

'Then where were you between half-past three and half-past four?'

'In the evacuation tent, like I said.'

'With Cully Teversham?'

Tiddly Wop said nothing. His silence confirmed the truth.

Joseph waited. He would dearly like to have believed him, but he could not afford even a single lie, no matter how much it was better or easier than the truth.

Tiddly Wop sighed. 'You aren't going to leave it, are you, Chaplain?'

'No. Where were you, Tiddly?'

'In the evacuation tent! It's just that Cully weren't there. He said he was to cover for me.'

'Why?'

Tiddly looked at Joseph, his eyes begging for a leniency, an understanding. ''Cos I pulled him off the wire at Passchendaele an' he reckons he owes me something. I didn't ask him for that. Don't drop him in it, Chaplain, please?'

'Who else was in the evacuation tent, Tiddly?'

'No one. I swear! But before you go blaming Cully, or thinking he did anything, he was with Snowy Nunn that time, but Snowy's gone back up the front again. And that's the truth!'

Joseph believed him. He understood the debt of honour. Any man who owed his life to someone else never forgot it. Cully was like tens of thousands of others. Joseph had not known Tiddly Wop had saved him. It was just one more piece of heroism done for its own sake, no recognition expected or wished for. It was what one did for friends.

'Yes,' Joseph acknowledged. 'Where was Moira Jessop?'

'I don't know. But she wasn't in the evacuation tent.'

Joseph thanked him and left him in order to go to find Moira Jessop and question her again.

She was asleep, taking advantage of a brief respite. She had worked all night and he felt unkind disturbing her, but there was no time for such considerations. Added to which, of course, if she were woken for an emergency he would not be able to speak to her anyway.

'What is it, Chaplain?' she said, fumbling to straighten her dress and collect her thoughts. She sat upright and scraped her hair back into something like neatness, even if it was unflatteringly tight.

'I need to talk to you about Sarah Price,' he said, standing in front of her.

Her face clouded. 'I don't know anything more than I've already told you. She flirted with the Germans.' Her face pulled into lines of distaste, her lips tight. She was sitting more stiffly now, the grey fabric of her dress stretched a little over her shoulders. 'Of course I wouldn't say she deserved it, but she certainly invited it in a way none of the rest of us would think of. She had no . . . modesty. It lowered all of us in the men's eyes.'

'What did she do?' he asked. That was not what he had been going to say, but he was curious and disturbed by Moira's comment.

'I told you,' she replied. 'She flirted with them. Far more than looked after them or attended to their wounds.'

'Are you certain?'

She was angry now. 'If you doubt me, ask Allie Robinson,' she challenged him. 'She knows it was cheap and disgusting. For heaven's sake, these are the men who slaughtered our own boys whose bodies are shattered by shrapnel, torn on the wires, riddled with bullets, frozen to death. Who in God's name does she think did it to them?' Her face was white, her voice sharp and rising out of control.

'I expect she knew that, even if she forgot it for the moment,'

Joseph said gently. He could understand Moira's anger and the fear of chaos that welled up inside her. One could become drowned in pain, desperate for any kind of right and wrong, anything at all that made sense of something too terrible to bear. The nurses dealt with the worst of it, endlessly, night after night, and they endured the same miserable rations, exhausting hours and endless hunger, weariness and cold as the men. Sometimes people forget that simply because they were seldom shot at, and they did not have to shoot back. Their task was always one of mercy. None of them would lie awake in the night sweating with horror as the face of a dying man swam in front of them, and they knew they had killed him. Joseph had held men who wept with terror and guilt over that. The nightmares would never leave some of them.

But they had their own nightmares, their own drowning in helplessness. Had the women at home even the faintest idea of their courage, or strength, the steel of endurance that had entered their lives day and night?

'I don't know anything,' Moira repeated stiffly. 'I already told you.'

'Yes, you do,' Joseph said firmly. 'You know where you were, and it was not the evacuation tent. It's time for the truth.'

She looked startled, drawing in breath to deny it. Then she met his eyes, and knew he was not going to accept that. The resistance drained away. 'I was with Private Eames,' she said very quietly. She did not explain, but it was unnecessary: her implication was perfectly clear.

'Where?' He tried to keep judgement out of his voice.

'Does it really matter?' The challenge was back, as if he were asking from some prurient curiosity.

'Yes, it does matter,' he replied. 'The only hope we have of finding out where people actually were is to get as much of the truth as possible, and weed out the lies. Unfortunately you are far from the only one to say they were somewhere they weren't.'

She blushed hotly. 'I don't know who killed her!'

'Somebody does. Where were you?'

'On the far side of the water drums.' It was almost an accusation in return, as if he were to blame for driving her to it. It was a muddy and miserable spot; they could not have been doing more than kissing at the most. Perhaps that was what she meant him to know.

'Out of sight of the Germans' hut,' he observed aloud.

'Yes.'

'For how long?'

'I don't know. Ten minutes, or fifteen.'

He automatically assumed it could have been more. She would err on the side that excused her, and – perhaps of greater importance – that excused Eames, who had left his post.

'I won't report it this time, if I can avoid it,' he said to her. 'But if that time is crucial to Sarah's murder, then I might have to.'

'I didn't have anything to do with it!' she said indignantly. 'Nor did Private Eames.'

'Yes, he did, Nurse Jessop. He was away from his duty, and so he cannot account for what happened around the German prisoners' hut. One of them may have come out. Also, of course, Lance-Corporal Benbow cannot account for himself either. And he lied, because he said they were together.'

Moira was now very shaken. She had obviously not allowed her mind to travel so far. But she was angry, and she refused to apologize. Joseph left her sitting on the cot, miserable and defensive.

He confirmed what she had said with Eames, then sought out Benbow and confronted him with his lie.

Benbow looked acutely uncomfortable, and a tide of guilt swept up his lean face. 'He was having a bit of a fling with Nurse Jessop,' he said, not looking directly at Joseph. 'Didn't see it mattered. He wasn't gone long.'

'How long, do you know?'

Benbow hesitated.

'You don't know,' Joseph said for him. 'Which means you are not accounted for either, and possibly not the German prisoners you swore so vehemently you were guarding. It's time for the truth, Benbow. It would be better if you gave it to me honestly rather than my having to drag it out of others. Any lie is a form of guilt at this point, whatever you are lying to conceal: your error, or anyone else's.'

Benbow looked wretched. 'I don't know how long he was gone,' he said in a low, hard voice. 'I wasn't there either, not when he came back. I think it was only a few minutes we were both gone.'

'You think?' Joseph said softly. 'Did you lie to cover Eames, or yourself?'

'Both.' Benbow hesitated again. 'I was with Sarah Price, but only at the water. I helped her carry a bucket, and stopped to talk to her for a few minutes. She was looking after some of the German wounded. I was angry with her for flirting with them. She seemed to prefer them to us.' His hands were clenched and the muscles were tight in his neck and jaw. 'It was then that I realized why. She liked to tease them, flirt, bait them a bit. Fun, she called it. But the poor bastards couldn't do anything about it. Most of them were too badly shot up, and scared stiff of what would happen to them – even more, to their women at home – and she liked that.'

'You're not painting a picture of a very pleasant young woman,' Joseph observed.

Benbow glared at him, then gave a short bark of laughter. 'It's a true one.'

'I am assuming, Lance-Corporal, that you knew her fairly well?'

Benbow coloured again. 'She was around a lot.'

Joseph said no more on the subject, but nor did he promise Benbow not to report it, if it should become necessary. Instead he went to speak with the German prisoners, to see if any of them could corroborate how long Eames or Benbow were absent from duty.

He asked Schenckendorff first. He looked pale still, but his foot was less inflamed and his fever appeared to have gone. Now he faced the possibility of being tried for murder and hanged, and his eyes held a black humour at the irony of it, but he had summoned all the strength he had to mask his fear.

He corroborated Benbow's story, hope flaring up for an instant that somehow it would help prove his own innocence, then dying when Joseph did not say so.

'I'm closer to the truth,' Joseph said quietly. 'But I'm not there yet.'

'I did not do it,' Schenckendorff replied. 'I stood outside on the earth for a little while, and felt the rain. I spoke to no one. The girl who was killed was the one who came in here and laughed and joked with our men? A very pretty girl, but shallow, I think, perhaps frightened, and cruel at times. It is terrible that she was killed. I'm sorry. Stupidity does not deserve such a fearful punishment. We are all stupid at times, led blindly by our hopes or fears. Too busy looking at what we are running away from to see what we are running into.'

Joseph said nothing. Schenckendorff could have been speaking of a dozen different things – physical, emotional, or moral. In another time and place he could have liked the man, even been friends. Now all that mattered was to clear him of blame so they could get him to London in time.

Joseph rose to leave, and as he was walking past the cots one of the men spoke to him in excellent English, calling him by name. Joseph stopped. There was something familiar about the voice, but he could not place it.

'Chaplain?' the man repeated. He was lean and dark with prominent features, handsome in his own way.

'Do I know you?' Joseph asked, puzzled.

The man smiled. His head was bandaged and there was still blood oozing over his right ear. There was also heavy padding on his right shoulder and arm. 'Feldwebel Eisenmann,' he answered. 'We discussed English football in no-man's-land, nineteen fifteen. I'm glad to see that you are all right. Can you tell me if my friend Lance-Corporal Goldstone is still alive, please?'

Joseph remembered the incident with a sudden glow of warmth. It had been terrifying one moment, overwhelmingly funny the next, ludicrous. They had discussed Arsenal's dismal defence against Chelsea, as if it actually mattered – a moment of beautiful sanity in the middle of hell. Two Jews and a Church of England Chaplain lost in a waste of mud and corpses, talking about a game, and parting as friends.

'Yes, he is, Feldwebel,' Joseph replied. 'He got a blighty one about a year ago. Lost his left foot, but he's adjusting well. I hear from him every so often. I'll write and tell him I saw you.'

'Tell him I lost my right ear,' Eisenmann said. 'He'll see the joke to that. He always said I couldn't sing. By the way, I have a message for you.' He smiled, a sweet, gentle look in his eyes. 'From a man called Sam. Tall fellow, dark hair. Did some work in Germany, and said he's going to stay there, at least for the time being. Asked you if you'd do him a favour, and tell his brother the truth. Do you understand that? And he said, "Be happy." Tell a good joke, and eat a chocolate biscuit for him.'

Joseph felt the warmth flood through him and the tears prickle in his eyes. Of all the friends the war had taken from him, he missed Sam Wetherall the most. 'Yes, the most excellent sense,' he replied. 'Thank you, Feldwebel. I am much in your debt.' He turned and left before emotion overtook him. He wanted to be alone outside, to walk in the rain along the old trenches, to recapture memory and the companionships that had been the best of it, perhaps to have time to live his own grief. He wanted to remember the voices, the laughter, the eyes of all that he knew so well who would stay here long after the rest of them had gone home, when the good and bad of war had drifted into the past and become stories told to people who had no idea what it had really been like.

Judith also was working on everything she could. The increasingly clear picture of Sarah Price that emerged was easy to understand, and to pity, but less easy to like.

'Loose,' Allie said pithily. 'Heaven knows, anyone can under-stand falling in love. We're all lonely, frightened, and very much aware that what we lose the chance for now we may never have again. But Sarah didn't love. In a way you could say she was always lying, promising something she didn't even have, much less intend to give!' Her face was bleak with anger and a consuming pain. 'By being what she was, cruel and vulgar, she betrayed us all.'

'Betrayed us?' Judith repeated with confusion. She was not understanding.

Allie stared at her with frustration bordering on contempt. 'The men who died out here, the wounded and broken – for everyone they loved at home, we must be worthy of their sacrifice. That's the greatest debt we can ever have. She wasn't! She mocked them. She had no loyalty.' She looked away. There was a bitterness and a deep, harsh anger in her voice. 'Over centuries men and women have given all they had to make the England we love. If we let ourselves become cheap and grubby now, we betray the dead not just of this war, but of all wars. Every sacrifice made in two thousand years is wasted. What irony if we beat the Germans, then let the prize slip out of our own hands into the mud to be trodden on.'

'You can give it away for yourself,' Judith said quite clearly. 'You can't give it away for others.'

Allie spun round and glared at her. 'Of course you can, you stupid woman! You can give it away for all the people who follow you! What are you going to teach your children? Are you going to teach them honour and chastity and how to care for others and be loyal and patient and decent? Or how to take everything you can for yourself, make sure you know all of your rights – and none of your duties?'

Judith opened her mouth to argue, then knew it was useless.

And Allie had some justice on her side. A generation that forgets its beliefs cannot pass them on. It was the depth of Allie's emotion that startled her, and made her a little afraid.

It was only after she had walked hunched against the wind and was back in Joseph's bunker comparing her notes that she realized Allie had said she was with Cavan working in the tent for lying wounded at the same time as she had also said she was in the resuscitation tent. And one of the orderlies had confirmed the second story.

Why would Allie say that if it were not true? And why had Cavan confirmed it? She sat on the edge of the cot and read through the accounts again, some in her own hand, some in Joseph's. Note by note, it was clear that Cavan and Allie were lying; the orderlies' stories fitted in with everything else. She could not believe Cavan, of all people, was guilty, even if, according to several people, he had known Sarah and at times laughed and joked with her, and perhaps a little bit more. She was easy to like – if you did not witness her cruelty – and she asked for nothing in return. She was not seeking any kind of commitment. That's what he had implied.

Dreading the answers, Judith forced herself to find Cavan and ask him. He was in the operating tent and she had to wait. Finally he came out into the resuscitation tent, his arms still bloody and his hair wet where he had dashed water over his face to keep himself awake. Judith felt guilty for bothering him, but she needed to know. Schenckendorff had to be saved, and Lizzie's grief was far worse than any brief embarrassment Cavan might experience.

Cavan smiled. He looked pleased to see her.

'I've been speaking to Allie,' she said straight away.

'She's a good nurse,' he responded, but his attention was

directed towards the man just brought in, who was not yet stirring from unconsciousness.

She looked at Cavan. Was it weariness in him, the fatigue they all felt now that the fighting was nearly over? There would only be days to go now. He was one man whose job was assured. He might get a few weeks' leave, but he would always be needed. His future was more certain than anyone else's, except perhaps Joseph's. He too would always be needed, although whether he would ever consider a peacetime ministry she did not know. He had refused it before the war, unable to face the griefs and turmoil, the moral tangles of other people's lives. He had had no answers to his own loss, no passionate faith with which to bear the pain of others and be certain enough of God to offer healing.

None of that had anything to do with her being honest now with Cavan.

'Why did you let Allie lie to protect you at the time Sarah was killed?' she said bluntly.

Cavan stiffened and turned round slowly. His face was pale and there was a very clear flare of anger in his heavy-lidded eyes. 'Just who do you think you are, questioning people like this?' he said abruptly. 'It's none of your business, Judith. I put up with a certain amount when your brother was accused, but now it's just some German, and you are overstepping yourself.'

'Probably,' she said tartly, stung by the coldness in him. 'If you prefer me to go and tell Jacobson, I can do. Allie lied, and you didn't say anything, so in effect you lied also. I understand lying. I do it myself to protect those I care for, especially if I believe absolutely in their innocence. But I won't see an innocent man hanged, German or British, or anything else. Either tell me, or tell Jacobson, the choice is yours.'

He was angry, very angry. She had not seen it in him before and it startled her, but she refused to back away.

'Allie is protecting me,' he said icily. 'I was exhausted and I took a few minutes outside alone to collect myself. I didn't say she lied because I was grateful, and I didn't want to get her into trouble. I don't know if your self-righteousness can understand that, or have any pity for it.'

The word 'pity' struck a spark in her mind. Suddenly she understood something she should have seen before. Allie Robinson was in love with Cavan, and he did not feel the same for her. He knew it, and was ashamed. Perhaps he had allowed her to misunderstand a word, a gesture, a long time of sharing desperate struggles, long watches over the wounded or the dying. It was that guilt that made him so angry. That terrible need not to be alone, to reach out to some human comfort in the inner turmoil of the mind, was not the same as love, at least not love between a man and a woman. But the illusion of love could spring from it, and the aching, devouring hunger.

'I see,' she said gently. 'Yes, I see. Thank you. Did anyone else know you were outside?'

His look softened. Something else showed in his eyes for a moment, a warmth that flared and died almost before she recognized it. 'Not so far as I know.'

The nights were drawing in. It was long past the equinox, and by late afternoon an autumn sun burned orange across the west. Veils of rain smudged grey, driving in hard and cold. Matthew, Joseph and Judith sat on the two cots. Judith had told them what she had learned.

Joseph chewed his lip. 'So we have accounted for everyone except Cavan, Benbow, and Barshey Gee.'

Judith was stunned. 'Barshey Gee? Don't be ridiculous, Joseph. Barshey wouldn't do that to anyone.' She felt the blood burning up her face. She had lied to protect Wil Sloan, saying she was working on her ambulance, and he was there with her. Actually she had finished it early and gone to sit inside, out of the wind and rain. Barshey had brought her a mug of hot tea. She had watched him shorten the flame, and wait until the water boiled. It had taken a long time. After that he had walked back to the ambulance with her and they had talked.

'I don't believe he did it either,' Joseph said grimly. 'But he lied, Judith.'

'Did he?' The words stuck on her tongue. 'What did he say?'

'That he made you a mug of tea in the walking wounded tent, then gone out with you to your ambulance. He said Wil Sloan wasn't there. You said he was, and you didn't mention Barshey.'

Matthew looked unhappy. 'That's a stupid lie, Joe. Why would Barshey say anything that could be disproved so easily? He had to know we'd all talk together. Why Judith? Any other VAD we might not have believed, but to say it was her was idiotic!'

Quick, ugly thoughts raced through Judith's mind; memories of how frightened Wil had been, his words about men afraid of the violence within themselves, the rage that betrayed their control. No, that was nonsense! She knew Wil too closely to allow that, even as overtired imagination.

Joseph was staring at her. She had told others to tell the truth. She had despised Allie for lying to protect Cavan, and seen his pity and guilt for her.

She lifted her eyes to meet Joseph's. It had to be now. 'Barshey didn't lie. I did. I'm sorry.' She swallowed. 'I wanted to protect Wil because I knew they would suspect him. He has a temper. Barshey made the tea inside, and then came out with it to the ambulance, just as he said. It had been raining and he wasn't even really wet, not at first. He was soaked like the rest of us by the time we went back.' She saw Joseph's face. 'I know! I'm sorry!' She was tangled in lies, as if in the arms of an octopus. As soon as she freed herself from one she was gripped by another. Now she had had to betray Wil when she had said she would not.

'And could it have been Wil?' Matthew said gravely. 'This time the truth, please?'

'We all have our debts, Matthew,' Joseph shook his head. 'We can't choose when they come due.' He touched Judith's arm in a moment's warmth, then leaned away again.

'I suppose so,' Judith whispered.

'So Cavan, Benbow or Wil Sloan,' Joseph looked from one to the other of them questioningly.

'Benbow,' Judith answered. 'I refuse to believe it was Cavan or Wil. So do you. We've known them for four years. Cavan has saved more lives than any other doctor on this part of the Front. He'd have had the VC if it weren't for that idiot Northrup. Even then he put his men before himself and stayed behind to answer the charge.'

'That doesn't mean he wouldn't rape a woman,' Matthew pointed out.

'Of course it doesn't!' Judith shouted at him, her voice rising in a kind of desperate denial. 'But it was Benbow. It has to have been.'

'Probably,' Joseph agreed. 'But we haven't proved it.'

Matthew's response was prevented by Mason banging on the makeshift lintel and pulling open the curtain.

'Come in,' Joseph invited him, although Mason was already down the first step. As he came into the full lamplight, they saw his face was haggard, his wide mouth pulled into a tight line. He looked briefly from one to the other of them.

'It's a hell of a lot worse,' he said without waiting for any of them to speak. 'Someone above Hook has ordered Jacobson off the case and put a military policeman in charge. Hook's furious, but there's nothing he can do. This bloke's already arrived, fellow called Onslow. He's ordered all investigation to cease and Schenckendorff is to be shipped out tomorrow. He doesn't give a damn whether he's medically fit or not.'

'The case is not proved,' Matthew protested. 'It's only a charge. There's far too little evidence to bring it to trial.'

Judith looked at Joseph, and saw in his eyes that he was more used to military police, and the needs of war. There was no such hope in him, no trust of reason or law.

'We can't prove Schenckendorff is innocent,' he said, looking from Matthew to Judith. 'That's the only thing that would do now.'

'There isn't any proof!' Mason's voice was tight with anger. 'What a bloody irony!' They were all thinking the same thing. Blind chance, a chain of individual lies and debts, and a military policeman ruled more by ambition than justice, and the Peacemaker had won again.

'What have we been fighting for?' Joseph said softly, 'if in the end we hang an innocent man for our convenience, to save us the trouble of finding the truth, and the discomfort of facing an answer we don't like? We could have saved the slaughter and simply surrendered in the first place.'

Judith put her head in her hands, and knew that she must go and speak to Lizzie. It was no longer possible for Lizzie to remain silent about her own rape.

# Chapter Nine

Joseph spent a wretched night. It seemed after all their efforts they were finally defeated. He had pleaded with Major Onslow, who was a pale, hazel-eyed man with close-clipped hair and lean body. Onslow had listened with civility, and then said he was sorry but the matter had dragged on too long. The crime was a hideous one, even by the standards of violence they had become tragically used to. Now at last they were looking forward to peace, it could come within days, and this matter must be settled. It was not only for the sake of justice, but for the men and women of this casualty clearing station whose morale had suffered profoundly.

Nothing Joseph could say about injustice, lack of evidence, even the possibility of someone else being guilty, had altered Onslow's judgement in the slightest. Schenckendorff would be moved out some time the following day, as soon as safe conduct could be arranged. He must be protected. For the sake of the men here, they must not be allowed to harm him. But his transportation would be early afternoon, at the latest.

Joseph had lain awake, knowing that Matthew was awake in the other bunk, but neither of them could think of anything more to suggest, so each sought sleep fitfully and with little success.

In the morning Matthew went out early without saying what he intended to do, and Joseph wrote two condolence letters left over from the previous day. He had just finished them when there was a brief rap on the lintel. Without waiting for a reply, Lizzie came down the steps.

She was hollow-eyed and bereft of colour. His first thought was death – Stan Tidyman, who had lost his leg? Had the amputation been too much of a shock to a body already exhausted?

'Who is it?' he said, offering her his chair and moving to sit on the bunk.

'No one,' she replied, accepting the seat awkwardly, as if she would rather have remained standing. 'That's not why I've come.'

'What is it?' What else could have happened? He had not had time to tell her about Schenckendorff last night. She had been on duty and busy with the wounded.

In short, cutting words she told him, sparing herself no fact, however harsh. She did not once look up at him or offer any excuses or blame. It was simply an account of a sudden rape in which she was violated and left bruised in body and soul, hurting beyond anything she could have imagined, soiled for ever. Something was left damaged inside her, which could never be repaired. And now she was carrying the man's child, as if she had been fused together with him in one terrible act, and a living person had been created so she could never forget. She had no idea who the rapist was. Still she did not look up or meet Joseph's eyes.

'It happened before Schenckendorff ever came through the lines,' she finished in a flat, tight voice. 'He could not have been the one. I need to tell Onslow that, so he doesn't charge him and take him away.'

Joseph was so shattered that he felt as if he too had been attacked deep inside himself, scorched by filth he could never be rid of. And yet no one had touched him. He would rather they had done this to him, than to her. He had no idea what to say or do that would ever reach her pain, let alone comfort it. He was overwhelmed, robbed of everything except the throbbing red wound of it. Even rage had not come yet. It would. He would want to kill the man, beat him senseless, then castrate him when he was conscious and aware of every movement of the knife, everything he lost for ever.

Would that help? Would it ease anything?

Lizzie was waiting for him to look at her, to say something. He realized with shock that she was not certain that he believed her. Incredibly, she was afraid he could even think it was a lie constructed to cover some moral lapse of her own.

What could he say? Words were so clumsy, inadequate to express any of the desperate emotion inside him. She needed to be believed. She could hardly care now that he loved her. The thought that the creature who had murdered Sarah Price had also been violently intimate with Lizzie, leaving his seed inside to grow and become her child, left him seared with horror. But he must think of her, not himself. Anything he felt could hardly matter to her now.

'Joseph?' Her voice was shaking. The terror in her was so

consuming he could feel it in the room. 'Will you come with me to Onslow?'

He must say something, the right thing. There was only this one chance; he could never take back a mistake. He reached out and touched the tips of her fingers with his own. It was the lightest possible brush of skin on skin.

'We'll find another way to clear Schenckendorff . . .' he began, and knew immediately that it could not be true. There was no more time.

She shook her head, in a tiny jerk of movement as if her muscles were locked. 'I've waited as long as I can. I have to do it. You know it's right. Don't make it harder. I just had to tell you myself before I did it.' She stood up, then her body swayed for a moment, and she caught her balance. 'I couldn't live with anything else, and neither could you.' She turned very slowly and walked to the door.

Joseph was too late to stand up, but he was not sure that his legs would hold him anyway. He knew she was right. Schenckendorff had come through the lines to surrender himself and betray the Peacemaker, with all that that cost him, because his honour demanded it. If she allowed him to hang for a crime she knew he had not committed it would poison the rest of her life, and Joseph's too if he colluded in such an act of cowardice.

And yet every part of him wanted to protect her. His mind screamed at him to find another way, any way, but not this. Please God, let there be something else they could do! But even as he cried out he knew there was not, and he was wasting time protesting while he allowed her to go to Onslow alone. He should be with her, beside her. What it cost him was irrelevant, and was nothing compared to the cost to her.

He stood up and parted the sacking, climbing the steps, his legs as heavy as if he were struggling through the thick mud of no-man's-land. He went outside and followed after her, knowing which way she would have gone. He caught up with her as she opened the door to the hut where Onslow had made his office, and they went in together.

Onslow was sitting behind a table with half a dozen sheets of paper on it. He looked surprised to see them, and somewhat irritated. He addressed Joseph first. 'Yes, Chaplain. Please don't waste your time and mine asking me to delay charging the German, or with any more theories as to who else could be guilty. You are not serving your men, or your regiment's honour.'

'Sir—' Joseph began.

'We need this wretched business to be over and put as far from our minds as possible,' Onslow said tartly, cutting across him, his hand up as if to silence him physically. 'You should write to the poor girl's family, if you have not done so already, then turn your attention to the living. There are more than enough wounded who need your help . . . your undivided help, Captain Reavley.' He still had not done more than glance at Lizzie.

Now she stepped forward. Joseph could see something of what it cost her to stand so stiffly to attention, shoulders squared.

'Captain Reavley came only to support me in what I have to tell you, Major Onslow,' she said clearly. 'He knew nothing of it, until I felt obliged to inform him just now.'

Onslow drew in his breath to interrupt her also, but something in her face and her bearing stopped him. He made an attempt at patience, but it was brief.

Lizzie plunged on. 'Unfortunately Sarah Price was not the

only woman to be assaulted. There was an earlier rape, extremely unpleasant, but very much less violent—'

This time he did interrupt. 'Nothing was reported, Miss . . . ?'

'Mrs Blaine,' she said. 'I know it was not reported.' Her voice dipped.

Joseph ached to be able to say it for her, explain, force Onslow to understand, but he knew he must not. It would rob Lizzie of the only dignity or control she had in the matter. He stood rigidly, his hands by his sides, clenched so his nails dug into his palms. The silence in the tent was oppressive, the air stale.

'It is very . . . difficult to report such a thing.' Lizzie's voice sank in spite of her will to keep it strong.

Onslow's face darkened with anger. 'Mrs Blaine, rape is a very serious crime! Not to report it is completely irresponsible. I am very sorry that such a thing should have happened, and if you tell me who the woman is, we shall add that to the charge.' He jerked his hands, as if freeing himself from some restraint. 'Although of course I cannot unless the victim herself tells me. Please point out to her that it is her duty, and perhaps if she had had the courage to come forward at the time, we might have caught the man then, and Sarah Price would still be alive.'

It cost Joseph such an effort of will to keep silent, that he could feel the blood throbbing in his temples as if the violence of it must be shaking his body. He wanted to beat Onslow until he lay senseless.

Lizzie struggled to force the words through her lips. 'I was the woman, sir. I have no idea who it was who raped me. Had I known, I would have reported it . . .'

Onslow looked taken aback, but it did not alter the anger in him. His face was red, his eyes bright and hard. 'Then your

266

accusation now is pointless, and too late, Mrs Blaine.' He stood up and walked around the table towards her, looking her up and down as though to see if she were injured.

Joseph was trembling, the sweat hot and then cold on his skin.

'It has every point!' Lizzie's voice was choked with tears. 'It happened over a month ago, before Colonel Schenckendorff was anywhere near here. It could not possibly have been he.'

Onslow took a moment to realize the full import of what she had said, and then it struck him. He froze. 'You mean you have allowed me to accuse and imprison an innocent man, while you said nothing?' he shouted at her.

'I . . . I hoped he would be proved innocent in some other way,' she whispered. 'I—'

'You hoped?' he demanded incredulously, his eyebrows arched high. '*You hoped?*' he repeated. 'If you had spoken at the time we would have investigated then, when the trail was fresh. At the very least we would have known there was a rapist loose in the clearing station, and women would have taken the proper precautions for safety. Sarah Price would still be alive, and we would not have wasted weeks questioning and accusing and finally locking up the wrong man! Have you any concept of what you have—'

'Yes!' she cried out, tears running down her face.

'Yes, of course I know. Why do you think I came to you now? But I don't know who it was . . .'

'You should have come—' Onslow began.

Joseph lost his temper with the sheer, blind cruelty of the man. Had he no idea of the intimacy of the violation? Onslow was still talking about Sarah and how she might have been saved. Lizzie was standing motionless, not knowing how to defend herself. Joseph lunged forward and hit Onslow hard, throwing all his weight behind the blow. Onslow staggered backwards, crashing into the canvas, losing his balance and falling sideways on to the floor.

'Joseph! No!' Lizzie shouted, throwing herself at him and clinging on so he could not strike again, and they both lurched to a standstill.

Onslow blinked and lay still for several seconds before raising himself on to one elbow. He drew in his breath and shook his head. Then very slowly he clambered to his feet, still half leaning against the wall, dizzy with shock and pain from the blow.

Joseph was so angry that if Onslow had turned to Lizzie and spoken he would have hit him again, even though the realization was beginning to sink in that he had struck a superior officer and could find himself court-martialled and possibly even dishonourably discharged.

Onslow was staring at him. He might want to apologize, try to explain, but nothing could excuse what Onslow had done to Lizzie, and Joseph would not yield. He was a chaplain, not a career soldier, and Lizzie was more important to him than any calling. He stared back at Onslow without wavering.

Lizzie too must have been desperate to think of something to say. She looked from one to the other of them, her face ashen.

Onslow straightened his tunic and brushed himself down. 'I'm sorry, Mrs Blaine,' he said quietly. 'I am quite sure you feel your omission more than sufficiently. I should not have mentioned it. I cannot imagine the suffering you have already endured, and the insensitivity of some people's remarks. I apologize that I added to them.'

'You were right to blame me, sir,' she said, her voice trembling.

'I thought perhaps it might have been my own fault, that somehow I had unintentionally allowed someone to believe I held a regard for them that I didn't. We . . . we all tend to think somehow we were stupid, careless . . . but I have no idea who it was. I've gone over and over it in my mind, and I don't know. It's too late now to say who was here then, I realize that. I was so ashamed . . . I wanted to pretend it hadn't happened. I'm sorry.'

Joseph waited for Onslow to agree, but instead he turned to Joseph, his face already beginning to swell from the blow. 'You should watch your temper, Chaplain. Not every senior officer may appreciate your remarkable service to the men here, or realize that to charge you with assault at such a time, when the morale of the whole unit is so fragile, would not be in the army's best interest. You are very fortunate that I do.' He put his hand to his cheek and touched it gingerly. 'If anyone enquires, I shall say that I fell. You would be wise to be quite unaware of the whole incident.'

'Yes, sir.' Joseph was now suddenly embarrassed. Onslow was a better man than he had given him credit for, simply out of his depth with the subject of rape. And like most people, he disliked intensely having made a very public stand on an issue and then being proved to be wrong. 'Thank you,' he added.

'Thank your record with the Cambridgeshires, Captain Reavley,' Onslow replied. 'You are loved by the men. I think if I were to charge you I would lose their support completely. I'm not fool enough for that.'

There was a certain pain in his voice, a knowledge of having been a fool in other things. He stood awkwardly, beginning to realize he had been hit very hard indeed. 'Now I have to make certain that Schenckendorff is released, and that everyone knows that he could not be guilty. I don't want him attacked – again.'

He turned to Lizzie. 'I regret that I shall have to tell them why, Mrs Blaine, because if I do not, they may not believe me, and someone will take a private vengeance on him. I will not mention your name, but it is possible someone may guess. There is no alternative. I cannot allow the man to be murdered in an "accident",' he emphasized the word, 'because I am not believed.'

'I understand,' she said hoarsely. 'That would be almost as bad as him being hanged. Thank you, sir.'

Onslow nodded.

Joseph and Lizzie turned and went back out into the rain.

Later, Joseph walked alone around the old supply trench, remembering the men he had known who were gone, so many of them dead. He thought of them in the good times, the jokes, the sharing, the long stories about home, the letters, the dreams for the future. Had they loved him as much as Onslow thought? He had loved them, and watched them die. Had he been any help in this nightmare?

What help was he now to Lizzie, whom he loved? He thought he had learned to deal with death, even with mutilation, which was sometimes even harder. But there was an element in rape that was different, a violation not just of the body but of the inner core that was unique to a woman. If it had been somebody else, possibly even Judith, he would not feel so wounded within himself. There would not be the horror, the . . . he had been going to use the word 'revulsion' in his mind. Part of him wanted to run away from all of it, the whole issue – even from Lizzie, as if she had been spoiled for him.

But she had done nothing wrong, and he knew that. She was a victim, brutalized by a violent man, randomly – unless there was something in her vitality, a moment's kindness misunderstood, possibly even something as stupid as a passing resemblance to someone else he knew, which had sparked his act? It could have been anything.

But even if she had allowed a moment's carelessness, or worse, she was still a victim. If he turned away from her because that man had touched her, known her, was it not totally selfish, nothing to do with anything but his own feelings, not love at all? He would make her a victim again, doubly so, by rejecting her as if she were unclean.

He knew with complete, sickening finality that to do so would not only devastate her, it would destroy the bedrock of all his own faith, which had sustained him throughout the war. It had made the endless boredom endurable, the sudden blood-red agony, the nights in no-man's-land with men caught on the wires and torn apart by bullets, left hanging there, bleeding to death. He had sat cradling in his arms the broken bodies of those he had loved. He had seen them starving, freezing to death, drowned in mud, gagging and vomiting up their own lungs from poison gas, and he had not turned away, not said he could not bear it.

Was he now going to turn away from Lizzie because he wanted to spend the rest of his life with her, passionately, intimately, and he could not bear that she had been raped? If this that had happened to her could kill his ability to love, then he had learned nothing, and there was no hope for any of the wounded, the damaged, the millions who would come home changed for ever. And who was not damaged, in some way perhaps more hidden, more inward to the soul?

He must overcome it. To fail at this bitter test was to lose it all. He leaned against the trench wall, his clasped hands resting on the clay.

'Father, help me to do what I cannot do alone.' In the silence of the wilderness and the miles of the dead, he asked again and again, until finally a kind of peace settled over him, and a stillness blossomed inside, growing stronger than the pain.

'Such misogyny doesn't happen without something starting him off,' Matthew said a couple of hours later as he and Joseph sat on a pile of sandbags that had collapsed from an old parapet. It was one of the places they could expect to be alone. Time was growing desperately short, not only to find the rapist before he struck again, but because the war news that poured in every day made it obvious that the armistice was no more than a couple of weeks away – perhaps not even that. If they were to unmask the Peacemaker in time to prevent his taking a primary part in the final negotiations, then they must begin the journey to the coast within a day or two.

In spite of his resolve, Joseph's emotions were so raw he was unsure how well he could control them. Subtlety was needed, not violence, even in words. A careless comment or accusation, an implied threat, could damage their investigation. He was sharply aware of it, but still he could feel the pain taking over inside him, and he was afraid it would slip out of his control.

Most likely to snap his frail mastery were the men he knew well but who were still lying to him, or to themselves, through old loyalties to those they had fought beside and whose most intimate griefs they knew, perhaps even shared.

He made an intense effort. He must make his mind dominate his emotions. Think! There were facts that still remained unaltered by what Lizzie had told him. The only men who were not accounted for at the time Sarah had been killed were Cavan, Benbow and Wil Sloan. Surely it must be Benbow. And yet the impossible did happen; people changed beyond imagination. Nothing could be assumed. It was not only illogical to do so, it was morally unjust.

'A man to whom something has happened that has changed his life,' Joseph said.

'Or at least his pattern of behaviour,' Matthew replied. 'The violence towards women has to have begun very recently, or he'd have been caught before.'

'I suppose so,' Joseph said slowly. 'The change could come slowly, as it has for everyone, and perhaps the thought of going home has made him realize how deep it is.'

Matthew looked puzzled.

'Take Judith, for example,' Joseph tried to explain. 'She isn't the only one, but can you imagine how an average man would feel faced with a wife like her?'

'I know she's my sister, but I've always thought she was beautiful,' Matthew replied. 'And rather fun. Awkward – but you get used to that. Underneath it she's pretty decent, if you're being serious. And you are, aren't you?'

'Yes. Very. She's also bright, articulate, and she's got more courage than most men I know. She's a better driver, and can mend an engine with almost anything that comes to hand. She's steady under fire, can give first aid to the wounded or the dying. She'd probably shoot a man if she had to, and I can't imagine her fainting or having a fit of the vapours if the world ended, let alone if the sort of inconvenience happened that used to send our aunts and grandmothers into a swoon.'

'I know. We've all changed,' Matthew agreed.

'Do you know it, really?' Joseph pressed. 'I think I'm only beginning to see how much. Are we going to be able to deal with it with some courage, and grace?'

Far over their heads a reconnaissance plane circled slowly and banked hard, swinging off to the east, looking like a dragonfly over an endless marsh of zigzag ditches in the mud.

'It isn't that sudden, Joe,' Matthew pointed out.

'He may not have had much chance until recently,' Joseph reasoned. 'If he were at the front line, and not injured, he wouldn't see anyone except the occasional ambulance driver, and maybe not even that.'

'You mean this was his first opportunity?' Matthew asked.

'Could be. Before then his violence was very properly turned towards the enemy.' He winced.

Joseph knew what he was thinking, but there was no time now to dwell on the effect of war on young men. Certainly there was nothing they could do about it. 'We have to find out what happened to someone that made his rage or sense of helplessness explode.' His memory reached back over the distress he had seen even in the last few years: the letters men had received from home on bereavement there also, the loss of other members of the family or close friends. The grief was hard and deep-scouring. Then there might be children they barely knew, babies born whom they might never see. But it was deceit that tore men apart, wounding irreparably: the sweetheart who could not or would not wait; and, worst by far, the wives who betrayed.

Matthew was watching him. His eyes squinted narrowly in a

sudden burst of sun dazzling where it caught the water in a series of craters, rippled by the east wind till the light danced. 'Don't you know, Joe, if you really think about it?' he asked quickly. 'Who's been cheated and left by a woman he loved, and should have been able to trust? Who's been belittled or laughed at? Everyone's been changed by what they've seen out here, even more by what they've done. Nobody is going to go home the same as they were before. Who has a wife that can't accept that?'

Joseph thought of them, one after the other, hearing again in his mind the tight, quiet voices of men for whom the gulf had become too great, whose friends were now strangers to whom they could no longer explain themselves, no longer share the laughter or the pain of the things that lay deepest. Perhaps it was the ultimate price of war, the change to the living more than the loss of the dead.

'It's Dante again,' he said aloud. 'Rewarded not for what we do, but by it – and by what we see, and what we see others do?'

Matthew said nothing.

'The "Inferno",' Joseph explained unnecessarily, wondering if some of Dante's wasted landscape of hell might look a bit like this. Did the River Styx look like this slow-moving, stagnant mud, filled with human remains from battles won and lost? That would symbolize despair very well. What about the forward lines now, all rage and noise, flame of gunfire and shattering destruction, the landscape of anger?

What about the uniquely human sins of corruption and betrayal? That was probably perfectly ordinary; with a smiling face, only the eyes were empty.

'Everything we do changes us, becomes part of what we are,' he said aloud. 'Do you think we'll ever get over this, Matthew?

Will we recover and become human again, innocent enough to have hope, to value human life and believe in a God who loves us, who has enough power to heal us, to affect anything that happens on earth? Or are we finally on the edge of the abyss, and falling?' The minute he had said it he wished he had not. It was selfish. Matthew was his younger brother, the one man above all others to whom he owed a better care than this, and some kind of protection from the darkness inside.

'Sorry,' he said aloud. 'I'll try to think who had bad news of some sort about a month ago. Whoever was closest to him will have noticed something. Trouble is, I'm the chaplain. If I know of it as a confidence there's only a limited amount I can repeat.' He pushed his hand over his forehead and back through his hair. 'What a bloody mess.'

Joseph sat in his bunker alone, trying to remember every private and wounding grief he had heard some man stammer out to him, looking for any kind of comfort, any sense of justice in their pain. Would the women who had loved these men accept what they had become, or would they be unable to cope with the memories? Would they even begin to understand the guilt of those who had survived when their friends had not?

Would the horror of killing an enemy soldier so much like a mirror-image of yourself make any kind of sense? He was not there because he wanted to be, any more than you were. On a still night you could hear him talking with his friends, laughing, singing.

No wonder you could not sleep. It was easy to see petty problems – a blocked drain, a disobedient child, a spilled jug of milk – as nothing at all. Life mattered. Friends, a whole body, someone to watch with you through the night.

Who had spoken of something bad enough to make him hate all women? Joseph thought of the men betrayed or deserted and went through their names one by one, ticking off each as he knew they were dead, too badly injured, gone home already, or somewhere else far forward of here.

Turner was the first of those left who seemed possible. His wife had left him for Turner's own brother, who had escaped military service because of flat feet, or something of the sort. Turner's rage had been almost uncontrollable. Joseph had thought it was directed against the war in general and the Germans in particular. But perhaps in time it had bent instead towards women.

And it seemed Culshaw was lying to protect him, again as one man did for his friend, perhaps not realizing there was anything more than a lapse of judgement, and of discipline.

'Of course he's bloody furious!' Culshaw had exploded. 'His own brother! Flat feet or cross-eyes, or some such damn thing! So he stays safe at home coining in the money on the black market while we're out here in the rats and the filth getting shot at. Sometimes I don't understand women at all. Have they got no honour, no sense of friendship, loyalty . . . anything?'

'Women are no more all alike than men are,' Joseph had answered him. 'Some men will sleep with anything that stays still long enough, and you know that as well as I do. Don't you think their wives feel just as used and betrayed?'

Culshaw had looked confused. 'Are you saying it's the same, Chaplain?'

Joseph had sighed. 'No,' he said wearily. He was honest enough to admit that, whatever reason or justice told him, it was not. His own reaction to Lizzie being raped forced him to acknowledge that reason had very little to do with the deepest passions, the intimacy of violation. 'No, it's not the same, Culshaw. If a man is betrayed by a woman he loved, he doesn't forget it, and he doesn't heal easily. And if a woman is raped by a man, she doesn't forget that either, or heal. Neither does any man who loved her. Have you considered that?'

Culshaw's face was very pale, the lines of exhaustion deep in his skin. 'I never saw it like that.'

'How did you see it?' Joseph had asked him.

Culshaw's eyes were wide. 'He didn't do that!' he breathed out the words. 'I swear! Jesus, do you think I'd have covered for him if he had? He skewered that German officer's foot, and he'd have beaten the hell out of any of the other prisoners, if we'd let him, but he never touched Sarah Price. You have to believe me!'

'I don't have to,' Joseph told him, disgust filling his mind at the senseless violence towards men already beaten by violence and shame.

'But it's the truth!' Culshaw protested desperately.

'Yes,' Joseph conceded. 'I dare say it is.'

Judith was thinking of the same things, but she at least faced the practical questions she had been wishing she could avoid. Material proof would have been so much easier, less viciously painful, but perhaps in the end it was always going to have come to this. She could not expect Joseph to do it, or Matthew, for that matter.

Now it could wait no longer. She told Wil she would be gone for a while, but gave him no other explanation.

She found Lizzie helping Allie Robinson. They were preparing some of the more seriously wounded for evacuation. There was an almost euphoric sense of release now that the railway station was open again and men could leave. It was as if a long paralysis were ended.

'Lizzie, I need to speak to you,' Judith said quietly. 'Sorry, but it's urgent.'

Allie looked at her sharply. 'When this is finished, Miss Reavley,' she said with a certain coolness. There was a warning in her eyes and her manner. Judith was overstepping her authority.

'It's urgent,' Judith repeated. 'I'm sorry, but there's no time to wait.'

Allie stiffened. 'If you have wounded, Miss Reavley, then you need either an orderly to help you, or a doctor. You do not need Mrs Blaine, who is already occupied here.'

Judith's emotions were raw with loathing of what she had to do. She felt guilty because of the pain she knew she was going to cause, and afraid Lizzie would hate her for it. Allie was a nuisance she had not foreseen and the irritation of it scraped her raw, but if she lost her temper it would only make it all more difficult, especially for Lizzie.

'I don't have wounded,' she replied as civilly as she could, but her voice had an edge to it and she could hear it herself.

'I thought not.' Allie smiled bleakly. 'Then you will have to wait.'

Judith took a deep breath and let it out slowly. 'It can't wait, Allie. It's important.'

Allie's eyebrows rose. 'To whom, Miss Reavley? To you?' The formal use of her name was a rebuke and her face had no warmth in it, no possibility of yielding.

'It's not your concern, Miss Robinson, but if you force the issue, to Major Onslow of the Military Police. It is a matter of information, which it is surely obvious I cannot discuss.' It was no more than half a lie.

Anger flared in Allie's eyes. 'Then why did you not say so in the first place?' she asked angrily. 'Just because you drive an ambulance around like a man does not give you the right to come in here giving orders. You forget yourself. You are going to find it extremely difficult after the war when you are not needed any more. You would be wise to learn how to behave like a woman again. You are in danger of becoming a complete misfit, unwanted by men and an embarrassment to women.'

Judith was stunned. The fury in Allie's manner had taken her completely by surprise. Was it her own fear speaking? Surely not. There were going to be years of skilled nursing ahead; peace would not affect that.

'Well, if it's so urgent, get on with it!' Allie snapped. 'Experience your authority. You won't have it much longer, make the most of it.'

Judith bit back her retaliation and looked at Lizzie. They went out together, Lizzie looking anxious and unhappy.

As soon as they were beyond the evacuation tent and in the open, the day bright and cold with frost in the wind, Lizzie spoke again.

'Does Major Onslow really want to see me?'

'No,' Judith said quickly. 'I do. But in a way it's half true. But not here. Your bunker or mine?'

'Mine's closer. What is it?'

'I'm sorry,' Judith said fiercely. 'I really am. I wouldn't do this if there were any other way.'

Lizzie walked in silence. It was a bad beginning. She was already afraid. They reached the bunker and went down the steps inside. It smelled of damp earth, enclosed space. The wooden slats on the floor were rotting, but still better than the bare mud.

'What is it?' Lizzie demanded again. 'Do they know something?' She did not sit down but remained standing, facing Judith in the gloom.

Judith could understand very easily how Lizzie might rather not know who had raped her, whose child she was carrying. Anonymity kept him one step removed. She wished with passion that she could leave it that way, or at least leave the choice to Lizzie.

'I'm sorry,' she said again. 'I am! They don't know, and all we can work out is that it had to be Cavan, Wil Sloan or Benbow.'

'How?' Even in the shadows the disbelief on Lizzie's face was obvious. 'It could have been anyone! I have no idea.'

'It couldn't have been just anyone who killed Sarah. Everybody else is ruled out.' It was brutal, but Lizzie had to know it was true. She had said so herself, to Onslow.

Lizzie sat down slowly on the bunk. Now she seemed unbearably tired, as if the strength inside her were totally used up. 'I don't know,' she said again. 'I'd hate to think it was Cavan, or Wil Sloan, but I can't say it was Benbow because I don't know! It might not have been.' She stared at Judith. 'When it comes to it, even the people we like can have terrible secrets that we have no idea of. I'm not going to say it was Benbow, just because Cavan and Wil are your friends. I'm sorry.'

Judith was momentarily stunned. It was the last thing she had thought of, at least consciously, but she could see how easily Lizzie must have thought of it.

'I don't want you to! That isn't what I meant at all. Of course I don't want it to be them, but if it is, then we must face it.'

'What do you want?'

Now was the moment. 'Onslow didn't ask you to go through it for him in detail, did he?'

'No!'

'Joseph wouldn't, or Matthew.' That was really a statement rather than a question. She knew the answer.

'No.' Lizzie's voice was quiet, but there was dread in it.

'Somebody must,' Judith said as gently as she could. 'You might remember something . . .'

'I don't! I don't know who it was! Just a man . . . a soldier. Judith, if I knew, don't you think I'd tell you?'

'Yes, of course you would. Just tell me anything. What time was it, roughly?'

'Some time between midnight and three. I can't remember now. We were busy.'

'What were you doing before it happened? Where were you?'

Lizzie hesitated. 'In the resuscitation tent. We'd just finished a bad one. We lost him.'

'Who did the operation?'

'Cavan, Bream, Moira Jessop.'

Judith felt cold. 'Then what?'

'We had the body taken away. Joseph wasn't here; he was up in the lines. I don't know where everybody went. I felt dreadful. We'd fought really hard. Thought he was going to make it. He was . . . about seventeen.' Her voice caught and she struggled to keep control of it. 'I went outside. I wanted to be alone and not have to look at anybody else's face. I . . .' She stopped, then started again. 'I was standing outside in the dark, somewhere beyond the evacuation tent, when I realized there was someone near me.'

'How?' Judith interrupted. 'How did you realize it? Did you see him?'

'No.' Lizzie thought for a moment. 'I heard his feet squelch in the mud. It wasn't so bad then, but it had rained earlier and there were a few places that never seemed to get dry.'

'Did he speak? Did you hear him breathing?'

'No, I don't think so. Does it matter now? I can't tell one person's breathing from another.' Lizzie's voice was strained, tight in her throat as memory brought it back to her.

'It might,' Judith insisted. 'Then what? Were you frightened?'

'No, of course I wasn't! I didn't think there was anything to be frightened of. Then the next thing I know he'd caught hold of me from behind, and . . . and twisted me round to face him. But before you ask, we were in shadow and it was cloudy. I didn't see his face at all. That's the truth.'

'How tall was he?' Judith asked.

'What?'

'How tall was he?' she repeated. 'A lot taller than you? A little?'

Lizzie shut her eyes. 'It doesn't matter, Judith. Cavan, Wil and Benbow are all much the same height, within an inch or two. They're all half a foot taller than I am.'

'I know. But he kissed you?'

'Yes! I told you!' Lizzie's voice was ragged, her control slipping.

Judith felt brutal, but she did not stop. 'Where were his hands?'

'Hands? I don't know! I . . .'

'Yes? What? Why didn't you twist away?'

'He held my face . . .'

'Smell,' Judith said instantly. 'What did his hands smell of?'

Lizzie froze, her eyes wide.

'Ether? Disinfectant? Blood?' Judith demanded.

'No . . . no, smoke, like cigarettes,' Lizzie replied. 'And oil?'

'What kind of oil?' Judith's voice was shaking now too. 'Think! Was it petrol, metallic oil, butter? What? Bring it back, exactly?'

'It wasn't Cavan, was it?' Lizzie said with certainty. 'He couldn't have got rid of the ether and disinfectant. Engine oil from Wil, gun oil from Benbow.'

'Yes. What was it?'

The silence was intense, as if the clay walls behind the wood shoring them up was somehow absorbing the sound, even their breath.

'I'm not sure. Bitter,' Lizzie said at last. 'I couldn't smell petrol, just tobacco, cigarette smoke, and a tiny bit of metallic oil. No . . . he . . .' Lizzie stopped with a gasp.

'What? What?'

'I heard him put it down . . .' Lizzie said with slow, gasping amazement. 'I remember . . . I heard him put it down. It unbalanced and fell against the duckboards. It was Benbow! It had to have been! Wil and Cavan don't have guns. And his tunic was rough, khaki. Cavan was still in his white coat.' She swallowed convulsively. 'Why didn't I know that before?'

'You didn't want to remember it. Who would?' Judith said simply. 'I'm sorry . . .'

Lizzie shook her head. 'No. Don't be. What should I do? I suppose I have to tell Onslow?' She was afraid, her fear palpable in the closed room.

'Not yet,' Judith replied. 'I'll tell Joseph first.' She heard Lizzie's sharp drawing-in of breath, and understood. 'He has to know some time. Get it over. I'll do it. At least you won't be afraid of everyone now. But don't be alone . . . promise?'

Lizzie gave a very slight smile. 'I promise.'

'Come on then. Now! Come with me back to Allie. She's a

pretty good bitch at times, but at least you know where you stand with her.'

'Benbow? Are you sure?' Matthew asked.

Joseph repeated the essence of what Judith had told him. He tried to keep his emotion out of it, think of it as a string of facts, imprison his imagination so none of it was real.

'Sounds pretty solid,' Matthew said gravely. 'I'm glad it wasn't Cavan or Wil Sloan. I'm sorry, Joe. Do you want to face him, or would you rather not?'

'We'll have to go to Onslow anyway,' Joseph pointed out. 'I hit him. I should do that.'

Matthew frowned. 'Are you sure?'

'Yes. Come on, if I don't do that I'm going to fall long before the last fence.' Joseph made himself smile. He was the eldest. It was his responsibility. He was the one who loved Lizzie. 'I'll go now.'

But it proved to be far harder than he had anticipated. Onslow accepted the evidence without argument, but when he had Benbow brought in it was a very different matter. He looked haggard, ashen-faced, and, standing feet away, Joseph could smell the fear in him.

'I didn't kill Sarah Price!' he protested, struggling uselessly against the manacles that held his hands tight behind his back. 'I didn't, I swear to God! I never touched her!' He wrenched himself round to face Joseph. 'Chaplain, I swear! All right, Moira Jessop played me around rotten, an' I took her, all right, an' I weren't none too gentle, fought like a wild cat, but that was a month ago, more. I never touched Sarah Price. Jesus! What do you think I am? She was sliced to bits!'

'You raped Moira Jessop?' Onslow said incredulously. He stared from Benbow to Joseph, and back again.

'Where?' Joseph demanded. 'Exactly where? What time?'

Benbow looked stunned. 'Out . . . outside the evacuation tent,' he stammered.

'Were you carrying a rifle?' Joseph asked.

'I never hurt her!' Benbow shouted. 'I swear—'

'Did you drop it?'

'Yes! I don't know. I must 'ave. Why? I never used any kind of knife on 'er. I never even hit 'er. I just . . .' His face was grey, his eyes wild. 'I didn't! She led me on, played . . . Oh God!'

'Did she see your face?' Onslow asked.

'She couldn't 'ave. It was dark,' Benbow responded. 'Could hardly see where you were going.'

Onslow looked across at Joseph again.

'How do you know it was Moira Jessop?' Joseph asked Benbow.

'I . . . I followed 'er out of the . . .' Suddenly Benbow surged and gulped air.

'It wasn't,' Joseph said quietly. 'You forced yourself on another woman, one who had never given you the slightest indication that she had any interest in you at all.'

Benbow stood silently, blinking as if blinded.

'And Sarah Price?' Onslow asked again.

'I never touched 'er. I swear to God,' Benbow replied hoarsely.

Joseph nodded slowly. There was no proof. He was not sure whether to believe it or not, but it was possible that the man who had raped Lizzie and the man who had murdered Sarah were not the same person.

Onslow looked profoundly unhappy. 'That will be for a jury to decide,' he said grimly. 'Take him away.'

After Benbow had been removed, Onslow faced Joseph. 'I'm sorry,' he emphasized. 'Perhaps Mrs Blaine will find some kind of relief, however small, in the knowledge that she was not the intended victim. I hope so.'

'Do you think it is possible he didn't kill Sarah Price?' Joseph said slowly, trying to work his way through the maze of facts, contradiction and anger.

'Frankly, I have no idea,' Onslow admitted. 'If I had to stake anything on it, I think it is possible, yes.'

'It has to be Benbow!' Matthew said savagely, staring at Joseph in disbelief. 'You can't think we have two rapists loose here?'

'I don't know what I think,' Joseph admitted. They were walking slowly along the rotting duckboards of the old supply trench coming back from the front line to the bunkers.

'Did Benbow have blood on him?' Matthew asked. 'Eames must have noticed.'

Joseph bit his lip. 'He says not, but Benbow was pretty wet and he had mud on his boots up to his knees. He says he slipped in one of the shallow craters. That could be true.'

Matthew swore. 'And I suppose Cavan was covered in blood from operating, and Wil Sloan from carrying in the wounded?'

'They would be,' Joseph agreed.

They discussed it further, achieving nothing. Finally Joseph left and walked on past the bunkers towards the admissions tent. The wind from the east was rising and in the gathering dusk the clear sky promised a frost. The colours were fragile and cold even over the ruined landscape to the west where the dying light was a clear lilac pink after the sun slipped below the horizon. The gunfire was too far away to be heard except as a distant rumble.

They had to solve this obscene crime. It could not be allowed to slip into oblivion because the war was ending and bit by bit the weary, soul-bruised men would be allowed to go home to whatever awaited them.

And what had made some desperate man slip from rape down the abyss to mutilation and slaughter? What happens in the mind of anyone to lose that last grip on any humanity? What he had done to Lizzie, believing her to be Moira, was crude and ugly, and deserved punishment. It was humiliating and destructive to do such a thing to any woman, whatever the provocation. But what someone had done to Sarah was bestial, outside the realms of sanity.

But how, Joseph thought, could he deal in ideas of sanity after the killing of the last five years? They had spent their nights and their days killing total strangers at any opportunity because they spoke a different language and were of a different culture. Not very different, just a little. It wasn't quite brother against brother, more like cousin against cousin. Is a thing sane if enough people do it?

No! They killed in war to defend the freedom to choose their own collective kind of life, of belief, of order in things. Rape was an act of hatred, of power to dominate. It was also a kind of invasion by force, but more intimate than an army's trespass on land.

Why Sarah? She had flirted quite openly with the German prisoners. Several people had said so, not necessarily with anger. But perhaps to someone it had been the ultimate offence?

Then another thought occurred to him, so ridiculous he dismissed it.

It must be Benbow, in spite of the lack of blood on him. Apart from anything else, he was carrying a rifle and bayonet. Every man on guard duty did. Neither Cavan nor Wil Sloan had such a weapon. Cavan would have a scalpel. But Joseph still refused to believe that Cavan could be guilty. No evidence short of an eye witness would make him accept that the man he knew had descended from the selfless courage of a year ago, unnoticed by anyone, into the pit of madness where he would rape a woman he knew and had worked beside, even cared for, not with his body but with the raw blade of a bayonet!

It would be like walking side by side with a friend, and turning to discover a creature beside you who had the devil's soul looking out of his eyes.

But Cavan could not account for his time. Allie Robinson had lied to protect him, and he had allowed her to until Joseph had caught him in it. He had said he had been in the evacuation tent, but he hadn't.

Joseph was sick with misery as if the evidence were closing in around him like an enemy in the dark. Any hour now it might strike the blow that could not be parried, the proof that could not be denied.

There was no point in asking Cavan himself, and he could keep Allie Robinson until last when she could no longer lie, no matter how bitter it was to admit that Cavan could have changed so tragically from the man he had once been.

He began his enquiries with Erica Barton-Jones. He found her with Stan Tidyman. The soldier still looked grey-faced, his eyes hollow, but he was wrapped up with a pillow and a blanket rolled tight to support him. He managed a faint smile.

Joseph asked after him briefly, then took Erica to one side, over in the corner of the tent beside a table piled with old blankets, bandages and other stores. They could hear the rain drumming on the canvas.

'The night Sarah was killed,' he said without preamble. 'Tell me what you can remember of where everyone was, just what you are certain of. From about midnight onward.'

'It was a bad night,' she said grimly. 'I can't tell you times, only where I was.'

'How many surgeons on duty?'

'Two – Captain Cavan and Captain Ellsworth – and there were anaesthetists and orderlies, of course.'

He did not tell her that he knew this already, or that all but Cavan were accounted for. 'Tell me what you recall,' he asked.

She repeated what she had said from the beginning, every case, what was done and an estimate of the time. He stopped her, questioned, made her repeat and be as precise as possible, everything checked against what others had said.

'What is it you expect, Chaplain?' she demanded exasperatedly. 'Going over and over it isn't going to help. I don't know who killed Sarah, or what snapped in somebody's head, or why it was her and not somebody else. Except that she was the one who flirted, but she certainly wasn't the only one who fell in love, or had normal human feelings.' Her face pinched and she turned half away from him. 'If you are looking for some unique sin in her that's going to make you feel there's any kind of justice in this, then you aren't going to find it. And quite frankly I think you are morally dishonest to try. There isn't any justice, and nobody with any . . . any courage . . . is going to believe there is.'

He was startled. He had not even considered such a thing. 'If it was always just, then there would be no courage necessary,' he pointed out. 'In fact not even possible. If being good would automatically make you safe, then it wouldn't even be good, it would just be sensible: buying safety, buying your way out of pain or failure, confusion, everything that hurts. Is that what you thought – that I was looking for sense in it?'

She stared at him, her face pale and tired in the half light. 'Aren't you? Aren't you longing to explain God, so we won't stop believing in Him?'

'No. I gave that up years ago, even before the war, let alone since.' He thought for an instant how he had felt after Eleanor's death, the anger and confusion, the long retreat from emotion into the religion of the brain. That was over now, a kind of little death from which he had been awoken. 'No,' he said again. 'I'm still looking for whoever killed Sarah because they have to be stopped. I'm not sure it's even anything to do with justice for her, or for them. It's a very practical matter of them being prevented from doing it again.'

She blinked. 'Sometimes I think you are so pointless, so divorced from the realities of life, well-meaning but essentially futile.' She gave a sigh. 'Then you come out with something that makes me feel that perhaps you are the only one who really is dealing with the truth, bigger than the little bits of reality we manage.'

'Sometimes,' he said with a slight smile.

She smiled back at him. 'I still don't know who did it.'

'Do you know if Cavan was in the evacuation tent when he said he was?'

'No, I don't.'

'Allie Robinson said he was, but she was lying, to cover for him,' he told her.

'That was stupid,' she said drily. 'She can't have been there herself. I saw her at about four o'clock, or shortly after, and she'd been in the admissions tent for some time.'

'No, she was in evacuation,' he corrected her. 'She was seen there by Benbow, and Eames as well.'

She shook her head. 'I saw her and she was covered in blood. She must have been in admissions. She was perfectly clean apart from a few spots on her skirt at about half-past three, and by the time any of the wounded get to evacuation they're band-aged and fit to go, or they wouldn't be there. You only get soaked in blood like that either in admissions or in lying wounded, waiting for operations.' Then suddenly her eyes widened and she stared at him aghast.

He could not believe it. It was hideous, terrible, but he knew exactly what she was thinking. The images raced through his mind also, increasing, growing clearer and more real. The hatred was there, the sense of morality and meaning to life falling apart. It was not only in violence and death on every side, but then finally at the core, the very fount of creation, the reason that redeemed all else and gave hope for newness, cleanness in the world again.

Men were dead or damaged everywhere, the flower of a gener-ation. No one could count the number of women who would live alone, and childless. A new, harsher order had taken over, and it was terrifying. Women, the keepers of sanity, had themselves cast it aside. There was a way in which that was the ultimate betrayal, the end of hope itself.

That was why the bayonet had been used – woman punishing the suicide of womanhood. How had he not even guessed at that before? Sarah's playing with Cavan, and then flirting with the German prisoners was the final, unbearable offence, committed while British men were only yards away, bleeding to an agonizing death, awake and hideously aware of all of it.

Erica was still staring at him, but there was no struggle left in her eyes. She knew it was true. 'I'm sorry,' she said gravely. 'I didn't see it either, and I should have. I was so sure it was a man. I thought it was Benbow. I saw certain . . . certain things he did, a way he looked at some of the women, especially Moira Jessop. That isn't evidence, and I misjudged him. I even thought of warning her not to tease him. I would have wronged him, wouldn't I?' She gave a bleak grimace of self-criticism.

Joseph did not answer. It was all past, and it would not help. He needed to find Onslow, and Jacobson too. Jacobson deserved to know. They would have to arrest Allie Robinson, and release all the men kept here, sending the wounded home and the few able-bodied back to the fighting. The station itself would be moved forward to where it was still needed.

'A woman?' Onslow said slowly, as if the very word were information to him, let alone the idea.

Patiently, allowing the horror to fill his words, Joseph explained to him the passion of betrayal that he believed Allie had seen: the ultimate obscenity of a woman like Sarah threatening to defile the very source of life, of nurture, of every hope to make everything clean and new.

'If there is no home to go back to, no one to love, to forgive and to start again, what was the pain all for?' he finished.

'Can we prove it?' Onslow asked, his voice hushed.

'Not easily, but I think so,' Joseph answered. 'But we must certainly try.'

Onslow wiped his hand over his brow. 'Come on, then. We'd better go and find her.' His hand went automatically to the revolver at his belt, reassuring himself it was there.

Joseph could not tell him whether it was unnecessary.

Allie Robinson was in the operating tent. Cavan was busy suturing a lacerated foot. He barely looked up.

Allie saw Joseph's face, and Onslow just behind him. She stiffened, her eyes wide.

Onslow walked forward slowly, moving a little towards the operating table so he cut her off from it, placing himself between her and the soldier whose foot was being stitched.

She saw the finality in his expression. She stepped back, closer to the table with the instruments on it, scalpel, forceps, needles, clamps.

'Don't do that,' Onslow said quietly. 'It's all over, Miss Robinson. Don't make it worse.'

'Worse?' she said, as if he had asked her a question. 'What could be worse? We've destroyed everything. What we haven't killed or maimed, we've defiled beyond help. There isn't anything left to win or lose. Our civilization is dead. Nothing is clean or modest or gentle as it used to be. It's all strident, dirty. We've forgotten who we are, and when you do that, there's nothing worth having at all. It's all dirt and blood.' She took another step back.

'Miss Robinson!' Onslow said loudly, his voice high with alarm.

But it was too late. She swung round and grasped a scalpel, looked at him for an instant, then plunged it into her chest. She was a good nurse; she had seen lots of men torn open by shrapnel. She knew exactly where to strike. The blood gushed out scarlet and she crumpled over to the floor; and did not move again.

The soldier on the table fainted.

Cavan went as white as his coat and gagged, holding his hands over his mouth, the needle dangling by its thread.

Onslow sighed. 'Sorry,' he apologized. 'I should have stopped that. Not that it would have helped, really.'

Joseph bent and straightened Allie out, removing the scalpel. The blood was still pouring, but it would stop soon. She was already dead. He felt sad and helpless.

'Poor creature,' he said quietly. 'And it won't change anything. We'll still have to find a way to heal.'

# Chapter Ten

Now they must race for the coast. There were only days to get Schenckendorff to London. Judith and Lizzie were volunteers, and could leave without difficulty. Mason could do as he chose. Matthew was due to return to London. Only Joseph was regular army, and for him to leave would be desertion.

'You have to,' Matthew said simply.

'I'll tell Colonel Hook—' Joseph began.

'You can't!' Matthew's expression left no room for argument or negotiation. 'We're this close, Joseph.' He held up his hand, fingers and thumb half an inch apart. 'The Peacemaker has eyes and ears everywhere. Hook has the power to stop us all. We can't take the chance.'

'Colonel Hook!' Joseph was incredulous. They were all crammed into his bunker, which was so confined they could not sit without touching each other. Only Schenckendorff was missing. Joseph looked at Mason, having to twist round to do it.

Mason's face was bleak. 'Anyone,' he said simply. 'I don't know who else believes the Peacemaker, or I'd tell you. We have to just leave. Fill cans with as much petrol as we can get hold of, as much food, and go. We could still lose it all.'

Joseph gave in. It was legally desertion, and it felt like it: no goodbyes, no explanation. But it was his men he cared about, and if Hook explained to them, news of it could reach the Peacemaker in hours.

He sighed, and nodded briefly.

Matthew resumed making plans.


Judith wanted to say goodbye to many people, particularly Cavan, and above all, Wil Sloan, but she too was aware of the danger. However she did it, or whatever she said, someone would notice and say something. Word would be passed around before they were more than a few miles away. For her, as for Joseph, any risk, however small, was too much. No one else could know how ruthless the Peacemaker was, or how far his knowledge and his alliances had spread.

So she said nothing, and felt disloyal as, shivering in the dark, she drove the ambulance out of the casualty clearing station on to the mud track to pick up Joseph and Matthew. They were supporting Schenckendorff between them, as he was still unable to put his weight on his injured foot. A few yards further on they were joined by Lizzie and Mason, climbing in the back of the ambulance hastily and closing the doors as Judith accelerated and made for the road.

Mason sat beside her. He alone was of no immediate use in the back where Lizzie was swallowing her occasional morning nausea and attending to Schenckendorff's injured foot. Joseph and Matthew were talking quietly about a route back through Belgium, and then across the Channel. Time was short. It was already 3 November, and a ceasefire could be declared within days. Matthew had a little money, but where to find further supplies was a far greater problem than paying for them. The availability of food and petrol was beyond being simply a matter of the price.

Judith drove steadily, with concentration. She worried not only about fuel but also about spare parts if they should have any sort of breakdown, not to mention accident. The ambulance was on its last legs anyway. Once away from the army lines with their supply stores, there would be nowhere to get oil, or any of the parts she might need. She had had no compunction about taking with her all that she could, begging, borrowing, or removing without the owner's consent three new plugs. Had she been able to explain the urgency, she was quite sure they would have been given willingly.

Now they drove through the fine, dry night. The air became colder in the open front of the vehicle, and the wind from the north swirled around, creeping in between folds of coats and scarves, numbing hands and whipping the blood in cheeks and brows.

Mason was used to it. He had spent the last four years in every kind of vehicle, on every battle front from the deserts of Arabia to the Arctic snows of Russia. As he sat here now, moving along the ruined roads of Belgium on the last journey of his own battle, he had a smile on his face and he seemed almost relaxed.

Judith looked sideways at him once or twice and saw the change in him. She was almost frighteningly happy to think that it was his feeling for her that had caused it. She wanted it to be so much that she could neither believe nor disbelieve it. And also she felt guilty, because it would cost him a high and terrible price. In exposing the Peacemaker he would be confessing to his own part in the treason. Only now was she realizing the meaning of that. There was peace ahead, and justice that would finally call Dermot Sandwell to account for the betrayal of his countrymen, and the murders of all those who had stood in his way.

And there was honour for Matthew and for Schenckendorff. Perhaps for Mason there would be at least the acceptance of a faith in life he had denied before, even fought against. But there would be no future for him with Judith. What he was going to admit to amounted to treason, and the only punishment for that was execution. That thought hurt her terribly.

She stared into the darkness ahead. The road was nearly dry. At the sides were occasional poplars. Many of them were little more than stumps, but now and then a few had branches, leafless like broken bones. Clear patches in the sky let the moonlight gleam fitfully, showing a landscape of craters and stretches of mud, and now and then the jagged walls of a bombed-out building. The ambulance passed a canal, its walls breached, the flood water flat and pale and irregularly shaped as it seeped away into the fields, sometimes lapping right up to the raised edges of the road.

She would not have changed Mason, or had him sink back into the cynicism of before. She remembered their quarrel at the court martial, the sense of futility that seemed to touch all his thoughts. It was not simply that he believed Joseph's efforts were pointless, but that they were foolish, in a way even contemptible because they were rooted in a refusal to face reality. He had thought both she and Joseph were cowards, clinging on to faith in a God who did not exist, because they had not the courage to live alone in the universe.

Why had he changed? Yes, he was in love with her. But so was she in love with him. No matter how much you loved someone, you could not alter who you were in order to be comfortable with them. If you loved the right person it should make you stronger, braver, gentler, perhaps eventually wiser. It should never make you deny your intelligence or forsake your integrity. What were you worth if you would do that?

She looked sideways at him again, trying to read his face in the few moments she could spare from watching the road. His eyes were wide and dark, staring ahead of him, and now there was a deep sadness in the curve of his mouth.

He must have been aware of her – because he turned and smiled.

'It isn't for me, is it, that you're doing this?' she said with something close to certainty, willing it to be so.

'No,' he said without hesitation. 'Because of you, perhaps – you and Joseph – but because I have to satisfy myself.'

She felt something of the fear ease out of her, the knots loosen.

'Were you afraid it was for you?' he asked, and this time there was amusement in his voice. 'That then you would owe me something?' He did not add that you cannot owe love; she knew he was thinking it, just as she was. She felt the heat in her face and was glad of the concealing darkness. There was only the occasional yellow glare of lamps as they passed some lone farmhouse still standing, or a group of people stopped temporarily, huddled around a fire, now and again vehicle lights going the other way.

Perhaps at last they understood each other in the deepest things; the values that are woven into nature, the need to be at peace with who you are, together or alone.

As if the emotion were too strong, and the time too short,

Mason moved away from it. 'I know you've dressed Schenckendorff as a British VAD, but you'd better not let him speak. He still sounds German to me. I'll wager any Belgian in the country knows German when he hears it. They have years of hate to avenge. They aren't going to forget it. Does Joseph really think they will?'

'No,' she said simply. 'Have you got a better idea?'

'No I haven't. But we'd better be right. We're going to have to stop for fuel sometime. We won't make it all the way to the coast on what we have. One mistake will be the last.'

'I know.' It was what she had been dreading. Even the basic difficulty of finding fuel could be enough to delay their journey fatally, let alone if the ambulance broke down and she could not find the parts to mend it, or had not the skill. Even any prolonged time in one place put them in danger of exposure. At best they might be taken for British deserters. Once anyone realized Schenckendorff was German, they might all be suspected.

'Judith?' Mason said quietly, his voice breaking through his thoughts.

'Yes?'

'We'll make it.' He was smiling. 'You, of all people, are not going to fall at the last fence.'

'Why not? It can happen.'

'There are three of you!' His smile was broader now, a kind of happiness in him.

'There are six of us,' she corrected him, slightly puzzled.

'Three Reavleys! That should be enough to take on the world, let alone the odd corner of Belgium,' he retorted.

She glanced at him and saw the laughter under the surface, and also the tenderness in his face, even in the pale, shifting reflections of light from the road. He was not mocking her; he wanted to mean it, wanted to hope.

The first stop came after about five hours. They were in flat country, further from the fighting, but this land had been occupied by enemy troops and the roads had been heavily bombed. One small river had spread wide, flooding the area behind the broken bridge and the scattered debris that had blocked it. There was nothing to do but go around the water-logged fields, which took them several miles out of their way, costing precious time and petrol. That meant they now needed to get more fuel. They dare not run too low.

They stopped at the next village and Judith made the request from a mechanic attempting to mend a battered van. She was in uniform and felt consumed with guilt when the few cans were given willingly. They had assumed that her passengers were wounded men being taken to the nearest port to ship to England. One man asked if the railway line had been bombed, and that was why they had come this way. He looked surprised that this sort of difficulty should crop up this late in the war.

'Zeppelin?' he said questioningly. 'Stupid! They'll lose now whatever they do. It's nearly over.' His voice choked. He was elderly with a heavy, ugly face and gentle eyes.

'Very nearly,' Judith agreed. She wanted to tell him the truth – he did not deserve any more lies – but she dared not. 'No more bombs that I know of,' she equivocated. 'Just too many people, thousands of them everywhere. It's all clogged up, and we need to be quick.'

'Badly wounded?' he asked sympathetically.

That lie might catch up with them. 'Some wounded,' she said, praying he would believe her. 'Some pretty urgent dispatches.

Kill two birds with one stone.' Then suddenly she wondered if he was familiar with the phrase, or might wildly misunderstand her. 'Two jobs in one,' she explained.

He smiled, bringing sudden light to his heavy features. 'I know. We say much the same. Good luck.'

More broken bridges drove them further north, where the Belgians had opened the dykes and let the sea fight the invader where they could not. The armies marching in had found a different kind of ruin, one they could hardly equal.

A grey dawn saw them creeping forward through shattered villages. The houses gutted by fire and bomb blast, some little more than mounds of rubble scarred black, perhaps a chimney breast still standing, or here and there a doorframe. The fields around them were sour, the men who would have worked them dead, or too mutilated to labour any more. The bones of animals shone pale, picked clean by scavengers.

They saw a group of buildings, half in ruins. It had once been a thriving farm with barn, cow byre, pigsties and henhouses.

They stopped and asked for breakfast, willing to pay for it.

An old woman came out of what was left of her house. She saw the two women in VAD uniform and recognized it immediately, her gaunt, sagging face lightening.

'What you need?' she said in thickly accented English.

Judith smiled at her. She could see from her worn broken-nailed hands, and the pallor of her skin under the weathering, that she had almost nothing, and yet for British soldiers she was willing to part with it.

'Water so we can make some tea,' Judith replied. 'And if you have bread of any kind . . . ?' She was suddenly uncertain whether an offer of payment would be welcome, or considered an insult.

The woman was waiting, as if she expected to be asked for more.

Joseph came up beside her. 'We have a little jam,' he said to the woman. 'Army ration, not very good, but we would be happy if you would share it with us. Tea, bread and jam. It could be worse.'

'Yes, yes, yes!' the woman said happily, nodding her head. 'Bread is not much good either, but with jam, will be fine. Yes, yes.'

'Thank you,' Judith murmured to Joseph as the woman hurried off to fetch what bread she had.

'I liberated a few tins,' he said. 'With Barshey's help.'

'You didn't tell him—' she began.

'Just told him I needed it. He didn't ask why. Got me a couple of tins of Maconochie's as well. Won't last long, but it's something.'

'You pinched army stores!' She rolled her eyes. 'There's hope for you yet!'

He did not answer, and suddenly she wondered if she had hurt him. It was something she would have said before the war, before she knew him so very well, understanding what he did and why, knowing the hurt he did not show, the pity he knew better than to display because it did not help. She had always admired him, but found him distant and a little intimidating. He was the eldest, she the youngest. He conformed, she rebelled. Except that was far too facile a judgement. He also rebelled, in his own way. Hannah was the only one who really conformed. And yet she was going to find the changes of war the hardest of all, because the old ways she had loved and which had been natural to her were gone for ever.

No one could conform now, or be comfortable; there was no standard left with which to conform.

'I'm sorry,' she said aloud. She did not know how to retreat without making it worse.

He smiled at her. There was warmth in it, even amusement. 'It's all right. You can't think of everything.'

'What?' she was confused.

'Jam,' he replied, laughing at her. 'You liberated the petrol and the spark plugs – ever practical. I have the jam.' He turned and walked back to the ambulance and there was even a very slight swagger in his step.

The meal was anything but easy. They ate in the farmhouse kitchen. It was the one room in the house the woman had taken the care and labour to repair. She had even found from somewhere odd tiles to replace the shattered ones in the floor. There was hot water, clean from the well in the yard, and it made the tea impossibly fragrant after the sour water they were used to. But the bread was coarse and nearly black, and without butter. It needed Joseph's tin of army jam to make it palatable at all. It did not go far among seven of them. Even so, they saved the hardest and driest of the crusts for the scrawny dog that lay on the tiles watching them, eyes following every mouthful.

They all knew the story they had to tell. Mason was better to be himself. It was always possible his face might even be recognized. His reports were famous all over the world, occasionally with a picture of him at the top of his column in most of the newspapers. Matthew and Joseph were in uniform; Joseph in particular needed no explanation. Judith and Lizzie similarly – their purpose was universal. Schenckendorff was the difficulty. Matthew had found a VAD uniform that fitted him and simply taken it; to request it would have needed explaining, which would in turn have raised further questions he could not answer. But in spite of his injured foot, Schenckendorff's posture was that of an officer. He was born and bred to it, and he did not know how to abandon it in a few days. His accent was slight, but it was distinctive.

But far more than that, as Judith sat at the old wooden table eating the black bread and smelling the fragrance of the tea, she was aware of the dismay in him, perhaps even the guilt. There had once been men in this house. The evidence of them was still here in the carefully carved, slightly irregular wooden bowls on the dresser, which was itself handmade to fit exactly into the space available for it. There was a low nursing chair in the other corner, as a mother might use, holding a baby when she had other children at her knees. There was a handmade wooden engine on one of the shelves. No doubt there were other arte-facts outside where once men had milked cows, dug the earth, harvested.

She saw Schenckendorff's eyes take it all in as hers had done, and the grief in his face. He was eating more and more slowly, as if to accept this gift of hospitality choked him. Was it pity, or the guilt of having deceived the farmwoman? She would never have given it to him if she had known he was German. It could not be only because it was sour and stale. However, Joseph had said often that Germany was every bit as devastated as Belgium or France. That had been true when he had gone through the lines last year. How much worse must it be now?

The old woman was talking to Mason, her attention moment-arily absorbed.

'You must eat it,' Judith whispered to Schenckendorff.

306

He turned a little to look at her. There were shadows around his eyes and a pallor to the skin round his nose and mouth. This must have been caused by more than the pain of his foot, which Lizzie had assured her was improving. It was because it had been his own people who had wasted this land, just as now the Allies would be wasting his, and the people he loved.

He swallowed with difficulty, and took another mouthful.

She reached for the pot and poured him the last of the tea. He needed it more than the others. Everywhere around them was ruin and loss. More lay ahead and he would see all of it: a land that smelled of death.

Was he thinking of the old treaty that never been ratified? He and the Peacemaker had tried so hard to prevent all this. Would betrayal and dominion really have been so very much worse? Did this old woman, who gave them black bread and tea made with clean water, care who made the laws in Brussels, or who collected the taxes, if her husband and her sons were home and safe, and her land bore its harvest, her cattle their milk? No one had asked her what she thought, or wanted.

Was that what was going through Schenckendorff's mind now: not guilt at the ruin but guilt that he and the Peacemaker had failed to prevent it all? When he looked at Matthew and Joseph did he see the two men who, above all others, had foiled the treaty that might have arrested war? Were they heroes, in his eyes? Or men whose patriotism was too small and too blind to allow them to see the whole of humanity, and the future that could save or destroy them all?

She looked at him, studying the slow way he ate, the courtesy in his manners and the distance between the few words he said, the brief communication only when necessary.

They finished as quickly as they could and thanked the woman, hurrying out with no time for extra words, all afraid in case something gave them away.

They pressed on westwards, moving slowly because the roads were so badly cratered that Judith dare not go more than twenty or twenty-five miles an hour. It rained again, washing mud everywhere, wetting the driver and whoever sat beside her.

It grew dark about five o'clock. Heavier clouds rolled in from the north like grey smears across the sky, wind-drawn curtains of rain hiding the trees. Mason had gone back into the body of the ambulance and Joseph was beside Judith.

'How's Schenckendorff?' she asked him.

'His foot hurts, but I don't think it's any worse,' he replied, hunching himself up a little and pulling his overcoat closer around him. 'He's not feverish, but he looks miserable. It must hurt. Wounds to the feet do.'

'Do you think that's why he looks so unhappy?' She swerved to avoid a pothole filled with water that she noticed only just in time. 'Sorry,' she said automatically.

'Do you think he's dreading getting to London?' he asked. 'He's bound to. In a way he's riding to his own execution, even if it is of choice.' His voice was low, muted with a kind of awe.

'I hadn't even got that far,' she replied. 'Although I suppose he has to be. Will they execute him, Joseph? He's done no more than fight for his country, as we all have. You shoot a man for that during the war, while he's armed, but you don't execute him for it afterwards. There's no crime in it.' She refused to think about Mason's situation. As the hours went by, that was becoming more and more difficult. It was not only that she loved him: his passion and subtlety; his energy of mind; and the honesty that had driven him to act where so many others merely dreamed and bemoaned their own helplessness. As she at last faced the issues with a cool head, and the will to consider and believe other ideas, she realized the moral questions were not so easy to sweep entirely to one side or the other.

She would still have fought, been blown to bits in Flanders, rather than live a life of guilt and regret under the domination of anyone else. But driving through the ruins of Belgium, passing graveyards filled with endless white crosses all the same, she could see that it was mistaken, but not monstrous, to have considered a different path.

Perhaps Joseph was also thinking about Mason, because he said nothing.

'I was wondering about guilt,' Judith said aloud. 'Did you watch Schenckendorff's face as he ate the bread today? He looked at her farm, and it almost choked him. Don't you think he would have thought that it would still be standing if we hadn't found the treaty, and there'd been no war?'

'There would still have been a war,' he said quickly, staring ahead at the rain now beating on the windscreen. The raindrops were swishing around and blowing inside, bitterly cold. The headlamps shone yellow in the gathering gloom, shining on puddles on the rutted road, broken trees and fallen debris at the sides. 'It might have been months later, or even years, but it would have come.'

'Do you think so?'

'The balance of power was too precarious to last.' Joseph spoke thoughtfully, feeling his way. 'There were too many promises that could never have been kept, too many alliances weighing one against another. Germany might have conquered most of Europe in a military sense, but there would always be a resistance. Possibly it would gather strength in time. There'd be sabotage to anything vulnerable, such a railways, bridges, fuel supplies. They would need a vast occupying army and a network of secret informers and police for years, if not indefinitely. And there would be all the other ugly sides of oppression and government by force: informers, betrayals, large-scale imprisonment; censorship of all communications, and probably limitation of travel; curfew after dark; suppression of all artistic or literary opinion that questioned anything.

'In Britain I dare say it would be even worse. It might descend to civil war before there was any kind of order. The death toll would be appalling. It would make our troubles in Ireland look small. Canada might accept British rule, but America never would. Whatever armies anyone sent, they'd fight to the end.'

He shook his head. 'And the rise of socialism internationally was going to create revolution if we didn't each unite our own country against an enemy outside. The revolution in Russia was probably inevitable. Austro-Hungary was falling apart. Hungary would have demanded its independence sooner or later. If Princip hadn't shot the Archduke and Duchess, something else would have sparked it off.'

'Do you suppose Schenckendorff sees it that way?' Judith asked doubtfully. 'He believed he could succeed, in the beginning.'

'Of course. We're wiser now, and I dare say sadder.' Joseph swivelled sideways to look at her. 'Are you afraid Schenckendorff will change his mind when he gets to London?'

'Haven't you thought of it?' she responded.

He hesitated.

She felt a surge of guilt. In her awareness of Schenckendorff's feelings, and the threat he posed to them in Belgium, she had temporarily forgotten about Lizzie. She wondered how Joseph must be feeling, watching her struggle to hide the nausea she suffered, especially in the mornings, and the emotions that must be in both of them. Apprehending Allie Robinson had changed nothing about Lizzie's rape or the reality of its effects. Of course they knew now that the rapist was not the person who had killed Sarah, but the relief of that was only short-lived. Everything else was just as it had been before.

'I'm sorry,' she said, meaning it intensely. 'It's only a small part of everything, isn't it.' That was not a question, it was an admission of truth. She was trying not to think of personal things, above all not about love, or the time after this was over and they could start living in peace, picking up daily routines again, and choice – and loneliness. There would be very few men left for anyone to marry, and those there were would not find her such an attractive prospect, any more than she would them. It had been hard enough before, when she was in her early twenties. Now, four and a half years later, it was going to be impossible.

Apart from the scarcity of available men, she would compare them all with Mason. At first they would bore her to tears; then she would begin to hate them, because they were there and alive, and he was not. They would be so flat and tame compared to him.

It was easier to concentrate on getting Schenckendorff back to London to expose the Peacemaker, than to worry about food and petrol, and how to mend the ambulance if it broke down, and how to make sure the Belgians didn't guess who they were.

They drove on through the darkness. Judith was growing very tired. She was used to long hours driving, more often at night than during the day, and always in difficult conditions. However, her eyes felt gritty, and her head ached as if she were wearing a helmet that was heavy and too tight. They would have to stop soon, or she would risk losing control, which could be lethal.

Within half an hour they found a ruined farmhouse. It was too badly shelled to live in, but there was a sheltered place within the old dairy that was dry and out of the wind where the men would make themselves places to rest. They had a meal of Maconochie's and some army-ration biscuits, washed down with tea. It was all prepared by Joseph, since he was the only one used to such chores. Mason had seen army cooking done, of course, as had Schenckendorff, but neither had actually boiled water in a dixie can over a flame, all balanced in a tin. It was more difficult than it looked and required a lot of patience.

Judith considered working on the engine, but knew she was exhausted enough to make mistakes. If something slipped from her clumsy fingers, was replaced crookedly, or not tightened far enough, they could break down fatally.

She was asleep within moments of lying down in the back of the ambulance, but she woke stiff and uncomfortable while it was still dark. She could hear Lizzie moving slightly on the other side, a couple of feet away, but she did not know if she was awake too, or just stretching or turning in restlessness, dreaming of fear or loss.

There had been no time for the two of them to talk, and she did not know what to say anyhow. She did not even know if Lizzie wanted to keep the baby, or if she would be relieved if she lost it. Perhaps both were true, at different times. One thing she was certain about; she had seen it in Lizzie's face, in a dozen small actions even in the short times they had all been together:

312

she loved Joseph. And – perhaps in a more lasting way, the thing that would carry them over the pain, the doubt, the times of failure – she liked him. She was not looking for a solution to her own need, or an answer to any difficulty; she liked him for himself. It was there in the quick, rueful laughter, a brief moment of teasing, the acceptance of help, and of criticism. Underneath the present fear, and the knowledge of future pain, she was comfortable with him.

Judith lay on her back on the hard surface, stared up into the complete darkness of the ambulance and let the near silence wrap around her. It was almost like being at home again after a long and violent journey. There was no sound but the rain on the roof, and that was intermittent now. Perhaps by morning it would have stopped altogether.

That comfort was the kind of feeling she had about Mason also – at least most of the time. And when she looked at his face, she saw certainty in him, as if he had found at last something he had been looking for for longer than he knew.

But he must be afraid, underneath the courage. He could not imagine the Prime Minister would accept his unmasking of the Peacemaker – with all his own involvement in the plot, and his knowledge that it intended to bring about the surrender of Britain – and then simply allow him to leave scot-free. The fact that he had imagined it was for the purpose of a greater world peace was immaterial. Just the knowledge of such plans, in wartime, was treason, and the punishment for treason had always been death. She closed her eyes tightly, even though she could see nothing in the dark anyway. Death by hanging. These few days of exhaustion in the rain and the ruin of Belgium, the Channel crossing, and then the drive to London, were all the time they had left together.

But then, for how many women was that true? She was only one more who would lose the man she loved. It was selfish and cowardly to cry as if she were the only one. She was one of millions, all over Europe, all over the world. It was the price of the battle she had never doubted they should fight. But that did nothing to lessen the pain. Every man she looked at she would wish were he: every man with thick, dark hair, or who stood very straight and turned with grace, or who spoke of wild open spaces as if they were antechambers of heaven.

Would he change his mind about surrendering himself when he got to London, and the final moment closed in on them, irreversible at last? Would past loyalties and old dreams overtake his present sense of duty, and he would find he could not say the words that would hang the Peacemaker?

Or was it imaginable that he was going with them to turn at the last moment and betray them, and save Sandwell, so he could help create a peace that would allow Germany to rise again, soon, and resurrect the old plan for dominion?

That was a wild and useless thought, and she would be better asleep. She must work on the ambulance engine before they set off and then drive all day again. Whatever any of them did, it must be what conscience demanded of them. Nothing else would bring happiness of any sort, or peace of heart, or the ability to love or trust anything.

In the morning it was clear and colder. They breakfasted on tea and the last of the bread they had brought with them, with plum jam. The bread was hard and stale, but no one complained. Uppermost in Judith's mind was the fact that they would have to buy or beg everything from now on, and that could be another two days, if they had any problems. Time was pressing urgently. It was already 5 November – Guy Fawkes Day at home, when bonfires were lit and fireworks let off to celebrate the fact that the plot to blow up Parliament, and kill all its members, had been foiled. A celebration of freedom and the defeat of treason and murder. Did anyone still remember what it was about? Or was it just an excuse to have fun?

The ambulance would not start. Judith cleaned the spark plugs, and it made no difference. It was hard to quell the panic inside her. It felt like a fluttering in her stomach and a tightening of her throat so it was difficult to breathe. No one else had any idea how to help, but she had expected that from the beginning. Mason could observe, assess, write brilliantly. Matthew could plan, judge men, think ahead, unravel truth and lies, and he was a good driver, but he never mended his own cars. Schenckendorff was a colonel. Colonels did not maintain their own cars. Lizzie was a nurse, and a pretty good driver too, according to Joseph, who was more than a little biased. And Joseph himself was good at medical emergencies, a fair army cook – at least with a candle and a tin – and a better soldier than he knew. But mechanics of any sort were a closed book to him.

She worked quietly, steadying her hands with an effort of will. At least it was light, and not raining. She changed the plugs. It was sooner than she would have wished to. Now they had nothing in reserve.

Joseph was watching her.

'Perhaps you should say a prayer for it,' she said ruefully. 'Otherwise we shall have to descend to stealing. Highway robbery.'

'Do you know what parts we need?' he asked, his face puckered with doubt.

She saw the comical side of it. 'I was thinking of a trade,' she replied, picking up the crank handle ready to attempt starting the engine.

'Trade?' he was puzzled. 'Still doesn't help, if we don't know what we need.'

'Their vehicle for ours,' she replied. 'I told you, highway robbery.' She passed him the crank handle. 'Please?'

At the third attempt it spluttered into life. They looked at each other, laughing, drenched with relief, and clambered in.

After they had gone forty-five miles west, they found the roads more crowded with other vehicles and people on foot. It began to look as if the country there were making something of a recovery.

They managed to find a roadside café at which to buy a meal. It was meagre – no eggs, no meat, only dumplings seasoned with herbs – but it was sufficient to sustain them. They spoke little and listened to the conversation around them. There had been other victories. Judith watched Schenckendorff's face as someone spoke of Allied troops pressing forward rapidly now, with terrible loss of German life. She saw the sudden flash of pain in him, and then the effort to hide it and pretend to feel pleasure, like the people around them. They were cheering, as if each death or mutilation were some kind of victory in itself, a payment for all the loss over the last years: the dead they would never even find, let alone bury.

Then the conversation shifted. There was other news that was more frightening. Spanish influenza had struck, and thousands of people were dying. No one could count how many, and the disease was spreading. Paris was particularly hard hit.

They left the café with a new sense of darkness on the horizon, unknown and closing in. Joseph walked closer to Lizzie. Mason touched Judith's arm, and stood beside her as if to help her up into the driver's seat, although he knew better than to do so. Instead he went to the front and cranked the engine.

Inside the ambulance, as it set off again, Joseph sat with Lizzie, absorbed in quiet conversation. Matthew sat opposite Schenckendorff and wanted to think of something to say, but all conversation seemed trivial compared with the enormity of the truth.

At lunchtime, they stopped for necessities and to eat some of their rations. They had pulled in at the side of the road, leaving the engine running in case it was reluctant to start again. All of them were aware of its frailty. They looked for clean water to drink, and found nothing. There was no time to light a candle and heat any. Thirst would have to wait.

Matthew and Schenckendorff walked back together from the semi-privacy of a clump of trees, picking their way through rough grass. The land was flat, cut by canals where once there had been straight lines of trees. It was more orderly countryside than in England; it looked man-made. Someone had created these avenues and dykes, these farmhouses with their stone walls dipping down into water. In Cambridgeshire, even in the fen country where there was water everywhere and it was as flat as a table, the paths were winding and the rivers seeped in all directions, as though taking as long as possible to reach the sea. People had got lost there since the last stand of the Saxons against the Norman invaders in 1066. They were a people who fought to the last ditch and dyke, to the last island and quicksand, the final stand.

Schenckendorff was limping badly. He should not have been

walking on that foot. It must hurt like hell, but he had never complained. Matthew caught up and they walked side by side.

'Where are you from?' Matthew asked conversationally.

'Heidelberg,' Schenckendorff replied. 'It's a very old city, steep, overlooking the Neckar.' He smiled slightly. 'It's nothing like this.' He left the wealth of comparison unsaid, but Matthew guessed at what might be racing through his mind.

Schenckendorff glanced at him, and saw it in his eyes. 'And you are from Cambridgeshire,' he said as if it were all some easy exchange of two men passing the time of day. 'Flat like this, but far more eccentric, more full of individual oddities that go back to your Domesday Book, and before. Nobody has ever forced you to change them. You are very stubborn.' He gave a little shrug. 'It used to annoy me. Now I have changed my mind. I think perhaps it is good. You found some kind of identity in being different, something to stand on and believe it worth paying the greatest price to save. If you give up the right to be different, maybe sooner or later you give up the right to think at all, and then perhaps you are dead anyway. You haven't had your life taken from you, you gave it up yourself – for nothing.'

Matthew stopped in the rough grass by the edge of the road, staring at him.

Schenckendorff smiled. 'You were wondering if I will change my mind when I get to London. I know. You all are. You would be foolish if it had not at least crossed your minds. You must take every possibility into account. I won't change. The cost of the peace I thought of is too high, and I am not sure now that it is peace at all.' His face shadowed. 'I think it might be the beginning of a slow death. Life – real, growing, passionate life – is not peaceful. Learning hurts, and has costs.

My one-time friend Sandwell misunderstood that, and he lost sight of the purpose of it all.'

Matthew waited.

'Individuals matter,' Schenckendorff said quietly. 'Moments of joy, a man's victory over the darkness within himself, a perception of beauty, whether it is of the eye or the mind. I think we had better get back into the ambulance. Your remarkable sister is waiting to leave.'

Some of the same thoughts had crossed Joseph's mind, but now his thoughts were preoccupied with Lizzie. As a child he had watched his mother endure the same distress, but she had been in her own home, secure and deeply loved, and the children she was carrying were wanted.

For Lizzie it was in every way different. She was alone, facing an unknown future and a child she must dread. Would she think of the violence, assault, degradation every time she looked at its face? Could she possibly learn to love it, to be tender, to laugh, to find joy in its growth, its achievements? 'It.' Would it be harder if it were a boy?

Now she was sick again, desperate for privacy, and surrounded by men, two of whom she barely knew. They were always in a hurry, feeling the urgency all the time, the need to move, the knowledge that if they made even one slip they could be stopped, imprisoned, or perhaps even executed summarily. The hunger for revenge was in the air like the smell of decay.

How could he help her? She was walking back over the grass, a little shakily. Her face was bleached of all colour and her hair was straggling out of its pins. He ached to comfort her, but might he be making promises he could not keep? Could he love that child as if it were his own, and never even for a moment look at it and hate it because Benbow was its father?

He remembered how he felt as a child: the certainty of his father's interest, his time and attention. He thought of countless hours shared: in listening to his father's long, rambling funny stories; in pottering in the garden feeling he was helping, learning to distinguish weeds from flowers. Later there had been more complicated discoveries about the first thoughts in philosophy, feeling his way towards wisdom. He remembered long walks in comfortable silence, always certain he was not only loved, but liked, valued, believed in, a necessary part in the greater happiness. Arguments meant nothing; the security was always there, underneath, like a deep ocean, with an inexhaustible current.

A warmth opened up inside him, a steadiness that had been absent for some time – he could not remember how long. It was back again now, a bedrock on which every good thing could be built. Lizzie's child deserved that, everyone did. Nothing less was enough.

He walked towards Lizzie and took her arm, lending her his strength. She looked up at him quickly and he met her gaze without wavering.

She saw the knowledge of something new in him, a complete absence of fear. She took a deep breath and smiled at him, hope flaring up.

By evening, the rain was steady and hard. They were grateful to be offered both food and shelter at what before the war must have been an excellent café. During the occupation it had housed German soldiers. Now the original owners had taken it back and were trying to salvage all they could of the past.

'Broken!' Madame said furiously, picking up a blue and white china platter to arrange the food on. It had been cracked across the centre, and carefully glued together again. 'Everything is tired and dusty, and broken. I'd kill every last one of them, if I could.'

Joseph struggled for something to say. She clearly wanted justice, some answering pain to compensate for all that had been taken from her and from all the others she knew and had loved.

'I know,' he answered her. 'There's not much left.'

She grunted and regarded his chaplain's uniform with contempt. 'Aren't you going to tell me to have faith in God?' she demanded. 'Or at least remind me that we should be grateful to you British for fighting for us? That's what my husband tells me.'

'You don't do what you think is right for other people's sake,' he said. 'You do it for yourself.'

She was surprised. It robbed her momentarily of the response she had been going to give. 'I suppose you'd like something decent to eat?'

'Wouldn't we all? But we'll be grateful for anything,' he replied.

'Don't be grateful!' she snapped. 'I'm not giving it you.'

But when the meal came it was prepared not only with care, but with imagination and skill as well. Dark bread was set out on the mended blue and white platter, made to look inviting with a few leaves of parsley and red radishes. There were small dishes of something that resembled Brussels pâté, and others of pickled fish to add taste, and the suggestion of meat. The customers were all sitting around one long table, and she placed the dishes in the middle with a baleful glare, daring anyone to make a remark.

They thanked her, and shared it out in equal portions, although Lizzie gave half of hers to the others.

Monsieur came and stood in the doorway smoking a clay pipe with something dark and pungent in it. It might have been half tobacco, but smelled as if it were at least half dung.

'So what are you doing away from the fighting, then?' His English was thickly accented, but he had some confidence in the language. 'Isn't over yet, you know. Still some men out there being killed.'

They had expected this, and were prepared.

'Taking information back to London,' Matthew replied. 'It's urgent, and secret. Can't trust it to letters.'

'All six of you?' Monsieur clearly did not believe them. He looked at Mason. 'You're not a soldier. Why not? You look fit enough. Flat feet, have you? Short-sighted? Know what I tell people who are short-sighted? Get closer to the enemy, you'll see him all right when he's a bayonet-length away.'

Madame mumbled something unintelligible at him.

He ignored her and glared at Mason, waiting for an answer.

'War correspondent,' Mason said. 'Miss Reavley is an ambulance driver and Mrs Blaine is a nurse. Lieutenant-Colonel Reavley is an intelligence officer.' He indicated Schenckendorff. 'And Major Sherman is also. He's been behind the lines, and as you can see, been injured.'

Monsieur was mollified, but not happy. He looked at Schenckendorff doubtfully. 'What's any use behind the lines now?' he asked. 'Kill them, I say. Same as they killed us.'

Everyone stiffened. Joseph drew in his breath sharply, afraid of what Schenckendorff would answer. He loathed what the Belgian was saying, but perhaps – if this had been his land, and his people – he might have felt much the same.

Monsieur was waiting, a challenge in his eyes.

322

'Exactly,' Judith said, swallowing her mouthful of food with a gulp. 'We are not so different from them.'

Monsieur's face flushed hot red. 'Speak for yourself, woman! We are nothing like them. They are animals, pigs! They steal and they rape and they kill.'

Lizzie's spoon slid out of her hand, spilling gravy on the table.

Joseph searched frantically for something to say or do to cover it. Nothing came to his mind but fury.

Judith looked at the man. 'Yes, of course. I only see the wounded. I forget: the ones who are able to be, are violent. We are not like that. We don't steal, we don't hurt women, and we don't kill the unarmed.'

Mason bent his head to conceal his expression.

Madame glared at Schenckendorff, challenging him to argue. The silence grew.

'The hunger for revenge is natural,' he responded uncomfortably at last. 'Especially after so many years of being helpless.'

Monsieur glared at him. 'We're not helpless! Where do you come from? You have a funny accent. You don't sound English at all.'

Joseph's throat tightened. He dared not look at Matthew. He reached under the shelter of the tabletop, took Lizzie's hand, and felt her fingers grasp his.

'I'm not,' Schenckendorff said calmly. 'I'm Scots. From the Western Isles. We spoke Gaelic when I was young.'

Joseph prayed silently that no one else in the room had the faintest idea what Gaelic sounded like. Actually, he had none himself.

Monsieur seemed satisfied. 'Really? Western Isles, eh? Rains a lot, doesn't it?'

'Yes, I suppose so,' Schenckendorff went on, turning to the woman. 'You can make the most ordinary ingredients taste good. That is an art.'

'There's no more,' she said ungraciously, but there was a flush of pleasure in her cheeks and she very nearly smiled at him.

Joseph slept well. It was the first time he had had a real bed in over half a year, since he had been at home on his last leave in the spring.

He was woken violently by a banging on the door. Even before he could sit up it burst open and a large Belgian policeman stood just inside the room, a German pistol in his hand, pointing it at Joseph.

'Get up,' he ordered. 'Slowly. Don't touch your uniform!'

'I can't get up without my clothes,' Joseph pointed out. 'Who are you, and what's wrong? We're British Army officers and volunteers, going back to London with important information.' He was sick at the thought that perhaps he had actually been posted as a deserter, and Hook had sent out his information. Surely not so soon?

'Maybe. Maybe not.' The man moved towards Joseph cautiously and, with one hand, picked up his uniform blouse off the back of the chair where Joseph had left it. He shook it hard. Papers fell out of one of the pockets. He dropped the jacket and picked up the trousers, shaking them also.

'I'm not armed,' Joseph said patiently, controlling himself with difficulty. 'If you look at the collar, and the insignia, you'll see that I'm a chaplain. I don't carry weapons.'

'How do I know the uniform's yours?' the man demanded. 'Anyone could wear it.'

There was no reasonable argument to that. It was true. Going through the lines last year Joseph had worn a Swiss chaplain's uniform to which he had had no right, and found one for Morel, who had even less right to it. 'They could,' he conceded. 'But why bother? What is it you think I am? An army deserter, with a war correspondent, two army officers, a nurse and an ambulance driver?' He tried to convey the absurdity of it in his voice.

'No, I think you're a collaborator trying to get a German occupying commander out of Belgium before we can catch him and hang him, like he deserves,' the man replied quite calmly. 'We'll give you over to the families of those he murdered.'

Joseph looked at his face and saw the years of suffering burned into his heart, the deaths he was helpless to prevent and, more bitter than that, the corruption of fear and loneliness and greed that had destroyed what had once been clean. He had found weakness and disappointment, which peace would never have shown up. He did not want to forgive.

Joseph felt real fear, hot and sick inside him. Lizzie would be hurt, and Judith. They did not spare women. He and Matthew would be killed. They would never catch the Peacemaker now. Bitter, terrible irony – the Reavleys would never exact their own vengeance.

Would John Reavley have wanted vengeance? Probably not. When Joseph thought about it, after four years of mutilation and death, he felt he would definitely not have. It ended nothing. The Peacemaker must be stopped because of the damage he could still do; no more than that.

'There may be such people, I don't know,' he said quietly. How much of the truth should he tell? One lie, if caught, could kill them all. But they must all tell the same story, true or false.

'Let me get dressed, and we can all answer your questions. I presume you do not wish to imprison British Army officers on military duty? Or perhaps you do? Maybe it's you who are helping the occupiers to escape, and you think we will discover that, and—'

The policeman lifted the gun up and swung his arm round. Joseph only just managed to fend off the blow, but he did it hard, with his weight behind it, and the gun clattered to the floor. He thought for an instant of diving to get it first, and realized he would be just too late. He forced himself to stand still.

The policeman watched him, eyes hard and angry, then he bent and retrieved the gun, holding its muzzle pointing at Joseph's stomach. 'Wise,' he said between his teeth. 'Very wise. I'd have shot you.'

'I can see that,' Joseph answered. 'You would have had a lot of explaining to do to the British Army as to why you'd shot an unarmed priest in his bed, but it would have been a bit late to help me.'

'You say you're a priest. I say you're a collaborator.'

'By then it would be obvious that you didn't care. You just wanted to shoot someone, and you didn't have the guts to pick anyone who could fight back,' Joseph said with contempt. He was frightened, especially for Lizzie and Judith, but he was beginning to be angry as well. 'For heaven's sake, think about it! We're in British Army uniforms. The ambulance is pretty obviously a real one; you can see the state of it. There's years of blood on its boards, it's splintered with shot and any fool can see it's at least four years old.'

'Oh, it's real enough,' the man agreed. 'I don't doubt you

stole it from a real British hospital. But we got reliable information that you have a German officer with you who's one of those that led the invasion and occupation of our country. To collaborate with the enemy makes you one of them. Worse, you betrayed your own.' He said it with total conviction, the contempt in him scalding like acid. 'Put your clothes on, priest. You're going to answer to the Belgian people. Unless you want to come as you are?'

Ten minutes later they were all downstairs in the grey early morning light, shivering and silent. There were three more policemen, all with guns. Madame and Monsieur were there too, bristling with anger because they had been made fools of, their hospitality abused. Madame, her puffy face grey, her hair in a thin braid over her shoulder, glared at Joseph in particular, and spat, her loathing too deep for words.

The man who seemed to be in charge, who was narrow-shouldered and tall, assumed that Joseph was the leader, since he appeared to be the oldest in uniform. Mason he disregarded; and Schenckendorff was the focus of his suspicion.

'You say you are taking information back to London. That's absurd. Doesn't take six of you, and women, to do that. And if it's urgent, as you say, you wouldn't go in an ambulance that's old and ready to fall to bits. You've got no papers of authority, no money, no supplies, no extra fuel. If you were on genuine army business, you would be properly equipped. Now tell me the truth, and we might believe you.'

Joseph looked across at Matthew. At least nothing had been said about desertion. They might have one chance left, but it would be only one.

Judith was next to Lizzie, so close as to be almost supporting her. Joseph could only guess how ill Lizzie must feel at this hour.

Schenckendorff moved his weight from one foot to the other, to ease the pain in his foot. He looked as if he were trying to decide whether to speak or not.

Mason smiled, as if the whole thing were faintly ridiculous. But under the bravado his shoulders were stiff, and the graceful posture was only half convincing.

'What on earth is it you think we're doing?' he asked, eyebrows raised. 'Last week of the war, and after four years here, we're deserting now? We'd still be shot, you know. As lunatics, if nothing else.'

Joseph winced at mention of deserting. Was it a piece of bravado too far?

'We know what you're doing!' the narrow-shouldered man replied. 'You've captured a German commandant and you want him for yourselves. He's plundered our works of art, paintings, reliquaries, ornamental weapons, and if you spare his life, he'll give them to you. Well, we've caught you, and after we've tried you and you've told us where you've hidden our material treasures, we'll execute you as thieves, and him as the murderer he is.'

Matthew looked at Joseph, then at Schenckendorff. A single thought had occurred to them all.

'There may be such a man,' Matthew said in a voice that was very nearly level. Only Joseph, who had known him all his life, heard the fear in it. 'It is not Colonel von Schenckendorff, who I admit is German. But he is a senior officer in Berlin, and at no time was part of the occupation of Belgium. I am Lieutenant-Colonel Reavley of the British Secret Intelligence Service, and I am bringing him back to London where he can expose certain collaborators we have of our own. We are doing it this way, in an ambulance and without papers of authority, because the collaborators concerned have spies in many places, and are attempting to stop us naming them even now. If you attempt to prevent us, I can only assume that you are in league with these collaborators yourselves. Perhaps you owe your own people a more detailed account of your part in the occupation of your country than you have given them so far?'

The narrow-shouldered man was startled. A counter-attack was the last thing he had expected. He was thrown off balance.

'By all means try us,' Matthew pressed his advantage. 'We shall try each other!'

The Belgians looked confused.

'Don't listen to them!' Madame said bitterly. 'They'll talk their way out of it.' She looked at the leader. 'Aren't both your sons dead?' She turned to another of them. 'Isn't your sister a widow? You used to be rich. Where's your house? A pile of rubble. Wasn't your daughter raped before she killed herself? What do those people know of what war is really like? It's over, and they're going home again. Where are our homes, eh?' She swung her arm violently and only just missed knocking a chipped candle-stick off the mantel to the floor.

'Lock them up,' the leader ordered. 'We'll find the people who say this is the German commandant. Someone must know.'

Before anyone could move to obey him there was a knock on the door. Almost immediately it opened and Sergeant Hampton came in. He glanced around the faces and stopped when he recognized Joseph. 'Morning, Chaplain. You seem to be in a spot of bother.'

Joseph was weak with relief and astonishment. 'Yes,' he gulped, drawing in air as if he had suddenly come to the surface from being close to drowning. 'We are finding it hard to prove we are who we say.' Then, like sudden nausea, he realized that Hampton might have come to arrest him for desertion. At least the others could go on!

'Really?' Hampton looked at the Belgians. 'Captain Reavley is chaplain with the Cambridgeshires at Ypres,' he said solemnly. 'Lieutenant-Colonel Reavley there is with the Secret Intelligence Service. Mr Mason is one of our most distinguished war correspondents. Miss Reavley is an ambulance driver, and Mrs Blaine is a nurse. I can swear to this because I have been conducting an investigation in which they were of assistance. Fortunately it is all cleared up now.' He fished in his pocket and brought out his police identification. 'Sergeant Hampton of the British Military Police.' He showed it, but kept it in his hand.

'And him?' the narrow-shouldered man asked, looking at Schenckendorff. 'Can you swear for him too?'

'Of course. He is Colonel von Schenckendorff, whom they are escorting to London. I would not like to have to insist that you permit them to go on their way unhindered, but I shall have to become unpleasant about it if you do not.' He had a revolver in his hand and was holding it with the muzzle pointing up, a little towards the middle of the man's chest. The shot would undoubtedly have killed him. 'Let us part amicably,' he said with a chilly smile. 'This would be an ugly end to a war which we entered originally on your behalf, in order to keep a rather rash promise we made to you, before . . . all this.'

The Belgians looked at each other, uncertain now, and embarrassed.

Hampton did not wait. 'I suggest you go outside and get back into your ambulance,' he said to Matthew. 'I shall follow you, when I am certain there will be no . . . ill-considered behaviour.'

Matthew did not hesitate. He led the way, and the others went after them, Hampton bringing up the rear.

Lizzie looked ill. Judith put her arm around her, half holding her up. Matthew went to the front. 'I'll drive,' he said, giving Judith no chance to argue.

Mason cranked the engine, then, as it fired, got in beside Matthew.

Joseph helped Schenckendorff, who was limping badly. Hampton was the last to get into the back, slamming the door behind him.

They jerked forward, then picked up speed, bouncing and lurching over the potholes in the road and slithering where the surface was wet and covered with mud.

Joseph looked at Lizzie. She smiled at him, eyes bright with relief.

'Thank you,' Schenckendorff said sincerely to Hampton.

'How did you know where to find us?' Joseph asked him.

Hampton gave a slight grimace. 'Deduction,' he replied. 'And a few discreet questions. You've chosen the best route. I did the same.' A ghost of warmth crossed his face, enigmatic rather than friendly. 'You have friends.' He said something deeply uncomplimentary about the Belgians they had just left behind. 'Won't happen again,' he added, tapping his gun, which was now in the holster on his belt.

Joseph wondered if Hampton was actually part of some intelligence service rather than merely a military policeman seconded to Jacobson. If not, why had he bothered to come after them to be helpful, rather than to arrest Joseph for desertion, and possibly Judith for taking the ambulance? More than that, how had he known that Schenckendorff would be with them? Had they been far more careless than they thought? No one had seen them leave.

Did Matthew know that he could be trusted, and had told him? Hampton knew Matthew's true rank. But if Hampton had known Matthew, he would never have allowed Jacobson to suspect him of having killed Sarah Price.

He couldn't ask Matthew; he was in front at the wheel, separated from them by the back of the cab.

He glanced at Judith, next to the front wall, on the seat beyond Hampton.

She stared back at him, her eyes wide.

Schenckendorff and Lizzie were on the opposite side.

Schenckendorff must have picked up some look, some motion of anxiety in Joseph, perhaps in Judith also. Maybe he too was wondering how Hampton knew him.

Then suddenly it was obvious – he was an accomplice of the Peacemaker!

Hampton saw the revelation and understood. His hand went to his belt and the gun appeared, levelled at Joseph.

'You are a good detective, Chaplain, but not good enough. Short-sighted as always. A man with a small vision, loyalty to a little idea, in fact parochial. For a man who claims to serve God, you should think of the whole world, not just your own, narrow few. I cannot allow Schenckendorff to betray the greater cause.' He lifted the gun a little higher and moved it from Joseph to Schenckendorff.

It was at that moment that Judith stood up behind him and hit him as hard as she could over the head with the first-aid box.

He slumped forward, the gun slipping out of his fingers. But he was only stunned.

Lizzie dived for the gun and her hand closed over it inches before he reached it.

'You won't!' Hampton said with a sneer.

She pulled the trigger and the bullet struck him cleanly between the eyes. Then she dropped the gun on the floor, and was sick.

# Chapter Eleven

Lizzie was deeply shocked. Joseph took off his jacket and put it around her. Still she sat shivering and white-faced. She did not say anything at all, but Joseph knew what must be racing through her mind. He had seen young soldiers like this after they had shot their first enemy, even though it had been in battle, and all those around them had been doing exactly the same thing. This was different. Hampton was a man she had known, spoken to civilly over many days. He was as English as she was, and wearing a British uniform. She had stood less than a yard from him, looked in his face and killed him.

'Thank you,' he said softly. 'You've saved all of us, and I know it has been at great cost.'

'Schenckendorff,' she murmured, even though she knew that Schenckendorff himself, sitting in the back of the ambulance only a couple of feet away from her, had to hear all she said. 'Not the rest of us.'

Judith was outside. She had found some water, albeit muddy, and cleared up the mess where Lizzie had been sick. Matthew and Mason had taken Hampton's body, and Joseph had not even asked them what they intended to do with it.

It was Schenckendorff who answered Lizzie. 'If he had shot me, as he apparently intended to, he would not have allowed you to remain alive. He would have killed all of you, then very probably have made it look as if the ambulance had gone off the road. He might have set fire to it, rather than have it obvious that you were shot. Your courage saved the lives of all of us.'

Lizzie blinked and frowned at him. 'I suppose so. I hadn't thought of it, but you are right.' She smiled very slightly. 'That does make me feel far less . . . brutal.'

A slight amusement touched Schenckendorff's face, softening the lines around his eyes. Then the instant after it was followed by intense sadness.

She looked away, not to be intrusive.

Judith came back into the ambulance, her face anxious. 'Matthew and Richard aren't back yet,' she said, turning from Lizzie to Joseph. 'They don't need to bury him! You didn't tell them to, did you?'

'No, of course I didn't,' Joseph stood up awkwardly in the narrow space. 'I said to hide the body, that's all. Better he isn't found. We don't need any more trouble than we have. He may have spoken to the authorities about us and they'll follow up on him. We don't want them to find him. I'll go and see what they're doing.'

But he had barely straightened up outside in the road when he saw Matthew and Mason a dozen yards away walking briskly across the rough grass towards him. They were both mud-stained, and Mason's jacket sleeve was torn.

'Finished,' Matthew said as they reached the ambulance. 'Took his identification and insignia of rank off him and burned them. That's what took the time. Hard to get wet cloth to ignite, but we can't afford to be caught with it . . . if he's got allies. Is Judith all right to drive, or shall I? That engine sounds very rough.'

'Then she'd better,' Joseph replied. 'She knows it. If anyone can nurse it along, she can.'

'Right.' Matthew opened up the back doors and climbed inside.

'I'll ride with her,' Mason made it a statement, not an offer.

A few minutes later the engine was cranked again. It sputtered to life and they lurched uncertainly forward, then it stalled. It took four attempts before they were finally on their way, moving at about twenty-five miles an hour in the cold morning sunlight.

'I think we have to face the fact that the Peacemaker knows Schenckendorff has crossed sides,' Mason said after five minutes of silence as they wound their way with difficulty through a small village. The streets were crowded with carts and people walking: some soldiers, some refugees returning to stare in dismay at once familiar houses now crumbled to stained and ugly ruin.

'Do you think he'll send someone else after us?' Judith asked.

'We can't afford to take it for granted that Hampton was the only one,' Mason replied. 'It's a toss-up which is better: speed on the better and more obvious roads, or discretion in taking byways, perhaps even having to ford the odd stream and follow a few farm tracks.'

'Wouldn't an ambulance on a farm track draw attention?' she asked. She was worried now. This road was bad enough, and the engine was misfiring. She had no more spark plugs, and anything else that went wrong would be beyond her ability to mend. 'And we'll need more fuel in another fifteen miles.' She smiled grimly. 'We might be better to fight, if we have to, then try running. The poor old thing's not got it in her any more.'

'We need to reach the coast by tomorrow night, if we can,' he said, a sudden sadness in his voice. 'We've still got to make it from Dover to London, or from wherever we land.'

'Did you like Dermot Sandwell?' she asked as quietly as she could, and still be heard over the noise of the engine. They were through the town and on to open, flat road again. 'I met him once,' she added, thinking back to 1915 and a brief leave in London. 'He was different, powerful, as if he had a brilliant mind. I remember his eyes: pale blue and very bright.'

Mason thought for a moment or two before he answered. 'I don't think "like" is the right word,' he said finally. 'I admired him. I thought he had a greater vision than the rest of us, and the courage to do what he believed was right for all mankind, not just a narrow few. Other politicians were always so partisan, playing to the crowd. Sandwell was above that. He didn't really care if he was liked or not, or even if the majority understood him or saw his vision.'

Judith drove with difficulty for half a mile, veering right and left to avoid all the rubble in the road, and potholes that were deep enough to break an axle. She was thinking about Mason, and how the disillusion must hurt him. It had been a great dream, selfless. At least that was how he had seen it at the outset.

'How did you know him?' she asked when the road was less dangerous and she could increase speed a little.

'After Africa,' he answered. 'We were both involved in the Boer War, although we didn't meet then. At that time it seemed terrible.'

She looked sideways at him and saw pity and self-mockery in his face. He must have been aware of her glance, because he turned to meet her eyes, and smiled. The tenderness in them was overwhelming, the pain for all that was impossible, and that he longed for.

She caught her breath and tears blinded her eyes. She veered sideways and hit a pothole, jarring the ambulance. She swore, partly in fury with herself.

He started to laugh, the emotion in him too powerful to contain.

She laughed with him, and managed to stop it from turning into weeping. They had today and tomorrow, and that was infinitely precious. This short time must not be spoiled with a word, a look, an instant of self-pity or blame that they would afterwards regret. Above all there must be no cowardice.

'No, I don't think I did like him,' Mason said at last. 'But I loved the dream. Now it's time to wake up.' He put his hand over her shoulder and she felt the warmth of it through her clothes. 'I hate to admit it,' he added, 'but I rather like Schenckendorff. There's nothing manipulative about him.'

She smiled, and avoided a chicken in the road. 'So do I. In his own way he has a nice sense of humour.'

In the early afternoon, they came to a village that seemed unusually deserted on the outskirts. But as they reached the square in the centre, they found there were at least thirty people gathered together. Most of them were watching while half a dozen crowded together, pushing and jostling, arms raised, flailing against one person who cowered beneath the blows, unable to resist.

Judith jerked the ambulance to a stop and Mason jumped out.

A moment later the back door opened and Joseph and Matthew scrambled out, apparently afraid it was they who had been attacked.

Joseph started straight towards the crowd, who were shouting and snarling at the figure, now fallen to the ground and being kicked. They parted to allow him through, thinking he wanted to join them.

'You lost someone? You deserve to die!' a heavy-boned woman cried out. 'Kick her for me! Kick her for my son!' Her voice became choked in a racking sob.

Another woman let out an animal cry of hate, which was word-less and raw with pain.

Joseph found himself pushed to the front, only feet away from the figure huddled to the ground. Her head was shaven, and the few remnants of her clothes were torn and covered with blood.

Joseph stared at her. She was a woman of not more than thirty, and slight. Now she was bare-foot, and looked as if she had been dragged along the ground.

Joseph was sick with revulsion at the violence. He stared around him at the people, their faces gloating, vivid with hate.

'What in God's name are you doing?' he demanded.

The man nearest him spat one word. 'Collaborator!'

Others took up the cry, adding taunts and curses. It was the worst accusation of all, worse than 'enemy', even than 'spy'. It was the lowest form of human life, the final betrayal. Still Joseph was horrified that they could do this to her. Without thinking of the danger of attracting their anger, he bent and lifted up the woman on the ground, pulling first at her shoulder, gently, to turn her so she could rise.

Her face was beaten; her nose broken and bloody, her eyes half swollen shut, her teeth chipped and lips torn. Even so, he recognized her, because the one time he had seen her had been so powerfully engraved in his memory. It had been last year, in Paris, when he had needed to find Punch Fuller to get his evidence for the court martial. Sam Wetherall had asked her help. Her name was Monique, and she worked for the French, spying against the Germans in the heart of their command, risking her life every day.

'Monique . . .' he said softly. 'Monique . . .'

She blinked once, her eyes focusing with difficulty. 'Did you find him?' she whispered, her words distorted by her shattered face.

'Yes, I found him. Thank you.' She knew him. There could be no doubt it was she.

Joseph cradled her in his arms, trying to think desperately what he could do for any of her injuries. How bad were they? She was covered in blood and it was still oozing through her thin dress, but – far more urgent than that – how bad was the bruising, what bones were broken?

'Collaborator!' A man spat on the ground. 'Get out of the way, monsieur. I am going to hang her. You too, if you stand in the path of justice.'

'She worked for the Germans,' a woman said harshly. She looked no more than thirty herself. 'Pig! Filth!' She aimed a kick but was too far away to reach.

Another man lashed out, and he was closer. His boot caught Monique in the chest, and she gasped and cried out. She slipped from Joseph's arms on to the cobbles. Her eyes rolled back and she stopped moving, blood running from her mouth.

The man regained his balance and lifted his foot to do it again. Joseph shot to his feet and hit the man as hard as he could with his fist, all his weight behind it. 'She's not a collaborator, you fool!' he shouted. 'She's part of the resistance!' He hit the man again, and again, feeling his fist strike bone, then soft flesh: yielding, sagging, dead weight. Still he didn't stop. 'She was braver and better than any of you, you cowards!'

The man staggered and fell backwards on to the stones himself, but Joseph didn't stop. He lunged after him and hauled him to his feet, then hit him again, one fist and then the other. His own hands were bleeding, but he didn't care. Another man came at him, and he hit him too, full in the face, sending him reeling backwards, then again, knocking him to the ground. He was bending over him, ready to strike when he felt arms holding him, stopping him moving, sending him off balance.

He heaved himself away and spun around, to lash out, and saw with surprise that it was Matthew. Then Mason caught him from behind and pinned his arms to his sides.

Judith was on the ground by Monique. The crowd was staring at Joseph, shocked into silence.

Judith laid Monique down gently. 'It's too late,' she said, looking at Joseph. 'She's dead.'

Joseph stiffened.

Mason held him more tightly.

Lizzie and Schenckendorff were standing on the edge of the crowd, their faces white.

'You know her?' Matthew asked, looking at Joseph with extra-ordinary tenderness.

'Yes. I met her in Paris, last year. She worked for our intelligence there. She risked her life to help her country, and these stupid animals have murdered her.' He was finding it difficult to breathe, as if there were a great weight tightening around his chest, crushing him. The distance blurred in his vision, figures becoming fuzzy and distorted.

'Not a collaborator?' someone asked quietly.

'We didn't know,' someone else tried to excuse themselves.

'No, you didn't!' Joseph grated the words between clenched teeth. 'And you didn't care. You murdered her anyway.'

'But we didn't . . . we thought . . .' The man's words tailed off in the withering blaze of Joseph's eyes.

'Tell her that!' Joseph said bitterly.

'Joseph, she's dead,' Matthew's voice was gentle, insistent.

'I know!' Joseph shouted, ending in a sob. He struggled for breath. They were all dead: his mother and father, Sebastian Allard, the man who had brought the treaty from Germany in the first place, Owen Cullingford, Charlie Gee, that damned reporter in his arrogance, Theo Blaine, Shanley Corcoran, Tucky Nunn, half the men of the Cambridgeshire regiment that he had grown up with, the young men from St John's College, half the armies of Europe torn and blinded and choked in their own blood. Now Monique: stupidly, senselessly murdered after all she had done for her own people. It was unbearable.

He was too late to save her, or to save those stupid, ugly people from their own fate. They could not undo what they had done. Had he really helped anyone? Those who believed, or those who didn't? The sick, the frightened, the hopeless, anyone at all?

He had kept a grip on all the despair that threatened him like a towering, consuming darkness all the years of war. He had not wept for his own pain, but now it could not be denied. It tore through him like a storm, sweeping reason, self-mastery and consciousness of others away like a tidal wave. He wept for all of them: every lost and terrified soul of the last, dreadful years.

Matthew held him, and the crowd swirled around, confused and ashamed, frightened by the power of what they had done. Suddenly they understood that it was irretrievable, and one by one they also saw that it was undeniable. Ignorance did not pardon them.

Matthew took Joseph back to the ambulance. Someone brought him a stiff jolt of cognac. It burned his throat and set a deep fire in his stomach. He was aware of people coming and going.

Matthew left, and it was Lizzie who sat beside him. She said nothing, simply held his hands. He had no idea where anyone else was, or what they were doing.

Finally his mind cleared and the vision of Monique's bleeding, disfigured face faded from his vision. He began to think, to remember other people, other losses that were also what he grieved for, young men whose deaths would always be woven into his mind and his memory.

He had wanted to serve, to lessen the suffering, to give people the hope and the love of God in the darkest places they would pass through. He would have given his own life, if it had been asked, but it had not. He was barely even injured, except the once in 1916.

He had promised God in the beginning that he would keep faith, but he would not attempt to feel everyone's grief. That he could not bear. It was too much to ask of everyone.

But in Gethsemane that was exactly what Christ had asked – 'Watch with Me'. It was what He asked of everyone.

Joseph remembered all the men he had sat with in their pain, their fear, their loneliness, their acceptance of death. He had cared intensely. So often all he could do was simply be there. He could not ease their agony, take away their terror of mutilation, of failure, of the last unknown step of death. He could not promise victory, or offer any reasons for the horror of it, or explain why God allowed such hell to be.

He had crouched in the mud of no-man's-land, freezing and sodden wet, smelled the stink of decaying flesh, of gas, of death, and all he could do was promise, 'I will not leave you.'

And in that moment it came to him with absolute certainty that what he wanted, needed, was to stay with Lizzie. He could do it, and love the child because it was hers, and because it needed to be loved, as everyone needs to be. He could give it the love his father had given him: wholeheartedly, generously, because he wanted to. He – or she – would never for an instant imagine they were the product of violence or pain. They would not be unwanted, so they would never feel it more deeply than the growing pains we all know, the finding of identity in the world.

He turned to Lizzie and smiled, then pulled his hands from hers, wincing as his lacerated skin was touched, then he took hers again and held them gently, more firmly. 'When we get home,' he said, 'there'll be a lot to do, a lot of people who'll need help, and more courage than they may think they have now. There are not only the wounded in body, but in heart and hope as well. There'll be disappointments, changes that are very diffi-cult to accept. I expect there will be injustices and a great deal of loneliness. The bad things of war will be gone, but so will the good things: the friendships, the purpose, the knowledge of who you are and what you are doing, and that it matters.'

'I know,' she answered him. 'I had planned to go on nursing . . . until . . .' She stopped, a slow colour working up her cheeks. She was afraid of pity, and he saw it in her eyes.

How could he ask her to marry him without her fearing, even for an instant, that that was what it was – pity – not love?

'I would very much rather that you helped me,' he told her. 'I am not sure that I can do it without you, and I am perfectly certain that I don't wish to. But with you, and the child, I might make a reasonably good job of it. I've learned something about what a real ministry is.'

She looked at him, searching his eyes slowly, very carefully.

He smiled, knowing there was nothing in him that he needed to hide from her. She knew his weaknesses already, as he knew hers, and he knew that in the end they would bind them together, not apart.

'I think that would be a good idea,' she said at last. 'We might make quite a passable job of it.'

Happiness opened up inside him like a great dawning light. He leaned forward and kissed her, and realized with surprise how long he had wanted to do that, and how sweet it was.

He had only just let her go when Matthew opened the door.

'Are you all right?' Matthew asked, then decided that the question was unnecessary.

'Yes . . . thank you,' Joseph replied. 'We should go. We can't be far from the coast now, but there isn't much time.'

'We've got a lot more help,' Matthew told him. 'Food, petrol and someone to show us the best roads. We could make it tonight.'

Joseph was startled. 'How did you do that?'

'Guilt,' Matthew answered simply. 'They felt like hell.'

Joseph was embarrassed. For the first time in years he had completely lost control of himself. He had wanted to kill the man who had kicked Monique. He might have, if Matthew had not stopped him. That was a frightening thought. He had

had no idea that there was so much rage inside him, or bottled up pain.

'The man I . . . hit, is he all right?'

Matthew rolled his eyes and shrugged. 'He'll live, but you broke his nose and jaw and two or three ribs. Good thing he's fairly heavily built, or you might have done worse. You took him totally by surprise. He didn't imagine the priest would try to kill him, or you might not have come out of it so well.'

'You don't need to labour the point,' Joseph said a little tartly. 'His behaviour was unforgivable.'

'That rather is the point, Joe.' Matthew looked at him steadily, not moving from the spot where he stood. 'You can't leave them like this. You've pretty well consigned them to hell, and left them in no doubt that you meant it. That isn't how you'd like it to stay.' He said it with certainty, no shadow in his eyes.

Joseph did not want to go back and face them again. It was deeply embarrassing, and he did not forgive them for what they had done to Monique. He could not tell them it was excusable. It would betray his own beliefs, and no one with an ounce of sense would believe him anyway.

'I can't offer them any forgiveness,' he said. 'There's no penance I know of that's going to heal what they just did. To say there is would be a lie.'

'There's always a way back, Joe, from anywhere,' Matthew replied. 'You told me that. If you can't help them, what hope is there for any of us?'

'It's time to begin,' Lizzie said, touching Joseph's hand lightly. 'You don't have to lie to them. Tell them how hard it will be, just don't say it's impossible.'

He climbed out of the ambulance, standing a little unsteadily at first, then turned and thanked her. Matthew was waiting. He followed him to where the villagers were collected together with a pile of food in boxes and three cans of petrol. They were the most precious things they had; perhaps a week's supply. There were also spark plugs and a small tin of oil. They looked frightened, and hopeful.

Suddenly Joseph wanted to tell them they were forgiven, but that was weariness, gratitude and pity speaking, the desire to escape, and none of those made it the right thing to do. It was facile, an escape for himself.

'Thank you,' he said to them, looking at the pile of food and petrol. 'We know what a great gift it is, and how much it represents of what you have. I would like to say that it will redeem you from what you did to Monique, but it would not be true. You don't deserve that. Like all of us, you need honesty. The way back from such a sin is longer and far harder than that, which you know as well as I do. But never forget that the way does exist, and you can walk it if you wish to enough. I can't tell you how to find it, because I don't know. But your chance to pay the price will come, if you want it enough to look for it, and accept it.'

They stared at him, shifting awkwardly from foot to foot. No one spoke. Hope sprang to life in one or two faces. In others it died. They had been expecting something easier.

'I apologize for standing in judgement of you,' Joseph went on. 'I have no right to. That is something you will have to do for yourselves. You know what you did, and why, and what drove you. And you know she didn't deserve it. Begin by not lying to yourselves. What I say is true, for you, for me, for everyone.'

One of the older men nodded. Then he turned to others and

they signalled agreement also. They said their goodbyes formally, and seemed relieved to see the ambulance begin its journey to the coast, with one young woman of the village in the cab beside Judith to guide them for the next ten miles. No one asked how she would get back.

They reached the harbour a little after sundown. The salt wind off the sea smelled clean and bitterly cold, but there was an excitement to the taste of it, an energy in the wind and tide.

It took considerable bargaining, and ultimately a threat on Matthew's part, but by midnight they were on their way across the Channel. Most of them attempted to sleep, but Matthew paced the deck looking out over the dark water. The foam rose and fell, patterns shifting on the surface. He remembered standing like this on the deck of the *Cormorant*, before the Battle of Jutland, knowing that any moment it could erupt in white water, then flame and unimaginable noise. There would be twisted metal, screams, the smell of burning corticene, and juddering, pitching ground as the ship reeled. Always at the end lay the threat of being swallowed by that black sea and sucked down, never to be released.

There were only days to go until the end, and yet ships were still being sunk, all hands lost. It was a kind of wild madness he did not understand. What was there left to win or lose now? Only hate, the most pointless of all passions.

He kept looking ahead, trying to discern the dark outline of land ahead. They were making for Harwich, not Dover, so there would be no familiar cliffs to see, but they had been grateful to take the first transport that would take them, and the ambulance too. They couldn't have simply abandoned the vehicle. It would be an added difficulty to try to get rail transport with as little money as they had been able to gather, and on a crowded train it might be impossible to conceal the fact that Schenckendorff was German.

It was still before dawn when at last Matthew saw the low, black line of land ahead. An hour later they were on the windswept quay with the ambulance which, to their intense relief, had started after the third attempt.

'We should be in London by early afternoon, unless we run into major difficulties,' Matthew said, shivering as the wind blew spray up off the water. They were all tired, and the cold bit into them. It was now his responsibility to make certain that they persuaded Shearing, and then the Prime Minister, of Sandwell's guilt. They would have only one chance, and Sandwell already knew they were coming. The danger was far from over; in fact this could be the worst part. Victory was so close that emotions that had been held in check for years were now boiling to the surface. There was hope and a desperate fragility almost perceptible in the air.

Would Sandwell try again? Of course. But how? Overt violence would be harder now that they were in England. Anything he did would have to look like an accident. Was it possible Sandwell did not yet know that Hampton had failed? Probably not. He would have some prearranged signal, a time to contact each other. Hampton's silence would be answer enough.

'We need to get to London as soon as we can,' he said. 'Thank heaven we have the ambulance and don't need to use trains, or risk getting separated, or lost in a crowd where we'd be far more vulnerable.'

He saw Lizzie start, and realized she had thought they were

already safe. She was standing next to Joseph, and unconsciously she moved closer to him.

'Sorry,' Matthew said briefly. 'He'll assume we are home, and he knows what for. He'll have worked out by now that Hampton failed. We need to keep close together, and on our guard. I've still got Hampton's gun, but I don't imagine any attack will be as obvious as that.' He turned to Mason. 'You know him. What's your best guess as to what he'll do now?'

Mason thought for several moments. 'He might try to stop us between here and London. It would be too good a chance to miss, unless he has no one he can trust . . .'

'We can't rely on that,' Joseph said instantly.

'Agreed,' Matthew nodded. 'Then maybe we'd better travel separately. Finding three or four men to reach us would be very much harder. And since we've travelled together so far, he won't be expecting it.'

'That's not all,' Mason went on. 'There's only one thing we can do in the end, which is accuse him openly. He'll be expecting that. It's the last throw of the dice left, so to speak. He'll be prepared for it. I don't know whether he'll try to say the Peacemaker is someone else.' He smiled with bitter amusement. 'Possibly even me. He might do it well enough to confuse events for a while. Or he might deny there was ever such a conspiracy at all. That's why we need to have the original treaty that your father took in nineteen fourteen.' He turned to Joseph. 'You still have it in Cambridgeshire, don't you?'

Matthew felt a moment of alarm. They were so close to the Peacemaker at last, but was it possible there was a final twist, and it was not Sandwell, but Mason's slight, almost half-hearted jest was the truth? Was Mason himself the leader, and perhaps

Sandwell and Schenckendorff followers? No, that was ridiculous. Mason was in love with Judith, deeply in love. He was not attempting to hide it now: this was the last time they would have together.

He looked at Joseph, wanting to know his thoughts, wishing he could speak to him alone.

Mason was waiting.

'Joe—' Matthew started.

'Yes,' Joseph cut across him. 'I know where it is.'

Too late. They were committed. Had Joseph thought of Mason's possible complicity, or was his religious naïvety still too powerful for him to consider that the man Judith loved could yet betray them?

'Better not tell us where,' Matthew said. 'That way we can't accidentally betray it.'

Mason smiled. 'Understood,' he said wryly. 'Joseph should get the treaty and we'll all meet somewhere in London. The rest of us should travel separately too as much as possible. Perhaps Judith and I, and Matthew with Schenckendorff, and Lizzie with them to see to Schenckendorff's foot. You take the ambulance. You can drive it, can't you?' The last question was directed towards Matthew.

Matthew hesitated. He did not want Mason to direct what they did, and yet he could not think of a better alternative. If they stayed together they were one target. They could not hope to convince Lloyd George without Schenckendorff, Mason and the treaty. It had to be either he or Joseph who went to St Giles to get the treaty from the gunroom. Judith didn't know one end of a gun from the other, and the last thing he would allow was Mason to go with her.

'Right,' he said. 'I'll take the ambulance with Lizzie and Schenckendorff and I'll meet you at my flat, Mason. You and Judith go by train to London. Joseph, take the train to Cambridge and then to St Giles. We'll wait for you in London. Go to the intelligence service office and ask for me.'

Goodbyes were brief as they pulled up outside the railway station. Judith and Mason went to wait for the first train to London, Joseph to Cambridge.

As Joseph sat by the window in the train – given a seat willingly because of his uniform – he watched the countryside slip past him. For a moment he could delude himself that nothing had changed. The soft slopes of the land rolled away to the horizon, dotted with occasional copses of trees. The late harvest fields were stubble gold, one or two ploughed ready for a winter crop, the earth dark and shining, black soil rich. The villages looked as they always had: many roofs steeply thatched; square church towers, Saxon solid; the little streets winding. Here and there he saw the flash of light on a duck pond in the centre of a green. The leaves were bronze where they still remained. Most were already shed in copper-coloured drifts on the ground.

He ached with a love for the ancient, familiar beauty of it. To come and go as he wished, here in these lanes and across this land, was what they had fought and died for. It was far from perfect, because people made mistakes, but there was a freedom here that had been learned and paid for over the centuries. It was the right, not only in law but in practice, to disagree, to be different, inventive, sometimes to be wrong, and still be a part of the fabric that was treasured. There was honour and tolerance throughout all the errors and wrongs of history, and that must be saved, whatever the cost.

The train pulled into Cambridge station and he asked about the next train to Selborne St Giles. It was too long to wait for. It would take him hours to get there and back. Nor did he have sufficient money. Even as it was, he was going to have to borrow from Hannah the train fare from Cambridge to London. He would not even entertain the thought that she might not be home.

His mind raced. Who could he ask to drive him, with precious petrol, first to St Giles, and then back to Cambridge? Who did he know?

St John's. That was the only answer. There must be somebody there he still knew. The question was, would they have a car, and petrol to put in it? Aidan Thyer would be the best chance, and there was no time to waste starting with others he might prefer. He remembered ruefully that Thyer was one of those he had suspected of being the Peacemaker. He had never been ruled out. The only thing he could do now was trust that Schenckendorff was telling the truth, and Mason also. Good men could lie, if the cause were great enough; he knew and understood that, but it was too late to dither.

He walked rapidly through the ancient streets, past the colleges he knew and had loved so long. Most of them were centuries old, built of towering stone, carved, bearing their coats of arms proudly. Behind them the green grass of the Backs sloped down to the river where four summers ago young men had pushed flat-bottomed boats along the quiet waters. Pretty girls had sat in the sterns, trailing their fingers in the stream, muslin dresses stirred by the breeze, hats shading their faces. Now there were no young men in sight, and girls had short hair, skirts not far below their knees, and they were working on buses, in factories and on the land. How short a time it had taken for the world to change utterly.

The Master's lodgings at St John's looked exactly as it always had, probably for at least three hundred years. The quad was silent. There were no leaves on the trees.

Joseph knocked on the door. If Aidan and Connie were in, they would answer it themselves. Nobody had servants any more. The silence closed in around him. Would they still even have a car? If they did, would Aidan be willing to help Joseph? Would he just drop everything, demand no explanations, and give up his day to drive Joseph to St Giles, wait, and then bring him back?

What if he were one of those who sympathized with the Peacemaker? Victory could slip out of their hands at any moment up to the very last.

The door opened. It was Aidan Thyer himself. He still looked elegant and faintly mystified, as if he had sustained some unexpected wound and was wondering how to deal with it. Was it still because he loved Connie more than she could ever love him? Or was it the loss of so many of his young men before they had fulfilled the promise or the hope of their lives?

'Joseph?' he said in amazement. 'Joseph Reavley! My dear fellow, come in.' He stepped back, holding the door wide. The light shone on his pale hair and the subtle lines of his face. 'What can I do for you? Is it acceptable to ask what you are doing home so soon before the end? I hope it is not bad news of your family?' Sudden deep concern shadowed his eyes.

'No, thank you,' Joseph followed him inside. 'We are all fine, so far as I know. But I have an urgent errand. I need to get to St Giles as soon as I can, and then back to the station to London. It is very urgent indeed, and I need help.' There was no time to waste in prevarication, and he would not have known how to do it anyway. 'Can you drive me, please? And if you can't, do you know someone who would?'

Thyer regarded him with concern. 'Of course I will. Are you sure you are all right?'

'Yes.' Then suddenly it occurred to him that Thyer might wonder if it were one of the Cambridge students he knew in trouble. 'It's not personal business at all,' he added. 'It's something I have to collect, and get to London today.'

Thyer nodded. 'Would you like anything to eat first, or even to drink? You look as if you have been up all night.'

'Yes, I dare say I do,' Joseph agreed ruefully. 'But I haven't time. Perhaps after.'

'I'll get the keys, and tell Connie. She'll be glad to hear at least that you are all right.'

Thyer returned a few moments later, accompanied by his wife. As always, Connie was delighted to see Joseph, but she understood that it could be no more than hello and goodbye. She had made a quick sandwich for him, and offered it to him now, wrapped in a piece of paper.

'Only bread and what I would like to call pâté, but it's really meat paste,' she apologized.

He thanked her and suddenly realized he was ravenously hungry.

She watched him, smiling, and handed him a glass of lemonade, knowing anything hot to drink would take possibly more time than he was willing to afford.

Standing just inside the Master's lodgings, looking at Connie, gave Joseph a startling sense of timelessness. She was still beautiful in her own warm, generous way. And there was still the restlessness in her eyes, although the edge of it had softened, and she looked towards Thyer more often than he remembered her doing before.

It was as if only months had passed since he had stood here in the summer of 1914, and spoken of war and peace with such innocence. No one had imagined the world could change so much, in so short a time. The past they had known was gone for ever. He knew it here in its fullness for the first time. In this quiet hallway looking into the quad where nothing changed, he realized the enormity of the change in everything else.

'Joseph?' Thyer asked. 'Are you ready?'

'Yes . . . thank you.' Joseph gave the empty glass back to Connie and bade her goodbye. He followed Thyer across the first quad and then the second into the street to where the car was parked.

The drive to Selborne St Giles was swift. Not once did Thyer ask him what was the purpose of his sudden and urgent journey, nor did they talk of those they knew who were dead. Instead Thyer discussed politics, in particular the character of Lloyd George, and the new ideas of widening the political franchise to include all men, property owners or not, and even many women.

'Times are changing at an extraordinary pace,' he said with a slight frown. 'I hope we can keep up with them without too many casualties. The men coming home aren't going to recognize the land they left behind, and may possibly not like it entirely. Women have all kinds of jobs now, and we need them to remain doing them. We can't now send them back to the kitchen.' He shook his head slightly. 'A great number of them will not marry because there is no one for them to have. They have no choice but to earn their own way. We cannot make that impossible for them.'

Joseph did not reply.

'And there are very few places for servants. We've learned to do without them,' Thyer went on. 'Jack's as good as his master. We discovered that in the trenches. There are an awful lot of "Jacks" to whom we owe our lives. I dare say you know that better than I do.'

Joseph smiled, and agreed. They were racing through the November countryside at a far higher speed than Joseph would have expected from the Master. He had always thought of him as a trifle staid, a scholar with little action in him. Perhaps he had been wrong.

They passed the quiet fields of the farm where Charlie and Barshey Gee had grown up, then that of Snowy and Tucky Nunn. The blacksmith's forge was open, Plugger Arnold's father bent over the anvil. It was all desperately familiar, and Joseph would have given all he possessed if the men he had known and loved could have come home again with him.

The street was quiet. There were half a dozen women in it, coats closed tight against the wind. The green was deserted, the duck pond flat and bright in the momentary sun.

They pulled up outside the house where Joseph had grown up, from which John and Alys Reavley had left that morning the world had changed, when Gavrilo Princip had fired a shot in Sarajevo that had ended history and begun the present, and Sebastian Allard had committed a wild, misconceived murder on the Hauxton Road.

'I'll not be long,' Joseph said briefly. 'One day I'll tell you exactly what all this is about.' He climbed out and walked a little shakily to the door and knocked. He had already made up his mind that, if Hannah were not home, he would break in, and leave her a note to explain what he had done.

He had raised his hand to knock again when the door opened. She stood just inside. She looked so like her mother that for a moment Joseph was stunned, just as taken aback as she was. Then she threw herself into his arms and hugged him, and he held her hard and close.

'It's all right,' he said, still holding her. 'I've come for the treaty. We know who the Peacemaker is, and we have to prove it to Lloyd George, and then it will be over. I have dozens of things to tell you, but Matthew and Judith are waiting for me in London, and there's no time now.'

She pulled back and stared at him. 'Who is it?'

'Dermot Sandwell.'

'The Minister? It can't be!'

'Now you see why I have to prove it.'

She did not argue. She could see the certainty in his face, and simply stood back and followed him through the house to the gunroom at the back. The door was locked, as it had been since 1914. He opened it and took down his father's old punt gun and broke it, then very carefully eased out the rolled-up piece of paper from inside the barrel.

'Has that been there all the time?' she asked in amazement.

'Yes. That's where Father hid it. We thought it the safest place, since they had searched the house during the funeral, remember?'

'You didn't tell me!'

'Safer for you not to know.' He smiled briefly. 'Have you heard from Archie lately?'

'Yes, he's due leave in about three weeks.'

'Give my love to Tom and Luke and Jenny. It'll all be over in a matter of days now. Then we can begin to build again and help the people who've been hurt more than they know how to bear.'

'A ministry again?' There was light in her face.

'Yes. I'm going to marry Lizzie Blaine.'

She smiled. 'Good. Very good. I thought you might.'

He kissed her quickly on the cheek, then put the treaty into the inside of his tunic and strode back to the car.

One day he would tell Aidan Thyer at least some of the truth, but not now. At Cambridge station he thanked him again, and went immediately to the platform to catch the next train to London. The journey still held the vestige of a sense of escape, which he was ashamed of. He should not have suspected Thyer, and yet he had a definite sense of relief to be alone again, anonymous among the other uniforms scattered here and there. Around him were men on leave, and men wounded, some too seriously ever to return to battle. It could be months, or even years, before the last stragglers returned. And of course so many would not.

When the train pulled into London, he alighted. He paid for the extravagance of a taxi, which earned a few black looks, since he was obviously able-bodied and didn't apparently need it.

The city looked weary, and even in the fitful sunlight there was a greyness to it. There were hardly any men in the streets except the old and the very young. There were women in all sorts of places that a couple of years ago would have been unthinkable: driving buses and lorries, even in police uniform. They looked busy, competent. The few who were fashionable had changed beyond recognition. The kind, feminine glamour that was designed for idleness was utterly gone. Now beauty was subdued, and extremely practical – short skirts, quiet colours.

The air seemed charged with emotion. A kind of expectancy lay behind the simplest exchange: a request for direction, the purchase of a newspaper. Joseph felt a moment of terrible pity for them, a fear that nothing was going to live up to the dream of what peace would be like when it came at last.

Very soon, when the armistice was announced, he expected the womenfolk to experience an almost unbearable excitement, anticipating welcoming home their men. Then, as they settled into a new life, they would have to rise to the challenge of redefining their roles as men and women, and their positions in society.

There was nothing in his life sweeter and more precious than the hope that Lizzie would be with him, sharing the work of rebuilding individual lives, communities again, helping people come to terms with change and loss.

The taxi stopped a block away from Matthew's office building. Joseph got out and paid, thanking the man, then turned and walked as swiftly as he could, grateful that the taxi had pulled away from the kerb. He went to the entrance and was admitted immediately he identified himself.

He was kept waiting in the outer room only moments before Matthew appeared, his face filled with relief. 'Got it?' he asked.

'Of course. Is everyone here?'

'Yes. No trouble?'

'None at all. You?'

Matthew smiled. 'Nothing that matters now.'

'What happened?' Joseph demanded.

'Difficulty getting petrol,' Matthew replied. 'Once we were

stopped by police and I was terrified it was another attempt by the Peacemaker, but it was just because I was going too fast. Come upstairs and we'll show Shearing the treaty.' He turned and led the way.

Inside Shearing's office Judith, Lizzie, Mason, and Schenckendorff were already waiting. Calder Shearing stood behind his desk, his face dark and tense, his eyes bright.

Wordlessly Joseph handed him the treaty between the Kaiser of Germany and the King of England with which the Peacemaker had proposed to create an Anglo-German empire to dominate the world, and lay peace in it by betraying France and the Low Countries to Germany, with Britain taking back all the old Empire, including the Americas.

Shearing read it, his face filling first with quiet, bitter amazement, and then with fury. He picked up his telephone and placed a call to Number 10 Downing Street. When he was finished he looked at them one by one.

'Are you ready, gentlemen?' he asked, although his glance included Judith and Lizzie. 'The Prime Minister will see us.'

# Chapter Twelve

In deference to Schenckendorff's injured foot – which was still severely painful – they travelled in two cars. Alighting outside Number 10 Downing Street, they were shown in immediately.

David Lloyd George was not a tall man, but he had a dynamism of character and a music in his voice that commanded attention. His inner energy, even after the terrible years of struggle, filled and dominated the room. He looked from one to the other of them. His main interest fell first on Mason, then on Schenckendorff, but he did not fail to notice the women, especially Judith. He had never in his life failed to perceive the beauty of a woman, and far too seldom had he failed to appreciate it.

'Well?' he asked Shearing. 'This had better be quick, and it had better be damned good! Which of you is going to explain to me what the devil you are talking about?'

Shearing indicated Matthew. 'Lieutenant-Colonel Matthew Reavley, one of my men.' He did not bother to introduce the others yet. They could be mentioned as their parts in the story arose.

Matthew stepped forward. 'Sir—'

'Speak, man!' Lloyd George commanded, waving his hand to order the rest of them to sit – or as many of them as there were chairs for. 'Forget the niceties. What is this tale of yours?'

Matthew began. 'On the night of June the twenty-seventh, nineteen fourteen, my father, John Reavley, telephoned me from Selborne St Giles in Cambridgeshire, to say that he had found a document which could change the history of the world, and shame Britain for ever, if it were put into effect. He said he would bring it to me the following day.'

Lloyd George blinked. 'Twenty-seventh of June nineteen fourteen?'

'Yes, sir. My mother and father set out the next day, and were murdered on the way, in a car accident. It was the same day as the assassination of the Archduke and Duchess in Sarajevo. After much difficulty, and tragically more murders, my brother, Joseph, and I found where my father hid the document. We read it and replaced it where it was.'

'Why in God's name—' Lloyd George glared at Shearing, and stopped abruptly. 'What was it, and why does it matter now?'

Wordlessly Joseph took the treaty out of his inner pocket and spread it on the table before the Prime Minister.

Lloyd George read it. The blood drained from his face, leaving it as white as his hair. 'God Almighty!' he said in a shaking voice. He swallowed and looked up at Joseph, still standing in front of him. 'You had this throughout the war?'

'Yes, sir. We had no idea who was behind it, only that he had great power and was willing to murder to put this plan into effect. He tried all through the war to bring about an Allied surrender so that this empire of his could still come about. We codenamed him "the Peacemaker" because we believed that the avoidance of war was his purpose, even if it meant robbing us of both freedom and honour to do so. We now know that he wishes to influence the terms of the armistice so that Germany can rise again quickly, rebuild its armies, and the plan still be carried through.'

'Never!' Lloyd George said instantly. 'We must find out who he is, and hang him as a traitor.'

Matthew resumed the story. 'We have tried all through the war to do that, sir. Only now have we succeeded, and only because some of the men who believed in peace and were unaware of the true extent of the cost he was prepared to pay for it have finally seen what he is, and are willing to come forward to unmask him, regardless of the cost to themselves.'

Lloyd George turned instantly to Schenckendorff, the only man in the room he did not know anything about. He wore a British volunteer uniform, but the command in his bearing, and the obviously painful injury to his foot, which was still heavily bandaged, marked him as other than he seemed.

Schenckendorff stood up, without the slightest wince even as he put his weight on his foot, and bowed. His face was tight and pale with the cost of it. 'Manfred von Schenckendorff, sir. It was I who obtained the Kaiser's signature to the treaty. At the time I believed it was for the peace of Europe and so that we might rule without war for all the years to come. Now I know that that dream was never possible. I have seen both your country and my own lose the best men of a generation, and wash the earth in blood. I have come through the lines to where Chaplain

Reavley fought in Ypres in order to expose my cousin, my British counterpart, so this never happens again. Because if he is not stopped, he will engineer a peace which is only a hiatus between this war and the next.'

'Your cousin?' Lloyd George asked tensely.

'Dermot Sandwell. His mother and mine were sisters,' Schenckendorff replied. Then, seeing the disbelief in Lloyd George's face, he added. 'Beautiful women, Irish, not English or German.'

'For God's sake!' Lloyd George exploded. 'Sandwell's one of the best, most loyal man we have! That's preposterous.' He looked at Shearing with increasing anger. 'What possessed you to believe this poppycock, man? Have you no more sense—'

Mason stepped forward, freeing himself from Judith's arm. He stood to the right of Schenckendorff, facing the Prime Minister. His voice shook as he began to speak, then it gathered emotion and strength.

'My name is Richard Mason, sir, war correspondent. As a young man I reported on the Boer War, and was horrified beyond my power or ability ever to forget the brutality and waste of life I saw there. So was Dermot Sandwell. I met him shortly afterwards, and we both swore that such slaughter should never happen again. I believed that there must be a better way, even if it had to be brought about by deceit, and a conspiracy of men who had more power than our soldiers or politicians. I was prepared to give my life to that cause. All through the war I reported to Sandwell to help at least part of his activities, in an attempt to bring the carnage to an end, and create a peace that would last.'

Lloyd George stared at him in incredulity and something close to dismay.

'What Colonel von Schenckendorff says is true, sir,' Mason continued. 'I could give you chapter and verse of it, were there time, but there isn't. Colonel von Schenckendorff and I are willing to give our lives to pay the price of our delusion. Matthew, Joseph and Judith Reavley have followed in the steps of their father to lay this open, and show that we fight our wars, we do not appease. Their passion and belief have shown now that it can and must be done. I will face Sandwell. He cannot deny me; I know far too much.'

Lloyd George sighed and his face was masked with a deep grief. It was clear that he no longer denied it to himself.

There was a deferential but insistent knocking on the door.

'What is it?' he demanded.

A man put his head round it. 'Mr Sandwell is here, sir.'

'Good! Just the man I want. Send him in,' Lloyd George ordered. 'And have the policeman at the door come inside.'

The man looked startled.

'Do it!' Lloyd George shouted.

Less than two minutes later the door opened again and Dermot Sandwell came into the room. He was tall and startlingly elegant. His fair hair was polished smooth, his eyes a curious, pale and brilliant blue. He looked first at the Prime Minister, then at Mason and Schenckendorff. The others he ignored. His face, already lean, seemed to tighten and fade to a pallor so bleached he looked about to faint, but he stood rigidly straight.

The door behind him closed with a sharp snick.

It was Schenckendorff who spoke. His pronunciation was precise, his English so perfect it was almost without accent. Only the pain thickened his voice. 'It is over, Dermot. The slaughter of nations and the murder of individuals has come to an end,

366

and those of us who tried to force on them a peace without honour must pay the price. I saw the same vision as you did, in the beginning, but now it is finished. We cannot do this again; we must not. If you will not stop yourself, then I will stop you.'

Sandwell stared at him, the shock in his face turning to scalding contempt. 'Coward,' he said simply. 'I trusted you with a vision of Europe without war, and you have betrayed me. If we had succeeded, if that idiot John Reavley had had a larger mind unfettered by the petty prejudices of nationalism, we could have saved the lives of thirty million men who now lie dead or mutilated across the world. Think of that, Manfred, when you weep for Germany. We were betrayed in the beginning by lesser men, too blinded by what they thought was patriotism to see the whole of humanity. Now it seems I stand alone. That does not make me any the less right.'

He turned to face the Prime Minister, then caught sight of Mason. 'And it seems you have turned out to be no more than a Little Englander after all, in spite of the horror and the death that you have seen. In the end you ran back to your own small square of the earth, blind to the rest of it.' He looked at Joseph. 'Of you I expected no better. You are your father's son. We might have hoped a man who professes a Christian religion would have a larger view, but we hoped in vain.'

Lloyd George rose to his feet. 'I trusted you, Dermot. It pains me to find you a traitor of such monumental proportions. You will hang for this.'

Sandwell gave a bark of laughter. 'Don't be absurd! You dare not prosecute me. What will you say? That I tried to save the world from this . . . this charnel house of blood and ruin, but I failed because of the short-sightedness of a few men who thought more of England than they did of humanity? And now that you have won, and we are up to our knees in the corpses of our own men, you are going to kill me too, because I would have saved them? How long do you think an exhausted and bereaved country will thank you for that?'

'Your proposed treaty was infamous,' Lloyd George said bitterly. 'It would have been a peace without honour.'

Sandwell's eyebrows rose high over his brilliant eyes. 'Tell that to the millions of women with fathers, uncles, brothers, husbands and sons whose broken bodies lie buried in the fields of France. See if they agree with you.'

Lloyd George's hands closed over the piece of paper, which rolled back upon itself after four and a half years inside the barrel of the punt gun.

Sandwell stared at it as he finally realized what it was. He made a movement towards it, and then froze. Very slowly he turned to Matthew.

'Yes,' Matthew replied, staring back at him. 'We had it all the time. My father hid it where all your searches failed to find it.'

'Then the blood of millions is on your hands,' Sandwell replied between his teeth. 'The best and the bravest of the nations of the earth lie crushed beneath the weight of your stupidity.'

'You are wrong,' Joseph answered him with absolute conviction. 'I do not believe our King would have signed it, but if he had, it would not have bound us, not all of us. There would always have been some who would pay for the freedom for us to make our own laws, speak our differences aloud, follow the faith we choose, make our own mistakes, laugh at ourselves and try again. If we pay with our lives, then so be it. We will not pay with the slow death of our minds or the withering of our souls.'

'You patronizing idiot!' Sandwell spat at him. 'Do you think anybody cares for that kind of empty sermon now? Death is real! It's broken bodies, men blinded, crippled, choked on their own blood! It's corpses riddled with bullets, frozen to death. It's not high-minded valour, you fool! Look at reality! Say that to the mutilated, the blind, if you dare!'

'I dare,' Joseph replied unflinchingly. 'I know them as you never will, or you would not have misjudged them so completely. Again and again you were wrong. You did not understand their courage, their loyalty, their friendship, their love of the right to come and go as they like, to keep their ancient customs, the little ways that make life sweet. Men and nations will always seek the right to make their own choices, whatever the cost. You can guide, but you cannot rule. You misjudged humanity in general, and Britain in particular.

'But worse than that, and far worse, you confused the ends with the means until they became one in your mind. You destroyed the very spark of life that you wanted to give us. Without the freedom to be right or wrong, to choose your own way rather than the way forced upon you, there is no virtue, no courage, no honour or laughter or love worth having. Men with far less intellect than yours know that in their blood and their bones, and they will die rather than sell it to you and your dreams of dominion. And that is what they have become. It is not the wisdom or the intent of power that corrupts, it is the totality of power that can no longer be curbed.'

Sandwell stared at Joseph with a hatred so violent his whole slender body trembled with it, then he hit him as hard as he could.

Joseph staggered backwards, overbalanced and fell, his head striking the floor with a crack. He lay still.

Judith went ashen. Lizzie drew in her breath with a sob and started forward, but Matthew blocked her way.

Sandwell moved forward to hit Joseph again. Matthew suddenly saw in Joseph's motionless body all the dead men he had loved: his father, Sebastian Allard, Owen Cullingford and all the others once full of passion and dreams, who had talked and laughed and cared so much. He struck Sandwell in the middle of the back, and as he swayed, caught him and spun him around. He hit him with the blow he had been taught and never expected to use, hard under the nose, driving the bone into his brain.

Sandwell slithered to the floor, and when Matthew bent over him he was not breathing. Without rising to his feet he turned to Joseph. Lizzie was beside him and Joseph was coughing, struggling to get his breath and to sit up. He looked dazed and unsteady, but unquestionably alive.

Matthew was overcome by a wave of relief so intense he felt dizzy. He realized that for an instant he had thought Joseph was dead. The crack of bone on the hard wood of the floor filled him with a fear just like the terrible grief he had felt for his father.

'Joe?' he said huskily.

Joseph groaned and put his hand to his head, then he stared beyond Matthew to the Peacemaker lying on the floor. 'You hit him,' he observed. 'Thank you. I think I really angered him. He wanted to kill me.'

Matthew looked at the figure almost at his feet, sprawled out, one leg under the other. He seemed smaller than when standing up. His brilliant eyes were open and staring sightlessly.

'He is dead,' Schenckendorff said quietly. 'I think perhaps that is a good thing.' He looked at Joseph. 'I hope you are not badly hurt. You are quite right: you angered him, because what you said is true. Great men use power as little as possible. It takes supreme humility to allow others to disagree, and to make their own mistakes. The right to be wrong is worth dying to protect, because without it all our virtues are empty. What we have not paid for slips through our fingers, because we do not value it enough to do what is necessary to keep it.' He held out his hand to Joseph.

Joseph took it and clasped it tightly.

Schenckendorff stood to attention and faced Lloyd George.

'I am at your service, sir,' he said stiffly.

Lloyd George was still standing, pale-faced. 'Thank you,' he said simply. 'You are a prisoner of war. You will be treated accordingly, and in time repatriated. I am mindful of how much we owe you, and it will not be forgotten.' He walked to the door and spoke to the man outside.

Minutes later Schenckendorff said goodbye to them. Matthew and Joseph saluted him. Two more men came to take the body of the Peacemaker.

'Heart attack,' the Prime Minister told them, even though it was patently obvious that that was not the cause of Sandwell's death. No one argued or made the slightest movement to intervene as the men carried the body out. The door closed behind them, and those left in the room faced the Prime Minister.

Joseph's head ached appallingly but his vision had cleared. All he could think of was Judith, and how she would bear it when Mason was arrested. Since she was no blood relation of Mason's, she might not even see him again. Were he in her place, and it was Lizzie who would be taken away to face trial and execution, he would not know how to endure it. And yet there was nothing he could do to help. Mason was as alone as if there were no one else in the building.

Mason stared at Lloyd George, waiting, his face white, eyes steady.

Lloyd George chewed his lip and very slowly shook his head. 'This grieves me,' he said softly. 'You were the bravest and the best of all our war correspondents. You went to every field of conflict. Your words framed the way we at home saw and felt the pain of our men, and their valour. Through your experience we have shared what our men endured, and the spirit they carried with them. You were the voice of those who could not and now never will speak for themselves.'

Mason swayed a little. Joseph held Judith's arm to prevent her going to him.

'We are weary of war,' Lloyd George went on. 'We are heartsick, bereaved, and frightened of a future that is stranger and more complex and difficult than ever we have faced before. We do not need to know that one of the voices that comforted us and led us through our darkest hours was that of a traitor. I shall hide that – not for your sake, but for the sake of my country. You will never speak of it again. No one in this room will.' He looked from one to the other of them, and saw agreement in their silence.

'Your punishment,' he went on, addressing Mason, 'is that you will leave these shores and never return. You are no longer an Englishman.'

Mason drew his breath in with a gasp, as if he had been struck a blow that took the breath from his body, but he did not complain.

Judith was clinging on to Joseph so hard her fingers hurt his arm, but he was aware only of what Mason must be feeling: the absolute and final rejection. He would never again walk the moors and see the wind-riven skies, hear the curlews call, return to the cobbled streets and the familiar speech, take ale with his friends in the village pub.

The silence was thick with the knowledge of what it is to be alone.

Judith let go of Joseph's arm and stepped forward. She touched Mason and at last he looked at her. She had never seen greater pain.

'I'm coming with you,' she said, having made the decision without even questioning it.

'You can't . . .' he began.

'I'm not asking you,' she replied. 'I'm telling you. I'll say goodbye to Hannah, pack a few things, then we'll go to America. Start again. There'll be work to do there too.'

He drew in his breath to argue, and changed his mind, and in any case was too overwhelmed to speak. He nodded, and gripped her hand so hard she momentarily pulled away. Then he realized what he was doing, and was suddenly, passionately gentle. 'Thank you,' was all he said.

Lloyd George nodded. 'Wait outside,' he instructed, his voice hoarse with emotion.

When they were gone, he returned to Matthew. 'You have done a good job, Reavley. I knew your father. He was a fine man, and honest. He loathed the secret services, but he would have been proud of you. Your country will never know what you have done, or what it may have cost you, but we are in your debt.' He held out his hand.

Matthew took it. 'Thank you, sir. I hope he would.'

Lloyd George nodded. 'Don't doubt it. We are in a new age, and those who wield secrets are as necessary to us as those who wield swords.' He turned to Lizzie. 'Or those who heal, and try to make the best of the damage we have done.'

Finally he turned to Joseph. 'And you, sir, have kept the faith. You have helped us heal the wounds of the soul. Without that, the rest is pointless. But it is not the end. This is only the middle.'

'I know, sir,' Joseph replied. 'There is a long ministry ahead. But first I must go back to my men in Flanders, before the end.'

'Of course you must,' Lloyd George agreed. 'Be with your regiment.'

Outside, in the November dusk, it was time for goodbyes. There was nothing to say. They were used to parting, but nothing ever eased the hurt of it or made the first pulling away less like a tearing of the heart. Judith clung long to Matthew, and even longer to Joseph, but still the moment had to come. She walked away beside Mason, her head high. The streetlight caught the bones of her cheek and the wide, vulnerable mouth, smiling, lips trembling. Then the shadows took them both.

Lizzie kissed Joseph and then moved away, and took Matthew's arm.

'We'll see you soon,' she said firmly.

Matthew saluted. Joseph saluted back, then turned and walked towards the railway station for Dover, and the crossing back to France.

On the morning of 11 November, Joseph crouched in a new, hastily constructed dugout. It was no more than a foxhole. He stared across the stretch of no-man's-land, far to the east of the old one at Ypres. The guns were still firing. Heavy artillery shells gouged up the earth. Snipers picked off the odd, careless soldier who raised his head too high.

Morel was twenty yards along to the right, Tiddly Wop behind him. The sun caught Snowy Nunn's fair hair.

'Knew you'd come back, Chaplain,' Barshey Gee said beside Joseph.

Joseph turned to look at him.

Gunfire roared again, obliterating Barshey's words.

Joseph shook his head to indicate that he had not heard.

'You'd not leave us,' Barshey repeated in the sudden stillness.

Joseph looked at his watch. It was eleven o'clock.

The silence went on. There was no answering fire. All along the line was silent – everywhere.

Slowly men stood up, tentatively at first, then more and more, until there were tens of thousands of them, as far as the eye could see, in every direction. Someone cheered, and another, and another, until there was a roar that filled the air and echoed across Europe from the mountains to the sea.